For my wife Margie

and my children and grandchild:

Sam and Jacques, Gregory and Patrick,

Chris and Roberta, Mike, Lexi and Jordan

Canvas
Under the Sky

Robin Binckes

Dearest Jim,
    Many happy returns
of the day & may you
be spared for many more
to come.
    Stay the wonderful
man you are

Destiny
xxx

30° South Publishers

Robin Binckes was born in East Griqualand, South Africa in 1941. Schooled in Umtata, Transkei, he did his national service at the South African Navy Gymnasium. He has promoted major sporting events, spent a decade in the food industry and was a peace monitor in the townships during the 1993 strife. Motivated by the late historical orator David Rattray, he now runs a tour-guide company, 'Spear of the Nation'.

Published in 2011 by 30° South Publishers (Pty) Ltd.

16 Ivy Road, Pinetown 3610

South Africa

www.30degreessouth.co.za

info@30degreessouth.co.za

Copyright © Robin Binckes, 2011

Design and origination by 30° South Publishers (Pty) Ltd.

Printed and bound by Pinetown Printers, Durban

ISBN 978-1-920143-63-3

Chapter One

The overloaded wagon groaned as Pa heaved up the last of our purchases.

"Look out for my wagon!" yelled Sloam Sinovitch, the owner and trader. He stretched his arms as though to catch the boxes piled precariously on the wooden vehicle.

After a week in Cape Town we were ready to start our five-hundred-mile, three-week ride back to our home on the frontier. In return for the wagon, Pa and I would provide armed protection to the smous and his wagon against robbers, runaway slaves and any other ne'er-do-wells who might be tempted to rob us.

Already loaded with the trader's wares, selected for mass appeal—or maximum profit—the wagon settled further on its wheels as we piled on fabrics for the women, barrels of gunpowder, a plough, forks and spades, dresses for Ma and my three sisters and smart breeches and shirts for my two older brothers, bags of spices, boxes of dried fruit, tins of coffee, planks, nails, saws and hammers—for the long-awaited construction of a permanent farmhouse—and seeds and even fruit trees. Sloam watched in alarm as the load grew. I smiled to myself, waiting for the mountain of assorted goods to collapse and topple off the wagon. Like circus acrobats balancing on each others' shoulders, the formation held.

Pa grinned at Sloam. "Stop worrying man. I told you it would be fine. Hurry up Rauch, let's get going." He hauled himself up onto the wagon, wriggling into the seat as he tried to find a space large enough to accommodate his bulky frame. Finally wedging himself between a pile of women's clothing and a drum of gunpowder, he gave a satisfied smile, ready for the journey.

It was early morning. A small crowd, including Emily Calverley, her nose reddened from crying, had gathered to see us off. Pa looked embarrassed but secretly I think he was quite pleased. He flustered a bit and blew his nose loudly on his handkerchief. I busied myself getting the horses ready, pretending not to notice. Earlier he had given Emily one last hug, his hands lingering on her well-shaped buttocks. The way they shifted alluringly under her dress had not escaped my notice either.

"Don't worry about a thing," said Pa to the concerned Sloam. "These wagons can carry a lot more than this; they were built by Boers!" He leaned off the wagon and gave Sloam, a man half his size, a hearty slap on the back, sending him off balance. Sloam staggered, took two steps forward then recovered. His face turned puce as he visualized his future profits lying in ruin on the side of the road. He didn't respond; instead he rechecked and retightened the ropes that criss-crossed the load, straining against the goods. The softer packages oozed between the ropes under the tarpaulin, reminding me of a fat man vainly attempting to restrain a bulging gut with a long-suffering belt. Sloam kept his concerns to himself. Nobody argued with Pa.

A wave of excitement welled up in me. I was going home. As we rode out of Cape Town, the wagon creaked and strained, wheels rumbling on cobbles still moist from the morning dew. The horses' hooves clattered and echoed up the lanes. The sun struggled to burn off the gloom of the predawn darkness, but as it strengthened the clouds were gently daubed with streaks of translucent pink. Soon the rolling tablecloth of white cloud covering Table Mountain would be in place. Strands of thin mist drifted in threads down the valleys and ravines, exploring the tucks and folds of the flat-topped mountain. To our left the sea was dark; a light southeasterly ruffled the surface, whisking up small patches of white froth.

The empty streets stirred with the sounds of hawkers, merchants and slaves. Dogs bounded alongside the wagon until they gave up the chase, panting with the effort. The sound of a city awakening was pierced with the shrieks of seagulls pinning their wings to their sides and plunging into the chilly Atlantic waters in search of food.

Grey's hooves clattered on the cobbles as he friskily carried me through the outskirts of the town. He shook his head occasionally, snorting out puffs of early morning steam. The scent of jasmine in the gardens blended with that of citrus and crushed herbs from the indigenous fynbos. Clinging to this delicate fragrance was the smell of fresh horses and warm leather saddles.

The smooth, monotonous rock of the saddle lulled me into reminiscencing on the events of the past week. As my thoughts paused on each one, I realized I would never forget this week. I had seen things that I couldn't do justice to by way of explanation. Time had lingered and it felt we had been away from our farm and family a lot longer. I felt I'd seen the world … perhaps even grown up a bit. Many a man three times my age on the frontier had never been to Cape Town and here was I, a boy of seventeen.

The wagon hampered our return, making it a great deal slower than our ride west. I thought of Amelia, and Ma. I was sure they would be delighted with their gifts. A smile crept over my face at the thought of the welcome awaiting our return.

Late on the twentieth day, after an uneventful journey, the horses seemed to sense, as they do, home, quickening their pace without urging. My heart beat a light tattoo in my chest at the thought of seeing Amelia and sharing out the presents with Ma and the others. Pa and I were in high spirits. Even Sloam's morose face lit up a few shades which made him look about as happy as someone attending a loved one's funeral.

"Nearly home," Pa shouted over his shoulder.

"Big storm coming," I called back as a flash of lightning cut the threatening clouds blowing toward us. "I hope we make it before the rain comes, otherwise we'll get soaked."

A sudden gust of wind rippled through the long grass, bending it into submission. Storm clouds, black and heavy, threatened a drenching. The streamers of rain on the horizon and the slow, soft rumble of approaching thunder rolling across the sky and clapping like a gun salute, couldn't dampen our spirits.

"I can't wait to see the women decked out in their finery. They'll be as grand as those upper-class English women we saw in Cape Town," Pa called back at me as he trotted ahead.

I think he was referring to Emily Calverley.

"Wait until Frans and Dirk see the breeches and shoes we've bought, as well as everything else," I said. I made no comment about the building materials ... we all knew that they would mean a great deal more work for us three boys and would not be as welcome as the clothing and gifts.

Then we were on our farm.

⤙⤙⤙

We passed the first of our fields as Pa reined Thunder in, glancing back at me. His face darkened. Despite the fast-approaching storm, silence settled upon us—heavy and uncomfortable—with foreboding. The fields were quiet. Too quiet.

Pa pulled up his horse, slowing almost to a stop. "What's going on?" He cast a worried look. "Something's wrong. Where are the sheep and cattle? Something's very wrong." This last he muttered to himself as he kicked Thunder in the ribs and lashed his reins, urging the horse on. "Kom! Maak gou! Hurry up!" he barked, spurring Thunder into a gallop.

I kicked Grey's flanks, lunging forward, leaving the smous trundling along in the wagon, vanishing in our dust.

I scanned the farm. Pa was right. Something was definitely amiss. Recent frontier history made it almost impossible not to fear the worst. Before we crested the final hill overlooking our thatch-and-mud hartebeeshuisie, we passed a field and our suspicions were confirmed. Short, black stubble laid waste the land where once our crops had flourished.

I drew level with Pa. Leaning forward in our saddles we urged the horses on ... faster ... in the vain hope that speed would alter the inevitable. Hooves drummed the ground as we hurried toward the homestead. My breath came in short, desperate rasps. We reached the top of the rise at full tilt. Pa yanked his reins, "Whoa!" He brought Thunder to a stop in a cloud of dust. I pulled Grey up alongside him.

All was still as the sun dipped. A backdrop of folded, creased hills rolling down gently to the lazy Kap River, whispered deceitfully that everything was just as it had been.

But it wasn't, and it never would be again.

We lowered our gaze to where the hartebeeshuisie had stood. In the middle of the charred land a cruel scar marked the place where our house had stood. A few crumbling stone walls, blackened by smoke, stood sentinel over the burned ruins. The first big drops splashed around us but we paid the storm no heed. We sat on our horses, staring, slumped, disbelieving as the rain lashed at us. Still we sat.

"Nee! Liewe Here, nee!" The anguished, breathy plea forced its way from Pa's lips. "Dear Lord, no!"

Everything was gone, the hartebeeshuisie burned to the ground as was the hut of our Hottentot, Gieletjie, and his wife Thandi.

The Xhosa had attacked again.

"Dit kan nie wees nie. It can't be." Pa jerked his reins and spurred his horse on to take him closer.

There was worse to come.

My temple throbbed and my vision blurred. The bile rose in my mouth. I leaned forward, gripping Grey's neck as I retched. Following Pa cautiously I think I realized what we were going to find. My mouth was dry, my tongue sticking to the roof. I tried to swallow. As we approached the ruins we were met by the stale, acrid smell of ash from burned cloth and bones. The pouring rain could not dampen the stench.

I could taste the smell. I shivered.

Pa screamed a long wailing, "Neeeeee! *Dit* moet nie wees nie!" He leaped off Thunder and scrambled to the ruins.

I watched, helpless. He stumbled the last few yards through the teeming rain to where fresh piles of earth with crude wooden crosses marked the eight new graves in a corner of what had been the garden.

Mounds of soil were piled in two groups of four, with five yards between the two sets. Pa ran from one mound to the next, holding the crude wooden crosses in his hand as if to break them off and deny the truth of the names on them. He frantically studied the harsh, black lettering, soaking up the names. He knelt by the first grave, his hat clutched against his chest and paused as he read the name. Then he covered his face in his hands as sobs wracked his body. The inscription read:

Annetjie Beukes

April 6th, 1794–October 30th, 1834

His body shuddered violently, his cries like the moans of a wounded animal. He turned his face to the heavens, imploring God to erase the events that had led to this moment. The full shock of what had happened hit me. I spewed a long yellow stream of vomit next to one of the graves as I read the names. Ma and the three girls—Helena, Hannah and Maria— were gone. So too were Gieletjie's sons, Peet and Rots, and the slaves Anna and Marcia.

I could not cry. No tears would come. My chest felt as if it had been struck a mighty blow. My legs buckled and I fell to the ground next to Pa. He turned to me, his face twisted in anguish, hugged me to his bosom and held me, his hat crunched between us, and sobbed, all the while gently rocking. His salty tears smeared against my mouth.

The storm was all around us. Giant drops of rain plopped loudly on the charred earth. The heavens themselves wept at the events they had witnessed. The storm gathered power as night fell, increasing in intensity until the drops became sheets lashed by the wind. Stronger gusts drove the deluge harder into our faces, whipping us with its fury, stinging our cheeks. Then the squall passed and the tempo changed to a solid beat, easing slightly for a moment or two, only to lash down furiously again with the next squall. We didn't care. Within ten minutes the storm was at its most violent. Thunder rolled and roared with the interval between a startling flash of lightning and a clap of thunder only a second. Forks of lightning punched through the blackness of the sky as they frolicked like marionettes accompanied by an orchestra of fire.

We sat, drenched through, next to the graves. Pa paid no attention to the elements, his sobs bursting from deep within. I stared at a grave. Rivulets of water trickled down the mound of earth covering Ma, turning it into a muddy heap. A flash of lightning lit up the sky and illuminated the landscape.

Sloam sat silently, hunched under the wagon. He watched us, like characters in a frozen tableau. I am not sure how long we sat there; we were unaware of anything except the physical ache and emptiness inside us.

Many hours later, as I stared unseeing into the shadows, the blackness squeezed out the shape of a man as he emerged from the darkness, his face occasionally lit up by the lightning. It was Gieletjie, our Hottentot worker, leading a horse. His lined face showed how he had aged since we had parted only six weeks back. He had been waiting for our return to break the bad news, not entrusting the task to another soul.

"Ek is so jammer, baas," he said. "I am so sorry. Ten days ago the kaffirs attacked. I tried to help and so did all the boys but there were just too many of them. The missus shot and shot but then they burned down the huisie and them with it. It was almost an accident ... the Xhosa don't kill women and children. I don't think they meant to kill them ..." He paused not wanting to say the words. "Still … they are dead. Your cattle and sheep are also gone; maybe only fifty cattle and a hundred sheep are left. I've put them in the bottom paddock, those that are left. Your sons are not hurt. Not in their bodies, anyway. They are with the Engelse, the Thompsons. Baas Thompson say when you ready you come there to stay."

Pa continued to rock back and forth in silence. Gieletjie said nothing more but squatted on his haunches with the rain dribbling down his face. He waited for Pa's command.

Much later that ghastly night I helped Pa to his feet. Gieletjie and I rounded up the horses and after we had stumbled and scrambled in the blackness and the rain, we hitched Grey and Thunder to Sloam's wagon.

Sloam had nodded off, head slumped forward and chin resting on his chest. He jerked awake as our boots squelched through the puddles. Water ran off the brim of his hat. We climbed onto the wagon.

"Come on Sloam," I said. "We are going to the English people's farm … the Thompsons. It's about two hours' ride from here."

Sloam started to speak, "I am so, so sorr …"

I cut him short. "Leave it! There's nothing to be said. Come, maak gou!"

I sat next to Sloam, while Pa and Gieletjie made room in the back and squeezed in between the wares. Sloam cracked his whip and the oxen leaned forward, straining in their harnesses against the driving rain. As we made our way through the darkness and the squalls of rain driving into our faces I realized that all we owned in the world was behind us in that wagon.

In the back Gieletjie talked to Pa. I couldn't hear what he was saying but the tone was gentle and soothing.

A flame flared from Pa's tonteldoos, his tinderbox, and I heard Pa sucking on his pipe. The sickly sweet smell of dagga mixed with the tobacco, signalled the treatment Gieletjie had dispensed for sorrow. I held out my hand to Gieletjie. He placed a rolled leaf of marijuana in my outstretched palm. I lit up. Sloam's face flickered in the light of the tonteldoos; I could see him nod approvingly. I inhaled deeply and let the smoke fill my lungs, sucking the full effect of the drug into my bloodstream. My head lightened and after two or three deep draws, I began to feel the floating upshot of the dagga. We would be alright. The boys were still alive. I even smiled to myself at the thought of seeing Amelia again. I felt myself relax. The pain hadn't gone but it had become bearable. The dagga was doing its work. I looked back at Pa and Gieletjie and could see that Pa too was allowing the drug to ease the pain.

We rode silently. Pa was asleep, cradled in Gieletjie's arms, stroking his hair and murmuring soothing sounds as one would to a baby. Water dripped from his hat, the drops falling off the brim in a rhythmic pattern … drop … drop … drop, dribble … drop … drop … drop, dribble, the pattern repeated over and over as the water gathered in the brim and spilled over.

Chapter Two

I was born on April 8th, 1817, three years and two days before the first English settlers arrived in Algoa Bay. They called me Rauch. It means smoke. Perhaps they had a foreboding of the flames of violence and passion that lay ahead of me. Perhaps they just liked the name.

I was the third son of Jakob Beukes, a wild, tough and fearless descendant of Admiral Jakob Beukes, a wild, tough and fearless Dutch buccaneer. The Dutch, who wisely recognized that he would make a better ally than an enemy, made him an admiral. He met his maker off Trinidad in 1657, a ball from a French musket ripping a hole the size of a fist into his chest through his gold-braided jacket. That was five years after his countrymen, the Dutch, settled in the Cape of Good Hope.

The Jakob Beukes who fathered me was not a pirate but in every other way he matched the best and the worst of his notorious naval ancestor. People who met us always remarked how similar we were in appearance. Pa was forty years old but looked fifty-five, aged by his time on the frontier, fighting the kaffirs. He had lived a life under the scorching sun and in the saddle. Six feet two inches tall and a hundred and seventy-eight pounds, much of it muscle, he had fair hair, bleached by the sun and grey-blue eyes, lined from being screwed up against the glare of the sun over many summers. His smile was wide and so were his hands; they could fold into fists big enough to shatter the jawbone of an ox with one blow. A straight, strong nose above a full mouth made him almost handsome. He, like all Boers, could do three things well: ride horses, shoot and pray. And like every other Boer he had another distinct advantage: he believed God was on his side.

On the other hand, my mother, Annetjie, was a gentle soul but like many women of her day her quiet demeanour belied a character of tempered steel, an inner core of strength which ensured that my siblings and I knew exactly who it was that headed the household. Attractive in her time, the harshness of life had left its thumbprint on her features. Her bone structure showed the beauty that had once been manifest. She had borne eight children, burying two of them. The harshness of the summer sun combined with thirty-eight winters, many of them spent under the stars, had lined her face and roughened her hands. Sometimes when she laughed, which didn't seem that often, I saw a sparkle in her eye and a flash of humour. For a fleeting moment she looked almost beautiful. Then the shutters would come down and the lips would come together again, tight and straight, more in keeping with the appearance of a woman of the frontier.

She too believed God was on my father's side in everything he did, except when it came to an argument, then God was on her side. In such cases Pa needed more than God. Both were born on the frontier, of Dutch settlers who had come out from Delft in Holland in 1770 to seek a better life. Somehow I don't think they found it.

Both families, the Beukeses on my father's side, and de Haases on my mother's, were part of a group of the early trek boers who had slowly, slowly, inch by inch, made their way up the Cape coast, to claim, by conflict, a piece of land from the Khoi. Sometimes, travelling in their tiny wagons, they made all of a half mile a day. Those wagons were the bees of the open veld, pollinating the earth with the early settlers as some stopped and stayed and others moved on in search of grazing, land and respite from the laws and interference of the Dutch East India Company.

Our piece of land was initially some seven thousand acres. It was defined by the time it took for a man to walk thirty minutes north, south, east and west from a central point. By war and conquest the land we now called our own was bigger by half than my grandfather's original claim. Pa had called the farm De Hoop. Hope.

Our small hartebeeshuisie, made of mud and straw, nestled on the side of one of the grass-clad rolling hills which characterized the frontier area. The hills rolled and folded into gorges and ravines channelled by rivers which ran to the sea only twelve miles distant. On fine summer evenings we sat on the mud-and-dung-smeared stoep, looking down as mist from the sea swirled up the Kap River which meandered through the valley between the green hills below.

A hundred yards upstream the sluggish brown water squeezed through a gorge and gurgled and sprayed over rapids. Sometimes in the still evening air we could hear the sounds of a large mullet as it slapped at the water's surface, fleeing the hungry jaws of a giant kob. When there had been rain up-country our little Kap turned into a raging torrent, sometimes as wide as a hundred yards. Tree stumps and branches, dead cattle and sheep, legs stiffly pointing to the heavens, were sent rolling, tumbling and bobbing in the foaming waters down to the sea. Pa told us that once he had even seen a dead Xhosa tribesman swept along by the angry river.

Our river ran parallel with the Cape Colony's boundary, the Great Fish River, just four and a half miles away. On the other side of the Great Fish lived the Xhosa, a black, brooding mass of anger tinged with fear, jealously guarding their land, waiting for the opportunity to seize from us what they believed was theirs. We were scared of them and they were scared of us.

Our little house was humble. Pa kept saying that when he made some money we would soon build a grand home like those I had seen in Grahamstown. Somehow he never seemed to make it. The house had two rooms, one for us to sleep in and the other, the larger living room, had a fireplace for those Eastern Cape winter nights when the damp and the cold eat into your very marrow. In the big room we sat around the fire at night and ate our meal. This is where we prayed and played.

Ma and Pa slept on a mattress in the corner of the smaller room behind a screen of reeds. We children slept on the mud floor. We weren't supposed to be able to see where Ma and Pa slept. Sometimes at night, if I looked very hard after my eyes had grown accustomed to the dark, the shapes of

Ma and Pa would merge. Through the reed barrier I would see his white backside rhythmically rise and fall. If I strained my ears I could hear as he grunted and panted, almost smothering Ma's soft moans. I was never sure whether the moans were of protest or delight. I was always surprised at the number of times that that backside would rise and fall. Sometimes his breathing was punctuated by words and louder grunts, mouthed against my Ma's neck as he slammed into her. It didn't take much watching for me to feel a stirring in my own loins and for my hands to find their way under the sheepskin blanket to clasp my own erection and begin my own pleasurable journey. One time I laughed as I thought of the three of us enjoying the same sensation. Another time, amid a frenzy of movement, Ma gently whispered, "Hurry! Please!" then almost reluctantly, "Yes! Yes!" She seemed to lift him as her body arched. His backside seemed suspended in the dark, a white patch in the gloom. Then I heard him groan and my groans, choked back in case I was heard, joined Pa's as I ejaculated into my hand. I always had to check to see if my brothers had seen me.

I knew that my three younger sisters on the far side of the room—Helena the youngest and the prettiest at only five years old (she had already stolen the hearts of all the men in the family), Maria, who at seven, was the splitting image of Ma and Hannah the oldest, who was at eight the most serious of the three—would be oblivious to the activity. Frans and Dirk, older than me, would certainly have known what I was doing. One night when I was thirteen, I watched as Dirk, then seventeen, did it. Until the day I killed him he was unaware that there was an audience watching the audience. Of course, being a Calvinist family, we never spoke about such subjects. Sex was for procreation. I always prayed afterward for forgiveness from our Lord, so I am sure that made it alright.

Our farm, the centre of my world, consisted of my immediate family, three hundred head of cattle, about a thousand sheep, two women slaves, Anna September and her daughter Katrina, the same age as me, and Marcia

Madagascar. Katrina had inherited her mother's East Indian looks: brown skinned and striking features, she was not beautiful. Black eyebrows, hazel eyes, a large sensuous mouth with wide lips that made a man want to cover them with his, and a tall, slim build. Her breasts dwarfed those of my sisters and even Ma's. All these features on a luscious, full body caused many a man older than me to turn his head. My heart beat faster when she looked at me with her big hazel eyes, even though she was a slave. I was torn between looking her in the eyes and at her nipples which made little tents in the fabric of her dress. Katrina helped the two older slave women and Ma around the house.

Then there was our servant, the Hottentot. Gieletjie and his wife and three sons lived in their thatched hut near the hartebeeshuisie. They spent their days working in the fields and tending the animals. As we grew up, most of our time was spent working side by side with Gieletjie, his wife Thandi, and the boys, Peet, Kleinman and Rots.

Though we were the baas's children, we too worked the fields, planting and harvesting mielies or looking after the cattle. Ma taught us to read and write; I suspected that she had taught Pa as well, at least enough to read the Bible which he used to do in front of the family every evening before bedtime. Occasionally Pa would tell us stories. Those were memorable times, with the flickering lamp offsetting the light from the flames which danced in the fireplace. We sat in a semi-circle around Pa, rocking gently in his rocking chair. He used to smoke his long pipe. Sometimes I think he mixed in a bit of dagga with his tobacco. Gieletjie always had that slightly sweet smell of the weed about him. On these occasions the pipe would be used to gesticulate and punctuate his stories. During the pauses, Pa would suck hard on his pipe which made gentle gurgling sounds. Ma sat and crocheted on his right-hand side, while we all craned forward to hear better. She would cast little glances at us to see if we were paying attention. The shadows at the far ends of the room were cold and dark and made the circle of light blanketing us seem comforting and warm. There was dead silence while Pa spoke. His stories were enhamced by the crackle from the fire as the logs burned down and rolled into new positions, with showers of sparks shooting up like millions of fireflies and briefly lighting up the gloom, before returning us to semi-darkness. We all had our favourite stories. Mine were about the coming of the English settlers in 1820. Pa had been in one of the ninety-six wagons driven by frontier farmers under a man called Piet Retief who went to Algoa Bay to fetch the settlers. He had a host of stories to tell about this adventure.

I liked hearing the story when I was older because by then I had met and, unbeknown to her, fallen in love with the daughter of one of these settler families, Amelia Thompson, the daughter of our English neighbour. I was besotted with Amelia and at every opportunity tried to attract her attention.

The Thompsons had been allocated a piece of land only two hours' horseback ride away so we were virtually neighbours. They seemed to struggle. Pa said it was because they were not boers like us and were not familiar with the land and how to survive from it. Sometimes the slaves would be allowed to listen to the story, even though they were coloured people. But that was only if my Pa had just finished praying when he started his story. I think his talking to the Lord made him more tolerant.

Our days were very full. The lifestyle made us boys as tough as string biltong. We rose before it was light to milk the cows and worked in the fields all day in all weather. At seventeen I was strong for my age and stood a finger above six foot in my stockinged feet. I was reasonably good-looking, with a strong nose, fair hair and my father's blue eyes. I was fit and hard and could ride a horse as well as any man. With my Sanna front-end-loading musket I could drop a rabbit from a hundred yards nine times out of ten, stone dead with a shot through its heart. I could load and shoot three times in a minute, riding my horse at a gallop, which was better than most boys of my age, but not all.

Then there were the kaffirs to watch for. That never stopped. They were over the river which gave us some sense of security, but we knew that when they came for us, that barrier would be crossed without a falter in their war steps. Besides, they knew they were onto a good thing with the Governor and the missionaries on their side who always blamed us boers for everything bad that happened. The powers that be seldom took into account the fact that the Xhosa constantly stole our mielies and rustled our cattle. They always blamed us when we stole back our own cattle. I found it strange that we had God on our side and the kaffirs had the missionaries, who only worked for God, on theirs. The authorities seemed to pay a great deal more attention to God's disciples than to God himself.

There had already been five major conflicts with the Xhosa. Their leader was the powerful chief, Hintsa. Pa kept telling us that, apart from the raids which frequently took place, we should all be ready because a big war was going to break out again.

Whenever Pa talked to our closest neighbour, Simon Plettenberg, the conversation inevitably turned to the subject. "Ever since the British came they have been scared to act. You know as well as I do, that if the British came here in any force they could crush the Xhosa. They lack the will and backbone. We should wipe them out once and for all. That would end this nonsense," Pa would say. He would spit tobacco juice onto the grass, to emphasize the point. Simon's eye would follow its flight with a look of concern; sometimes it would hit my bare feet if I was standing too close. Simon would nod his head knowingly in agreement.

Nobody disagreed with my Pa.

⋞⋞⋞

Early in the year of 1834 a new subject crept into conversations, first with Simon Plettenberg and then with Ma. It seemed there were plenty of rumours around that the British were going to grant the slaves their freedom.

"I don't know what we will do about Anna, Marcia and Katrina, if we have to allow them to be free," said Pa. "Mind you, they say that we will be paid compensation. How much, I don't know, but at least we will get something. Sometimes I think that might be better than having them under our feet all the time and having to feed them. They will also have to work for us as apprentices for four years, so they say."

It was after one of these conversations that I think the idea of a journey, some sixteen days and five hundred miles of horseback ride to Cape Town, started taking root in Pa's mind. "We need to buy more seed and goods and I want to find out what's happening in the world. I would also like to see my brother. Grahamstown would be a lot easier and closer, but then my brother doesn't live in Grahamstown, does he?" said Pa to Ma, sucking hard on his unlit pipe, a habit which surfaced whenever he felt unsure of himself when talking to Ma. He explained, rather nervously, that she was staying behind with my two brothers and three sisters.

As the youngest boy and because we were so alike in looks and character, I had always been the favourite son. That ensured my invitation to accompany him on the journey. I had never been to Cape Town, nor had any of my brothers or sisters. In fact I didn't know anyone who had been to Cape Town. The night that Pa told us that I was going with him, Frans and Dirk both peed on my bedclothes to demonstrate how they felt about the decision. I just laughed. Nothing could have dampened my excitement.

Six weeks after the conversation with Plettenberg, my father and I set off on horseback for Cape Town, I on Grey and Pa on Thunder. As we waved goodbye to the family, even the slaves came to see us off and Gieletjie and his boys, already hard at work in the fields, joined in the farewells, waving as we passed. Pa seemed to know everyone in the country. When we didn't stay in a little village inn, our night stops were with a succession of friends whom he had known for years on the frontier. Everyone was pleased to see him and there was much back-slapping and raucous laughter. There was a bond between these people, forged by years of common hardship and danger.

Frequently when we set off in the morning on the next leg of the journey, Pa would look the worse for wear, with bloodshot eyes and, I am pretty sure, a pounding headache from talking and drinking brandy well into the early hours. After such evenings I saw him wince with pain as we rode. Riding a horse wasn't the best treatment for a hangover. During these evening sessions I was allowed to sit with the men and listen. The conversation would be about the natives and the reluctance of the British to act. At times they would lower their voices as if afraid they'd be overheard, although I was never sure who would overhear them as there wasn't a living soul for miles around.

Two nights before we arrived in Cape Town we stayed with the van Zyls who farmed outside the village of Swellendam. Pa was in fine form. He was excited about arriving in Cape Town. We were sitting around the fire after dinner.

Koos van Zyl said, "You would think that the English would care a bit more about their own people, wouldn't you? After all, they brought them out here fourteen years ago and now they won't even help protect them against the Xhosa."

Pa nodded in agreement. "Ja, but most of those people who came out are now in Cape Town or Grahamstown. They aren't farmers' backsides, and of course they got no, or should I say very little, assistance from the British. Mind you," he said reflectively, "there are still some up there on the frontier. We have people near us, the Thompsons, who are still trying to make a go of it. But hell, man! they really struggle. After all these years

I still have to go over there and help them with the harvest. You know, us boers have got the soil under our fingernails. Not the English though." He took a large swallow of brandy.

Koos took a swig himself and said thoughtfully, "You know, Jakob, I believe there is talk that some of the farmers are going to pack up and leave."

"Pack up and leave?" asked Pa disbelievingly. He threw his head back and laughed. "Where the hell are they going to go? *This* is their land. Where on earth would they go?"

Koos retorted quietly, "Away from British rule; away from the colony."

Pa looked dumbstruck. "You mean, outside the colony? They would be mad to do that. What about the Xhosa? If they left they would be killed very, very quickly. Where would they live? Mind you, I don't suppose they would have to pay these damned taxes ... if they survived. What a thing. Can you believe it? And, Koos ... tell me, do you really think they are serious? How many times have you heard this story? Do you think there's any truth in it?" Pa became quite agitated at the thought of people leaving and heading off into who knew where.

I noticed that his pipe had gone out but he was still drawing on it as he did when unnerved by Ma, totally unaware that his nicotine supply had ceased.

As we rode out the gate the next morning, Pa shouted back, "Koos! I am going to find out if there is any truth in this story. Who are these people who are so unhappy that they want to leave? Give me names so I can find out."

"Apparently one is Trichardt, the other is van Rensburg. Some say they have already left, but there are many others," Koos shouted.

Pa shook his head in astonishment. I heard him muttering some hours later, "Leave the colony? Break with the British? I wonder if the devil we know isn't better than the one we don't?"

That night he told me again how fourteen years ago he had been asked by the government in the Cape to travel to Algoa Bay to meet the settlers and transport them to their farms. "Eighteen Twenty settlers they call them. I call them the eighteen twenty fools. One hundred acres they gave them. I mean, what can a man do with a hundred acres? In an area called the Zuurveld? Our farm is a hundred times bigger. Would you buy a farm even if it was for only ten pounds in an area called the Zuurveld?" I shook my head, as if he was waiting for my reply. "You'd have to be mad." He paused reflectively, sucking on his pipe. "Or desperate."

"They didn't tell those poor people the full story … if they told them anything at all. I mean, you and I know that you have to have a piece of land at least over a thousand acres in an area like that to farm." He snorted as he spoke. "The most important thing of all they conveniently left out. The fact that the area selected for them was a war zone and they were going to act as a buffer between the Xhosa and the Cape. Because of the unemployment in England they had sixty thousand fools who wanted to come. In the end they brought just fewer than five thousand. If half a dozen of them had farming experience, it was a lot." Then he corrected himself, musing, "Perhaps they weren't fools? Just desperate. There was no work for them in England and a lot of them were soldiers and had no prospects of a job; just desperate people looking for a better life. I suppose it's a bit like these people wanting to leave the colony forever … desperate and in search of a better life."

He pointed with his pipe. "Anyway, I went down with Oom Peet Botha and Veldt Kommandant Piet Retief and a whole lot of others to fetch them." He glanced at me to see that I was following. "It was early April when we got to Algoa Bay after a ten-day journey; there were all the tents where the settlers were being housed. Four ships in the bay that had brought the first lot of settlers. They had spent four months at sea. They were very relieved when they arrived, I can assure you. Conditions on the ships were shocking. A lot of them were sick with scurvy. You know, that after fetching them in the wagons, for days after we left Algoa Bay the womenfolk kept complaining that they felt as though my wagon was pitching like a ship!"

There was silence while he re-lit his pipe, emitting clouds of blue smoke as he sucked before continuing. The first few words sounded as if they came from the smoke cloud; you couldn't see Pa at all. "I had two families with me, the Calverleys and the Mosses. All from somewhere called the north of England. With the children there were twelve of them. The women—you should have seen them in their lovely long dresses and big bonnets—hell, they looked like they were going to the Grahamstown show."

I had only been to the Grahamstown races and never the show, so I wasn't too sure how they looked but understood that they must have appeared quite grand. I nodded agreement, showing that I could picture them.

"They were so excited, just like you going to Cape Town," he said with a grin. "Everything was so new to them. They said they hadn't seen such lovely land in their lives because everything looked so fertile. Most of the time they just stared wide eyed at the passing scenery. I remember Mrs Calverley saying 'Look! Some of the crops planted here are knee high already.' Two days later some of the crops were ready for harvesting. And then we passed some fields which had been burned by the Xhosa. I don't think they realized what they were looking at. Later when we passed a burned-out homestead and the rotting, stinking corpse of one of the kaffirs who had been shot in a raid, with flies buzzing all around, they understood."

There was silence while we both pictured the scene.

"Ten days it took us to get to their farms. Farms? You must be joking! The government had pegged their land out. One hundred acres was what they got. You couldn't call that a farm. I offloaded them. Of course, I helped them off the wagons with their big sea trunks. Mrs Calverley had tears in her eyes when she looked around at what would soon be her home. She said to me, 'You know Jakob, last night I realized the enormous divide which exists between the land that was my home and this land where I cannot even recognize the stars in the sky.'"

"Why did she say that?" I asked.

He answered smugly, as if he was pleased I had asked, "Because they have different stars in the skies over England. We are in the southern hemisphere and they are in the north. Their stars are totally different."

He paused again as he collected his thoughts after my interruption. "Do you know, I had to leave quickly? Not even a coffee did I stay for. The thing is ... I felt so sorry for them because they looked so foolish and they knew it. As I cracked my whip and rode away, I thought I should warn them what lay ahead so I shouted, 'Remember! When you plant your seed, take your guns with you.' The last I saw of Mrs Calverley was her sitting on one of those big sea trunks in her long flowing dress, her bonnet on her head, and tears streaming down her face as she realized what the future held. I felt really bad leaving them. Well, they didn't last long. I think they are now in Cape Town." He had been talking quite softly, but this last he said in a lively tone. "Perhaps we can find them in Cape Town and pay a visit, eh? That Emily Calverley was a fine-looking woman, even though she was English." Pa dashed a quick glance at me. He knew he'd said too much and feared that I might tell Ma. "The Thompsons, though, have got guts. They might be lousy farmers but they're still there." He gazed into the distance. "It's a pity they are English because that little filly Amelia would have been just right for you. Ag! No, not really," he corrected himself. "She appears to be a little bit wild and I doubt whether you could tame her," he said with a sideways glance.

I felt my face going red and looked away.

The next day, after crossing the last range of mountains, we approached the outskirts of Cape Town. We rode down the Great Road, Sir Lowry's Pass, into Cape Town. As we approached my nostrils picked up a foul smell on the morning breeze. It grew stronger as we neared the castle which dominated the area. The stench was one which I had experienced before. I couldn't place it. I searched through the corridors of my memory. When we saw the gallows ahead and what was left of the man hanging from them, I realized that it was the smell of death. A body hung from the gibbet next to the road, with what was left of the head dangling at an unnatural angle, a grim warning to those who contemplated evil deeds and to those who had yet to consider them. Four scraggy-necked vultures pecked urgently at the remains, heads bent forward as razor-sharp beaks tore off pieces of rotting human flesh. I was shocked at the callousness of a society that left a corpse to rot in the sun. At least where I came from we would bury even the kaffirs if they didn't take their bodies back. The sun was warm but I shivered as we rode past.

Pa too kept his eyes focused in front of him. "We'd better not do anything wrong, seun," he said, "or else we'll end up like that." He didn't smile.

My excitement mounted as I entered that strange Aladdin's Cave of the Tavern of the Seas. It didn't take me long to put the forbidding sight behind me. Pa looked at me and laughed excitedly when he saw the wonder in my eyes. I think he was as awed as I. We trotted down the dirt road entering the settlement, passing whitewashed houses. Cape Town was a bustling town of twenty thousand people and totally different to anything I had ever seen. As we progressed deeper into the town, water channels appeared on each side of the street. There were more and more people. The finely dressed folk looked at us with as much amazement as Pa and I felt staring at them. With a start I realized that our clothes were very different. They were dressed more like our English neighbours, the Thompsons: men in frock coats and tail coats, wearing breeches to the knees or trousers to their boots, top hats or beaver hats, carrying canes; women who walked as gracefully as swans in dresses with high waists in bright colours of mulberry, lilac, blue, and even the colour of the willow tree next to the river where we swam. Sleeves which were puffed out and tall bonnets made of straw which followed the hair line; feather plumes on the bonnets finished them off with a flourish. Nothing like what our women wore on the frontier. With our worn-out breeches, hide waistcoats and jackets and our broad-brimmed hats, we were from another world; even the slaves accompanying their masters or the children walking hand in hand with their nannies, were better dressed than us.

It didn't bother me. I was too excited. The streets bustled with noise and colour everywhere. Mixed in with the feathers, bonnets, long dresses, parasols, canes, top hats, frock coats, breeches and boots was a wide range of smart military and even smarter naval uniforms. Swinging kilts in a variety of tartans under sporrans which swung gaily from side to side, naval braid and shiny brass buttons and buckles, epaulettes and medals. Like lizards slithering around the rocks and weaving their way through the grass were the Khoi hawkers with their wares piled on their heads as they threaded their way through the throng.

The houses were different: white walls, no stoeps. Some were double storey. And the shops! Mrs Barker's on the corner of Burg and Castle streets had windows through which I could see the goods that she had on sale. None of the shops in Grahamstown had display windows. My mouth hung open in astonishment. I looked at Pa. He was shaking his head.

It was hard to take it all in. I had never seen tiles used for roofs instead of thatching grass. I looked through the big glass windows of the houses as we rode by. From my elevated position on Grey, I could see large and spacious rooms. Occasionally there were people in the rooms going about their daily lives. Staircases and plastered ceilings contrasted with the beams that I was accustomed to.

Pa laughed out loud as he observed me. I actually think he pretended not to be awed. "It's the Engelse. This is how they build houses. Even some of the boers live like this," he added in wonder. Then nervously, "We must find out how to get to my brother, Oom Willem's house. I wonder where Long Street is?"

On we rode, now in the town proper. Past the Grand Parade along Strand Street, past the jail, then by pure chance we stopped at a crossroads. Pa removed his hat in a sweeping motion, looking very grand. I think all the finery around him persuaded him that he should put on his best manners as he asked a distinguished-looking gentleman, who actually turned out to be a slave, "Excuse me, mijnheer. I am looking for Long Street, number twenty-two?"

"Daar voor jou," came the immediate but surly response.

I looked ahead. My heart thumped with excitement. We were looking at my uncle's house. I knew that he was quite important, being an opperkoopman, a senior official with the British administration, but had no idea he was this important.

The house I feasted my eyes upon was three storeys high. Five windows set in the walls, like eyes, two at the top and three below, indicated the second and third floors, while on the ground floor two windows were positioned on each side of a big wooden door. In the front garden were flowers and a small pool with tiny fish which darted here and there. And we were going to stay here! Even if nothing else good happened on the trip and I witnessed nothing more that was new or exciting, what I had seen had already made the journey worthwhile.

Oom Willem, a large, ruddy-faced, friendly man, greeted us heartily at the door, called for a slave to fetch our horses and invited us inside. "Liewe Hemel!" he said as we entered, "Good heavens! Is this little Rauch? Well, my boy, it's about time that you tasted civilization instead of that life your father chooses up on the frontier. What a big lad you've turned out to be. Mind you," he added, looking at Pa, "I suppose I shouldn't be surprised, should I? Nothing stays the same. Things are really changing here as well. You know that they are going to free the slaves on the first of December?" Without waiting for a reply he went on, "Some of the farmers have been offered half of what their slaves are valued at. Why, old van Reenen out in Stellenbosch has slaves valued at five hundred pounds and they are only going to pay him two hundred and fifty, so the story goes. Plus, they must claim their money from agents in England. A lot of damned nonsense! Although I work for the government I can understand how upset our people are about this. How will it affect you?" he asked Pa as we walked down the passage.

"We have two women and Katrina, the daughter of one of them. Her father was executed six years ago for running away. Since then they have almost become part of the family. You know, on the frontier, as long as they do their work, everyone's happy. I think they enjoy being with us," said Pa. He stopped and looked at Oom Willem quizzically. "I hear they are going to make them stay apprenticed to us for four years?"

Oom Willem nodded, "What's the difference? Give them their freedom."

"The one we spoke to on the way here was as surly as can be. Maybe it's time. They wouldn't speak to us like that on the frontier, I can assure you," said Pa with a humourless laugh.

Oom Willem ushered us into a room which I later learned was called the drawing room. It was decorated with floral wallpaper. I ran my hand over it; it felt soft and smooth. It was embossed with ripples and raised lines. I had never seen wallpaper before. Draped velvet curtains, edge-to-edge carpeting with a hearth rug in front of a fireplace in which a fire burned vigorously, despite the heat of the day outside. A beautiful Grecian sofa and chintz-upholstered chairs with thin-legged tables beside each one, and in the corner a lovely looking lady, my aunt, Tant Sarie Beukes, aged about thirty-five, creating the most gentle, melodic sounds on a harp. I thought with some embarrassment how crudely we lived on the frontier. We had no refinements like these.

That night I was astounded when dinner was served by an immaculately dressed male slave and two white women. I nearly choked on my food when I saw the two women ... I had never been served by a white person in my life. When Oom Willem saw our unconcealed looks of amazement, he explained, "There is a great deal of unemployment in England so these girls have come out as what is called indentured labour. Much better than slaves and far more willing … about everything!" I saw him wink at Pa. I knew what he meant. Aunt Sarie's lips curled slightly in a resigned manner as she caught the glance.

After dinner, as we sat around the big dining-room table, the conversation turned to politics. Pa and Willem became extremely animated when discussing the recent talk of people leaving the colony.

"The latest is that the church is asking them not to go," said Oom Willem. "They say that they are not going to allow a dominee to accompany them. That means no Nagmaal or christenings or marriages or anything."

Pa looked dumbfounded. "What do you think will happen?" he asked.

"I don't know," replied Oom Willem, "But things are getting very serious. We hear that Uys, Maritz and Rudolph have already been in contact with the Zulus. Others have been looking north. There is already argument among the people as to which direction is best. There is a lot of discontent about the government among the people in your area. Quite frankly, there are many people who say if they want to go, then let them go and good riddance. I think they're being unreasonable by going. The English mean well. Our people should give them a chance. We hear from the missionaries that most of the violence on the frontier is caused by you boers anyway. If you'd just stop raiding the Xhosa and stealing their cattle, things would be fine. Anyway we have Sir Benjamin d'Urban here now. Maybe he'll be able to sort it all out."

Pa looked as if he was going to explode. His face went quite red but then, as if remembering that he couldn't be rude to his host, controlled himself and retorted quietly, "Ja, I can understand what you say. They pay your salary." He glanced around as if seeing all the surrounding trappings of wealth for the first time.

"It's not as simple as that. Our lands …" Oom Willem stopped, realizing that he had offended Pa. He smiled. "Come. We are all tired. I think it's time for bed."

We were ushered to our room upstairs. I didn't like to look out of the window as it was so high off the ground. We each had a four-poster bed with a canopy. Once Pa and I were alone we looked at the beds and burst out laughing. I took off my boots and bounced up and down, testing the softness. The springs squeaked and strained as I sank deep into the down-filled covers. "It feels like I am going to drown in this bed. It folds you in," I giggled.

That night Pa tossed and turned the whole night through, unaccustomed as he was to sleeping in a soft, springy bed. I took my bedclothes off the bed and slept on the floor, like a log.

Our time in Cape Town flew by. Everything was so different to the life I was accustomed to. It turned out that Oom Willem knew Emily Calverley and her family, the people Pa had transported to the frontier fourteen years before. Mrs Calverley was now a widow and lived in a very smart area on the road to Green Point. Pa seemed delighted with this news. I think he was even more pleased to hear that she was now a widow, not that I had ever heard him speak of a Mr Calverley.

On our first morning in Cape Town, while Pa made what he called a courtesy visit to Emily Calverley, I strolled through the streets and soaked up the atmosphere of the bustling, vibrant, town. "I wish Ma and the others could see me now," I thought to myself.

Around the area where we were staying, despite the grandeur of our accommodation, we were surrounded by a maze of steegs—lanes, alleys, squares and culs de sac—with a stench of raw sewage. I was grateful that Oom Willem had obviously done well. His lifestyle contrasted strongly with that of the average person in the Cape. We were living in luxury compared to most. Everywhere I went I heard the language of the English. The accents, though I did not know it then, were of the lower, working classes of London and the north of England. Free blacks, slaves, military and naval officers rubbed shoulders with ordinary soldiers—many in kilts—and sailors. Khoi hawkers, traders and smouses weaved their way between fine-looking gentlemen and shoddy beggars. Society ladies attended by slaves mingled with prostitutes. Everywhere I looked there were people, people and more people and colour, noise and bustle. Where we came from, people of different colours and social classes did not carry on their lives together in such fashion.

Pa's visit to Emily Calverley lasted most of the first day. He obviously thought it his duty to visit her quite often during our week-long stay. He frequently spruced himself up and disappeared for several hours at a time. He always returned in excellent humour and, more than once, mixed with the smell of brandy on his breath I detected the lingering scent of perfume. I think he became quite supportive of Emily Calverley. It was a good thing that Mr Calverley had been killed in a hunting accident five years before, otherwise he might have been hunting a different sort of game and Pa himself could have been on the wrong end of a barrel. When Pa wasn't visiting Emily Calverley on one of his frequent duty visits, as he called them, the two of us went shopping and explored the town.

Three days after our arrival, Tant Sarie introduced us to the finest tailor in town and showed us the shops where we could purchase all the goods on Pa's shopping list. She also showed me where I could buy a suitable gift for Amelia and helped me choose a tiny gold cross on a thin chain. It wasn't real gold but I was well pleased with my purchase. For an extra four pence I had 'Amelia' engraved onto it.

Tant Sarie took us to a shop in Long Street owned by a Frenchman. There were stuffed animals on show: hippopotamus, lion, rhinoceros and leopard. We had only ever seen these animals in the wild. They were so realistic that as we walked into the shop I saw Pa recoil in fright. Sarie watched our reactions with amusement. We had a long list of clothes to buy for my brothers as well as for Pa and me. Tant Sarie took us to a friend of hers, a British tailor, Arthur Millar. Pa was quite cross as Oom Willem had told him there were about thirty-eight Dutch or German tailors in Cape Town so he couldn't understand why we had to support an Englishman. Apart from the Thompsons, Pa wasn't too keen on the English. When he saw what a fuss was made of the two of us because we were with Tant Sarie and when he saw the quality of Mr Millar's clothes, he changed his mind. He changed it again for the worse when he received the bill. A pair of breeches cost him ten shillings, the equivalent of six days' pay for an average worker.

Pa also had trouble working out the value of his money as he wasn't used to the pounds, shillings and pence of the English. On the frontier we still spoke about rix dollars and shjillings. It had been only two years since the English had changed the currency. Pa was close to tears when he saw the prices.

On one of my walking excursions I made my way down to the waterfront. It was evening. I stood on the breakwater and watched the little fishing boats bobbing and rolling in the Atlantic rollers as they made their way back after a day at sea. Those that had been successful wallowed deeper in the water like fat ducks after a feeding frenzy while those with less fortune seemed to skim across the top of the waves. As they tied up to the wharf the fishermen jumped ashore, their sea boots squelching as they stamped on dry land with noisy shouts to those left aboard: "Gooi die vis, manne." The piles of fish formed shiny silvery heaps which shone as they caught the rays of the setting sun. After haggling ferociously with the fishermen, the fishmongers loaded their stock onto handcarts and almost immediately began trading with the gathering throngs. Shouts of "Fresh fish", the sounds of fish horns, prices yelled out and the names of fish created a babble of noise, conjuring up images of the deep: "Kabbeljou ... geelstert ... dhamba ... snoek ... come on people! Get it while it's fresh!"

The bustle was interrupted when a couple of fishmongers began chasing after two pigs and three mangy dogs, attracted by the smell of fish innards. One of the men swung a hefty kick with a solid boot at one of the pigs, which disappeared in a chorus of squeals, curly tail suddenly straightened by the well-placed kick. The stench of rotting entrails was most unpleasant so I did not linger long.

At the top of the Heerengracht a crowd of people caught my eye, standing near a water pump, huddled together. Curious, I gently elbowed my way forward. About six rows from the front I craned my neck, glad that I was quite tall. I could see a group of about eight scruffy, sad-looking boys with two girls. I estimated that their ages ranged between ten and fifteen. All had their eyes downcast and looked in a pitiful state.

A man stood in front, shouting out their attributes, "Look at this fine muscular lad …" He squeezed the puny muscles of a boy's arm. When any potential employer showed interest the child was roughly shoved in his direction. These were white children.

"Are they slaves?" I asked the man next to me.

"They may as well be," was the whispered reply. "These are poor children from England who have been brought out to give them a chance in life. The Children's Friend Society in London sends them out. Most of them are from destitute families in England; they are supposed to be getting a chance in life. Some chance!" he snorted. "Many of them are young criminals but I suppose this is better than being in a workhouse. For myself, I wouldn't want one as a servant. They are more trouble than they are worth. They run away more than the slaves."

I shook my head. I did not enjoy watching the humiliation and so left.

Night was fast approaching when I found myself next to the Company Gardens in Wale Street. As I took in the excitement of the town in the setting sun I became aware of the most magnificent building I had ever seen. It was so stately and elegant that it took my breath away. It was St George's Cathedral—tall, stately and elegant—with a clock tower and a spire. The architecture was majestically different. Behind the cathedral, the dark blue of Table Mountain towered over the town.

That evening over dinner, served by the two white women and the slave, Oom Willem informed us that we were invited to join him the next day at the races. "There are a great number of new horses that the English have brought in from India," he said. "They have these new soldiers here that we call the Indians. They love their horse racing and gambling … sometimes I think they prefer horse racing to dancing and women! Anyway, we will spend the day at the Green Point races and you can try and make back some of that money that that tailor Millar took from you."

Pa's eyes lit up at the thought that he might combine horse racing with a visit to widow Calverley whose house was on the way.

The next afternoon we rode with Oom Willem in his carriage. I was quite bored watching the races. Fortunately it was a lovely warm day. I enjoyed soaking up the sun and watching the splendour and finery of the people far more than I did the horses. Neither Pa nor I had money for gambling. Oom Willem on the other hand seemed to delight in the excitement and didn't seem at all unhappy when he lost.

Late in the afternoon Pa and I decided to leave him at the track and walk home. As we entered Burg Street dusk was falling, the street lamps already lit, glowing through the evening sea mist. We heard a commotion down one of the steegs. Men were shouting and cheering.

"Let's see what's going on," said Pa, quickening his pace.

We pushed our way through a crowd of about fifty people, mainly Malay slaves and sailors from a variety of nations, mixed with a sprinkling of Khoi servants. The men were crowded around an open area about ten yards square. Two giant cockerels, one red and the other white, were fighting to the death. The birds had sharpened artificial metal spurs attached to their own. We were watching one of the oldest sports in the world, a cock fight, and we were in the cockpit. Red and white wings flapped, almost folding into each other. Feathers flew. A slave was holding the spectators' wagers. Against a wall lay the mangled, bloody corpse of the most recent loser. The two birds were sparring, heads craned forward, feathers ruffled, circling each other, looking for the opening. Suddenly the white bird struck with lightning speed; there was a flash of metal and blood squirted and spattered as the spurs ripped into his opponent's body. With a single flap of his wings, the white bird flew onto his opponent's back and furiously slashed and pecked at the head. Blood pumped from the red cockerel's neck, speckling the whiteness of the stronger bird. The onlookers cheered and screamed in a frenzy of excitement. As the red bird fell to his side with the white cockerel ruthlessly slashing, clawing and pecking, a hush descended over the crowd. The red bird jerked, its legs straight out in front of its body, shivered violently three times and then fell still. It was all over. A loud cheer rose from the supporters of the white bird as a crowd huddled around the promoter to collect their winnings. The excitement over until the next two birds duelled to the death, Pa and I wandered off unnoticed and made our way down Waterkant Street.

"I need a drink after that," said Pa. He stopped opposite a sign over a door advertising 'Het Blaauwe Anker', one of some seventy public houses in the Tavern of the Seas. Pa turned to me, "Oom Willem will still be some time, so we needn't rush back. It's time that you learned to suip! Come, let's drink."

I wasn't too enthusiastic but had no option but to follow. We ducked through the narrow wooden door. I had never been in a tavern before. The smoke and noise hit me like a wall. Despite the early hour the small smoke-filled room was alive with the humming of conversation, shouts and laughter. My nostrils twitched at the unpleasant odour of stale pipe smoke, sour beer, vomit and lingering farts. The sound of breaking glass heralded our arrival as a drunken sailor dropped a bottle onto the stone floor with a crash. Nobody paid any attention. I looked around at the crowd, mainly sailors and quite a few free blacks, as well as slaves and poorer whites. A number of drunks sat motionless, heads sunk deep into their chests; some were sitting at tables with their heads resting on their arms, dead to the world, oblivious to their daily cares. The main room was packed with men crowded around wooden tables, some seated, some standing. In an alcove, through a blue haze of tobacco smoke, I made out the figures of a group of men smoking what Pa told me later was opium. Games were taking place, all of which involved betting and arguing, cards, dice, dominoes and skittles. Some men played, others were content to watch and shout rowdy, unsolicited advice. A scuffle broke out as two men argued over the winnings of a hand of cards.

Pa paid the three pence for half a pint of brandy after having to wait for a good few minutes for his turn to be served. Holding our beakers and our jug of brandy, we squeezed into two empty chairs at a table in a corner, where we had a good view of the tavern's activities. Pa poured brandy into the two tumblers, looked me straight in the eye, raised his glass and said, "Geluk seun!" He downed it in a single gulp. I watched him and did the same. The brandy burned its way down my gullet like hell's fire, scorching a trail down my throat and into my stomach. I lost my breath, spluttering and choking. The sensation spread down my body and seemed even to curl my toes. My eyes streamed and my spluttering brought raucous shouts of amusement from those nearby who had witnessed my first attempts at drinking. Pa pounded my back and laughed heartily. I tried to cover my embarrassment by immediately filling my glass again and gulping down another large tot. It had the same effect. Somehow, this time, I didn't seem to worry so much about being embarrassed.

We sat observing the activities around us as I slipped into a mild state of intoxication, feeling a warm glow inside. From time to time a number of women approached the tables, interrupting the gaming. Sometimes they would move onto the next group but occasionally, a man would stand up to the raucous jeers of his companions and leave the room, hand in hand with a woman. I looked at Pa questioningly.

"They earn money selling sex," said Pa, in answer to my unasked question. "The better ones have rooms next door which they rent, where the men you see leaving sleep with them."

Next to us an argument broke out between one of the women and a drunken sailor. She was a slave seeking an income and had approached the table offering her services.

"Two shillings is all you are worth, you old hag," sneered the sailor.

"Jou wit canailje, you white trash! Wie wil met jou saamen gaan? Who would want to go with you? "Kammene kas, kammene kunte!" she yelled. "No cash, no cunt!"

The sailor jumped up, knocking his chair over and slapped the woman across the face, cutting her lip. She grabbed a bottle, smashed it on the edge of the table and then, almost in the same movement, rammed the jagged ends of the broken bottle into the sailor's face. He let out a scream of agony, doubling over, covering his face with his hands. Bright red blood seeped through his fingers, dripping onto the stone floor. Two of his companions grabbed the woman, twisted her arms behind her back and propelled her—spitting, screaming and kicking like a banshee—to the door. The injured sailor was hustled from the room by his friends to receive some sort of medical treatment. He would be scarred for life. He, like me, wouldn't forget the night.

The disturbance over, the hubbub of conversation started up again. The more brandy I drank, the rosier the world appeared. Pa also seemed to be enjoying himself. He was flushed and had a fixed smile on his face. We weren't talking at all. Everything seemed right in my world. Above the babble of conversation in the tavern I heard 'rattatatat ... rattatatat ... rattatatat!'—the sound of kettledrums calling the sailors back to their ships. I watched as a few of the more law-abiding characters started making for the door, while the majority carried on drinking. As a group of sailors passed us, one fell against our table and shouted out almost in desperation,

"Nog eens gestooft te worden!" His mates bundled him out of the door and into the night, with him still pleading for one last drink.

Pa looked at me and then at the empty flask. Reluctantly he surrendered to convention, stood up from the table, wiped his mouth with the back of his hand and said, "Kom, seun. It's time to head back."

We walked out into the cool night air. From the direction of Waterkant Street, the sound of gentle singing could be heard. A group of Malay slaves hove into view, singing sadly of a land far away and loved ones left behind, of open spaces where children ran free and laughed, of running waters and whispered dreams, of warm sunlight and tender kisses, of waves caressing the shore, of tears of sadness and promises of forever, of leaving, never to return, of loneliness. The sound of men and women singing in harmony was the most beautiful sound I had ever heard. I could feel the hairs on my arms standing up.

As the slaves passed and the music faded, Pa broke the spell. "Well, Rauch, we have seen some things today, haven't we? I wonder if we will ever be able to tell your brothers and sisters of all we have witnessed."

I knew what he meant. I doubted that I would ever be able to convey what I had experienced ...

Back in our lodging in Long Street, Pa collapsed on his bed still fully clothed with his boots on. He was soon dead to the world. I lay on my bed on the floor in my clothes. I closed my eyes.

Tomorrow we were going home.

Chapter Three

And now we had returned to find that our lives would never be the same. Cape Town was another world, as after midnight on that ghastly night, with Pa still cradled in Gieletjie's arms, we approached the light of the Thompsons' farm. Despite the rain, they must have heard the sound of the wagon approaching. Gieletjie stayed with the oxen, while we dashed through the rain to the house and the warmth and dryness the cheerful light promised.

Framed by the doorway, lit from the lamp in the passage, was the Englishman, Brian Thompson, wearing a long nightshirt. Behind him was the concerned, pretty face of his wife Mary, also clad in her nightdress. "Come in, come in," said Brian, holding his arms out in welcome.

"I'll put the coffee on," said Mary.

The Thompsons' house was similar to the English houses we had seen in the Cape. Not like our boer houses with a voorkamer, the living room where everything happened. Here, leading from the front door and running through the house to the kitchen at the back was a passage. Doors guarded the rooms.

A door opened and there stood the Thompsons' only child, fifteen-year-old Amelia, holding a candle. My heart did a drum roll as I saw her. The light from the candle cast a glow on a pretty, slightly freckled face, framed by golden curls. Through the coarse flannel cloth of her nightgown I could see her nipples pressing against the fabric. I felt awkward in her presence, although the dagga had made me bolder.

"Greetings, Amelia. How are you? You look nice. I have brought you a present." I wanted to bite my tongue as I said it but it was too late.

Amelia smiled and looking directly at me, said, "But you are the only present I need, Rauch—to have you here safe and sound."

She seemed so grown up. Although I was a full two years older, I felt like the younger of the two. I handed her the gold cross, wrapped in a cloth. She looked at it and then at me with blue eyes full of warmth. "Thank you, Rauch. I will treasure it forever. Please help me put it on."

Holding the two ends of the chain on each side of her neck, she turned around so that I could fasten the clip at the back. As I touched her skin at the nape of her neck my fingers felt like they were all thumbs.

When I had finished she turned, smiled sweetly and said softly, "Thank you, Rauch. That is very sweet of you."

My heart surged. Amelia led us into the lounge. We dripped puddles of water onto the stone floor. Frans and Dirk had been woken by our arrival. Despite being twenty-one and nineteen respectively they were unable to hold back the tears. Frans sobbed openly and I could see Dirk struggling not to cry. He lost the battle and tears streamed down his cheeks. I felt my throat constrict and my own eyes brimmed with tears. I tried not to wipe my eyes but the tears welled up until they overflowed and coursed uncontrollably down my cheeks. Pa cried in great wracking sobs that seemed to shake every bone and sinew in his body. The remaining four members of our family hugged each other, sharing our grief, while the Thompsons and Sloam left us alone.

"They even killed our little Helena. What harm could she ever have done to the Xhosa?" sobbed Frans.

Pa shook his head like a wounded animal. After we had comforted each other, the Thompsons came back into the room and stood watching us almost awkwardly. I looked around as if seeing my family for the first time. Frans and Dirk were wearing only breeches. I noticed how similar we four were in build and appearance: fair hair, blue eyes and strong features. Frans's locks were slightly curly while the rest of us had straight hair. Pa's was speckled with grey like a pigeon egg. All about the same height and weight.

We drank the steaming coffee made by the slave Katrina who had been woken by the Thompsons and who had tears of sadness coursing down her dark cheeks. As she passed me a mug, one of her tears plopped gently into the coffee. I said nothing.

Brian Thompson spoke: "We did what we could but by the time we got to your place it was all over. All we could do was bury the dead. We waited for a couple of days in case you came back, but then, when you didn't arrive, of course we had to do it. You know," he looked sad and embarrassed, glancing away before completing the sentence, "the smell was starting … so we …" He shrugged his shoulders hopelessly.

"We got the minister from Bathurst to say prayers for them. I hope you don't mind … it was in English. I am sure that God didn't mind." He looked overcome with embarrassment. No one said anything. Then, as he got onto safer ground, his words tumbled out, "You can stay here. We have already got your slave girl Katrina here; she is sleeping with our two slaves in the hartebeeshuisie outside. Frans and Dirk are sleeping in one of the wagons at the back of the house and you two can join them and stay for as long as it takes you to rebuild your house."

"Yes, stay … please!" said Amelia, looking directly at me.

I could feel myself going red and looked away. I saw Dirk exchange glances with her, as a slight smile flitted across his face.

"They have been very good to us," said Dirk. Again a glance in Amelia's direction, "I don't know what we would have done without help from the Thompsons."

Pa seemed to snap himself out of his state of shock. "Tomorrow we start rebuilding. We appreciate your goodness," he said, turning to Thompson. "There are four of us and Gieletjie, so it will not take long. We will get out of your way as soon as we can. For now, we say, thank you. Come boys. Let's offload our goods from Sloam's wagon so that he can make an early start in the morning. But first let us pray."

We held hands. Amelia next to me squeezed mine as Pa prayed to God and thanked him for our safe return. I wondered why he didn't mention what God had allowed to happen to the rest of our family. I glanced up while Pa prayed. Amelia had her eyes open and was watching me. I smiled. She smiled back.

When he had finished, the four of us went out with lanterns. It had stopped raining. Gieletjie had outspanned the oxen and had joined Thompsons' Hottentots in their huts.

We took the presents that had been meant for our family, together with the gunpowder and building equipment which we had bought in the Cape, and put them in one of the Thompsons' back rooms. How different our homecoming had been to what we had planned.

ക്ക്ക

For the next sixty-three nights we slept in the spare wagon next to the house. We shared out the clothes we had bought for my sisters and Ma between Mary, Amelia and Katrina, with the odd gift to Thandi. We gave the new clothes to Frans and Dirk.

Then we loaded up a Cape cart, loaned to us by Brian Thompson, and with our building materials piled high, set off on horseback to the ruins of our house. Pa selected a new site, higher up the hill. It looked down on the eight new graves. "This time we are going to build a proper house, like those in the Cape," he said.

The four of us set to work. We searched for straight tree trunks in the nearby forest, chopping down the trees and using the horses to drag giant bundles of five or six trunks to our new site. The walls were to be a full twenty-four inches wide, using timber beams, stone and clay. All materials first had to be located and then transported by horseback and wagon.

The four of us, assisted by Gieletjie and two other Hottentots loaned to us by the Thompsons, toiled daily from sunrise to sunset. As we worked, wearing only breeches, the sun burned our bodies a rich brown. The heavy manual labour ensured that arms became muscular and taut. The work also took our minds off what had happened. Pa was a great deal quieter and kept more to himself than he had done before. Sometimes it looked as though he was lost in another world. Despite this, there were times when it seemed as though the pain of his loss was diminishing. Whether it was the work or our collective loss, we seemed much closer as a family. Some days we would work in silence where the only sounds were the grunts of effort and curt instructions from Pa. Yet despite the lack of words there was a bonding between us.

Occasionally we would be interrupted by the arrival of Amelia, riding her pony, Daisy. We all stopped work, watching as she approached, sitting straight-backed like the English do; not riding like us boers. The English always looked like little tin soldiers on their horses. Amelia, encouraged by her mother, dressed in English style rather than a boer's. She always seemed more relaxed and less severe than my sisters had looked. The English clothing was somehow softer and more feminine. There were days when Amelia wouldn't even wear a kappie, a bonnet. Her long, curly, golden hair would be done up in braids and piled on her head. Her dress, which came down to her ankles with frilly petticoats underneath, was usually brightly coloured, in stark contrast to the drab browns and blacks that our women wore. On her feet she wore veldskoene, but on her they looked dainty and ladylike compared to the handmade riempieskoene worn by the Boer women which made their feet look slow and clumsy.

Sometimes she would sit and watch us as we worked and then, if Pa said so, we would all go down to the river at the bottom of the farm just before the sunset and swim in the fast-flowing waters as the sun slipped behind the hills, washing the waters of the Kap with a pinkish glow. The four of us would go into the reeds, where Amelia couldn't see us, strip down to our underwear and then slide into the welcoming cool waters. We would swim to Amelia sitting on the bank, watching, usually chewing on a piece of grass, smiling at our efforts to impress her. Sometimes her dress and numerous petticoats would be slightly drawn up so that we could see her calf almost up to the knee. She didn't seem to care. Nor did we.

It was at times like this that even Pa seemed to snap out of his melancholy. The four of us would be high spirited, shouting and splashing each other, diving under the water, casting glances at Amelia to see if she was watching and seeing who could swim farthest under water. I, as the youngest and the one in love with Amelia, tried hardest of all to outdo the others. Amelia and I seemed to grow a great deal closer. I had never plucked up the courage to tell her how I felt. To be honest, I didn't think it was necessary. I am sure she knew.

She knew how to flirt as well. One evening after we had been swimming, the others rode back to the Thompsons' homestead ahead of us. Amelia and I rode behind in the dust which cloaked us from view. Suddenly Amelia stopped her horse. "I think Daisy has a stone in her hoof."

She climbed down. I stopped and jumped off Grey. She bent down and lifted up Daisy's front right hoof and examined it. "All looks fine to me," she said. Then she turned to me. "So do you, Rauch."

That made me feel good. She smiled and turned to get on her pony. As she did she appeared to stumble and trip, falling sideways. I jumped to prevent her falling but was too late. She fell onto the grass, half backward, her legs splayed and her dress and petticoats riding up, exposing bloomers which came to about four inches above her knees. She landed with her arms stretched backward to stop herself from hitting the ground too hard. She sat dead still, leaning back, resting on her elbows and allowing me to feast my eyes on her limbs. She made no effort to cover them. I could see the shape of her well-formed legs. Just below the elastic of her bloomers, I saw the start of her white thigh. She watched me with a smile. Our eyes locked and then mine darted back to that bit of creamy thigh.

"That's enough, don't you think?" she said as she slowly and deliberately pulled her dress down, firming it down with the palms of her hands.

That ended my mental journey of delight. She scrambled up and leaning forward, placed a gentle kiss on my lips before laughing, "Oh! You are funny, Rauch. You should see your face!" She jumped on her horse and galloped home.

Her taste and smell lingered for hours. That night as Pa said prayers I could see her looking at me from beneath her fluttering eyelids while pretending to have her eyes closed. I could still taste and smell her as I closed my eyes to sleep that night. Thinking of her aroused me and my hands seemed to have a will of their own. Of course I asked the Lord for forgiveness afterward. I am sure that He understood.

One morning, before the sun was up, I went over to the rondavel where the two slaves and Katrina lived. I called Katrina to make coffee. There was no response. I pushed open the door. As I peered into the gloom of the smoke-filled interior, from the light of the last embers of the fire in the middle of the mud floor, I could see that there were two shapes under the covers. One was Katrina. I strained my eyes and made out the other: my brother, Dirk.

I shouted, "Katrina! Staan op! Dis tyd om koffie te maak!"

She stirred and pulled her long black hair away from her face. Her eyes flashed a challenge. She threw the bedclothes aside and got up. Despite my fascination with Amelia, Katrina's sultry looks always set my heart racing. Together with the flash of her brown legs, the sight of my brother lying next to her sent a pang of jealousy through me. I never said a word to either of them. I now knew why when frequently I awoke at night, I would feel rather than see that the sleeping position next to me was unoccupied. Dirk was not there. He was obviously visiting Katrina. I wondered how long she had been sleeping with him.

Six weeks after the attack on the homestead, Pa was still nursing his pain. Sometimes in the night, Pa's space was also empty. I imagined that he just wanted to be on his own and think about Ma and the girls and his loneliness.

ὣ ὣ ὣ

Our days were long as we toiled under a burning sun. We completed the walls of the house in four weeks. We sat on the beams of the half-finished roof, doing the thatching. My highlight of any day was when Amelia rode down and brought us a jug of cold water. She always poured mine last and our hands would sometimes touch, sending a shiver down my spine as she let her hand linger. Frequently our hands touched when no one was looking. Sometimes she brushed past me, touching me with her breasts. I did not complain. I saw that her hands sometimes also seemed to linger when she touched Dirk. I remember thinking that she was a tease. I was never sure whether she really liked me or whether it was all men. That my brothers were much older didn't seem to bother her.

Days were frequently topped off by a swim in the river and an evening meal around the fire after we arrived back at the Thompsons at dusk. We would smell the wood fire and the aroma of the potjie stew bubbling over the fire that Katrina had prepared for us. Sometimes Amelia would swim with us. If not, she would join us for the evening meal, looking lovely and fresh.

After supper Mr Thompson, if he felt in the mood, entertained us by playing his fiddle, a boereliedjie if he was feeling cheerful and, slow, beautiful, classical music from far away if he was feeling sad or pensive. When he played like that my mind went back to the singing of the Malay slaves in the Cape. His mood, carried to us by the music, was contagious. He could change our mood by the rhythm and selection of the pieces he played. Sometimes if we recognized the piece we would join in singing.

The classical pieces were only for Mr Thompson, Mary and Amelia. They sounded so beautiful but none of us could whistle or hum the melodies.

On an evening such as this at the beginning of December we arrived at the Thompsons to find the Landdrost from Bathurst, Meneer Snyman, waiting for us. Brian Thompson called to us when we were still some distance off. "Come, kêrels! Johann has news from the Cape." Unable to contain himself, he shouted, "The English have freed the slaves! All the slaves are free from the first of December. It's happened already!"

Katrina and Mr Thompson's slaves stood listening nearby, looking very unsure of themselves and what to do next. I looked at Katrina. In the glow of the firelight, she was magnificent. She reminded me of an Arabian mare. When she was angry or unsure she would bristle like a hunting dog on scent. Now her nostrils flared as she tossed her thick black hair and gazed at Pa in expectation, with flashing, burning eyes of coal, as if challenging him to react to the news.

Pa took it in philosophically. "We have been expecting this. I'm not sorry. Katrina, you are no longer our slave."

Katrina looked horrified. "What am I then?" she asked.

"You now work for us, like Gieletjie," said Pa. "I have to keep you working for me as an apprentice for four more years; only then can you go free. That is the law."

Katrina looked quite relieved and said, "There is nowhere I can go to anyway. My home is here with this family. It is all I have ever known. Anyway, what is the difference between Gieletjie and me? We both work for you. I don't want anything else, so nothing has changed."

I could see from the expression on Dirk's face that for him a lot had changed. Better to sleep with a free woman than a slave. That night change started.

After the evening meal, Katrina sat with us and the Landdrost, listening to Brian Thompson playing the fiddle, not as a slave but as a servant. She chose to sit next to me on a log, between me and Pa. There wasn't much space so she sat close to me. I felt her thigh against mine and felt her press against me. I responded with a gentle push back. Amelia cast slivers of glass in my direction; Dirk didn't look too pleased either. The music that night was soft and gentle but we didn't sing; we just listened.

After the music finished and we had prayed, Pa and Hans and the Thompsons accompanied the Landdrost into the house to drink brandy and catch up on all the latest news from the Cape, of people leaving the colony. Dirk and I were left next to the fire with Katrina and Amelia. Dirk beckoned Katrina with a movement of his head in the direction of our wagon. Katrina applied pressure against my thigh one last time and then glanced at me and stood up. She followed Dirk into the night.

Amelia looked at me. Her eyes seemed full of promise. The jealousy shown a few minutes ago seemed to have disappeared. She ran her tongue over her bottom lip, stood up, moved into the shadows out of the firelight and looked back at me. I followed her into the darkness. She stopped a few paces into the blackness. Behind me, I could still see the fire blazing but we were no longer part of that light. She turned to me as I reached her and then slowly lowered herself backward to sit in the grass. We were in grass, long from half a summer of rains. We were completely hidden. She held out her arms to me. I needed no further encouragement and put my arms around her. In the flickering light I saw that her eyes were closed and her lips slightly parted, inviting me to taste them. I kissed her long and gently at first but very quickly the gentle kiss turned into one of excitement. I could feel myself becoming aroused. Already excited by Katrina's thigh, the feel of Amelia's mouth on mine made my breathing come faster. I could actually taste her. Her mouth opened and I felt her tongue exploring my mouth. It was the most delicious feeling I had ever experienced. Her breath was hot and sweet, her breathing quickening as we kissed, deep and hard.

I learned quickly. My body seemed to know exactly what to do. As we sat kissing, my hand went to her breasts. It seemed the natural thing to do. She didn't push it away. I could feel her pert, upright breasts through the fabric of her dress. I caressed them gently and could feel her nipples stiffening. She breathed heavily. I felt her hand rub down the front of my breeches. As she moved her hand up and down in a steady rhythm I knew that she could feel the rod of stiffness. I didn't care. I lifted up her dress. I ran my hand up past her knee, expecting to meet her bloomers. Nothing! All I could feel was the silky softness of her thigh as my hand moved higher and higher under the petticoats. My hands were clammy with excitement as they continued the journey upward. She started to make tiny noises as my hand reached its destination. I could feel her soft hair. I started to rub the wetness between her legs. She opened them to allow better access. Her hand was still busy rubbing me through my breeches. I wanted to stop and take my breeches off and plunge myself into her depths but didn't want to take my hand away from the promise to come. I could feel her wetness on my fingers. Her head was thrown back. She arched her back as I played with her and she with me. I pulled her dress further up, around her waist. Even in the dark I could see her beautiful thighs and the dark patch between her legs where my hand had been busy. I forced myself to stand up and began unbuckling my belt. As I started to pull down my breeches, Amelia seemed to snap from her intoxicated state. She raised herself up onto her elbows and whispered fiercely. "What are you doing? Stop! Now! No! No! We can't do this! We are not married!"

My heart sank. My erection collapsed. Not married? What on earth was she talking about? From her reaction I don't think that I was the first man to feel that secret garden between her thighs. If the experience was new to me, it certainly wasn't to her.

"Come, we must go back. My father will be worrying about me."

I knew the only thing that Mr Thompson would be worrying about was whether or not he was going to get another brandy when the one he was drinking was finished. She stood up, straightened her petticoats and her dress and kissed me gently on the mouth. Thinking that she had changed her mind, I kissed her harder and moved my tongue into her mouth. She laughed and nibbled it with her teeth. She again reached down and grabbed me through my breeches and rubbed ... hard. I had already stiffened again and ejaculated in my breeches. I shuddered as I exploded. I could feel the wetness down my front.

She stepped away from me and laughed. "Too much for you, hey Rauch? Well, that'll give you something to look forward to in the future. If you enjoyed that I am sure that you will enjoy the real thing; I know that I will." She looked at me smiling. "Come, it's done. Let's go."

I was too embarrassed to respond, and when she took my hand in hers and led me back to the fire, I was very quiet. I was worried that she and the others would notice the wet patch spread over the front of my trousers. I went straight to my wagon.

Lying in bed that night I could smell her scent on my hand. As I thought of the magnificent treasures that awaited me and the vision of that patch between her legs, the memory was so vivid that it took less than a dozen strokes of my right hand. After asking forgiveness from the Lord, I went to sleep feeling quite drained.

The new homestead was ready for us to move into on December 18th, 1834. I will never forget the day. There wasn't much to move into the house as most of our furniture and personal possessions had been burned. What we had was loaded onto the Thompsons' wagon and, after saying our farewells, the four of us, with Gieletjie, Thandi, Katrina and our horses, made our way to our new house.

After the wonderful night when I had come so close to making love to Amelia, I was more in love with her than ever but she had appeared a little distracted and distant. I put it down to the fact that she was feeling sad as we were leaving. As she waved farewell I saw that she was fingering the little gold cross nestling below the neckline of her dress. It made me feel good.

On the trip to the new house, talk was still about the news that Johann Snyman had brought us a week earlier.

"Apparently, Andries Potgieter, Piet Uys and Johann Pretorius have all sent scouts on secret expeditions outside the colony, to explore where it might be suitable and safe to move to," said Pa.

"Why secret?" asked Frans.

"The government doesn't want us leaving, so people are scared that they will charge those who leave as rebels. I am sure that the authorities will make life difficult for anyone who considers it," said Pa. After a brief silence, he glanced at each of us. "We must watch what happens. Who knows? We've already lost half our family. If things don't get any better here, maybe we will join them and go as well." He cracked his whip over the span of oxen.

We continued in silence which grew heavier as we passed the graves of our mother and sisters before climbing the hill to the homestead. The eight graves, now covered with green grass, appeared lonely. I had never considered the possibility that we might actually leave our land behind, particularly as our family was now buried in it.

It was late afternoon when we arrived. Despite the hospitality shown by the Thompsons and the presence of Amelia, it was good to be at De Hoop again, our own home. I took my Sanna and rode off in the evening light to shoot an impala for the pot. The sky was painted a brilliant pink. An hour later, with an impala slung over Grey, my track took me close to the swimming place at the river. It had been a hot day so I decided to cool down. I rode quietly, lost in my thoughts. Just before the river there was a clearing. Despite the failing light, I could see a man and woman in the grass. Amelia was facing me, lying on her back. There was no doubt in my mind that Dirk was the man on top of her, his breeches around his ankles. Amelia's head was thrown back, her legs wide apart with knees raised. Her dress was around her waist and her arms around his back. Her hands clawed at his naked buttocks as if to give his thrusts more force and feeling. Her obvious pleasure and wild abandonment struck me like a sledgehammer in the pit of my stomach. The world spun in front of my eyes and I jerked back in the saddle.

Then she saw me, over his shoulder. Her eyes widened in shock and she started to wriggle, to move out from under him. He, thrusting away like a piston, must have thought that her reaction was a signal of her immense enjoyment. He drove into her even harder. I pulled hard on the reins, wheeled Grey around and kicked my heels into his flanks. My eyes blinded by tears of rage, hate and betrayal, I galloped as fast as I could back to the homestead. I knew that I could not stay there. I knew too that I hated Dirk and Amelia. I stormed into the house in a blind rage. In the kitchen, Katrina was stacking provisions in a cupboard which the Thompsons had given us. She immediately noticed that something was wrong.

"What …?" she started

I grabbed her and pulled her to me, wanting to do anything to hit back at Dirk. As I tried to kiss her, she pulled away and shoved both hands against my chest. I saw red. I grabbed at the top of her dress and ripped it open, revealing magnificent dusky, full, ripe breasts with dark brown nipples, standing erect. I was breathing heavily with a combination of rage and desire. Her eyes flashed with anger. She tried to cover her breasts with one hand, pulling at the torn fabric. With the other she grabbed a knife.

"Come one step closer or ever try that again and I will cut your throat from here to here," she hissed, gesturing with the knife against her throat. "I say when I want to be fucked!"

I stopped as Dirk ran into the kitchen. "What the hell is going on?" he shouted. "What do you think you are doing?"

All the rage in me exploded. I was sure that I could smell Amelia on him. My fist smashed into him, full in the face, with all the strength that I could muster. Katrina screamed. Blood spurted from his broken nose. He spat out two teeth. I hit him again. His eyes dazed, he staggered backward. I moved forward but this time he was ready for me. His fist rammed into my right cheek and immediately I felt my eye closing. I grabbed the knife from the floor where Katrina had dropped it. I moved forward to stab my older brother. His right foot came up and caught me in the testicles. The pain was excruciating.

"That'll teach you to try and fuck my girl" he shouted.

I collapsed on the floor, doubled over in pain. The fight was finished. One last kick to the head from Dirk's boot ensured that I knew it was all over. They left me lying there, sobbing, alone and in pain, long into the night and long after the physical pain had eased.

When I woke before dawn the next morning, still lying on the floor, my first thought was of Amelia lying beneath Dirk with that look of desire on her face. It was as if that scene was now permanently burned into my brain. My eye had closed up completely, my head throbbed from Dirk's final kick and my balls ached from his boot. It was clear to me that I couldn't stay in the same house. What was even clearer was that I never wanted to see Amelia again. I quietly slipped into the room where my father and brothers slept, grabbed a satchel, shoved a few clothes into it, then went out into the darkness.

ॐॐॐ

I saddled up Grey and only then did I start to think about where I was going. The Thompsons were out of the question. I decided to ride to the frontier fort at Caffre Drift on the Fish River, some two and a half miles away. I knew I would be welcomed. Some of the officers had hunted pheasant and quail on our farm and I had got on well with the twenty-five-year-old Lieutenant Gibson who was garrisoned at the fort with his English wife, Joan, and their two-year-old baby, Chrissie.

I arrived as the sun was starting to peep over the thick bush surrounding the fort.

"Halt! Who goes there?" shouted a guard, wakened from his half slumber as he peered out at me.

"Rauch Beukes", I shouted in reply. "From the farm, De Hoop." I couldn't help being pleased that my time spent with Amelia had improved my English. The gate of the stockade was opened for me as I rode in and I found myself inside the barrack square.

"Where do I find Lieutenant Gibson?" I inquired of a passing soldier.

"He is on duty in the guardroom"

Entering the guardroom I saw Lieutenant Bill Gibson engaged in what appeared to be a serious discussion with another officer and half a dozen men. He broke off his conversation and turned to me. His face lit up in recognition. "Hello Boertjie," he said. "What are you doing here?" He saw my swollen eye which was taking on a deeper colouring of purple. "By God! Who hit you?"

I felt my face redden in embarrassment but didn't wish to share the story with a room full of strangers. "That doesn't matter. Can I stay here for a few days … there has been a bit of a problem at the farm?"

"One more civvy isn't going to break us for a few days. We'll keep it quiet from Colonel England in Grahamstown though, as he's a bit of a difficult sod." Gibson's face then lit up. "You could be the answer to a prayer. You know the land and also the Xhosa. We've had some mixed reports and would like to establish whether they are true or not. Two days ago we caught a kaffir stealing cattle up the river. He's in the black hole as punishment and we gave him a bloody good beating as well. He tells us that Maqoma, the Xhosa chief, is planning to attack Grahamstown before the next full moon. We think it's a load of nonsense but we want someone to visit the missionaries across the Fish and establish whether or not there's any foundation to the stories. What do you think? Will you do it? We will provide you with an extra horse and provisions and two troopers to accompany you?"

"When do you want me to go?"

"As soon as possible," answered Gibson.

Two hours later, after a good breakfast and accompanied by two Redcoats, Taylor and Hanson, I set off, pleased to be occupying myself with something useful.

The tide was low and we were able to cross the Fish directly below the fort, something not possible at high tide. The three of us set off cautiously as we didn't want to alert the natives to our presence—easier said than done as we had to travel through thick bush, making it extremely difficult to be quiet. We rode with guns primed and senses alert in case of attack. My first objective was to reach John Brownlee at his mission station on the banks of the Buffalo River and then, dependent on what we learned, to move to a couple more stations. The missionaries lived among the Xhosa and would be the best source to substantiate the rumours. We travelled northeast in the direction of the Buffalo, riding slowly, constantly scanning the surrounding bush.

From time to time we saw groups of people in the distance. There seemed to be many more Xhosa than I was used to seeing in this part of the world but not once did any of them challenge us, melting into the undergrowth instead.

Despite our unhindered progress I felt uneasy. "There is something afoot," I said to the troopers. "I have never seen this kind of behaviour."

The troopers, fresh out from England, glanced at each other nervously. Taylor said, "Shouldn't we go back to the post and tell them?"

"Tell them what?" I retorted. "No, better we get to see John Brownlee; he has his ear to the ground. If anything is happening he will have wind of it."

When we arrived at the mission station the next day we were met by a friendly John Brownlee. The missionaries were always pleased to see the boers or the settlers and to catch up on any news. By now the whole frontier knew what had happened to Ma and the girls.

"Sorry to hear about your family," said Brownlee, "You will stay here with us tonight? Where are you going? What are you doing this side of the Fish? Must be important if you have two Redcoats with you?" he asked with a wink.

I was tempted to tell him that I was probably the one doing the guarding—guarding the two troopers. That night, sitting next to the fire after we had eaten a large kudu potjie and mielies I asked Brownlee whether he'd heard any rumours of a possible attack by the Xhosa on the colony.

"What? You must be mad!" he said in astonishment. "No! No! I don't believe anything like that is likely to happen. I live here among the Xhosa and I'm sure it would be impossible to keep anything of that nature a secret. Where did you get such a story?"

I explained about the prisoner at Caffre Drift.

"Definitely, nothing! I think that they are starting to embrace the word of our Lord. I don't believe they want war. The Xhosa have already been defeated by the army and I can't see them taking up arms again. The only thing I *will* say is that there seems to be a larger number of them around than normal. Maybe my work is starting to pay off and they are gathering to celebrate the birth of our Lord at Christmas in five days time?" he joked. "Anyway, I am going up to the Burnshill Mission to collect my sons, Charles and James, in a couple of days. I wouldn't be leaving here if there was any thought of danger. I think Lieutenant Gibson must be getting jumpy. Has he been drinking again?" he asked.

It was common knowledge that the troops in the isolated forts drank heavily, often out of boredom, and led a life that was frowned upon by the missionaries.

"In fact," he went on, "I will be going to see two other missionaries, Gottlieb Kayser and Richard Thompson, as well. Save your effort and go back to the fort and tell Gibson that he must stay off the bottle. If I find out anything different to what I have already told you, I will send a rider to tell you. I can swear to you, on my Holy Bible, that what I have told you is correct."

His prayers before we retired that night were for the souls of the natives and their conversion to the ways of the Lord. I didn't think Pa would have liked to share his Lord with the kaffirs. Again that night when I closed my eyes I saw Dirk on Amelia, her mouth opened lasciviously, eyes half closed and her face an expression of pure sexual pleasure.

Convinced by Brownlee's confident argument, I decided to return ahead of the troopers first thing the next morning, a Sunday, to convey the good news so that preparations for Christmas, only four days away, could be made by the one hundred and twelve men, women and children of the fort. I set off before Brownlee began his prayers with the heathen for Sunday morning church. I saw that his little church was already quite full.

On the ride back, I again saw many Xhosa, again melting away in front of me. I became more convinced that Brownlee was correct and quickly rode back to Fort Caffre, relaxed and pleased to be the bearer of good tidings. Riding alone, I was able to arrive at dusk the same day.

I entered the stockade and reported to Lieutenant Gibson. "Brownlee says that he has seen no evidence of any problem. He says that he is visiting the other mission stations and will check with them but is pretty sure there is nothing going on."

Gibson appeared relieved. "Well, that is certainly good news. I must say I respect Brownlee's opinion, so that little bit of information lifts a load off my shoulders. Thank you, Rauch. Now, we have found you some accommodation in one of the old stables. Will that do for you if you aren't yet ready to go home?"

I fixed a bed from the hay and made myself as comfortable as I could, before strolling over to join Lieutenant Gibson and his wife in his quarters for their evening meal. I was halfway across the parade ground when shouts of alarm from the guards stopped me in my tracks as the stockade gates swung open in a clatter of hooves and a cloud of dust. Trooper Hanson rode in, leading Taylor's horse by the reins with Taylor's lifeless body draped over the horse. Three assegais protruded from his back, pink blood smeared down the side of the horse, wet from sweat and the water of the river; Hanson had swum the Fish rather than wait for low tide.

"Look out!" shouted Hanson. "The bastards are coming! We've 'ad it! There are millions of the savages. They've already attacked the missionaries on the other side of the river. There is killing all over! Get out! Run for it!"

In the setting sun I caught the faint acrid smell of burning grass. I realized that I had noticed it earlier: burning huts. Troopers ran for their guns. A bugle sounded and Lieutenant Gibson came running from his quarters, buckling his belt, a pistol to hand. "You stupid sod!" he shouted at me, his face red with anger, "How can you say everything is fine? Look at Taylor! He's dead! How could you be so bloody stupid? I told you to find out what was happening. We're done for. You'd better get out of here and warn the farmers. If the Xhosa are attacking, your family and the others must be warned."

Hanson swung from his horse, his face white with terror. "They've attacked some of the mission stations, killing traders who sought shelter there. I've never seen so many of the buggers. They're on the rampage, heading to cross the Fish at Trompetters Drift. Thank 'eavens the tide is in otherwise they could cross 'ere and finish us all."

"How can you be sure?" Gibson shouted at the terrified trooper.

"Strewth! I saw 'em, sir! Millions there must 'ave been. Millions." he said repeating the number as if he needed convincing. "They're all dressed for war in their feathers ... and covered in that bloody red war clay. Some of 'em even 'ad guns! I've never seen so many of 'em, sir ... We're done for if they come across the river 'ere." He was babbling.

"Pull yourself together, man. You'll panic the people. We'll abandon camp and make for Bathurst." Turning to me, "You'd better go and warn the farmers ... now! You've probably got a lead of about an hour. Go!" he snapped. Then he looked at me again, the anger still in his eyes, "Christ, Boertjie, how could you have been so blind not to realize what was happening?"

I swallowed hard, unable to respond, my throat tight with shame. I grabbed my things, ran to the stables, mounted Grey and galloped out of the stockade into the night and away from the advancing hordes which I could now hear on the other side of the river as they moved into position, the sounds of thousands of Xhosa warriors moving through the grass.

The sixth Kaffir War had started.

Chapter Four

I could see the glow from at least five burning homesteads on the opposite bank of the Fish River as I rode out of Fort Caffre. The smell of burning assailed my nostrils and smoke stung my eyes. I rode through the night as fast as I could. It was over before I had time to contemplate the circumstances of my departure a few days before. It seemed an age had passed since I had left home. As I drew closer to the homestead I could see figures moving about on the roof. Pa, Frans and Gieletjie were pouring water onto the thatch to dampen it.

Pa shouted. "Don't shoot! It's Rauch."

Guns were pointing at me from two windows. At one were Katrina, Dirk and Amelia and at the other Mary and Brian Thompson, all holding Sannas.

I dismounted. "The Xhosa are attacking," I shouted, running inside.

"We know," Dirk replied.

Inside the darkened house I saw our neighbours, the Plettenbergs. Slaves from the Thompsons and Plettenbergs were crowded into the front room. Everyone was busy, shoving what little furniture we had against the doors or boarding up the windows that were not needed to shoot from.

"We've left our place," said Simon Plettenberg. "They can have it. We'll make a stand here with you. We have a better chance together. How far away are they?"

"About half an hour now," I answered as Simon prepared one of an arsenal of guns.

I felt Amelia looking at me. "Hello Rauchie," she said with the hint of a smile.

I ignored her and took up a position at the Thompsons' window, looking out into the dark.

Pa and the others came down off the roof. "That should stop the thatch from burning for a while," said Pa. "Let them come."

All went quiet, the silence broken only by whispers in the darkened room. I ignored Dirk and Amelia and focused my attention on what was happening outside. In the distance we saw a glow light up the sky. A shower of sparks rose into the blackness of the sky as the Plettenbergs' farm was torched. Then from the other side another glow as the Thompsons' place went up in flames.

I heard Brian Thompson moan quietly. "Oh no," he whispered almost to himself.

Dirk shouted, "Here they come!"

What seemed to be thousands of shapes emerged from the shadows, the light from flaming torches illuminating a long snake of warriors in full battle dress, with the approaching line stretching as far as the eye could see. Whistling and chanting, they came closer in a great surge like a rogue wave in a high sea.

Dirk was the first to shoot. Bodies fell. We all opened fire, aiming first at those carrying the torches and then just firing into the dark mass. They were packed so close and thick that wherever our bullets struck a man fell, sometimes more. The room was full of swirling smoke as we fired repeatedly. Men went down but as soon as one fell, he was replaced by another. The wave of attackers stopped about forty yards from us. We continued firing. The women loaded and primed the guns, passing them into our ready hands.

One of the torches detached itself from the dark mass and tumbled through the dark, followed by another and then another. They were throwing the flares onto the roof to try and burn us out. However, the water did the trick, although bits of smouldering thatch did shower down on us as we fired. The Xhosa wave was all around us. Directly in front of the house, in our line of fire, we were stopping them. Then, to our surprise, we saw that the black wave of screaming and whistling humanity had already swirled around the house. The attack was passing us by, almost as if the Xhosa had more important things to do, although there were still stragglers attacking from the front. Two Xhosa crept up to Dirk's window.

"Look out Dirk," I cried. "Two of them are right on you!"

One of the Xhosa drew himself erect and pulling back his arm, aimed the sharp point of a stabbing spear at Dirk's throat.

"Shoot! Shoot!" shouted Pa, looking at me. I turned and swivelled my Sanna in the direction of the attacker just as he was about to drive the assegai into Dirk's throat. My finger tightened on the trigger. And then I glimpsed Amelia's expression. She was next to Dirk.

I froze.

Amelia had the same expression of surprise on her face when she had seen me a few days before. I had a flash memory of her face contorted with lust. I hesitated . . . then fired straight into the head of the Xhosa warrior. I was too late. The split second of hesitation was time enough for the assegai to plunge deep into Dirk's throat just below his Adam's apple. Blood spurted. His eyes widened in shock as he dropped his gun, his hands rising to clutch at the shaft of the spear protruding from his throat. His mouth opened wide as if gasping for air and I saw the gap in his mouth where I had knocked out his teeth a few days before. Then, with a cough, he fell to the ground, dead. Pa's gun roared a split second after mine and the other Xhosa took the shot straight in the temple and fell dead in front of us. I had killed my brother as surely as if the shot from my Sanna had blown off his head and not that of the Xhosa's.

Behind me I heard a woman scream. I turned to see Katrina with her hand clasped over her mouth, her eyes wide with horror as she stared at Dirk's body. Pa ran and knelt down next to Dirk, cradling him in his arms. I stood frozen, in shock, not knowing what to do. The firing of guns continued from the rest of the group. Stragglers from the mighty army dashed past the windows, catching up with their comrades who had already passed by the dwelling. The sounds of whistling and shouting continued as they rounded up the cattle and sheep before disappearing into the night in the direction of Algoa Bay.

"Oh no, no! He's gone!" shouted Pa. He looked at me accusingly, "Why, oh why, did you take so long to shoot?"

I couldn't answer. They were all looking at me. I couldn't tell them the truth. "I ... I .... couldn't sight him," I said lamely.

Pa stood up, looking down at his dead son, his back to me. Amelia ran up to Pa and threw her arms around him. Pa sobbed as she drew him near. Amelia's face was staring at me over Pa's shoulder. Her hands moved down his back to rest lightly on his buttocks.

I felt a sledgehammer of realization strike me between the eyes. I had seen the identical tableau before. Only then it was on the grass bank of the Kap. I now recognized the build and the back of Pa from that day. It was Pa, Pa I had seen lying between Amelia's legs and not Dirk. My mind whirled. My hands went clammy and for a second the world spun as I almost passed out from the shock.

How stupid had I been?

Dirk had never slept with Amelia. It had been Pa all along. I remembered the nights when he disappeared from the wagon. I thought it was to smoke his pipe and mourn for Ma. He and Amelia! Holy God! There I was feeling sorry for him and all the time he was sleeping with the girl that I loved. My father had betrayed me and the memory of our mother.

Everyone was crowded around Dirk's corpse. The women wailed in grief and shock. The men tried to console them. Katrina knelt next to Dirk's body and wept. I staggered outside, my eyes blinded by tears of sadness and rage. I felt sick with shame at what I had allowed to happen and rage and jealousy at what Amelia and Pa had been doing behind my back. Frans came out of the house. In the distance we could hear the Xhosa as they moved in search of more homesteads to attack.

"It wasn't your fault," he said when he saw the tears in my eyes. "The

Xhosa killed him. Forgive Pa. He blames you; there is no one else to blame. You did your best."

I looked at Frans, almost speechless. "Forgive Pa? Forgive Pa? I will never forgive him for what he has done to me. He made me kill Dirk! He made me kill him," I screamed. "It wasn't even Dirk in the first place."

Frans looked at me in amazement. "What do you mean?" he said, "The warrior killed Dirk. You didn't."

"He's been fucking Amelia," I blurted out. "I thought it was Dirk but it was him. Pa. He was the one. How could he do that to me?"

Frans looked aghast as he took in what I was saying and then as if to comfort me, "I wasn't sure whether to say anything to you. We all know how you feel about Amelia and I knew that you would be upset. Who would have thought that it would have led to this?"

"I have to get away from here. Amelia and Pa … hell! I don't know what to do … where to go … I can't stay here anymore. I hate them both. Now I've killed Dirk because of her. My life is over. What can I do?" I was distraught and couldn't think rationally. Tears streamed down my face. "Oh my God! What can I do? What *can* I do?"

Brian Thompson and Simon Plettenberg came out of the house and heard me ranting. "Right now, what we can all do is get the hell out of this place and make for Bathurst. I think that was the first wave of the attack, so before the next lot comes, let's get going," Brian said. "We don't have time to stand around here feeling sorry for ourselves. Quick! Let's go." There were four wagons behind the house belonging to the Thompsons and Plettenbergs. The in-spanned oxen had escaped attention from the Xhosa.

"We can't go and leave Dirk behind," Pa shouted as Amelia took his arm. He turned to return to Dirk's body.

Amelia pulled forcibly at him. "Leave it! We can't take the boy with us and we haven't time to bury him now." She looked across at me. "Rauch can do it all … it's his duty anyway."

Her comment hit me like the spear that had ended Dirk's life. I watched as Pa was led away by Amelia. Despite the urgency, he climbed slowly onto the wagon. He looked a broken man.

Led by Gieletjie, the sad little procession of wagons disappeared into the night in the direction of Bathurst and sanctuary, twelve miles away. Nobody asked me to join them.

I went back into the house. Dirk's body lay under a sheepskin kaross next to the window where he had fallen. I dragged him across the grass to where Ma and my sisters were buried. Gieletjie's hut was still smouldering, torched by the Xhosa. I scratched through the ashes of what had been his home until I found the spade, partly burned but still usable. In the dark, with a heavy heart, I began to dig a shallow grave alongside Ma's and the girls'. When I had finished, I wrapped his body in the kaross and rolled him into the grave. I shovelled earth onto him. The last I saw of Dirk before soil covered him forever was the gap in his teeth.

ঔ৵ঔ৵ঔ৵

I decided not to follow the others to Bathurst but instead chose to head for Grahamstown, more than thirty miles away. Riding alone in the dark I was constantly on the alert in case I came across any stray Xhosa. The army had swept past us. That night and over the next few days close to five hundred farms were burned to the ground. The darkness of night was broken by the sight of burning farms and homesteads. De Villiers, Snyman, Stoltz, Marais. All abandoned. It was total devastation. Homesteads burned to the ground, the ruins still smouldering as I rode past, with the acrid smell of smoke polluting the night air.

After riding for an hour I caught up with five wagons, carrying more than thirty people, also heading for Grahamstown. "Rauch Beukes! Is that you? Where are the others? Where is the rest of your family?" It was Koos

Snyman, a boy of my age, whose family's ruined homestead I had passed thirty minutes earlier.

I pulled up next to the wagon, hitched Grey to it and jumped on. There were about a dozen people huddled inside. My gaze was drawn to the sight of a wounded man lying with his head cradled in the arms of a woman. Blood seeped from a wound in his stomach which I guessed had been caused by a Xhosa spear. All were lost in their own worlds of terror and silence. Sobbing women were being comforted by distraught men. Some of the men had tears trickling down their cheeks.

I sat next to Koos and answered. "They have all gone ... I think to Bathurst. We've lost the farm ... again. The Thompsons' farm has gone as well. Dirk is dead. Killed by the kaffirs. Everything's finished. How many did you lose?" I asked, attempting to steer the conversation away from my family.

"None dead, but I'm not sure if my brother Adrian is going to make it," he said gesturing to the back of the wagon where Adrian lay unconscious. "He was stabbed by one of the kaffirs but managed to shoot the bastard. He's in a bad way, though. The farm is gone and so are all the cattle and sheep. Look over there," he pointed.

I followed his gaze as we topped the crest of a hill. The scene was devastating. Beacons of fire shone out of the darkness. The ruins of hopes and dreams blazed away. I counted twelve fires in the distance, marking the route of the mighty Xhosa army that was sweeping the land ahead of us.

The sun was peeping over the horizon as our convoy, which had swelled to twenty wagons, arrived in Grahamstown. During the night other refugees had joined us. Despite the early hour, Grahamstown was alive with activity. Wagons were everywhere. Sobbing women, crying children and bewildered men stood around in small groups. A crowd formed around one of the wagons in the market square and watched in stunned silence as the bodies of three farmers were removed. As new wagons rolled in, each carrying their sad load of human cargo, fresh tales of devastation and death spread through the town. Rumours of an imminent Xhosa attack on Grahamstown were spreading. I saw two men run by, white-faced, carrying pitchforks as weapons. People seemed to be rushing about not knowing where to go or what to do.

"Where are the soldiers?" I asked Koos. I knew that the 75th Regiment under Lieutenant Colonel Richard English was based in Grahamstown and had expected to see troops in the streets organizing the town's defence.

"Apparently they are all guarding their barracks on the eastern edge of town; they are no good to us. I think we will have to take care of ourselves."

Veldt Kornet Piet Retief, a friend of Pa's from the days when they met the 1820 settlers in Algoa Bay, rode up to our dispirited group. "Hello Rauch. Where's your Pa and the rest of the family?"

"Dirk's dead," I replied, "and the others have gone with the Thompsons and Plettenbergs to Bathurst. Our farm is gone. I don't know what's going to happen now."

"Well, I am looking for men to ride out to the farms and see if we can find any survivors," said Retief. "We need to bring the people into Grahamstown. They will be safer here than on their farms, even if the Xhosa do attack the town." Retief looked around him. "Anyone else who can shoot and ride?"

Koos put up his hand and the two of us joined twenty-eight other boer volunteers. We rode out of Grahamstown. From the hills surrounding the town, where groups of boers stood guard every few hundred yards, our view toward the Fish River was almost too ghastly to bear. Pillars of smoke rose into the sky and tiny specks of circling vultures signalled what we would find.

For the next few days my own grief, shame and anger were put aside as I witnessed terrible scenes of loss on farm after farm. Occasionally we found survivors who would be escorted to Grahamstown. Our mission took us from Fort Brown, around the Fish River area and then toward Bathurst.

On Christmas Day we were approaching Jan de Beer's farm when Retief shouted, "Look out, kêrels! The kaffirs are attacking old Jan's place!"

I looked ahead and saw a crowd of warriors surrounding de Beer's small homestead. We could hear gunshots. Retief galloped toward the fray. We followed. The Xhosa did not see or hear us approaching. Their shouts and whistles drowned the sound of our horses' hooves as we galloped closer. We opened fire from fifty yards. Our bullets struck down more than a dozen Xhosa in the first fusillade. With shouts of alarm the others scattered and ran into the thick bush.

"Leave them," shouted Retief. "Rather get the family out and to safety in Grahamstown."

Their wagons had been burned so we loaded Jan de Beer, his wife and three young children onto our horses, with a few items of clothing hurriedly shoved into bags.

Back in Grahamstown my burden of guilt returned and I became more and more depressed. My whole life had changed in a week. I felt completely without direction. I was angry with Pa and Amelia, guilty because I had allowed Dirk to die, ashamed that I had mistakenly thought that it was him and not Pa with Amelia. Determined to drown my sorrows in alcohol I made my way to the King's Head.

As I entered the inn a man burst from the doorway, almost colliding with me. "Have you heard the news?" he shouted. "The kaffirs have attacked Bathurst."

"How many people have been killed?" I asked, fearing the worst.

"I don't think any ... they all took refuge in the church. But they have taken all the cattle and horses. Retief is riding out there to bring them all back in convoy to Grahamstown. Apparently Salem has also been attacked. They will all be safer here, although God only knows for how long."

I sought out Retief and again joined his band of volunteers. As we rode into the little settlement of thirty houses that evening, we stopped at the

Wayside Inn. It had been a long ride from Grahamstown. We hitched our horses and made our way inside. There was chaos. People stood shoulder to shoulder. In addition to the men, the place was full of crying children and their mothers. We pushed our way to the bar.

I felt a hand clutching at me. "Rauch ... it's me ... Katrina!" She was standing squeezed between three English settlers. One had his hand resting on her buttocks.

"Hello Katrina," I said rather lamely. "Are you alright? Where are the others? Were any of you hurt?"

She shook her head. Her eyes were puffy from crying. "No, everyone's fine. Your Pa is with Amelia and the Thompsons. Frans is standing guard outside the village. I don't know where Gieletjie and Thandi are but they were fine when I last saw them."

I smelt the brandy on her breath. Despite her swollen eyes she still looked attractive. She really was a sultry woman whose curves had attracted the attention of a number of men in the room. The Englishman who had been feeling her bottom tried to pull her back into his circle of companions, but she moved closer to me, seeking protection. She leaned against me, hands at her sides, her full breasts pushed against my chest. I could feel myself becoming aroused by the closeness of her warm body.

While Koos struggled to get our drinks, Katrina told me what had happened since they had left me at the farm. She was standing so close to me that the people around us could not see her hands move around to my front. Nor did I realize what was happening until I felt her hand rub lightly over the front of my breeches. The positioning of her hand was no accident. I felt my face redden as she gently stroked, up and down. Because of the crush of bodies, I couldn't have moved even if I had wanted to.

Koos, oblivious to what was happening between Katrina and me, pushed his way through the crowd carrying two tumblers. He greeted her. "Hello Katrina. Thank the Lord you are not hurt."

"Your attention, please, ladies and gentlemen," came a command.

We turned in the direction of the voice. Katrina's hand resting where it was. It was Kommandant Jakobus Rademeyer, one of Retief's men, who had climbed onto a table. "We have come from Grahamstown to take you all out of Bathurst. We will escort you and your wagons and protect you from any further attacks. Tonight we will laager the wagons outside the village for safety and tomorrow morning at first light we leave for Grahamstown. We must leave Bathurst. You will be safer in Grahamstown."

There was a weak cheer from some of the men before the buzz of conversation rose again. Katrina's hazel eyes never left mine. We drank the brandy quickly. The raw alcohol burned its way down my throat. I wryly thought to myself how much things had changed since I last tasted the fiery spirit. It seemed a lifetime ago.

The bar started to empty as people went to their wagons to move them into the defensive laager to the east of the village. Katrina stayed standing close to me. As the crowd thinned she removed her hand and looked at me with a little smile. "I'd better get back to our wagon. If you come, there is more of that for you and of course you can see your precious Amelia and your Pa. Are you coming with me?" she asked quietly.

"No, I am on guard duty at midnight. Retief wants us to watch the wagons during the night." I was relieved at having a reason for not going with her. Appealing though the undisguised invitation from Katrina was it was outweighed by my reluctance to see Pa and Amelia together. The thought of seeing her with Pa filled me with jealousy and anger.

"I will see you tomorrow then … at least you are still very much alive," she said with a wry smile, reminding me of Dirk but also perhaps referring to what she had felt in my breeches.

Early the next morning the sounds of shouts, whistles and cracking of whips filled the air, signalling the departure of the convoy of more than a hundred wagons. Slowly it trundled out of Bathurst, leaving the deserted village behind. I was one of Retief's outriders, patrolling ahead of the wagons. Behind in the distance I saw the Thompsons' wagon and guessed that Pa and Amelia were in it. I hoped Amelia would see me and recognize the important role I was playing in keeping her safe.

That evening, when the convoy arrived in Grahamstown without incident, the townsfolk were still in a state of high anxiety in an air of gloom. Rumour was still rife and nobody knew what would happen next. Settlers and boers wandered the streets, armed with guns and pistols, knives, swords and bayonets in case of attack. Reports were coming in of military forts being abandoned as British troops too scurried back to Grahamstown, fearing for their lives.

Chapter Five

With the frontier region in chaos, Lieutenant Colonel Harry Smith rode into Grahamstown on January 6th to take control of military activities. His arrival, after a six-day ride from Cape Town, was heralded by the shouts of the town crier calling a public meeting on the market square for two o'clock the next day and the announcement that we were now subject to military law. Most of us were relieved; at least someone was taking charge.

I was in the King's Head with Koos when the news came. "That Charles Somerset has done nothing to get the situation under control," said Koos. "At least we now have some strong leadership. Let's see what Harry Smith has to say for himself."

The market square was packed with hundreds of curious settlers, boers and military personnel when the man who was to become Sir Harry Smith made his appearance. There was a buzz of anticipation as he climbed onto the platform. Resplendent in full dress uniform and looking extremely dapper despite the rigours of his ride, Smith made a marked impression on his audience.

He came straight to the point. "The situation here is not good. However, now that I am in charge things will get better. We will drive the kaffirs back over the Fish and peace will be restored."

A few desultory cheers greeted his words. I caught a glimpse of Pa and Brian Thompson listening with great interest on the other side of the square.

"You are now all under military law which means that I am in charge. Let no man here forget that. I am not here to make friends but to defeat the enemy. We need every man here to play his part. Therefore all males between sixteen and sixty will immediately register for active duty. At the tables over there you will register and be allocated your duties," he announced, waving in the direction of six tables manned by soldiers from the 75th Regiment. Over the hubbub of the crowd a few shouts of protest could be heard.

"Quiet!" ordered Smith. "I am not here to argue but to command. You are now under martial law and the first person—I care not who he may be—who does not promptly obey my command, will be tried by court martial and punished immediately."

A stunned silence greeted his words and then desultory clapping. Then a few more joined in. Then more …. and more. The clapping swelled to loud applause.

Harry Smith looked well pleased with himself and shouted over the applause, "Right! To the tables, men, and get to your duties."

Men pushed and shoved to get to the tables and register for military service. I saw Pa at one table and was careful to make sure that I was on the other side of the square so I didn't have to greet him.

For the next few months I saw little of life in Grahamstown. I had been allotted to serve under Kommandant Jacobus Ignatius Rademeyer and spent most of my time on patrol outside the town, part of a band of ten English settlers and thirty boers attempting to drive the elusive Xhosa back over the Fish. It was tiring and frustrating work as many of us felt that we were becoming nothing more than glorified herdsmen with much of the time spent recovering cattle taken by the Xhosa from the frontier boers and settlers. The tribesmen knew the terrain and were used to moving and hiding in the thick bush, while we struggled to come to terms with it.

This warfare, if it can be dignified by that name, continued sporadically for the next year. Occasionally we would get a chance to relax in Grahamstown. These rest and recuperation periods became dim memories, clouded in mists of alcohol. When things appeared bad I took to smoking the dagga pipe taken from a Xhosa warrior I had killed in a rare skirmish in the Fish River bush. It was the most effective way to get the events of the past few months out of my mind. I was still wracked with guilt and remorse and still bitter about Pa and Amelia. Talk was now rife of the migration of boers and speculation grew about the possibilities of life beyond the colony. Grahamstown was like a honeypot attracting bees. Community leaders were frequently seen visiting the town from places as far away as Graaff-Reinet.

One of these leaders was thirty-seven-year-old Andries Wilhelmus Pretorius, who had already established himself as a respected leader in his community. He had brought eight hundred men down to Grahamstown from Graaff-Reinet to fight the Xhosa. My favourite was Gerrit Maritz, a wealthy thirty-five-year-old wagon maker from Graaff-Reinet and the most colourful of the leaders. He had a keen sense of humour, dressed to impress the ladies and was always recognizable by the fur top hat he wore and the light blue wagon he drove. He was a big man, standing well over six foot, with a clean-shaven upper lip and a well-manicured, dark, tawny beard. When he was in town everyone knew it. Those who enjoyed his jokes didn't laugh when he challenged them though, as he was a forceful man who was used to getting his own way. My own kommandant, Piet Retief, was fifty-five years old and a fighter. He didn't have Maritz's polish but men respected him. He was a born leader but when you crossed him his dark, piercing gaze seemed to bore into your very soul. Whenever such leaders were in town, rumours and speculation grew until you would have thought that the whole frontier was on the point of deserting the Cape.

There were two events during that year which, despite the dagga and alcohol, burned their way into my memory. In the middle of March I rode into town late one afternoon, having just returned from two weeks' patrol in the Fort Willshire region. I was tired and hot and stopped as usual at the King's Head. I pushed my way into the smoke-filled saloon. The place was alive with activity, full of boers, soldiers and settlers. Prostitutes plied their trade as the noisy babble of conversation rose higher and higher. I jostled my way to the counter and ordered a brandy. Taking the first mouthful, I rolled the brandy around my mouth, savouring the warmth and flavour and then let the warm liquid slide down my throat. The alcohol began to work its miracle.

A hand fell on my shoulder and I heard a familiar voice say, "Hello, Rauch." It was Pa.

I spun round. He was standing with his arm around Amelia, the hint of a smile on his face. My heart leaped at the sight of her. I wished I could escape but it was too late. "Pa ... Amelia," I said, nodding a greeting. I swallowed the rest of the brandy in a gulp.

"It's been a long time," said Pa. "Too long. How are you? We hear of your brave deeds fighting the Xhosa. Retief himself tells me that you are a good soldier."

"Ja, ja ... I am sure that's right," I said sarcastically and half turned away, embarrassed that he still spoke to me like a boy.

"Hello Rauch. Still angry with me?" Amelia smiled at me quizzically, her head slightly cocked. She looked beautiful. Her strawberry-blond hair cascaded over her shoulders, framing her lightly freckled face like a golden halo. She was wearing a dress which showed off the smooth skin below the wishbone in her throat. The gold cross was not there.

Pa moved to the counter and ordered more brandies. He appeared to be in a jolly mood. While he faced the bar, his back to the room, Amelia looked directly at me, moved a step closer, looked into my eyes and quietly hissed, making sure that Pa would not hear: "I've missed you. Why did you leave me? We have unfinished business, don't we?" This last was said even more quietly, with unspoken promise in her eyes.

I stared at her. My eyes kept flicking to her silky flesh, to the spot where the cross had been. Pa pushed his way back, carrying the tumblers of brandy. Amelia moved away, breaking the intimacy created by her whispered invitation.

"Come. Drink, Rauch! We have something to tell you, something to celebrate." He lifted his glass as if to propose a toast. He looked at Amelia with a wide grin before downing his brandy. "We're getting married," he announced with a self-satisfied smile.

Amelia was watching me. I felt as if I had been shot in the chest. I was stunned for a few seconds while my brain tried to absorb the information. "Are you mad?" I blurted out, hardly able to believe what I'd heard. "You can't be serious! Amelia," I said, turning to her, "tell me this is not true."

She didn't answer but carried on gazing at me with that half-smile of hers.

"She is younger than *me*, for God's sake! Why pick her?" I was shaking with rage. "For heaven's sake! If you want a fuck, why not Katrina, she fucks everyone. Even Gieletjie has fucked her. What about that woman, Mrs Calverley, in Cape Town? You were fucking her when Ma was still alive. Surely you can choose someone else! How about those English women at Oom Willem's place in the Cape? I know that you were messing around with them as well. You don't have to pick my girl. Please, man! What is wrong with you? You disgust me. You are older than her father. And anyway she's mine!" This last was shouted into his face, the words streaming out.

"Shut your mouth. Don't you speak to me like that," snapped Pa.

I stared at the two of them. I couldn't believe it. Now my humiliation and loss were complete. I was hoping that my revelation of Pa's clandestine activities would shock Amelia into changing her mind. She didn't even raise an eyebrow.

She smiled sweetly and broke the silence. "I've never belonged to you, Rauch, or for that matter, to anyone. I love your father. You and I, though, will always be friends. I love you too ... I love you like a brother and I am sure we are going to get along fine. After all, we will be family." She reached out and took my hand.

I jerked it away as if scalded. "What have you two done to me?" I whispered hoarsely. My eyes were burning with tears and I could hardly breathe. A tight band bound my chest, the band tightening like a hangman's noose when the scarf around Pa's neck slipped aside and I saw a little gold cross hanging from a thin riempie round his neck. I stared at the cross and then at Amelia who stood there smirking as she realized what I had seen.

I reached out to grab the cross, "That is mine!"

Pa pulled away out of my reach, holding his hand over the cross.

"No, it's not," said Amelia angrily. "You gave it to me and I gave it to your father. It is mine to do with as I wish!"

"Fuck you both!" I shouted. The room went quiet.

As I threw the brandy into Pa's face, two men standing behind him grabbed him by the arms to prevent him lashing out at me. I spat into Amelia's face and walked out of the bar. I glanced back and saw Pa wiping the brandy from his eyes and Amelia wiping away my spit. I stormed out into the lane, feeling as though my world had collapsed.

Behind me, I heard running footsteps and out of the darkness a woman's voice called my name. It was Katrina. She grabbed my arm. I hadn't seen her since we had escorted her and the others from Bathurst back in December. I realized she had just come out of the King's Head and had witnessed what had taken place.

"Hello Rauch," she said and without waiting for me to return her greeting, "Where are you going?" still holding tightly onto my arm. Despite the fact that I had been drinking, I could smell alcohol on her breath.

"I don't know, I don't know. I must get away from here."

"Come with me," she said, pulling me in the direction of a row of rooms that we all knew were rented by prostitutes. "Come," she said as she slipped her arm around my waist and started to walk. I let her lead.

We went into a small, dingy room. She fumbled in the dark and lit a candle. In the flickering light I could make out an untidy bed and a bedside table. Clothes lay scattered on the floor and the unmade bed looked as though it had only recently been used. I looked at Katrina in the half light. She wasn't beautiful but her pitch-black hair shone in the candlelight, setting off her strong Malay features. Her voluptuous breasts strained against the fabric of her faded dress. I remembered how they had looked on the night when I had tried to kiss her. She smiled at me and her teeth flashed white in the candlelight. Then she did look beautiful.

"Don't be shocked, Rauch. This is where I live and how I earn a living. Your Pa let me go and there is no work for former slaves here. Anyway, I enjoy it … no, no, I love it … and I get to eat. But now, it's you that I want. For you there is no charge. I used to think about you even when I was with Dirk." She flashed a bold smile. "Here" she said, sitting down and patting the crumpled sheets beside her. "Come, sit next to me. Have you ever been with a woman, Rauch?" She didn't wait for a reply. "Let's forget about Amelia. I will show you how to forget her."

With a tonteldoos she lit a dagga pipe, similar to mine. I wondered whether Gieletjie had given it to her. She passed it to me. I sat close to her and drew in a deep breath of aromatic smoke. The water in the pipe gurgled in protest at the force of my inhalation. The drug started to relax me and I lay back, resting on the bed on my elbows. I wondered who the last man was and how many hours or minutes ago it had been. Katrina drew on the pipe and passed it back to me. Her saliva was on the mouthpiece. The taste of her, coupled with the dagga, heightened my senses. I inhaled more deeply.

She stood before me in the candlelight. Suddenly she bent forward, grabbed the hem of her dress and lifted it up over her head. Then she stood, quite still, in front of me. With the light behind her, she was etched against it in all her splendour. She was wearing only long, white drawers. I stared at her, running my tongue over my lips, my mouth drained of every drop of spittle. My hands were clammy with sweat. She looked at me with her large brown eyes, a slight smile on the edge of her lips. I couldn't take my eyes off her magnificent breasts with the hard, erect nipples, so invitingly close.

I felt as though I was going to burst. I stood and unbuckled my breeches. They dropped to the floor leaving me in my underwear, a large bulge straining toward her. Then I pulled the underwear down.

Katrina's eyes widened in shock and, I think, delight. Her face lit up. "Here! My God! I thought so … that night in Bathurst … I felt … my God! If I knew what you had I wouldn't have wasted my time on those little boys … including your Pa!"

As if prompted by the mention of my father's name, I reached forward roughly and grabbed her. She laughed at my haste. With one movement I pulled her onto the bed. She lay back submissively. I pulled my shirt over my head, knelt next to her and slipped off her drawers, tossing them onto the floor. She lay there, looking at me. She couldn't take her eyes off me.

I kissed her hard on the mouth. Her lips parted and she slid her tongue into mine. I could taste her. My hands stroked her mountainous breasts. She started to breathe hard. I sucked her nipples, marvelling at their size and erectness, putting a whole nipple into my mouth and sucking it like an orange. Her hips were starting to move up and down in anticipation. I raised myself to my knees and knelt between her strong, slender legs. Her hand guided me and I entered her. She gasped and then wrapped her legs around my waist as she tried to get as much of me as she could. Our bodies pushed together, our hips locked into each other, starting to grind in perfect rhythm, slowly at first and then faster and faster still. This was pure sex with no emotion. We were both panting with effort and desire. The bed creaked furiously as I drove myself into her time and again, harder and faster, faster and harder. My head was whirling from the dagga and the sex. Sweat trickled down my back as I rode Katrina, bucking and thrusting beneath me. I had never felt any sensation like it. All too soon I could feel that I was about to erupt. I thrust harder. Katrina arched to meet me.

"Now!" I shouted.

I thought her back was going to break as she shouted, "Yes! My Rauchie!

Yes, yes!" The muscles of her pelvis tightened. Like a giant wave crashing onto the beach, I exploded, emptying myself into her. But she had been wrong; I hadn't forgotten Amelia. I could see her before me as I flowed into Katrina.

I let out a sigh, spent. We lay exhausted on the bed, I on top of her. I must have dozed off into a gentle sleep. I woke a while later. Twice more that night, we journeyed together into paradise.

I woke the next morning to find the candle had burned down to a pool of wax. Tired and tender and amazed at what pleasures I had enjoyed, I looked at Katrina lying next to me. Her breasts still bore the marks of my hands. They rose and fell as she slept. She was a striking woman with a magnificent body and I felt tenderness because of the treasure she had shared with me.

She stirred, opened her eyes and looked at me, purring like a cat as she reached across and stroked my face. "My Rauchie," she said, gazing at me in a proprietary manner. "I wonder why they called you Rauch? What a strange name. Maybe I should be Vlam? There is no smoke without fire and I want to be that fire for your smoke."

From that moment, Katrina became Vlam to me. She was known as Rauch's whore to all and sundry as she became my sex partner for the next year. I didn't love her but I was in love with her physicality, the way she oozed sex. Having Vlam by my side was like having a possession, something I could use whenever I wished, which was often.

Vlam also became my companion, at times even accompanying me on patrol to the Fish River. Sometimes she stayed behind in her room in Grahamstown. She was always tired when I returned: for her sex wasn't just a job, it was an activity that she loved and couldn't get enough of. I'm sure I didn't realize quite how much.

My life consisted of an assortment of raids over the Fish River as a member of a boer commando, alternating with short drunken bouts in Grahamstown. On Harry Smith's orders, our task was to recover stolen cattle. There was very little action. The Xhosa were extremely elusive, accustomed as they were to the thick bush. They took great pleasure in taunting us from a safe distance:

"You are not men, you are but children. We are the warriors and the chiefs!"

Our frustrations at fighting this will-o'-the-wisp enemy mounted; it was clear that this war of attrition would have no resolution

Whenever I returned to Grahamstown I would seek solace in inns and alcohol and of course there was always Vlam. After drinking myself into oblivion I would stagger to her room to collapse onto the well-used bed. On more than one occasion, as I fell through the doorway after Vlam had reluctantly unbolted it, I would find some customer hastily buckling his breeches, casting nervous glances at me. Perhaps my senses were dulled by dagga and alcohol because only once did this seem to have any effect on me. Most times, after the startled visitor had scurried to safety, clutching his shoes and shirt, our sex was torrid and rough. It was as though she had been primed for me by the paying client. On the one occasion when it did bother me, I had been on the frontier for three straight weeks and, after a brief stop at the inn, I made my way to Vlam's room. Perhaps I wasn't as drunk as I normally was. Or perhaps it was the fact that the man lying naked on Vlam's bed was my friend, Lieutenant Bill Gibson, whom I had last seen the night the Xhosa attacked Fort Caffre.

"You!" I said. "Get out!"

"Hello, Boertjie", he said, smiling lazily, making no effort to move.

In my hand I had a sweepstok, a leather whip with a handle almost as short as my temper at that moment. I tore back the woollen blanket, leaving him stark naked on the bed. He made no attempt to cover his semi-erect cock. I stepped back two paces and with a sound like a pistol shot, cracked the sweepstok behind me, before flicking the whip. Years of practice had perfected my aim. The tip of the long, leather strip hissed through the air and, like a spitting snake, struck Gibson across his genitals. Blood spurted. He screamed with pain as his hands went down to protect himself. I adjusted my aim and the lash caught him under the right eye. A trickle of blood oozed from his cheek.

He leaped out of bed, close to tears of pain and indignation. "Jesus!" he shouted, as he grabbed his clothes. "How can you do that to me? I've paid your whore. For fuck's sake, how could I know you were back? Jesus, Boertjie … you aren't going to tell Joan, are you?"

"Get out of here!" I repeated, hoarsely. He scurried about, grabbing items of uniform, hastily pulling them on, with blood trickling down his cheek and from his crotch.

When he had stumbled into the night, I looked at Vlam and we both burst out laughing. "He will have some explaining to do to Joan as to how he came by whip marks on his balls and cock," I said. "Shame, he won't be using those for a while."

That night our sex was more passionate than ever. But despite all Katrina's charms and expertise in bed, for some reason I still longed for Amelia. The ache for her never diminished and the thought of her with Pa made my stomach churn. And always the phantom of Dirk floated before me. I was becoming more and more disgruntled with life. The rumours and talk of leaving the colony in search of a new life sounded attractive. There did not seem much left for me in British territory.

Then, toward the end of the year I heard from Frans whom I used to bump into occasionally in one or other tavern that Amelia and Pa had married. It was gut-wrenching.

A few months into the new year of 1835, I had to leave Vlam again, as Sir Benjamin d'Urban had decided to invade Kaffraria and attack the Xhosa. This time I couldn't take her with me.

Some days earlier I had been told by Kommandant Rademeyer that I had been selected as one of twelve boers who would form Harry Smith's personal escort. I was flattered and intrigued. I had heard a great deal about him so was excited and honoured at the thought of being part of his personal guard.

The destination for our two-thousand-strong army was the Amatola mountains where we hoped to make contact with and clear out the Xhosa. We marched out of Fort Willshire on March 30th, 1835, in a lumbering five-mile convoy. Riding next to Lieutenant Colonel Harry Smith I soon became aware of his sharp, foul tongue. To my surprise I found him to be self-absorbed and arrogant.

"You bloody boers," he announced one day to the world in general. "You're all the same, bloody chicken!"

There was dead silence as we rode on. I could feel my fellow boers' hackles rising, as were mine. Then Jan Greyling, with whom I had become friendly and who was about my age—and as cheeky—asked what we all wanted to ask: "Why is that, sir?" he said, his voice trembling slightly as he struggled to control his emotions.

Harry Smith looked at him in disgust. "Because you are all bloody scared of the kaffir. Look at those Hottentot soldiers … damned fine chaps. I call them my children. They will do anything I ask of them. But you bastards, ever since the bloody kaffirs got guns, you are scared as bloody hell. Cowardly pricks."

I saw Jan's face redden with anger. I cast him a warning glance but to no avail. He couldn't resist a retort and muttered quietly, but not quietly enough, "That's why a prick like you has to have us to guard you."

Smith reined in his horse, turned in his saddle and looked directly at Jan.

"What did you fucking say, boy?" he snarled.

"I said, if we are so bad, why have boers to guard you when you could have your own soldiers?"

"How dare you challenge me, you little bastard?"

Jan didn't respond.

"Answer me! I am speaking to you."

"I think you heard me, sir."

Harry Smith looked as though he might explode. "You cheeky sod" he shouted. "That's you finished with on this detail. I'll see that you get the birch. Arrest this man," he shouted at us.

By now we had all reined in our horses. We stared, unmoving, at our abusive commander.

"Arrest him … now!" he screamed.

No one moved. The tension could have been cut with a knife.

"Arrest him," cried Smith again, his voice shrill with frustration.

Again, we simply looked at him. Out of the corner of my eye I saw Kommandant Rademeyer loosen his Sanna from over his shoulder. This was a signal to the rest of us. Behind me I heard the clicks of hammers being pulled back. We always rode ready for action so our weapons were primed and ready to fire at all times.

Smith looked about him, disbelieving, as he realized the stand-off his anger had created. There was dead silence, broken only by the creak of leather and the occasional sound of clicking hooves as the horses, sensing the tension, shuffled position. Kommandant Rademeyer recognized that a confrontation between the commanding officer of an army of British soldiers and twelve boers could have but one consequence. "No need for that, colonel. None of my men is getting the birch," said Rademeyer. Turning to Jan, he winked gently and said, "Apologize to the colonel, Jan, otherwise we'll have to do what he says. Come on. We are here to fight the Xhosa, not each other."

Jan hesitated. I caught his eye and nodded, giving him some encouragement.

"I apologize, sir," he said.

Smith nodded gruffly, quite relieved that the stand-off was over, though he did not acknowledge Jan directly. Instead he turned to Kommandant Rademeyer. "You had better keep your men under control. Otherwise I will have to do it for you."

I saw Rademeyer's eyes flash in anger but he did not respond. The crisis was over.

From that day on, while we remained as the personal guards for Lieutenant Colonel Henry George Wakelyn Smith all twelve of us had lost respect for the foul-mouthed colonel and, despite his personal courage and commitment to fighting the Xhosa, none of us felt any loyalty to him.

We were divided into four divisions. Three were commanded by Englishmen, Henry Somerset, Colonel John Peddie, who had lost an arm, and Major William Cox. We fell under our own boer commander, Veldt Kommandant Stephanus van Wyk.

It was a frustrating time as we lumbered into the Amatolas. We never came into contact with the enemy. Whenever we came across a small settlement of Xhosa huts, surrounded by crops, the enemy was nowhere to be seen. They had vanished into thin air. We would torch the crops and huts and move on. The only sight of the enemy was in the distance beyond cannon range, tall warriors dressed in karosses, gesturing with their assegais to their own people hiding in the valleys below. For hours on end we laboured through the bush; sometimes we had to cut a path with axes for the convoy following us. Progress was slow and the work arduous and unpleasant.

To add to the lowering morale there were reports of dissent between Colonel Harry Smith and the governor, Sir Benjamin d'Urban. Smith was all for going ahead and crossing the Kei River to invade the Hintsa's territory. Sir Benjamin vacillated, changing his mind repeatedly. We had no respect for Smith but we all believed he was right. Our kommandant, van Wyk, had twice been sent to Hintsa with messages from Sir Benjamin to establish whether or not he intended fighting on the side of a Xhosa chief, Maqoma. Van Wyk had told Hintsa that all the cattle that had been taken across the Kei had to be returned to the colony. Hintsa failed to provide a satisfactory response.

As a result, on April 15th, 1835 we arrived on the banks of the Kei River. As our convoy slowly rumbled down to the river, thousands of Xhosa warriors began massing on the slopes of the opposite bank. Van Wyk and Smith stepped forward and walked to the water's edge while we sat on the ground and watched. A tall, imposing figure detached itself from the mass of warriors. This was Bhuru, Hintsa's brother. In front of him were three of his counsellors.

One stepped forward and shouted across the river, his voice carried to us by the gentle breeze. "What do you want, you swallows from over the sea?" he shouted. "You have no right to drink the waters of the Kei. This is Hintsa's land. You come no farther."

"Tell him we want an assurance that Hintsa will return our cattle and that he will not side with the other chiefs who are making war against us," Smith said to van Wyk. The response was shouted back.

The Xhosa counsellors went into a huddle to work out their response. After about thirty minutes of demands and counter-demands, an exasperated Harry Smith turned to us and with a word, commanded the two thousand troops, "Mount!"

With that we commenced the invasion of the lands across the Kei River, the country of the Gcaleka and of Hintsa, the Paramount Chief of the Xhosa.

Chapter Six

The tribesmen melted away as we crossed the sandy riverbed and there was no resistance as our convoy of wagons made its laborious way to the mission station of Butterworth. No sooner had we set up camp than the bugler sounded the alarm. There were shouts of, "Man your posts … the Xhosa are coming."

Approaching our camp were about seven hundred tribesmen, dressed for war and dancing in extended line, two deep, with shields held over their heads. They were grouped in three impis, whistling and dancing as they approached.

"Form up!" Smith bellowed.

The troops and we boers lined up with guns ready and aimed, waiting for the order to fire. My hands were sweating. This was the first time I had seen the Xhosa in such disciplined and regimented formation. It was a formidable sight. As they came closer their sinister whistling began like the rustling of leaves and ended as the sound of a storm lashing a forest, shaking their hide shields above their heads. Jan Greyling was standing next to me. I glanced at his face; it was as white as a sheet. There was dead silence in the ranks. Every man had his gun to his shoulder and was squinting down the barrel, taking aim. We waited, breathless, for the order to open fire.

The voice of Kommandant van Wyk sounded above the noise of the whistling and the roar of the storm created by the shields: "Moenie skiet nie! Hold your fire! Bugler! Sound the stand-down. These are Fingoes. They are not fighting us; these are our allies!"

Other voices joined van Wyk's, urging us not to fire. The relief was palpable. A cheer broke out. Whether this was to welcome the people also known as the Mfengu or whether out of sheer relief that our lives were no longer at threat, I never bothered to work out. Van Wyk was right: the Mfengu, an offshoot of the Xhosa, were the first of some seventeen thousand refugees who arrived over the next few weeks, having fled the martial Zulus who were rampaging farther north. They had asked Governor d'Urban for asylum in the colony in return for their support of the British against the Xhosa. Within a few days the area surrounding Butterworth was black with thousands of Mfengu and their cattle.

D'Urban had travelled up from the Cape and, as part of Smith's guard, Jan and I were able to hear the discussions that took place between them on their strategies to ensnare Hintsa.

"I think we should extend the Cape Colony boundary up to the Kei River," said d'Urban.

I glanced at Jan Greyling, whose eyebrows shot up in surprise.

"Governor, you couldn't be more right," said Smith. "The sooner you get the blessing of London the better. If we controlled the whole area we could certainly lick the Xhosa into shape."

"I have no intention of asking permission. In any event I intend moving deeper into Xhosa territory. Between the two of us we will corner that rascal Hintsa in his lair. Once we get him to order his chiefs to lay down their arms and get our stolen cattle back, we will have peace," said d'Urban

"I strongly disagree, governor," said Smith. "Against a conventional enemy you would be right. However, with the kaffirs, who are beasts of prey, you must disturb their earths, their breeding places." Noticing that he had d'Urban's attention, he hurriedly went on. "That is why I suggest you take a division or two and go deeper into the Trans-Kei area but leave me here. I will harass the Xhosa in their lairs and destroy them, so that those in hiding have nowhere to return to. Nobody knows how to fight these savages as I do … haven't I already proved that I am the greatest military commander to have fought these bastards? With these Mfengu at our disposal, Hintsa won't stand a chance."

D'Urban, though, had different ideas. "I am going to send the Mfengu over the Kei into the colony; I will make them British subjects. We will keep them on the frontier as a buffer between the Xhosa and ourselves. In the meantime, we will split our men and you can do as you request, burning and raiding here. One way or another we'll flush Hintsa out."

Both Jan and I were becoming increasingly disgruntled with our enforced participation in a war which didn't seem to have any prospect of ending soon. The night after we had eavesdropped on the conversation between Smith and the Governor, Jan whispered to me as we stood guard. "How long are we going to carry on with this?"

I shrugged and stared into the blackness of the night. I felt a pang of emotion at the thought of returning to life in Grahamstown. "I don't know. There isn't much else for us, is there? My family has split up and our homes are gone. We may as well spend our time fighting here as anything else." I was still tormented with guilt and anger. I couldn't face going back to that life. At least fighting the Xhosa was a course of action that no one questioned.

"I think I might join one of the groups leaving the colony," said Jan. "I believe that one of the leaders, Trichardt, is being hounded by the British because he's been selling guns to the Xhosa. They don't like Trichardt or the fact that he and his group have left. There's talk that they will prevent others from leaving. Still, I think I will go as well."

"Where will you go?" I asked.

"I don't know. From what I gather there are a few options. Potgieter is one. Uys another … or maybe Maritz … Retief, Liebenberg or even van Rensburg. Rumour has it that there is no shortage of plans. Of course," he added after a slight pause, "whether they will become a reality, who knows? They won't all go."

My ears pricked up at the names Retief and Maritz. The thought of starting a new, a different life and the adventure of discovering it had some appeal. I decided to investigate the possibilities the next time I took a break in Grahamstown. Perhaps I would pay a visit to Tarka or to Graaff-Reinet where it was said that every conversation in every tavern centred on leaving the colony.

In the meantime, the Mfengu situation led to a dramatic announcement by d'Urban. In a commanding voice, he announced to the massed troops, "As the representative of His Royal Highness, King William IV, I declare that, as of today, April the 24th, all Mfengu people are now British subjects. Furthermore, I have no option other than to declare war against Paramount Chief Hintsa and all his people. God save the King!"

For the next few weeks we carried out raids on Hintsa's people, the Gcaleka, taking cattle and burning huts while d'Urban drove deeper and deeper into Trans-Kei territory. On one of these raids, after we had burned the royal huts of Hintsa himself, without seeing any sign of the Great Chief, I was shocked to see Smith stealing royal ornaments from Nomsa's hut, the Chief's Great Wife. He looked most surprised when he realized that Jan and I were behind him while he was stuffing ornaments into a saddlebag.

"I'm taking these back for the governor," he explained feebly.

Jan and I simply glared at him in disgust.

The raids must have had an effect because a few days later a group of thirty horsemen approached the camp. It was Hintsa himself and his bodyguards. He had come seeking peace. There was a buzz of excitement in the camp as word spread of his arrival.

"Now maybe it will all be over and we can go back to living our lives," said Jan.

I didn't respond because I was too busy studying the chief. Hintsa, standing more than six feet six inches tall and wearing a magnificent leopard-skin cloak, looked every inch a leader. He was well built, upright in his bearing, with prominent eyes and lips and an aquiline nose. The skin of his face shone with animal fat. There were beads of perspiration on his brow, either from the ride or the stressful situation that he faced, I couldn't tell. He was adorned with brass and ivory bracelets, wore red and white beads around his powerful neck and carried a knobkerrie club and an assegai, while a sjambok bullwhip dangled from his wrist. He looked majestic. I could see that even Harry Smith was impressed.

"Beukes," shouted Smith. "Fetch three stools from my tent … and make it snappy!"

D'Urban, Smith and Hintsa sat down as d'Urban began to read a document which listed Hintsa's so-called crimes, stressing that as Paramount Chief he had failed in his responsibility to prevent the minor chiefs from waging war against the colony. Hintsa sat quietly and listened as Kommandant van Wyk translated d'Urban's charges and terms of peace. From time to time Hintsa breathed a great sigh but he spoke not a word. After hours of one-sided discussion, Smith invited Hintsa to dine in his tent. Van Wyk again acted as interpreter. He told us later that Smith had treated the chief with the same mercurial arrogance that he displayed toward his own men, veering from disdainful superiority to exaggerated jocularity. The upshot, though, was that Hintsa had agreed to Smith's terms. He undertook to deliver fifty thousand cattle and a thousand horses as compensation for the Xhosa attacks.

"Capital," Smith had exclaimed, according to van Wyk. "You are a capital chap!"

Van Wyk told us later with a wink, "You should have seen Smith. He was grinning like a clown and he kept slapping Hintsa on the back, calling him my dear friend! What a fool he is; he will never see those cattle and horses, Hintsa is just biding his time."

None of us appreciated how right van Wyk was.

The next morning we were all in formation once again as Smith, flanked by d'Urban and Hintsa, declared to the assembled throng, "Now let it be proclaimed throughout the land and the world that the Great Chief of the Xhosa, Paramount Chief Hintsa, has concluded peace with the Great King, King William of England. Let the cannons be fired!"

Three cannon shots boomed out in quick succession. Thus was an uneasy peace declared, a peace that lasted only days before word arrived at the camp that the Gcaleka were killing our allies, the Mfengu. Hintsa and his son, Sarili, had stayed behind in camp as volunteer hostages until the terms of the peace were met. The Mfengu, taking advantage of Hinta's absence, had begun stealing the Gcalekas' cattle.

Smith was outraged. "Fetch that bastard Hintsa," he shouted to Jan and me.

Earlier that day we had seen Smith and Hintsa, arm in arm, strolling through the camp, with Smith chuckling and calling him "my dear fellow". But now he had become "that bastard".

We entered Hintsa's tent, where he was engaged in earnest conversation with his counsellors. As we walked in, he looked up almost guiltily; I wondered what they had been plotting. Jan and I escorted Hintsa, surrounded by his bodyguards, to Smith's tent where three nooses had been suspended from the tent pole. There was no doubt what they were there for. Harry Smith ranted and swore abuse. Hintsa sat, regal and impassive, while Smith threatened him, Sarili and his brother, Bhuru, with hanging unless the raids stopped within three hours. At times a smile flicked over Hintsa's face. As captor Smith might have the upper hand but dignity, emotional control and mastery of the situation belonged to Hintsa. From that moment on Hintsa and his kin were no longer Smith's guests but his prisoners.

The Mfengu, meanwhile, were on the move. Early on the misty morning of May 9th, 1835, their song 'Siya Emlungweni'—We are going to the land of the white people—rang out as seventeen thousand Mfengu and twenty-two thousand cattle crossed the Kei into the colony, under the protection of the British, their new allies.

This was just one of the ripple effects of the *Mfecane*—a word meaning 'destroyed in total war'—which was sweeping across the sub-continent, leaving thousands dead and many more displaced. The Zulu king, Dingaan, and the breakaway Matabele under Chief Mzilikazi, were the two primary protagonists in a bloody struggle for territory and domination.

The next day, in the presence of Hintsa, Sarili and Bhurhu, with due pomp and ceremony and the firing of twenty-one cannon, d'Urban announced that the colony's border had been extended to include all the land as far as the Kei River. Hintsa was stunned. With that terse announcement and three cheers for King William, he had been stripped of his land and his people. Neither I, nor any of the boers, joined in the cheers for the English king.

After the ceremony, Smith again had us escort Hintsa to his tent. Again Smith ranted, threatening Hintsa with imprisonment on Robben Island unless he produced the cattle that had been promised.

Hintsa patiently heard Smith's tirade. When Smith paused in mid-sentence, Hintsa said calmly, "I will lead you to the cattle you want."

Smith immediately switched to being Hintsa's friend. "There you are! What a splendid fellow. Damned good show, sir! Damned good show. I knew you would see sense. You really are a splendid chap. By God! If you had had a proper education I believe we could have made a gentleman of you."

Hintsa stared at him in silence, his eyes filled with contempt.

Later that day Hintsa, escorted by Highlanders, Khoi guards, boer guards and a Corps of Guides made up of British settlers, led the group out of camp. We had no idea where we were going and over the next couple of days even Hintsa himself didn't appear to be too sure of his way. Smith and Hintsa rode out in front. I was behind them with Jan and some of the Corps of Guides.

Jan turned in his saddle and whispered, "I think he is leading us into a trap. Be careful!"

I nodded in agreement.

George Southey, a tough young settler in the Corps of Guides, joined in the conversation. "I think you're right. I've been watching Hintsa. He's leading Smith on a wild goose chase but Smith is too wrapped up in himself to realize it."

As we rode beside a stream at the bottom of a hill, Hintsa pulled up his horse. He dismounted and started to walk, leading his horse by the reins.

"What are you doing?" shouted Kommandant van Wyk in Xhosa.

"My horse is tired, I am giving him a rest," replied Hintsa, as he made his way up the hill, away from the river. Twenty minutes later he remounted.

"Look out," said Southey softly, "I think he is going to make a run for it. Load your guns."

We trotted slowly behind Hintsa. After about thirty minutes, when we were halfway to the top of the hill, Hintsa dug his heels into his horse's flanks and, with a shout, galloped away.

The chief had to pass Smith at the head of the column. Smith drew his pistol. "Hintsa, stop!" he cried. The two of them headed off at full gallop with the rest of us following as fast as we could. Smith gradually gained ground on the fleeing chief. He took aim with his pistol but there was no report. Misfire

But he was like a man possessed; he managed to draw his horse alongside Hintsa's, throwing his useless pistol at the chief's head. Hintsa ducked. Smith got so close that the chief did not have enough space in which to stab with his assegai. Smith grabbed Hintsa by the throat and with one violent thrust, threw him to the ground. Hintsa leaped to his feet and started to run down the hill toward the river.

"Shoot, damn you! Shoot!" shouted Smith.

"Shoot, George!"

Southey fired from the saddle at the fleeing man who was darting around like a rabbit.

"He's hit!" cried Jan as Hintsa fell to the ground.

"We've got 'im!" yelled George.

But he was wrong. Hintsa jumped to his feet and with blood running down his left leg, made for the comparative safety of a thicket on the riverbank.

"Damn you bastards!" Smith screamed, "Fire again … he's getting away!"

Again Southey discharged a shot, hitting Hintsa in the shoulder. The chief was a few paces short of the thick bush at the water's edge. With a superhuman effort he spurred himself on into the sanctuary of the bush and out of sight.

"Get him!" yelled Smith.

Southey, Jan Greyling, van Wyk, Lieutenant Paddy Balfour and I jumped off our horses and scrambled down the bank, an assegai clattering onto the rocks next to Southey, missing him by inches.

"There he is!" shouted Southey, spotting Hintsa in the river with only his head visible above the surface of the water. George raised his gun to fire as Hintsa stood up, his arms raised, blood spurting from the wound in his shoulder. His face was contorted with pain and terror as Southey aimed the rifle at his head from just three yards away.

Suddenly Hintsa cried out in Xhosa, "Musa ukundidubula … xolela!"

Southey spoke fluent Xhosa and understood perfectly Hintsa's "Don't shoot, forgive me" but his finger tightened on the trigger.

I desperately reached across to Southey. "Don't shoot him, you bastard! He has surrendered!"

But I was too late. Southey's rifle roared and Hintsa's head exploded as the bullet struck. I felt bits of brain and bone spatter against my cheeks and when I looked down my shirt was wet with Hintsa's blood.

Southey dragged the body to the bank. I was shaking with horror and disgust but there was worse to come. Southey laughingly took out his hunting knife and calmly cut away the dead chief's ear as a souvenir. Then he took Hintsa's brass ornaments and bracelets and put them in his pockets. Some of the others joined in. Jan and I watched, revolted, as soldiers grabbed whatever they could from the dead chief.

"This is sickening," said Jan. "I don't like the kaffirs but the chief had already surrendered. This war makes me want to vomit. This is nothing but a hyena scavenge."

Assistant Surgeon Ford of the 72nd Highlanders arrived on the scene, breathless. He pushed his way through the men to Hintsa's body. I was pleased to hear his command: "Stand back men. Stop that!" But he pulled a pair of dental pliers from his pocket and started to extract the dead chief's front teeth as keepsakes.

"You stop that!" shouted Kommandant van Wyk.

Ford looked up but carried on regardless.

Van Wyk lifted his gun, pointing it at Ford. "I said stop. Now! Or do you want to be next?"

The tension was broken by the arrival of an officer, Captain Wickham, who rode up to the unruly group. "The colonel wants you to bring the body to him at the top of the hill."

Ford stopped his dirty work and stepped away, glaring at van Wyk. Some of the soldiers wrapped the body in a kaross and draped it over the saddle of Lieutenant Balfour's horse. Blood seeped through the kaross as the procession made its way up the hill. Halfway up, Wickham again rode over and told the soldiers that Smith had changed his mind. "Leave the body. The colonel doesn't want to see it now."

Balfour shoved the mutilated body from his horse. We rode past in silence, without a backward glance. I never found out who found the body first: the hyenas or Hintsa's people.

"I'm sick and tired of all of this," said Jan as we rode back to camp. "I am going to go back to Grahamstown. Why should we be doing the dirty work? We don't even get paid. To hell with it! I am going to look outside the colony. I can't stand Smith and his cronies. One day they act like brothers to the kaffirs and the Khoi—even eating with them—and the next they are murdering them. You never know where you stand with an Englishman."

I then understood that I shared Jan's views. There was nothing for me in Grahamstown except my whore, Katrina. I was fond of her but I was certainly not in love with her. Then and there I made up my mind to head for Tarka or maybe Graaff-Reinet, to hear first hand from those who were quitting the colony. Then I would decide whether or not to join them.

Chapter Seven

Kommandant van Wyk walked up to Jan and me, a broad smile on his face. "It's over for us, this fighting for the English. They have decided to let us boers go back to our farms ... those of us that still have farms ... they need us to grow food. So, no more of this fighting for no pay ... we are free to go."

Our problem was solved. For two weeks we had been debating the idea of deserting and joining the boers who were planning to leave the colony. The downside had been the thought of being caught and facing a court martial. This was a far better solution. We decided to set off for Grahamstown that night.

We left the camp with a group of fellow boers after saying goodbye to the soldiers we had served with. It never occurred to us that we should say farewell to Lieutenant Colonel Harry Smith, the man we had been detailed to guard these past months. Few of us had time for the man, despite his courage, on account of his foul mouth and erratic behaviour. These seemed to outweigh his good points.

"I really couldn't care less whether or not I see the colonel again," I said to Jan.

Our role in the Frontier War ended, we rode through the night. I felt excited, my life was entering a new and different stage but I wondered what to do about Katrina. The thought of her exciteded me but I knew that leaving her behind would give me more flexibility and less encumbrance if I were to join the other migrants. I decided to make up my mind based on her reaction when I told her of my plans.

Two days later we arrived in Grahamstown as dawn was breaking. I made my way through the dark deserted streets, Grey's hooves on the cobbles making the only sound. A couple of drunks staggered past as I made my way to Katrina's lodgings. Not sure what I would find, I knocked on the door. No response. I knocked again, louder this time.

"Who's there?" came Katrina's voice.

"It's me, Vlam. It's Rauch. I'm back!"

There was a squeal of delight and the door flung open. Hair hanging in her face, she was dishevelled and sleepy-eyed, wearing only a pair of bloomers which she had hastily pulled on. Her ample breasts shone with sweat. She looked magnificent. After weeks in the bush living with only rough male company she was a goddess.

"Rauchie!" she cried with a broad smile. "You are back!"

I grabbed her in my arms, feeling her breasts against my chest. As I kissed her open mouth I peered over her shoulder and saw a figure in the bed, under the bedclothes. My heart sank.

Katrina lit a candle and I saw the mound under the covers stir. A tousled mop of what turned out to be long, blond hair appeared, followed by a beautiful, impish female face. The eyes that opened wide were a startling, bright blue. The wide lips broke into a smile, alluring in the candlelight. The gorgeous creature sat up in bed, holding the bedclothes up to her breasts as stared at me, quite relaxed.

She said in Dutch: "Hello. So you are Rauchie. My name's Marietjie."

I was much relieved to find the figure in the bed was female and not one of Vlam's customers.

"Hello Marietjie," I said. "Who are you? Where do you come from?"

Katrina looked amused. "Marietjie is a *very* good friend of mine … she's visiting me from Graaff-Reinet. Marietjie's father is leaving the colony. My family were slaves to her family before we came to yours. Even though Marietjie is much younger than me we used to play together, even then"

I knew that Katrina's father had been shot as a runaway slave before her mother came to work for us six years ago but I hadn't been aware that Katrina had been friends with the daughter. They must have noticed my look of surprise that a white girl would be sharing a bed with the mixed-race daughter of a slave.

Marietjie smiled and Katrina chuckled. "We have always been close, haven't we, skattie? She came down here with another family but wanted to stay a bit longer so when we bumped into each other I offered her a bed. She's getting married soon, to a soldier … an officer in the army."

"Maybe yes … maybe no." Marietjie smiled widely again.

I saw that the covers had slipped—maybe she hadn't noticed—but I could see the profile of a perfectly formed rounded breast with a dark brown nipple. As my eyes grew more accustomed to the gloom I could better appreciate Marietjie's looks, with her open face, large smiling mouth, long blond hair and freckles sprinkling the bridge of her upturned nose. I couldn't take my eyes off her as she returned my gaze with a slight smile, staring unflinchingly at me.

I became aware that Katrina was watching me. "Come on Rauchie, there are still three hours before sun-up … let's go to bed."

"Where shall I sleep?" I asked.

"Right here, with us. I'll be in the middle, between you and Marietjie. Come!" She squeezed up against Marietjie, leaving space for me. I blew out the candle, slipped off my pants and climbed into the warmth of the bed, feeling the heat of Katrina's voluptuous body. Her hands were all over me and her mouth smothered mine with kisses. Her tongue hungrily sought my mouth. Over Katrina's shoulder I could see Marietjie's eyes gazing straight into mine, an amused smile on her lips. It felt strange lying next to two naked women. Despite Katrina's expert touch I could not get an erection. Marietjie had discreetly turned her back but the damage was done, despite the fact that I desperately wanted Katrina.

Katrina whispered, "Lie on the floor."

I slipped out of bed, tossing a kaross onto the floor. Katrina followed, lying on top of me. My body began to respond. We made passionate love and weeks of pent-up desire exploded into her. It was good to be back. I fell sound asleep without returning the favour to Katrina. I must have slept for an hour and I woke with a jolt. I had been dreaming of Pa's white backside rising and falling as I had seen him on top of Ma … except that the woman under him now was Amelia. Katrina was no longer lying next to me when I got myself up. The two women were lying asleep on the bed. I rose quietly and as I dressed I became aware that Marietjiie was watching me.

She smiled sleepily. "Hello Rauch. How was your sleep on the floor?"

"Fine," I replied, feeling slightly embarrassed.

"That's good. Well, you can have your bed back tonight. I'm going to see my fiancé at Fort Brown and then I am going back to Graaff-Reinet. My fiancé is an officer," she said with a hint of pride.

"Watch out if he's an Englishman … rather get yourself a good boer," I said with a grin. "I don't trust the English."

She ignored my dig. "Oh, Roddy is a fine man. You would like him, I'm sure."

"What are you doing going back to Graaff-Reinet if your man is at Fort Brown?" I asked. Katrina was awake and lay listening to the conversation.

"My family's planning to leave the colony, so I'm helping with the preparations. There is much to be done. If I wasn't getting married in December I might even have gone with them. There really doesn't seem to be much for us here in the colony any longer. I am hoping that life will be better as an army officer's wife."

"I doubt that," I said. "From what I can gather life isn't easy in those forts. There are rumours that some of the soldiers have had enough and are deserting. From what I have seen, unless you are like Colonel Smith you don't get looked after very well. Anyway, I'm interested in leaving the colony as well. Maybe you could introduce me to some of the leaders who are planning to go … do you know them well? Perhaps they are members of your family?"

Before Marietjie could reply, Katrina interrupted excitedly, "Are we leaving here, Rauchie?"

"I may. I'm not sure yet. If I go, it will most probably be alone," I retorted sharply.

Katrina looked at me but made no answer. She turned away so I would not see her eyes brimming with tears.

"Does that mean you are riding back today?" I asked Marietjie.

"Yes, after I have been to Fort Brown."

"Would you mind if my friend, Jan Greyling, and I came with you? Perhaps you could introduce us to a few people in Graaff-Reinet?"

"Of course not. It will be my pleasure to have you accompany me. I wasn't that keen on a full two-days' ride across country. Of course I will introduce you. I hear though that the next group will be leaving from Tarka. My father is probably going, so you can start off by talking to him."

Two hours later, Marietjie on Eerste, her grey mare, Jan on Toekoms and I on Grey, set off for Fort Brown, some fifteen miles northeast of Grahamstown. As I waved goodbye to Katrina standing in front of her lodgings, I shouted, "I'll only be gone for a few days, so don't fret, Vlam."

She didn't reply and returned my wave despondently. I didn't see the tears trickling down her cheeks.

ல ல ல

The ride to Fort Brown took two hours. Marietjie was a pleasant and intelligent travelling companion. She told us about the dissatisfaction of the people in Graaff-Reinet. "It's really coming to a head now. Do you know that some people are being paid out only a third of what they were promised by the English for their slaves? Plus, they are passing laws that make coloured people the same as us!" Her face reddened as she realized what she had said, as Katrina was an ex-slave and coloured.

When she saw that I didn't react, she continued, "It's not only that. The people have to get their money back through agents in England." She snorted in disgust, "The English don't care about us; they see themselves as our superiors. You will see when you get to Graaff-Reinet. Many people throughout the district want to leave. The English are aware of this and there is even talk of them making it illegal. Already they are passing laws that we cannot transport gunpowder. Now we also have that lily-livered Andries Stockenström, as much a boer as the three of us, taking the side of the missionaries and the kaffirs. The rumour is that he's going to give evidence to the English parliament of injustices committed by us boers against the blacks and Hottentots." She paused for breath.

We rode in silence. After a minute or two she asked, "What do you think, Rauch? Do you think you will go?" She looked at me, an eyebrow raised.

"I'm not sure … If I talk to these leaders, then I can make up my mind. There isn't much keeping me here … I lost the woman I love to someone else, so I may as well leave my former life and the English far behind."

"You mean Amelia? You lost her to your Pa! Sies!" she exclaimed in disgust.

Jan and I exchanged glances. "How do you know?"

"Because now they are also in Graaff-Reinet and they talk of leaving as well. They have been there for a few months. Your Pa is a bywoner, a tenant farmer, on the Fouries' farm just outside the town. Do you know that they are married now?"

Although I'd heard this, the confirmation stunned me. I shook my head. "Married?" I thought to myself, "Then it's definitely over. There's no chance now that she and I will ever be together." I think this final piece of information decided me.

"Let's hope that I can find a group to join. But I have to earn some money first," I said.

"Well, you never know. Maybe I will convince Roddy to come as well. He is sick of how they are treated. No food. No replacements or new uniforms. While those snobs like Smith and his officers live like lords in

Grahamstown, you'll see how these poor soldiers have to live in the forts."

"I would rather that he didn't come," I said with a smile. I saw that Jan beside me was grinning, too. Marietjie glanced at me but didn't reply. She seemed a great deal older and wiser than her eighteen years.

We arrived at Fort Brown and found Roddy without much trouble. Second Lieutenant Roddy Turner looked a shocking sight. I couldn't believe that a British officer could be so shabby. His tall, skinny frame was clothed in a threadbare uniform. I glanced at other soldiers passing by. They looked just as bad, very different to Smith's men who always had enough food and uniforms to spare. These men looked like vagrants.

After Marietjie and Roddy had embraced—rather coolly I thought for an engaged couple—Marietjie introduced us. Roddy had a warm, friendly smile. He stood an inch or two above me, good-looking with rather unruly black, curly hair and a tanned open face with brown eyes which looked directly into yours while he spoke.

"I hope you brought us some food," he said to Marietjie. "I think they eat up our share in Grahamstown. We hardly get fed nowadays. The men are really down-hearted. Mind you, so are we officers. Look at us. Our clothes are in tatters, there are no replacements and scarcely any food gets to us here. Also, since the boers were released from military service and went back to their farms we have had nothing but trouble from the Hottentots; not to mention the Xhosa."

Marietjie produced some bread and fruit from her saddlebag and handed it to him. He started hungrily on the bread as we conversed. Marietjie told him who we were and that we would be accompanying her to Graaff-Reinet to explore the idea of leaving the colony.

"Don't speak about it too openly," Roddy mumbled through a mouthful of bread. "There is talk of outlawing the emigrants. We are supposed to report anyone we hear of, so do be careful," he warned. "When will you go?"

"I am not sure but definitely sometime soon," I replied.

"The same goes for me," added Jan.

"Well, we could well join you if you decide to go. I'm due for release from the army in May next year. If you haven't gone by then and you do decide to go, I might just come along too. What do you say, Marietjie?" Roddy said, looking at her, licking the last bit of food from his fingers.

"My family is already talking about it, so I think maybe we should go as well. Anyway let's see what the position is in Graaff-Reinet. By the time you get out the army you'll be nothing but skin and bone," Marietjie said, looking anxiously at Roddy. "It's one thing for your government to treat us boers with contempt but quite another to treat its own officers like slaves. I wouldn't fight for an army that doesn't look after its own."

Roddy looked embarrassed but did not respond. In the manner typical of a boer woman, Marietjie was calling the shots. I thought to myself that Roddy had quite a handful in this strikingly attractive woman.

An hour or so later we took our leave. Marietjie had been right. I liked Roddy. He seemed a very pleasant chap. A pity I thought, because I found his fiancée so appealing. The three of us set off on the two-and-a-half day trip to Graaff-Reinet. Night camps made a welcome break from the arduous ride. Sitting around the flickering flames of the fire in the evening Marietjie and I spoke long after Jan had crawled into his blankets. I found that this beautiful woman of iron could be extremely entertaining with her amusing stories of life in Graaff-Reinet.

"And so?" she said to me when I had roared with laughter at one of her tales, "what about Katrina, or Vlam as you call her?"

"Ag, no, Katrina is not really my woman."

"What do you mean 'not really my woman'?" she imitated.

I felt awkward as she gazed at me, waiting for an answer. Then to make things more awkward she added, "I heard the two of you in her room in Grahamstown and there is little doubt what you were doing."

I felt my face redden and hoped she wouldn't notice.

"Don't be embarrassed," she said, "I am not stupid, you know."

I could see that she was smiling.

I was silent. The night was busy with the sounds of crickets and frogs from the riverbank. I threw another log onto the fire. Sparks rose into the blackness and the log caught fire. Flames cast flickering shadows over us.

"So, then? You haven't answered me."

"Well, I suppose she might think that I am her man but I'm not really. She was a slave. She is a whore. I do find her attractive, though."

"That's why you use her, sleep with her? But you don't love her?"

"No. I don't." I paused. "She has slept with many others. I do like her and I will miss her. But she is not part of my life. My life in the future."

"I think you will break her heart if you leave her behind."

I glanced at her. The smile had gone.

"What about Amelia?" she asked. "Are you still pining for her?"

I didn't know how to respond. How could I tell her that Amelia was always in my thoughts but that since I had met her, Marietjie, I had found it a great deal easier to shift Amelia to the back of my mind? I felt I should take the initiative and break this line of questioning before I landed myself in trouble. "Well, what about you and Roddy? Where did you meet him? Do you love him?"

"He was based in Graaff-Reinet for a few weeks and I fell in love with him." She paused for what seemed a long time. "I'm not so sure anymore, I'm afraid. Everything seems to be changing."

I felt my heart skip a beat. The look in her eyes as she gazed steadily at me …

There was silence.

I said suddenly, "Well, we still have a fair way to travel tomorrow, so I think it's time for sleep." I stood up and dusted the dirt from the back of my trousers.

"Yes," said Marietjie as she stood up.

I held out my hand to help her to her feet. As I pulled her up she continued toward me, stopping very close to me. The fire hissed and spat as some green twigs were enveloped by flames. Marietjie looked beautiful in the firelight.

She put her hands on my shoulders and looked me right in the eyes. "Good night Rauch, sleep well." She turned her face up and kissed me on the mouth, softly but firmly. "Katrina has told me all about you, you know." She smiled broadly, her teeth flashing. "She's a very lucky girl if all she tells me is true."

I put my arms around her and pulled her to me. She didn't resist but stiffened slightly. I bent my head to kiss her again.

"No, not yet, Rauchie. I am still engaged to Roddy, and anything more would be unfair and disloyal to him. There is plenty of time … but I need to sort myself out first." She pushed me gently away.

I let her go, dropping my arms. As I walked to the other side of the fire she called out in a loud whisper, "I hope you have nice dreams."

I looked back and she was smiling, teasingly. I climbed into my bedclothes and within a minute my hand was working, relieving the built-up pressure. I slept like a log after asking forgiveness.

Chapter Eight

Night had fallen when the three of us trotted into Graaff-Reinet.

"You may as well come and stay at our place or have you somewhere else to stay?" said Marietjie.

"No, we would appreciate somewhere to sleep," I replied.

"Well, I am afraid you will have to sleep in the stables as we don't have room in the house … there will be straw to sleep on. You should be quite comfortable. I'm sure that we still have some potjie … there's always a stew on the stove. So, I'll feed you up and send the two of you to bed."

She was watching my face with a slightly concerned look in case her offer of accommodation sounded a rather poor option. I laughed, slapping Jan on the back. "That's wonderful. I could eat a horse I'm so hungry but after that I just want to sleep … it was a long ride. So, yes, we'll be very happy to sleep in the stables."

We met Marietjie's father and mother, Stefan and Marina Bronkhorst, while Marietjie served us some food next to the big iron stove in the cosy kitchen. They were warm, friendly people who laughed easily and made us feel welcome. Stefan Bronkhorst was a large man, standing well over six feet, bald and quite portly. In contrast Marina was a trim, attractive lady, with blond hair done up in the customary bun on the back of her head. It was obvious where Marietjie's looks had come from.

Stefan broke into a broad grin when he realized that I was Jakob's son. "That is wonderful. He and Amelia have been very welcome in Graaff-Reinet. So, you are the other son that I have heard about? I believe you were one of that fool Smith's personal guards on the frontier. No wonder you want to leave the colony!"

I was longing to ask after Amelia but bit my tongue.

"This whole place is full of rumours at the moment. Just about the only thing that people talk about is leaving. Particularly now that this business with the slaves has come to a head. People have to claim their compensation from agents in England but there are plenty of skelms trying to claim commission by getting the money out of the authorities. People who talk of leaving are arguing about whether they should go north into the interior or over the mountains into Natal."

"Perhaps you could introduce us to some of the people who are planning to go?" I asked.

He nodded. "First thing tomorrow I'll take you to see Gerrit Maritz. He will know who you should talk to." He paused. "He is very busy at the moment ... he's a wagon maker and of course the demand for wagons has become almost too much for him. In any event he'll know what's happening."

"I know Meneer Maritz," I replied, "We have seen him often, riding around Grahamstown in his blue wagon. He's quite a colourful character. Maybe he can find some work for us building wagons if he's so busy."

Jan nodded eagerly. "We both need work and will have to earn some money ... neither of us has anything other than our horses and what's in our saddlebags."

The next morning, after Jan and I had joined the Bronkhorst family for coffee and rusks, Stefan Bronkhurst accompanied us down the main road to the shed where Gerrit Maritz made his wagons. The distinctive pale blue wagon stood outside.

The frenzy of activity inside created an atmosphere of excitement and purpose. Men shouted above the sound of hammering and sawing, fires were blazing and the smell of scorched metal seared the nostrils. Hammers clanged on metal rims, nails were hammered into wooden planks and women sat sewing what turned out to be the canvas coverings for the wagons. Smoke poured from the fires that heated the metal rims before they were lowered into a bath of cold water, creating clouds of steam and hissing as they cooled and contracted to fit the wagon wheels. Jan and I looked around in amazement—there were seven wagons being built simultaneously.

"Hello Stefan," called a tall, well-dressed man on the far side of the shed. Gerrit Maritz wiped his hands on a cloth as he strode smiling toward us. He stuck his right hand out in greeting. I felt as though mine was being gripped in a steel trap.

"Môre Gerrit," said Stefan. "I've brought you two visitors. They rode up with Marietjie from Grahamstown. They are keen to talk to you if you have the time. This is Jan Greyling, and this here …" as he put his hand on my shoulder and winked at Maritz, "is young Beukes … Rauch. You know his father; he's married to that pretty little thing, Amelia."

"Of course! Now I recognize you. I have seen you often enough in Grahamstown. Last time I heard, you were fighting the kaffirs with Harry Smith, weren't you? What can I do for you, young men?"

"We'd like to talk to you about leaving," I said.

Maritz glanced around to see if anyone had heard but the words were muffled by the noise of hammering. "Don't say too much in here," he said softly, "There is a tavern three doors away where I am meeting some people this evening. If you're interested, join us at six o'clock."

I nodded in appreciation. "We will be there Meneer Maritz. Thank you very much." Then, realizing that I might not get the opportunity again, I blurted out, "Is there any chance that Jan and I could get some work here? We need to earn some money."

Maritz laughed. "So do we all. But it so happens that we are a bit short of good, hard-working men right now. I've never seen so many people interested in buying wagons. It's hard work and I need honest workers. If you are prepared to do anything I ask I will start the two of you tomorrow. I will pay you each fifty shillings for a month's work."

Fifty shillings! We hadn't earned a thing fighting the Xhosa. This sounded like a fortune. I glanced at Jan.

"Dankie, meneer. Thank you. You won't be sorry!" Jan beamed with delight.

We had work and had now met with one of the leaders. We found it hard to believe our good fortune.

"Off you go then," grinned Maritz. "I'll see you in the tavern this evening. Hendrik Potgieter is here from Tarka and is likely to be there as well, so you couldn't have timed your arrival better."

I was on the verge of a new adventure. I had made up my mind. Maybe moving away would help erase the memory of that awful night when Dirk had been killed. I didn't care what warnings and threats might be issued by the authorities, my future lay in the unexplored lands to the north. But every time I thought of my new life a cold hand touched my heart. Amelia was here with Pa. It was only a matter of time before I bumped into them. My stomach tightened.

When we arrived back at the Bronkhorst house, Marietjie was sweeping out the stables. She looked up at the sound of our footsteps. "No need to ask how you got on," she smiled, leaning her broom against the barn wall and standing with her hands on her hips. "It's written all over your faces."

"Well, we will know more tonight after we have been to the meeting in the tavern. Meneer Maritz has also offered us a job making wagons. He has so much business, so we are very fortunate … thanks to you and your father for introducing us."

"Well, I want to see where all this is going and whether or not I am going to be part of it, so you'd better pay attention to what they say tonight. When are you starting work? How will you be able to leave if you are working for Meneer Maritz?"

"We start tomorrow. We are just going to work until we have some money. It's certainly not going to stop us from going when the time comes. Have you decided whether you and Roddy are going?" This I asked more to establish whether Roddy featured in her future plans.

She turned away and picked up her broom. She replied without looking up but seemed to sweep the ground a great deal harder. "I will make up my mind irrespective of what he's doing. Maybe he'll come ... maybe he won't." She stopped sweeping and looked up. "You had better get there early tonight if you want a seat. From what I've heard the whole district will be there."

Jan and I strolled down to the tavern in the main street a full thirty minutes before the scheduled time. As we drew near we could see others arriving and had to push our way through a tightly packed crowd to get a position near the counter. Marietjie had been right. The air was filled with blue smoke from many pipes. An excited babble of sound drowned out any chance of normal conversation. The atmosphere was thick with anticipation. Men shouted over the crowd as they recognized friends and neighbours. People jostled to get served brandy. There must have been more than a hundred people in the tiny room. I smiled wryly to myself. There was absolutely no possibility of a seat. Jan managed to shout an order for two flasks of brandy over the noise.

"Retief and Pretorius as well as Maritz are going to be here." The news spread like wildfire. Jan and I exchanged glances. We downed our brandies and ordered more. Six o'clock came and went with no sign of the great men. Jan and I continued to drink. His face was already flushed. Suddenly the buzz rose to a new level as a small group of people elbowed their way through the mass. The crowd parted and fell silent. We craned our necks to see the new arrivals.

"Potgieter is the one with Maritz," said Jan. I looked at Potgieter. A tall man in his early forties, with a severe face, a high forehead with his dark hair cut in a fringe hiding part of his forehead. He was carrying a wide-brimmed straw hat which he had obviously just removed as the sweat stain still ringed his head. I didn't realize it at the time but this was one of the few times I would see him without his hat. He was wearing a blue moleskin suit and the short jacket of a Dopper, a member of a sect of the Dutch Reformed Church. A dark beard which did not fully cover his chin, balanced piercing blue eyes. The manner in which he carried himself made him look every inch a leader. I heard someone whisper loudly, "It's old Blaauwberg himself," referring to Potgieter's nickname, which meant blue mountain.

He and his companions made their way to the front of the crowd. There was no sign of Retief or Pretorius.

A man with long sideburns, younger than Potgieter, short and stout, clean-shaven and with fair hair combed forward, also dressed in a moleskin suit with the short jacket of the Dopper, clambered onto a table looking self-important.

"Kêrels! Kêrels!" he shouted.

"Shhhhhh!" came from across the room.

When the self-important one had everyone's attention, he stretched his arms forward, steepled his fingers and said, "Come, let us pray."

I looked questioningly at Jan, his head bowed and hands clasped in front of him as he whispered, "Sarel Cilliers. He is close to Potgieter. They are both Doppers. He thinks he's a minister."

As the last amen died away Cilliers addressed us: "Men, we all know the reason for our being here. I don't wish to alarm you but the authorities may well brand all who even discuss leaving the colony as rebels. If this worries you, then I suggest you leave now." He paused and looked around, as did we all, to see if anyone had followed his advice.

No one moved.

On looking around, my gaze settled on a figure at the far side of the room. The moment I saw him I could see that he'd seen me. It was Pa with my brother Frans. Pa dug Frans in the ribs and nodded in my direction. My stomach lurched as all the memories came flooding back. Our eyes locked. Neither of us showed any recognition or warmth to the other. I moved my gaze to Frans, nodded my head and smiled slightly in greeting. Frans smiled back. I was relieved that Amelia wasn't there. At the same time I longed to see her.

Cilliers had started speaking again and I turned to listen " ... clamp down on us. Some people have already left the colony. A group of people have gone with Louis Trichardt and another group with van Rensburg. They have crossed the Great River and are now beyond the control of the English."

A loud cheer went up from the men in the room and there were shouts of, "I'm going as well!", "Let's join Trichardt!" One man, fuelled by brandy, jumped onto a table at the back of the room and shouted, "Who's with me? I am going to join the Trichardts." There were shouts of support and some raised hands.

Cilliers saw that he was losing control. "Order! Order! Listen to me. In view of the attitude of the English there can be no discussion outside this room about what takes place here tonight. Agreed?"

This was met with a roar of agreement.

"Further, I urge you all to consider your participation with great care. So that you all know, we have recently sent ten men north of the Great River to claim land and have written to the authorities requesting permission to occupy that land outside the colony and still remain British subjects."

Again he was interrupted. The brandy was starting to take effect. "To hell with the British!" someone cried from the back. "When I go it is to escape the British, not to be one of them." There was a chorus of "Hear, hear," from around the room.

Cilliers warned, "Talk is cheap, men. Listen carefully to what I say. Life is going to be very hard. We have had expeditions exploring the lands on the other side of the mountains in what is called Natal, as well as across the rivers to the north but we only have limited information about what lies beyond. Some of you here tonight have fought the Xhosa. There are plenty of tribes in those parts who are just as aggressive. While we will go in peace and seek friends, we have already had reports of the warlike

Matabele under their leader Mzilikazi, who are killing thousands of kaffirs from other tribes. They will, in all likelihood, try and kill us as well. We have made contact with Dingaan in Natal but he is known to be a despot and is feared by all, so maybe life here under the English *is* better."

"Never!"

"Anyone is better than the English!"

"Look how they have cheated us over the slaves," the shouts rang out.

"No one knows that better than me," said Cilliers. "My slaves were valued at one thousand rix dollars. They have offered me three hundred and I must claim it from England. Plus they are charging me a commission!"

There were shouts of anger at the injustice of the payouts and Cilliers continued, holding his hand up for silence. "We have here, tonight, your own Gerrit Maritz, who is thinking of leading a group." Cilliers gestured to the smiling Maritz.

Again shouts broke out. "Count me with you Gerrit."

"Ja! That is a real man. Good old Maritz!"

"When are we going?"

Then someone with a sense of humour shouted, "I hope he'll have time to finish my wagon before he runs away from the English." There was a guffaw of laughter

Again Cilliers spoke. "You all seem to know our friend Meneer Maritz but please also welcome Hendrik Potgieter from Tarka who is also planning to leave with his family and whoever else has the means to join him."

There was a polite round of applause and scattered cheers. Potgieter looked even more solemn at this reception.

Cilliers continued, "There is much debate at present regarding whether to cross the fierce mountains and go into Natal where the English already are, or to head across the Great River into the territories to the north. Both areas have an abundance of land for grazing and farming. These are the things you must think about. Also, of course, you must realize that if you go there is no turning back. The English will not welcome you back and you may even be branded a traitor. There is talk of legislation to stop us leaving. You must all be aware of the risks ahead. Life in a wagon, which might sound exciting after a few flasks of brandy, will be arduous and dangerous. Many of you standing here tonight will not live to see your final destination. Some of you will have to bury your loved ones on the trail. The ministers of our church have threatened us with ex-communication which means that your children will not be Christians in the eyes of our Lord as they will not be able to be baptized. We will face dangerous animals and kaffirs who will see us as a threat, as did the Xhosa. You will be leaving forever, which means you have to sell your farms and maybe leave your possessions behind. You will only be able to take the things that you really need. And, of course, most of your space will be taken up with gunpowder."

The room was silent as the men digested this information. I saw some glancing anxiously at their companions.

"However, know this," said Cilliers. "We go with the blessing of our Lord, God our Father." He dropped to one knee, placed his right hand diagonally over his heart and closed his eyes. "Father we place our trust in you, that you will lead us to the Promised Land. That you will deliver us safely into the lands you have kept for us to prosper and grow and to find peace away from the injustices of the oppressors. Dear Lord our God, guide us in the path of righteousness, together with our loved ones, as we seek your eternal wisdom and guidance to make the right decisions as we leave the colony to seek a better life." He paused. "Grant us peace, Heavenly Father, and lead us by your light. Amen."

There was a roar of "Amen" as the men responded and the meeting broke up. Some left the room but most crowded round the table asking animated questions of Cilliers, Maritz and Potgieter. I was relieved to see that Pa and Frans had been among the first to leave.

Marietjie was waiting in the kitchen when we arrived back, flushed with brandy and information. "Some people have already left," I said as we entered the kitchen.

Marietjie and her mother Marina were sitting at the table sewing a tapestry. Marietjie looked up in the half light of the lamp. "Well that's not news; we already knew that," she said with a smile. The glow from the lamp on the table emphasized her features. She continued to sew. "What I want to know is, are you two definitely going and if so, where to?'

"Yes," I replied without hesitation. "But I am not sure whether Natal or the northern interior is a better option. Also, I think it depends on when they decide to leave. At present it's just talk, so we will have to see."

Jan broke in, "I might go before any groups go. There are plenty of people who have crossed the Great River already."

Marietjie looked at me for a few seconds. "And you? Are you going to wait? Are you going to take Katrina with you?"

"No," I said. "Katrina is not part of my plan. I will probably wait. There is much to be done beforehand. In any event we are both starting work in the morning for Meneer Maritz."

"Well, in that case, I think the two of you had better go to the stables and get some sleep. You'll need it if you're going to be working for Meneer Maritz."

At that moment the door opened and in walked Stefan Bronkhorst. He had also been at the meeting. He tossed his hat on the table and sat down next to the two women. "Well, it certainly seems as though it's going to happen. I'm not sure though if I'm that interested in going anymore. At my age ... better the devil you know than the one you don't. It seems like there could be a great deal of difficulties ... kaffirs, animals, disease ..." He paused and sighed.

His wife's eyes flashed in the lamplight. "What?" she asked incredulously. "Have I a coward for a husband?"

Stefan's face flushed.

"We *are* going," stressed Marina. "And the sooner the better. You had better see Maritz yourself tomorrow as we'll need a new wagon. We must also start buying the things we'll need … we won't be able to take much of this with us," she said, looking at the few pieces of furniture in the kitchen, "so we'd better start selling things off. There is much to be done."

Stefan looked taken aback, muttering, "Well, we'll see. There's lots of time to decide."

"There is no time," snapped Marina. "It is decided. We are going. The only doubtful point is whether Marietjie comes with us and the other four children, or whether she stays behind." She looked at Marietjie for a response.

"Roddy will be leaving the army next May, so everything depends on that. In the meantime I will help you with the preparations."

The atmosphere in the kitchen had become quite tense and I could see that Stefan felt slightly embarrassed at the way Marina had taken control.

"Goodnight everyone. I'm off to bed." Jan said, breaking the tension.

Made bold by brandy, I looked at Marietjie and said, "I'm going to bed as well."

"Good," she responded and put her tapestry on the table. "I need a breath of fresh air so I will walk with you. Anyway, there is something that I want to ask you."

I nodded goodnight to Stefan and Marina and went outside. It was a lovely, crisp winter evening. The sky was ablaze with stars with the moon lighting up the buildings. We walked in silence for a minute or two before I broke the silence.

"What is it that you wish to ask me?"

"Two things really. Firstly, although you might say it's none of my business: are you over your love for Amelia?" I raised my eyebrows in surprise but before I could answer her she continued, "… and secondly, if Meneer Maritz will give you a day off once you have started work for him, would you like to join me one day? We will take our horses and ride out of Graaff-Reinet and I will show you my favourite place. It is the most beautiful place in the world where you can see for miles and there is no one around … we can take a picnic and make a day of it."

I wasn't sure how to answer the first question so ignored it and said, "That sounds like a good idea. Of course I don't know what my hours of work will be but I am sure that sometime I will be given a day off. That will give me something to look forward to."

She smiled and stopped, ignoring the fact that I had not answered her about Amelia. "Well, that is done then. You can go the rest of the way on your own. I'm glad you have agreed to our trip. Don't say anything to Ma and Pa as they won't approve of me going with you, seeing as I am engaged to be married to Roddy."

My heart beat a little quicker at the thought of this little conspiracy. I hadn't answered the question about Amelia because I wasn't sure myself. It had been almost three months since that night in March when I'd thrown my drink in Pa's face and spat in Amelia's. I turned to Marietjie. "Of course, I won't say a word."

"Good," she said and before I could react she stepped forward, held my face gently, turned her face up and kissed me.

I reached out to embrace her but she stepped away with a laugh. "No, Rauch. I'm not ready for more than that." She turned on her heel and with her long skirts swishing around her ankles, strode back to the warmth of the kitchen. At the door, framed by the light inside, she stopped and looked back, blew me a kiss and was gone.

The next morning Jan and I strolled down Cradock Street to Gerrit Maritz's wagon-making business. As we drew near we could see a crowd gathered outside. It looked as though a fight was in progress.

"There's something wrong," I shouted at Jan as I broke into a run. The crowd surrounded two men I recognized from the night before. They were circling each other, fists raised and faces bloodied. I pushed my way through the crowd and grabbed one man from the back, holding him as he struggled to break away and land a blow on his opponent's face. Jan did the same with the other.

"He jumped the queue," the larger of the two claimed.

I looked around. The men had all been at the meeting and had come early to order wagons. There must have been more than fifty men anxiously waiting for Gerrit Maritz to see them.

The excitement over, the queue re-formed with the two bloodied antagonists at the back, cursing the other would-be buyers who were now in front of them. Jan and I entered the shed. My mouth dropped open in amazement. There were another twenty men lined up inside waiting to see Maritz. The people outside were merely the overflow. Maritz was at a table, writing furiously, while a customer sat opposite him.

He glanced up. "Good morning. I don't have time to talk now, as you can see. Go over and see Koos Fouché," he said, waving his hand toward a man working on a wagon wheel. "Koos will show you the ropes. Start on the wagon wheels and we'll see how you do. We're very busy, so we'll be working late tonight and every night." He paused and smiled, "That's if you still want the work."

The eight wagons under construction were eighteen feet long and six feet wide. The wheels on which Jan and I would work were shaped like saucers with the concave centres facing out. There were large wheels for the back and smaller ones for the front of the wagons. The larger wheels were about five feet high and fixed to a solid axle. Each had fourteen spokes made of hard assegai wood. The smaller wheels in front had only ten spokes. The outer rims were made from white and red pear wood and slanted out from the spokes to provide some springiness to the ride. On these rudimentary vehicles history would be made.

Chapter Nine

Jan and I toiled, making wagon wheels from six in the morning and finishing only well after night had fallen, sometimes as late as midnight. I enjoyed the work. It kept me occupied and of course it meant that I was earning money.

At night when we had locked up with Gerrit Maritz we would make our way back to the Bronkhorst home and after a hot meal in the kitchen, prepared by Marietjie or Marina, we would tumble into our straw beds and fall into a deep sleep. While we ate, Marietjie sat chatting to us while Jan and I wolfed down the delicious potjie. Like most of the trekker women, Marietjie and her mother had secret recipes which they were happy to lavish on us. Both were excellent cooks.

The weeks flew by. Rumour after rumour swept the town.

"The English are stopping people from leaving."

"The Trichardts and van Rensburgs are all dead."

"The authorities have stopped gunpowder from being transported."

"Ministers are refusing to baptize the children of people who plan to leave the colony."

"There are no wagons available."

"Farms are being given away, there are so many on the market."

"The province of Adelaide has been given back to the kaffirs."

"Forts have again been attacked by the Xhosa."

"Settlers have been arrested; they are being shot as traitors."

No one knew which were true and which were false.

Commerce boomed as people stocked up with goods for their journeys. Graaff-Reinet was a bustle of activity and Maritz's business was flourishing. We worked every day—apart from the Sabbath—for a full five months before Maritz came to speak to us. "Well boys! You have worked well and deserve a day off. You needn't come in on Saturday."

My spirits soared. I knew what I would be doing that day.

That evening at dinner, Jan announced, "Meneer Maritz has given us the day off on Saturday. I think I'm just going to sleep all day. What about you, Rauch?"

Marietjie was watching me, smiling as I looked at her, "Ag, I don't know about sleeping. If it's a nice day I might just take Grey and go and explore the countryside … it will be good to get out of town for a while and get some fresh air. I'm tired of being cooped up with those wagons day after day."

Early that Saturday morning I heard horses' hooves and a sharp whistle outside the stable. The sun had not yet risen, although there was enough pre-dawn light for me to see Marietjie sitting on Eerste. She looked beautiful. She was wearing an embroidered kappie; her long dress was pulled up and gathered in front of her so that I could make out the outlines of her well-shaped legs. Her feet were bare. Two saddlebags were slung across the horse.

She gestured. "Some food and drink, spare clothes in case we swim and something to sit on … are you ready?"

I mounted Grey and the two of us rode north through the quiet streets. "Where are we going?" I asked. 'Where is this favourite place of yours?"

"The Valley of Desolation," she smiled. "You will see … it will become your favourite place as well."

I let her lead the way, the sun starting to rise, promising a magnificent, clear day. We headed for a mountain about ten miles away and rode in silence at a leisurely pace, enjoying the quiet company. The worn bridle path became steeper and steeper as we rode up the mountainside. Near the top, after we had been riding for about two hours, Marietjie pulled up her horse. I stopped next to her.

"Here," she said, reaching out to me with a neckerchief in her hand, "I am going to blindfold you."

I laughed as she tied the neckerchief tightly around my eyes. She then took my reins and led Grey alongside Eerste. We walked for about five minutes. She stopped. There was not a sound. I could feel a slight breeze on my cheeks and the sweet smell of morning was heightened by my temporary loss of sight.

"There!" Marietjie said triumphantly as she whipped off the neckerchief.

I blinked as my eyes adjusted to the bright sunlight, and then I stared. Our horses were standing side by side on a ledge many hundreds of feet above a valley. We could see for miles. It was as if the whole world lay before us, far, far below. It was a magnificent sight: a patchwork quilt of greens and browns, tumbling rock formations and ribbons of blue streams.

Two black eagles circled their prey a few hundred yards below us but far above their unsuspecting targets. The sounds of herdsmen calling their cattle floated gently up to us. In the distance were the outlines of mauve-blue mountains etched against the morning sky and in front of them clouds of morning mist were rapidly dispersing in the warmth of the sun. I felt as if I was in heaven.

Marietjie watched me intently. "See what I mean?" she smiled.

I nodded, feasting my eyes on the panorama that stretched before us. "Whew," I whispered in awe. "This is really lovely. So this is your favourite place?"

"One of my favourite places. The best one is way down there," she pointed to the valley below. "We'll go there after we've had something to eat and drink."

We sat down on the ledge after tethering the horses. Our eyes drank in the view for what felt like hours.

Marietjie reached out and squeezed my hand. "I don't want to break the spell but shall we eat?"

After the cold boerewors and biltong, we ate the hard-boiled eggs she had prepared. The sun was now quite warm but we were cooled by a slight breeze as we sat in silence, revelling in the view. I had made a fire and we brewed hot, strong coffee which we drank black and sweet. I felt deeply at peace and the thought occurred to me that there surely must be a God to have created such a magnificent sight. I felt on top of the world drinking coffee with Marietjie. She had removed her kappie and loosened her bun to let her hair cascade over her shoulders. The breeze stirred the leaves around us, gently wafting her fine hair from time to time. Her face was turned away, showing off her striking profile. High cheekbones, soft smooth skin and a wide mouth that smiled easily, the sweep of her long, dark eyelashes—all contributed to her beauty. Her dress had a square neckline and although I couldn't quite make out the shape of her breasts, the memory of the glimpse I'd had in Katrina's room was still vivid.

She realized I was watching her. "So, do you like what you see?" she grinned, her neat white teeth flashing in the sunlight.

I nodded. "Yes and I can understand why you call this one of your most special places."

"Not the view, you fool!" she giggled. "Me!"

"Oh yes!" I replied quickly, "Much more than the view. You are truly beautiful."

She tossed her head and leaned back on her elbows, looking up at the sky. "Oh my … Rauch," she said, "everything has become very complicated since I met you." She glanced at me sideways and smiled, "Come. Let me show you my very special place."

I'd felt a stirring in my loins as she flirted shamelessly so I was quite relieved that she'd suggested we move as I wasn't quite sure how to handle this confident young lady. After packing the saddlebags we mounted our horses and meandered slowly down the steep slope into the valley below. Marietjie led the way. As we descended the breeze that we had enjoyed on top of the mountain diminished until it disappeared altogether. The day became hotter and hotter as we went deeper into the valley. I could feel the sun scorching my back through my shirt. I was glad of my wide-brimmed hat which at least gave my face some protection.

"Hot, isn't it?" I called out to Marietjie.

"Very hot …" She glanced back at me and smiled.

I made no answer but her meaning was clear. We rode on in silence for another hour, moving ever deeper into the valley.

"Almost there," Marietjie called without looking round.

We were approaching a stream that meandered along the valley. We followed the riverbank. I spurred Grey on to draw level with Marietjie. The riding was easier now on the level ground. Marietjie's face was slightly hidden as she'd put her kappie back on. Her hair still spilled down her back from beneath the bonnet.

"Here we are." She pulled up her horse.

Beside us, crystal clear waters gurgled over a bed of rocks a few feet below. Ahead of us was the mouth of a cave into which the stream disappeared. Marietjie climbed off her horse, tethered him and removed the saddlebag. Slinging it over her shoulder, she entered the cave. I followed. It was pitch black inside. I looked back, encouraged that I could still see bright sunlight through the mouth. I stood for a moment or two until my eyes became accustomed to the dark. Marietjie placed the saddlebag on the ground. A light flared as she lit a tonteldoos to light a candle which flickered, almost dying, and then, as the wick ignited fully, the light increased in intensity, revealing the cave. We were in a spectacular cavern of stalactites and stalagmites. The atmosphere was almost sacred. The walls shimmered with different colours, like the facets of a diamond reflecting the light. The stream bubbled at our feet as it emptied into a large pool. Marietjie threw a kaross onto a dry spot on the ground near the stream.

I was astounded by the magnificence of the cavern. "I don't need to ask you why this is your favourite place," I said.

She nodded briefly. She took something out of the saddlebag, bent over the stream and swished it through the water. Squatting, she pulled up her long dress, exposing her shapely calves and knees. She was filling a dagga pipe with water before stuffing it with dagga from the saddlebag and lighting it with the tonteldoos. I was sitting on the kaross, watching her preparations.

She paused and looked up at me. "I've brought you a flask of brandy. You like brandy, don't you?"

"Sometimes too much … you seem to have thought of everything," I grinned.

"Pretty much. I bet you didn't think that I'd enjoy smoking dagga and having an occasional dop?" She looked at me quizzically.

I shook my head.

The pipe was ready. Marietjie put the stem to her lips and inhaled deeply. Her eyes widened as the smoke filled her lungs. I could see that the drug had an immediate effect.

"Your turn," she said, passing me the pipe.

I inhaled. The smoke passed over the water in the pipe, cooling it and making it easier to breathe in. My head swam and as I sat on the kaross with this beautiful woman, I felt perfectly content with life. What a day we were having. I thought of the weeks of work in Gerrit Maritz's shed and smiled to myself at the contrast. We smoked happily, passing the pipe back and forth.

"Not too much, now," Marietjie said. "We still have to have a swim."

She got up and walked out of the candlelight into the darkness. On the far side of the pool I could just make out the shape of a giant rock that hid her from view. I puffed a few times on the pipe while I waited for her. I suddenly saw white flesh in the semi-dark. In three quick steps she dived head first into the pool in front of me. Her body shimmered as she swam under water, hands outstretched in front of her. Her legs thrashed, propelling her toward the bank where I was sitting. A tiny stream of bubbles marked her progress through the water. When I thought her lungs would surely burst, her head broke the surface, wet hair plastered to her face. I could see that she was wearing a pair of men's breeches which showed off a startlingly curvaceous figure. She wore nothing above the waist.

She kept herself afloat, paddling like a dog, and then with graceful but powerful strokes she swam to the bank. She held onto the side, looking up at me. "Give me a brandy now, please Rauch. I feel very naughty," she giggled.

I passed the flask and she took a large swig. With her head back she raised herself slightly in the water. Her breasts were taut and perfectly shaped, the erect nipples pointing proudly at me. I swallowed hard, realizing she must have noticed the expression on my face.

"That's so good," she announced. "The water is chilly but the brandy warms you from the inside. It's wonderful. Come on, Rauch, come join me," she said as she splashed me.

I scrambled to my feet and moved into the shadows to strip. I felt a pang of melancholy as I remembered the days with Amelia at the river on the farm before the Xhosa came. I was pleased that I was in the dark as the dagga and the sight of Marietjie had stimulated me. I kept my breeches on, hoping to hide the bulge as I dived headlong into the pool. The crisp, cold water took my breath away.

As my head broke the surface, I looked around for Marietjie. She was nowhere to be seen. I looked around for her. Panic gripped me. "Marietjie!" I shouted, peering into the recesses. "Marietjie! Where are you?" Just as I thought something terrible must have happened, I felt something grab my ankle.

"Aaaaaaagh!" I screamed in terror, pulling my legs up before realizing that Marietjie had dived under water and grabbed my ankle to give me a fright. I felt a bit silly when her head popped up. She was laughing so much that water got into her mouth and her laughter turned into a fit of coughing and spluttering interspersed with giggles. "Oh, Rauch, you're so funny! You got such a fright."

I managed an embarrassed smile. She trod water in front of me, her taut, sculpted breasts standing out.

"You've kept your breeches on."

"So have you … I'll take mine off, if you like," I said easily, knowing full well that the icy water had done for my erection what no power of thought could do. Despite still being aroused, it was quite safe to expose myself. I stayed in the water, unbuckled my breeches and wriggled out of them.

"What about you?" I asked.

Marietjie laughed, "There are some things I am not sharing with you," she laughed as she dived backward and using backstroke, swam energetically to the far side of the pool. Before she disappeared into the darker shadows out of the flickering light I could see her wet breasts glistening above the water. The light from the candle did not reach the far end of the pool but I could just make out Marietjie's shape as she pulled herself out of the water onto the bank. She disappeared behind the big rock.

I clambered out of the water and dried myself with my shirt which I then tied around my waist by the sleeves with the tail hanging in front to offer a degree of privacy. Despite the warmth outside, my teeth were chattering from the icy water. I picked up the flask and swigged a mouthful of brandy. The alcohol created a warm glow, starting deep inside and working its way outward.

Marietjie emerged from the darkness. She still had her breeches on but she needn't have bothered as the wet fabric clung to her, detailing every inch of her body. She had pulled back her wet hair so that it was swept over her ears. I saw that she was smiling as she drew close.

"That was wonderful, wasn't it?" she said, squeezing water from her hair at the nape of her neck. "You've gone all shy on me, Rauch," she admonished as she noticed my shirt. She looked me straight in the eyes, placed her hands on my shoulders and said simply, "I think I am falling in love with you, Rauch."

My legs felt that they could not hold me up any longer.

"Do you think you could love me in place of your beloved Amelia?"

Looking at her right then I would have defied any man to have said no, her body a picture of perfection. I didn't respond but held out my arms. She moved against me. I could feel her nipples almost rasping against my chest. Her hand reached around my back. With a single movement of her hand she untied my shirt sleeves. The shirt dropped to the ground while her hands gently caressed my naked buttocks, describing slow circles. I moved my hand up her body and started to caress her back, using the tips of my fingers. I felt small goose bumps appear under my fingers as she dug her nails into my back and pressed hard against me. Her breathing quickened. I slipped my hand under the wet breeches and felt the smooth cold flesh of her buttocks.

She let her head fall back and her breath came in long gasps. "God, no! Oh God, please stop. What are you doing to me?" she whispered loudly but without moving away.

Instead I could feel her nails digging into my buttocks as she pushed hard against me. We made love on the kaross. For the first time in my life I enjoyed the warmth and affection that went with pure lust. This was very different to anything I had experienced with Katrina and what I had always dreamed I would feel with Amelia. Our bodies moved in perfect harmony, our movements choreographed as that of one body.

I woke to find that the candle had died out. I felt beside me; Marietjie still lying there, stark naked and dead to the world. I shook her gently to wake her and pulled my clothes on. At the mouth of the cave I could see that the light outside was failing.

"Wake up, Marietjie. It's getting late and we still have to ride home," I said urgently.

She grabbed her clothes and in the dark I could see her outline as she started to dress, her lovely body disappearing into the folds of her long dress.

"Come on, then, let's go. I hope no one's going to ask where I've been today and, more importantly, with whom. I am engaged to be married, remember." With that she picked up the kaross and saddlebag and made her way outside.

There were still a couple of hours of light left as we mounted the horses and started for home. I felt joyful, relaxed and content. For the first time I had someone other than Amelia on my mind and I knew Marietjie felt the same way. She was smiling and as we rode side by side, holding hands. Occasionally, she glanced at me with her broad smile.

She made me feel good.

ঙ-ঙ-ঙ

Darkness was fast approaching as we made our way into town. As we reached the Bronkhorst house, I noticed a wagon outside and a group of people clustered around it. They appeared to be busy removing items from the wagon. My heart sank. I saw that Stefan Bronkhorst was one of them. As we drew closer, Stefan, alerted by our horses' hooves, looked up and recognized us. His face darkened. He detached himself from the group. I noticed that the others were removing a body on a stretcher from the back of the wagon.

Looking at Marietjie first he hissed in a loud whisper, "Where the donder have you been?" Then he looked at me. "Don't you know that my daughter is engaged?" Not waiting for a reply he confronted Marietjie and grabbed her wrist, pulling her to him. "Look who has come in the wagon: your fiancé, the Englishman, Roddy … or what is left of him."

A wave of shock hit me full in the stomach.

Marietjie went ashen. She swung herself swiftly off her horse. "Sorry Pa!" she whispered.

"I can smell brandy on your breath. What have you two been up to? You little hussy, I can guess. And you … betrothed! You bring shame on our family!"

The blood rushed back into Marietjie's face as she hurried to the wagon just as the men lowered the stretcher to the ground.

Turning to me, Stefan said, "How dare you abuse my hospitality? That is her betrothed lying there, while the two of you are God knows where and up to all sorts of nonsense. I can guess what's been going on. Thank God Roddy is unconscious and didn't see the two of you arrive. I'll deal with you later. We have to get him inside and call the doctor." He turned away and followed the men. One of those carrying the stretcher was Jan Greyling.

As they made their way up the steps to the house I saw a bloodied bandage tied around Roddy's head. He was ash white, his eyes closed; he looked at death's door. Marietjie was walking next to the stretcher, her hand gently stroking his tousled hair.

The magic of the day slipped a thousand miles away. Not knowing what else to do, I stabled Grey and went to my room to await Jan's return. I didn't have long to wait.

"That was good timing," he said angrily as he walked in. "Her father is furious with you. When will you start thinking with your brains instead of your balls?"

I ignored his comment. "What happened to Roddy?"

"He was on a patrol when the Xhosa attacked. Two soldiers were killed and Roddy was left for dead. They brought him here because they don't think the doctor can do much for him. He took an assegai in the stomach and his left leg has had it. As you saw they hacked his head open with a battle axe. He's in a bad way … probably a good thing, too!" he said, glaring at me. "Otherwise I think it might have been you on the stretcher!"

"What are they going to do with him?"

"Apparently Doctor van Rensburg is on his way. They think he might have to amputate the leg and who knows how bad the injury to his stomach might be. The blade of the assegai is still in there. You wouldn't believe it—the handle is sticking out. I think it might be better if he doesn't live, he's in such a bad state. Fortunately for him, he seems to drift in and out of consciousness."

Just then the figure of Stefan appeared in the doorway. "Look, Rauch. This is a bad time for us, as you can see. I am very disappointed in you. I liked you and now you have cheated on my family with my daughter. We are going to be very busy now, trying to help Roddy. I don't think we have room for you here any longer." He glanced at Jan, "The two of you can take your things and go".

My heart sank. Jan shot me a look that plainly said, "I told you so."

"I am sorry, Meneer Bronkhorst. Marietjie and I are good friends and we …"

He interrupted me, "Just friends, are you? You bring my eighteen-year-old daughter home stinking of booze like a man after a night out. As I said before, I think I can guess what the two of you have been up to. Sorry is not good enough. You probably encouraged her to drink and then took advantage of her. You should have considered the consequences before you planned your day out with little Marietjie!"

I did not respond. I began packing my belongings into a saddlebag. Jan did the same. Stefan Bronkhorst stood and watched us for a minute and then turned on his heel and went out into the night.

"Thanks a lot!" said Jan, angrily. "Now you've really done it! Where are we going to go?"

"To Meneer Maritz's place. We can sleep on the floor in the shed. We won't have so far to walk in the mornings …" I added feebly, trying to lighten the mood. But I felt anything but light-hearted.

When we were ready to leave, I said to Jan, "I can't leave here without a word to Marietjie."

"Marietjie! She's not interested in you at the moment. Don't you understand? Her fiancé is here and is gravely hurt. All she will want to do now is to care for him, you mark my words. Mind you, I don't know why she would fall for an English soldier when she could have had a boer like *you*."

I ignored his sarcasm but couldn't help but wonder the very same thing myself. As we were leaving, Marietjie ran out of the house. Her eyes were red and swollen from crying; she was distraught. "Pa told me you are going." She clutched my hand and gazed up at me. Her words tumbled out in a torrent. "I am so sorry, Rauch. Pa is furious with you … and me … and he blames you. I tried to explain but he won't listen. It is I who has caused this problem. I am so mixed up … I am so sorry for what has happened. I won't forget what we shared today. It was very special … but Roddy needs me now. The doctor is already here and is talking about amputating the leg as gangrene has set in. Poor man, he is still unconscious. I must go …"

Then, as if suddenly realizing that we were going, "Where will you go? Please come and see me … I must go … they are all inside and I must look after Roddy. Oh, oh dear, I am so very mixed up. I'm so sorry, Rauch. Please, but please do visit. The doctor says, he says that the blow on the head could be the worst of Roddy's injuries."

"Go to him," I said as if I didn't really care. With a sinking feeling in my stomach I turned away and rode off with Jan to seek new lodgings.

Chapter Ten

Jan and I soon settled into our new lodgings, sleeping on the floor behind Gerrit Maritz's wagon workshop. He had been understanding about our predicament, although I hadn't divulged the details. I was afraid to visit the Bronkhorsts. Much as I wanted to see Marietjie, I was nervous in case I bumped into her father. I often walked past in the hope of seeing her but I never did.

A full two months later, while working on the wheels of Meneer Potgieter's wagon, I was called by Maritz.

"Rauch!" I looked up from my work. "Someone wants to see you."

I could see a woman's dress through the open door. My heart beat faster. "It must be Marietjie," I thought, wiping my greasy hands on a rag as I made my way to Meneer Maritz's office. He left to give my visitor and me some privacy, saying with a wry smile, "She's waiting for you."

"Hello Rauchie," said Katrina, studying my face with her big brown eyes. "Are you pleased to see me?" My eyes were drawn to her swollen stomach. She was about six months pregnant. She saw the look of shock on my face. Before I could answer, Katrina laughed, rather hollowly. "You look as if you've seen a ghost," she said, glancing down and patting her stomach. "Don't worry; this is not why I'm here. I wanted to see you again. Why haven't you been in touch with me?"

"Hello Vlam," I said. I put my arms around her and kissed her gently on the mouth. "It's good to see you. How are you?"

"Bigger and better than ever," was the wry retort. "I'm staying with Marietjie. Bill Gibson rode here with me. He wanted to see Roddy ... they trained together, so he is here too."

I noticed a man standing outside the shed, watching us. Gibson was out of earshot and I acknowledged him with a half-hearted wave. I was dying to ask Katrina whether or not I was a father but was afraid of the answer.

"Well, why have you come ... apart from wanting to see me?" I asked.

"I am hoping that I can hook up with you again and leave the colony with you ... you are still going, aren't you? You see, Rauch, I still care about you ... and now ... the baby ..." Her eyes filled with tears. She looked at me questioningly.

"Look, I have to get back to work," I said. "I will meet you after work. Be here at eight o'clock and we can talk. How is Roddy getting along?" I added hastily, trying to change the subject. I had heard snippets of news about him and from what I knew he was recovering well.

"They amputated his leg at the knee and he is fast recovering from the stab wound in the stomach. The axe wound in his head is the worst. Although he seems to be recovering he behaves very strangely sometimes, so they think maybe his brain is damaged. He is out of bed now and sits in a chair but he seems moody and falls quickly into fits of temper. Poor Marietjie," she looked straight into my eyes, "she really has had a bad time and to make matters worse, for some reason she and her father hardly speak any more."

My face flushed as I wondered if Katrina knew that I was the cause of the rift.

That evening after work Jan and I stood outside, discussing the latest developments while waiting for Katrina, leaving Meneer Maritz inside poring over his books.

"Are you going to marry her?" Jan asked, looking quite concerned.

"No, I don't think so ... at least I don't want to. I don't love her and in any event who says the baby is mine? There is just as much chance that it's Bill Gibson's ... or maybe even yours ... or one of a dozen others ... who knows ... I don't want a bastard baby. I think I must get away from here and the sooner the better. First my Pa and Amelia, then I meet Marietjie ... now Katrina's turned up ..." I left the sentence trailing as Katrina arrived.

"Hello Jan," she said, kissing him on the cheek.

"Hello Rauchie," she greeted me, kissing my mouth.

"I'll leave you two, then," said Jan. He turned and smiled at me as if to say "Good luck".

Katrina took my hand and we strolled down the street. It was a warm summer's evening and there were quite a few people out. Many greeted me. Having worked for Gerrit Maritz for six months I had become friendly with a number of the townsfolk.

"Oh, Marietjie says I must give you her love," she said, looking at me to gauge my reaction. My face went red but she went on. "Shame, poor girl, she looks after that Roddy from morning till night. She's all skin and bone and doesn't look at all well herself. Her father keeps on at her all the time that she must take care of Roddy … that that's her responsibility since they are betrothed. Roddy has become quite unpleasant and rude. I used to like him but I think that blow on the head has made him a bit strange. I pity Marietjie having to marry him."

I stopped and looked at her in shock. "What do you mean, marry him?" I had quite forgotten that Marietjie was engaged or at least had put the idea out of my mind, considering the circumstances.

"Oh, it will happen in December. I think Marietjie feels now that she *has* to marry him after what happened." She looked at me sharply. "They were engaged anyway and I think that just because he is injured it would be very wrong of Marietjie if she didn't marry him. Anyway," she said squeezing my hand, "I didn't come here to talk about Marietjie. What about us?"

I felt sick at being reminded of Marietjie's impending marriage to Roddy and even sicker about the trap I found myself in with Katrina. My world was on the point of collapse, just as I had thought that it might be coming right.

"What do you mean … what about us?" I asked sharply.

"Well, I am going to have a baby in a few months' time. When are we going to get married? There is much to be done. When are we to leave the colony? We have a lot to prepare."

I felt even sicker as the reality sank home: she really did believe that we would live happily ever after. I stopped and faced her. "I am not taking you with me. I told you that before. Don't you listen?" Her eyes widened as she stared at me. "Who says that this baby is mine? It might be your friend Bill Gibson's or Jan's or even my Pa's—that wouldn't surprise me—or maybe even Gieletjie's. Why pick on me?"

"Because you are the only one that I really care about … you know that," she said defensively.

"That may well be but I don't want to marry you, Vlam. Because you have decided that you want me to marry you isn't quite good enough. You are my friend and I'll always be fond of you but I don't want to marry you!"

She stared at me angrily. "You *have* to marry me. You are the father of our child. You know that we are meant to be together … I am … I will always be your Vlam." She smiled through her tears.

"Katrina, you have a wide choice to pick from. Why choose me?" I felt sorry as soon as the words were out of my mouth but I rushed on. "I will not marry you! As far as I am concerned I am *not* the father. I am not marrying you and you are *not* coming with me. Do you understand?"

Tears trickled down her cheeks as her anger rose. She sniffed and dabbed her eyes with a handkerchief. "I *am* going to leave the colony and I *am* going to get married. If you don't want me then I'll find someone who does. I hate you for this, Rauch. I curse you for not marrying me!" She dropped my hand, turned on her heel and walked into the night.

My heart went out to her. I felt nauseous at the thought of how I was hurting her but I knew that if I agreed to her demands I would be sentencing myself to a life with a woman I did not love. I was sure I was doing the right thing, at least from my point of view, because I loved another woman. That woman, though, was no longer Amelia but Marietjie. My heart felt like lead at the thought of Marietjie marrying Roddy.

Jan was waiting for me as I walked despondently into the shed. He obviously had something on his mind as he was reading the Bible by the light of the candle. "How did it go?" he asked.

"Not well. I have to get away from here. Katrina is deeply hurt because I don't want to marry her and Marietjie is going to marry Roddy in December, even though he only has one leg and apparently is quite abusive to her. Everything is a mess. I must get away."

"Well I think our opportunity has come," he said excitedly.

"What do you mean?"

"While you were out with Katrina, Meneer Potgieter was here talking to Meneer Maritz. Apparently Meneer Potgieter has sent some of his family, the Trichardts and the van Rensburgs, out of the colony already and he himself is leaving in a few weeks to go up north. He is taking a large number of people. We can go with his group. This is the chance we have been waiting for."

"Where is he going?" I asked.

"North, across the Great River, far away from the English. He says that land there is plentiful and that there are no English." Jan's mouth twisted as though the very word 'English' was sour as a lemon in his mouth.

"I would rather go to Natal. They say it's like the Garden of Eden. Lush and beautiful … on the other hand, if he is leaving soon …"

"He is leaving in mid-December," said Jan, "and although Meneer Potgieter acknowledges that Natal is very attractive he was saying to Maritz that 'where there is sea, you have the English'." Jan mimicked Potgieter's gruff voice, before continuing, "Apparently the English have already set up a little settlement on the coast. Potgieter says he's not going anywhere where he has to answer to them. What do you think?"

"Well the idea of leaving in a few weeks' time is exciting. On the other hand, going with Meneer Potgieter and his crowd of religious fanatics is not so attractive, neither is the thought of going north. I think we must sleep on it. Anyway, who says that Potgieter will let us join him? We're not members of his church and to be frank I find their whole attitude to God and the Bible a bit tiresome. Let's sleep on it... maybe it's an option, who knows? I have to do *something*."

"I think we should ask him whether we can join him, Dopper church or not," replied Jan.

My head whirled as I lay on the straw. I finally dozed off into a troubled sleep but not until I heard the first cock crow of dawn. My last thought before sleep blanketed me was that I'd leave with Potgieter, religious zealot or not.

Next morning Jan and I explained to Gerrit Maritz what we wanted to do. He listened with the hint of a smile on his face as we outlined our wish to see Potgieter.

"Look, you two have been good workers. I won't stop you but why don't you wait a bit longer? Meneer Potgieter, old Blaauwberg, is not an easy man to get along with. I am hoping to leave soon myself and intend making for Natal ... a much better land for our people to settle. Also Blaauwberg is fanatically religious. I'm sure that the two of you are not quite of the same religious convictions, are you?" he smiled.

"We believe in the same God; that's about all I can say. When are you going?"

"Not till later next year."

"No, Meneer Maritz. I have made up my mind. Potgieter and his followers can't be that bad. I want to get away as soon as possible. So does Jan."

An hour later, with our pay in our pockets and a generous bonus of five pounds each, Jan and I were in our saddles ready to ride the one hundred miles from Graaff-Reinet to Tarka.

I had an idea. "Wait for me," I shouted to Jan and galloped off in the direction of the Bronkhorst house. I had to see Marietjie before we left. I clambered off Grey and knocked on the door, my heart pounding in case Meneer Bronkhorst should open it.

Worse, Roddy opened it. He stared at me, unsmiling. I was shocked by his appearance. He looked gaunt, his face grey. He stood propped in the doorway, resting on a crutch. He had one good leg and a wooden stump from the knee of the other. A livid scar ruined his appearance and the once smiling, open face looked surly and ill-tempered.

"Hello Roddy … how are you?"

He didn't answer at first. "What do you want here?" he spat bitterly after a time.

"I've come to say goodbye." I didn't add "to Marietjie".

"Well, I can't say that I'll be shedding any tears for you. Anyway, you have wasted your time. Marietjie is not here."

I could hear voices in the background. One was Katrina's, the other Marietjie's. I stood for a moment. There was silence between the two of us but it was obvious that Roddy knew that I had heard.

"I think you had better go," said Roddy "You aren't welcome here."

After a few more moments, I turned on my heel and without a backward glance, strode over to Grey.

Roddy shouted after me, "I'll tell Marietjie you came to say goodbye. I am sure she will be sorry to have missed you." I heard the door being slammed.

I rode to the shed where I had left Jan. "Let's go."

"Did you see her?" asked Jan.

"No. I saw her bloody fiancé, Roddy. He wouldn't let me near her."

As we rode I gradually felt my spirits lifting. It was as if my troubles diminished with every mile farther from Katrina. I kept thinking of Marietjie and wondered when I would see her again, if ever. We rode into the little village of Tarka in the early evening the following day. After asking directions to Potgieter's farm, Jan and I decided to continue on our way. It was only another half hour's ride.

The sun was setting as we approached the farm. A large group of people was clustered around the farmhouse. As we drew nearer we could hear singing; they were in the middle of a prayer meeting. We drew up our horses and waited for the meeting to finish.

"I'm not too sure about this," whispered Jan.

When the service was over Potgieter detached himself from the group and walked across to us. He was a powerful, serious man. His eyes seemed to look right through us as he greeted us. "Welcome. I recognize you. You were at the meeting that night in Graaff-Reinet with Sarel Cilliers, weren't you?"

"Thank you, Meneer Potgieter. Yes we were."

"What brings you here?"

"We believe that you are leaving the colony and we were wondering whether the two of us could join you," said Jan.

Blaauwberg looked from me to Jan and then back to me. He fixed me with a firm gaze and said quietly, "Let us pray, and thank the Lord. For it is He who has sent you to us. We leave in fourteen days, on Saturday, December 19th."

The three of us joined hands and closed our eyes. Potgieter led us in prayer and we thanked the Lord for his guidance. I closed my eyes then sneaked a look at Jan and saw that he was doing the same, looking at me. Jan winked. We smiled at each other and closed our eyes again. When we had finished praying Potgieter led us up to the house where people were drinking coffee, engaged in animated conversation.

"People," he shouted. There was immediate silence. "We have two young men here who will be joining us on our journey to the Promised Land. This is Jan Greyling and this, Rauch Beukes. Both these young men have had experience fighting the Xhosa. I know that they are both handy with a gun and, as you can see, they are sturdy young fellows." He turned to us. "I welcome the two of you to our trek. The Lord has sent you to us and this is a sign we must recognize. There is much preparation to be done before we depart, so four more hands will lighten the load. You are most welcome!"

There was a scattering of applause as men approached us, slapped us on the back, pumping our hands.

That night as we lay on the hay in the stables, Jan said "Well, this is it, Rauch. This looks to be the start of a whole new life. I hope we have done the right thing."

I didn't hear him finish the sentence. I was already asleep.

The next few days passed in a flurry of activity. Meneer Potgieter was right: there was much to be done. Provisions had to be procured in Tarka or occasionally from smouses with their range of wares. A number of prospective trekkers spent much of the time at Potgieter's farm, assisting in the preparations and we became friendly with many kindred spirits. In the evening we sat around the fire while Potgieter led us in prayer and then talked to each of the families about their preparations. We heard sad tales of farmers who had abandoned their farms due to a collapse in the land price, as so many people were trying to sell up. As one farmer said, they would rather ride away with nothing than accept an insulting offer of "an apple and an egg". Others sold their farms for as little as a wagon or a span of oxen, the number required to draw a wagon. It turned out that many who planned to go with Potgieter were family of some sort. I wondered why he had agreed to Jan and me accompanying them. I estimated that there were about sixty people in the trek party. Jan and I assisted wherever we could. For us it was a great deal easier. We had few possessions and therefore did not have the painful task of deciding what to leave behind. Many were the arguments I heard while walking past the wagons.

"What are you loading those planks of wood for?" I heard Petronella Botha asking of her husband, Petrus.

"My coffin."

She laughed. "Don't be silly ... what do you mean?"

"And what will you bury me in if I die on the journey?" Little did he know at the time how prophetic this was.

Great care had to be taken to ensure that the correct items were included. Furniture, tables, footstools, ropes and whips, cloths, brake-shoes for the wagons and tar. Then there were household items such as cutlery, kettles, pots, pans, buckets and water carriers. Chicken hoks containing live chickens were to be slung under the wagons. Lists were never-ending: blankets of hide and wool, spare shoes, needlework items, lantern oil, soap, medicines, fruit and vegetable seeds and tin and lead to make ammunition as well as whatever ammunition we could take with us. Every wagon had at least one giant family Bible which was kept accessible to be read every evening.

The activity grew ever more frenzied. The women sewed blankets, made pillows, cooked and dried fruit and biscuits and boiled sheeptail fat to make candles and soap. Wherever one looked in those hectic days of preparation there were sticks of beef biltong hanging in the breeze to dry. Men prepared wagons and melted tin plates and lead to make shot for their guns. The most important item of all was gunpowder.

At one of the evening discussions, Nikolaas Potgieter, Hendrik's younger brother, shocked us all after spending a day in Tarka. "They say that the English are setting up patrols to search people leaving the colony and that they will confiscate any gunpowder found on the wagons."

There was stunned silence. The trekkers looked from one to the other. Without gunpowder they would be lost.

"We will have to find a way to outsmart them," declared Potgieter over the hum of conversation. "I thought they might do something like this. Jan," he said, peering into the shadows where Jan and I were sitting, "you will take control of this part of the project. Tomorrow the women are going to sew skin bags and fill them with gunpowder. You, Jan, are going to load a wagon with the bags of gunpowder and take three slaves, Tokkie, Groot Kaatjie and Klein Kaatjie, to help you. You are to travel as fast as you can and bury the bags near the Great River, which we will then dig up when the main party passes through in about a week's time. Try and get as close to the river as you can."

Jan nodded in agreement.

"You, Rauch, are to take six wagons driven by the other slaves and Hottentots and ride urgently into Graaff-Reinet to see Meneer Maritz. Tell him that we need him to make us another deck on the bottoms of the wagons, about twelve inches under or over the floors. We will use that space to store the gunpowder and lead. Rauch, you ride at sun-up. Jan, you must wait until the women have finished sewing. Be sure to mark well the hiding place of the gunpowder," he admonished. "Our lives may very well depend on finding it."

My heart soared. I would be returning to Graaff-Reinet and one way or another I was determined to see Marietjie. This would probably be my last chance before we departed. Early next morning, before the sun rose, I said farewell to Jan, made arrangements to meet the wagon drivers in Graaff-Reinet and rode out on my own.

Chapter Eleven

I rode into Graaff-Reinet as the sun was setting and made straight for Gerrit Maritz's wagon shop. I found him hunched over a table working on some quotes.

He looked up as I entered. "Goodness, if it's not Rauch! Back already? Don't tell me those religious freaks are just too much for you!"

"No, no, not at all, Meneer Maritz. Meneer Potgieter has sent me to ask for your help. We have to find a way to hide gunpowder from the English patrols in case they try to confiscate it. The wagons will be here tomorrow and we need you to build false bottoms to hide the gunpowder." I explained what Potgieter had in mind while Gerrit Maritz listened attentively, nodding his head.

"Well, I am very busy as you can see. When is Potgieter leaving?"

"In about ten days' time, on December the nineteenth."

"When the wagons come tomorrow, I'll see what can be done," Maritz said reassuringly.

I heaved a sigh of relief, appreciating how lucky we were to have Maritz on side.

"I suppose you will be at the wedding on Saturday?" asked Maritz.

I was taken aback. "Wedding? What wedding?"

"Why, Roddy, the English soldier, and Marietjie Bronkhorst," he replied, looking surprised at my ignorance.

"But … but … he is injured, isn't he? Surely they can't get married … can they?" I stammered.

"Well," laughed Maritz. "He can't be that badly injured. I know he has only one leg but the other parts must be working … there is talk that she is already with child."

A wave of shock swept over me. I held onto the wagon wheel next to me to stop from falling over. So soon! She was marrying Roddy? I couldn't get my head around it. There must surely‚be some mistake. "No … I don't think I will be going," I stammered.

Maritz looked at me, puzzled. "Are you alright? What's the matter with you? You look as if you've seen a ghost."

"Something like that," I mumbled as I stumbled outside.

I found myself wandering in the direction of the Bronkhorsts' place. I had to see Marietjie. This was my last chance. I kept walking. I wasn't sure what I was going to do. Keeping to the shadows, I crept up to the house, watching the windows that were illuminated by lamplight, in the frail hope of seeing her. I moved to the back of the house where the bedrooms were. There was little to see as the curtains were drawn. After about half an hour of staring into the dark, my prayers were answered. I saw one of the darkened windows suddenly flickering with light as a lamp was carried into the room. A figure came to the window to draw the curtains. It was Marietjie. She closed the curtains, shutting me out again into the blackness of the night. I bent down, picked up a stone and threw it gently against the windowpane.

Ping! … no response.

I picked up a handful of pebbles and tossed them gently, sounding like buckshot in the stillness of the night. There was a brief delay before she appeared at the window, gazing out into the darkness. She couldn't see me in the shadows.

"Who's there?" she said in a loud whisper.

I stepped forward into the light, so that she could see me.

"It's me. Rauch!"

She let out a gasp. "Shhhhh! Don't let them hear you. There will be all sorts of trouble if they know you're here. I'll meet you at the stables." A few moments later the room was plunged into darkness.

I made my way to the stables and sat on a bale of hay. I didn't have long to wait before I heard her footsteps. "Here I am. Come here," I called quietly.

"Oh, Rauch, I am so pleased to see you!"

I took her in my arms. Her body was soft and warm against mine. We kissed gently and tenderly.

"I've missed you, Rauch. My God, I've missed you! Where have you been? No, don't answer. I know. Just kiss me. It's so, so good to be with you again."

I held her close and nuzzled her hair with my lips.

"Have you forgotten our day together?" she asked.

"Never … and I never will," I answered. "It was the best day of my life."

"I'm so glad. I was scared that it didn't mean as much to you as it did to me."

We held each other close, content to enjoy the physical contact. She had her arms around my neck, mine clasped behind her back. I pulled her closer to me and held her tightly.

"Come away with me," I said, impulsively.

She stepped back, breaking our embrace and looked at me with a smile. "I can't … you know that. I can't leave Roddy. Not after what he's been through. I'm going to have a baby and I am marrying Roddy on Saturday. It's too late, I'm afraid. His being so gravely wounded has changed everything."

"I thought you loved me," I said. "Now you are going to have his baby and become his wife. What about me? You've betrayed me!"

"I do love you. More than I have ever loved anyone, or ever will. But I cannot leave Roddy in the state that he's in."

I felt sick at the thought of her having Roddy's child and losing her forever. I decided to try once more. "Come away with me. We can go away when I've finished my business with Gerrit Maritz and then we can leave the colony forever … you and me. We will start a new life together. You know that I love you. I can't lose you now."

"It's too late. Roddy has plans to leave as well. I'm sorry, Rauch. I marry him on Saturday. It really is no good. You'd better leave now."

My heart sank. "I cannot think of you making love to him instead of me," was all I could think of saying.

"Don't think about it then," she said with a wry smile. "It hasn't happened since his injury and it never happened before. He is not capable … but only he, you and I know this."

For a second or two I didn't register what she'd said. "But … what about the baby?"

"Use your head, Rauch … you are the only one that I have made love with."

"That means … ?"

"Yes. The baby is yours, Rauch. I think Roddy knows … he's not a fool. I think he knows what happened that day in the Valley of Desolation."

My head whirled. For the second time in the space of a few hours I had to find something to support me as my legs turned to water. She was going to have my child. And Roddy knew! I was surprised that he hadn't blown my head off the last time he saw me.

I looked at Marietjie in amazement. She looked so beautiful, her blond curls framing her face and her deep blue eyes sparkling like the shimmering sea. I was filled with a feeling of deep love and tenderness.

There was an ache in the pit of my stomach. "That's even more reason why we should be together," I said. "I need you and now you are carrying our child."

Marietjie took my hand. "If it had just been a case of breaking up with Roddy under normal circumstances I would have done it. No question. But Roddy is completely alone. His injuries mean that he has to have someone to take care of him. It's not just his leg. By far the worst damage is to his head. Sometimes he has terrible headaches and almost cries with the pain. I feel so sorry for him. He needs me, I'm afraid. I was engaged to him at the time he was wounded so everyone, including me, feels I have a duty to care for him."

"To hell with what everyone else thinks!" I said angrily. "I am leaving in a week's time and want you to come with me … as my wife." I pulled her to me but she resisted.

"It's no good. We are getting married on Saturday. It's too late, Rauch. I will always love you and will care for the baby that you've given me. I'm sorry Rauch … I am really, really sorry." Her eyes filled with tears.

I knew there was no point in trying any longer. So near and yet so far. For the second time the woman I loved had been cruelly taken from me. We kissed tenderly and I held her close to my chest. I could feel that she was crying; shivery sobs rippled through her body. I held her in my arms and felt the wetness of her tears on my shoulder. I didn't ever want to let her go. Suddenly she reached up and kissed me firmly on the mouth. Before I could respond she pulled away, looked at me, blew a kiss and then turned and walked quickly away. My throat was tight with emotion and I had to blink back my own tears.

At the stable door she stopped, framed by the light of the moon, blew another kiss and whispered loudly, "Goodbye my love. We both will love you forever. Take care of yourself because many dangers lie ahead. Goodbye Rauch."

Then she was gone.

❦ ❦ ❦

The wagons arrived the next day and I threw myself into the task of working with Gerrit Maritz and his men, building false floors into each of the wagons. On the Friday before Marietjie was to marry Roddy, as Gerrit Maritz and I examined the last of the wagons, I looked up as a shadow fell at my feet. It was Katrina. My heart sank.

"Hello Rauch. I heard from Marietjie that you were here." Katrina was wearing a black dress and a plain white kappie. She looked heavy and dull in her pregnant state. Even her giant breasts seemed bulbous and unattractive.

"Hello, Vlam," I smiled, trying hard to disguise my feelings.

Gerrit Maritz moved to the other side of the shed, giving us some privacy.

"When are you leaving?" asked Katrina.

"I'm going back to Tarka tomorrow; we're leaving in about a week. Keep that to yourself. Why do you ask?"

"Take me with you, please, Rauch," she begged.

"No, Vlam. You are in no fit state to be starting a journey. In any event, I don't want you along. It's not a place or a trip for a woman; you know that."

"Well, why did you ask Marietjie to go with you?" she shot.

"That's not the point," I said, ducking the question. "You're going to have a baby."

"So is she. The difference is that this baby is yours and hers is Roddy's. I have a right to go with you. Why did you ask her, Rauch? You knew she was going to marry Roddy. You have made her unhappy. She came back in tears after she saw you. Roddy was furious that she spoke to you; he heard her telling me and I heard him slap her."

My heart stopped. I felt sick. "What do you mean? He hit her? Is she alright? How could he do that to her? The bastard!"

"It's not your affair," Katrina replied. "Anyway, they're getting married and I think that his betrothed should be more respectful of him, don't you?"

I was shocked. Roddy hit my Marietjie. Christ! Wait till I get my hands around his neck. I'll make him sorry for that!

Katrina twisted the knife further. "He often hits her, you know. I think he has gone slightly mad since that blow to the head. He's nothing like the Roddy of old." There was a pause as I absorbed this information. She repeated, "Take me with you, Rauch. It will be like old times. You enjoyed coming home to me in Grahamstown, didn't you? Well, it will be like that again. You know I can make you happy." Coquettishly she sidled close to me.

"No! For God's sake, can't you take no for an answer? I don't want you …
or your bastard child!" I turned on my heel.

Katrina stood for a few moments, looking at my back as I walked away,
before walking out of the shed. Had I seen her face I would have seen the
tears streaming down her puffy cheeks. Had I been closer I would have
heard her whisper: "Curse you, Rauch! You have left me with nothing …
except your bastard child in my belly."

๛๛๛

I left Graaff-Reinet that Saturday with a heavy heart, thinking of Marietjie
getting married that very day. How could she marry him after he struck
her? I was glad that I wouldn't be there to see them married. On the ride
back Marietjie filled my thoughts. I felt an enormous ache. I thought too
about Katrina and tried to put her out of my mind. I felt guilty for having
hurt her. It crossed my mind to wonder how Pa and Amelia were getting
along. I found I was able to think of Amelia without the pain I had felt
before … unlike Marietjie which was like a barb in my gut.

I arrived back at the Potgieter farm two days later, leading the six
wagons. We only had three days left to pack the wagons and make the final
preparations. The excitement of adventure was in the air as I rode through
the gates and was immediately swept up in the joyful atmosphere. Fires
were lit with the women preparing the evening meal.

"Welcome back," Gert Breedt greeted me.

The smell of cooking from the open pots and the wood smoke from the
fires felt warm and welcoming, a haze of scented smoke hanging over the
wagons. This was how it was going to be every day, I thought to myself.
This is now our life.

Jan was still on his mission, burying gunpowder along the route, so I
was on my own. A final prayer service had been called by Sarel Cilliers for

Friday night, the night of December 18th. It was exactly a year since I had surprised Pa and Amelia making love on the bank of the river. So much had changed since then. A wave of sadness washed over me as I thought of all I had lost. I stood at the back of the crowd of almost a hundred-strong who listened attentively to the words of Sarel Cilliers. Most of the trekkers, as we now called ourselves, were there. Nothing had been said but all were in their best finery for this last service before departing the colony and entering the unknown, forever. I looked at the faces: eyes closed in devotion, mouthing the prayers that Sarel Cilliers intoned, strong voices raised in song as they sang the chosen hymn; their faces shone with fervour as they sang out to the Lord, calling for his protection and guidance. I shivered at the sound and butterflies swirled in my stomach as I thought of what might lie ahead.

Lead us, O Heavenly Father, to thy Promised Land

Show us the way to the lands you have chosen for us

Protect us, O Holy Father, from the dangers of the heathen

Shelter us from the storms and all the perils of the elements

Fill us with thy strength and boldness as we are led by you into your Eden

Shield us from the weapons of our enemies

Help us honour your name with righteousness. Amen.

"Amen," roared the crowd. "Amen. Amen!"

I was swept up in the emotion of the moment and found myself shouting "Amen" as loudly as the rest. Even the little children, of which there must have been well over forty, showed respect, as if they too recognized the solemnity of the moment and the need not to interrupt this last plea to God to grant their families safety.

Early next morning, while it was still dark, I was part of a group of young men who led the way for the twenty families and thirty wagons that carried some eighty souls through the almost deserted village of Tarka, heading north.

The Great Trek had started in earnest.

As our wheels crunched over the stony road, the early morning dark was punctuated by pricks of light as lanterns flared in the houses we passed.

"Go with our Lord!" cried one old man, standing on his stoep in his nightshirt, holding a lantern above his head.

"God be with you!" called another.

"Come, quick, ma. Look!"

"Hurry, vrou ... come and see them go. They are going ... leaving the colony. They really are going."

People stood on their stoeps, holding their lanterns high, waving and clapping as we rode by. We waved back, proudly acknowledging their good wishes and enjoying the attention. I felt exhilarated by the fact that people thought us heroes. I sat straighter on my horse and held my head higher, noticing others doing the same. Moved by the emotion of the moment, I galloped ahead of the procession, whistling and waving my hat in the air. My troubles and sadness seemed to have dissipated, for now

In the still morning air the rattle and clatter of wheels over the stones and the jingle of harnesses dominated. Occasionally the crack of a whip wielded by one of the voorlopers, the servants who walked in front, rang out. As the morning sun started to light up the sky, cockerels began crowing from their little hokkies slung under the wagons. I looked back. We had been joined by a number of other wagons whose owners had been waiting for us to arrive at pre-designated meeting points. By the time the sun started to peek over the hills to the east, I counted another dozen wagons; never in my life had I seen so many travelling together. At the head of the procession, which stretched back well over a mile, the wagons in single file, was our group of horsemen. In many cases where a family had no servant, the span of oxen was led by one of the children. Each wagon was drawn by twelve to sixteen heaving, sweating beasts. Behind the wagon train came more than two thousand head of cattle, followed by perhaps twenty thousand sheep and goats, shepherded by the children and some thirty Hottentots. Whips cracked and herders shouted. A great cloud of red dust whirled up from the thousands of hooves. The earthy smell of sweaty cattle, urine, fresh cow dung and dust assailed my senses.

Initially the going was easy and we made good progress as we followed the track which would lead us through the colony to the Great River, also known as the Orange. As the sun began to set on that first day, we had covered some twenty miles and had been joined by many more wagons along the way. Over the next few days, as we drew farther away from the villages, progress became slower and harder but our numbers grew as ever more trekkers joined us.

We travelled in skofs, or shifts, of about three hours before taking a break to rest the oxen. No two days were ever the same but we usually managed four skofs in a day. If the moon was up and the weather was fine we could manage an additional skof after sunset.

After thirteen days of travelling, we reached the banks of the Orange on New Year's Eve. "There it is," cried Piet Jordaan, one of the men riding up front, leading the convoy. "On the other side of that river lies freedom!"

Those nearest Piet let out a cheer which was picked up by all behind him. The oxen seemed to put in extra effort as if smelling freedom the closer we drew to the river. But our joy was short-lived. There were cries of alarm as the first riders reached the river bank. "The river is in flood," shouted Piet. "There is no way across, we shall have to wait until the water level drops."

Potgieter rode up, squinting against the sun. His dark, brooding eyes surveyed the swirling brown waters that stretched over two hundred yards in front of us. Tree stumps, branches and debris of every kind tumbled and tossed in the angry, foaming waters, barring our way to freedom. The wagons came to a halt and people began making their way to the water's edge, waiting to hear Potgieter's opinion. "We will outspan here for a day or two. It will give us the opportunity to thank the Lord for our safe deliverance so far," he announced after careful consideration.

Disappointed as we were, it did seem a good time to have a rest. We had been travelling most days, except of course on the Sabbath, and when we had to stop for the lambing, as it was the season. It was a time to catch our breath, to repair damaged wheels, to make more candles and for the women to sew and mend clothing and prepare food for the next stretch.

Our convoy had grown as new families joined us, with their horses, cattle, sheep and goats and their worldly goods piled high on their wagons. Already, though, everyone seemed to accept that there was only one leader … and that was Hendrik Potgieter. All decisions were made by Potgieter who seemed to grow more arrogant, but also more God-fearing, as we journeyed farther north. He wasn't a warm person but even I had to acknowledge that we could not have had a better man in charge.

On our first evening on the riverbank, as I was sitting cross-legged next to the fire, having supper with Marthinus van der Merwe and his family, my friend Jan Greyling appeared out of the shadows.

"Hello Rauch," he greeted me with a big grin, and then, "Good evening, everyone!" to the van der Merwe family. There was a chorus of cheerful greetings.

"Good to see you, Jan!" I said as I leaped to my feet and pumped his hand. "How did you get along?"

"Well, we managed to get all the gunpowder up here. The bags are buried under a tree over there." He pointed to a thicket of trees about fifty yards from the river. "Good thing I didn't bury the powder any closer: it would have been underwater from the floods by now. We can dig it up tomorrow and share it out among the wagons. Not once were we stopped by British patrols, so we needn't have bothered. Still … better safe than sorry."

For the next few hours Jan and I exchanged news. When I told him about Katrina he pulled a face. "Shame, Rauch. You know she really would be company for you … and more than just company, too. I wouldn't have minded taking her with me," he leered before adding, "Did you see Marietjie?"

I explained what had happened and that by now she was married to Roddy even though he apparently beat her.

Jan appeared shocked. "Well, there you are. You may as well have brought Katrina with you. You've lost Marietjie forever. Hitting her? The man must have gone mad!"

Two days later Potgieter called a meeting on the southern bank of the Orange River. By this time there must have been about two hundred of us. More than half were children under the age of sixteen. We gathered round our leader, who opened the meeting with a prayer. "Amen!" we chorused in unison as Potgieter finished praying. He stood on a wagon to address us.

"People," he shouted. "As you can see, the river is in flood. Not as high as it was but still high enough to prevent us from crossing. We now have two options. The first is to stay here for what could be another week and wait for the waters to subside. Who knows, though … maybe there will be even more rain. The second is to carry on and make a plan to cross. I think we could build a raft and though it will be slow and dangerous we will be able to cross with the wagons and animals and continue our journey to the Promised Land. Over that river," he gestured, "lies freedom. What do you say?"

There were shouts of:

"Let's go!"

"Let's wait!"

"What difference will it make, just a few more days?"

Potgieter held up his hand for silence. The shouting died away. "I can hear there are different opinions. Let's take a vote. Raise hands, all those in favour of crossing now."

There was a show of hands. The vast majority was in favour of pressing on.

"Right, it is decided then. Before we do anything, all the men will go with Jan Greyling and dig up the hidden gunpowder and share it out among the wagons. I would suggest that every wagon carries one third of its freight weight in gunpowder. If it means leaving some of your goods behind to take gunpowder, then do so, for gunpowder will be our gold. We cannot live without it. Do not load it onto your wagons yet as we must unpack everything before the crossing."

For the next few hours we toiled, digging up the leather bags that contained the gunpowder. We shared it out among the sixty wagons. While we worked Potgieter approached us. I stopped loading, looking up at him expectantly.

"I need the strongest among you ... you Rauch and you Jan. We are going to need the trunks of those willows over there. Those trees will be perfect if we cut them down and lash them together in sufficient number. That will be our raft. Make sure that you choose the largest."

Jan and I set to the task together with eight other men. We identified the trees we were going to use and, as we'd done when we built our house on the frontier, marked them with an X. We selected trees which were at least thirty feet tall. Then we returned with axes. My mind went back to rebuilding our house. How much had happened since then. I felt a pang of sadness as I thought of Dirk, of Pa and Amelia.

We used horses to drag the timber to the water's edge while others stripped the trees of branches and leaves. After we had cleaned the trunks, we lashed them together, side by side. It was hard work but as we worked we became more proficient. Jan and I were in a team of three which lashed the logs together with riems, leather thongs. Another team was cutting down trees, another with the horses dragging the logs to us, with yet another cleaning and preparing the logs for lashing. By the time darkness was upon us we had managed to build a raft some twenty feet wide and just over thirty feet long, onto which we could squeeze five wagons.

That night Jan and I sat next to the fire with Nikolaas Grobbelaar and feasted on a delicious potjie of kudu and potatoes cooked by his wife, Dorothea. Their ten children ran noisily around us.

"Well, I think that the raft will get us over alright," said Nikolaas, who had been on the team with Jan and me.

"As long as you tied those knots properly," joked Jan.

"Ja," I said, "but it's going to take some time. I estimate that once we get organized and get the ropes over the river, it will take us at least half an hour to pull the raft to the other side, more time to offload the wagons and then back over the river again. Then we have to take all the freight, then the people. It's going to be a hell of a job."

"And what about the cattle, horses sheep and goats?" added Jan.

"Don't be silly, Jan. They must swim."

Jan looked slightly embarrassed, retorting, "Of course! I hope they can all swim. Why don't we let the women and children swim as well?" he laughed.

"There must be about sixty tons of goods that we need to get across. I hope the raft is up to it," said Nikolaas.

Dorothea busied herself picking up the plates, taking them off to be washed. We sat watching the flickering fire.

"And after we have crossed the Great River?" asked Jan. "What then?"

"Well, we've had word that there are more trekkers waiting to join us. Potgieter says that we are making for a mountain called Blesberg ... a mountain you can see for miles because the top of it is white with birdshit."

"We will outspan there for a few weeks while Potgieter pushes on with a small group to look for his cousins, the van Rensburgs, who left with the Trichardts some months back," said Nikolaas. Turning to me, he asked, "What about you, Rauch? Are you going to stay or will you try and join

Potgieter looking for his cousins? Of course, they could all be dead by now. Nobody's heard anything from them since they left. It must be a year at least. In some ways I envy you two." He looked around just as two of the bigger boys came tearing past us, laughing and shrieking. "See what I mean? Neither of you has any responsibilities; you're free to do as you please."

"What's that, Nikolaas?" snapped Dorothea, sitting in the shadows.

"No, no, nothing, my dear. I was just saying how sorry I was that these two have no family; it must be lonely travelling on one's own."

"You watch what you say, my man," said Dorothea, glaring at her husband with her hands on her hips, "Anyone would think that you had nothing to do with us having ten children."

"I think I might try to join Potgieter and the group going north," I said hastily. "Anyway there is time enough for that decision. Tomorrow we must start the crossing, so I am off to bed. Thank you, Mevrou Grobbelaar, for a lovely meal. Good night everyone."

That night I dreamed of Marietjie, again.

Chapter Twelve

It was early morning when eight of us manoeuvred the completed raft down to the water's edge. We had joined several leather riempies together to make a long rope, which we tied to each of the four corners of the raft. Although the river was still in spate the level had dropped enough for us to be confident that the fifty yards of rope from each corner would be enough to pull the raft to the shallows. We manhandled the craft into the muddy water. It floated! We let out a cheer.

Potgieter ordered, "Right. Bring the first five wagons."

One by one the wagons were pulled down to the water's edge by a span of oxen. Each had been unloaded with the contents placed neatly in piles up the bank—chairs, tables, beds, kists, food, guns and gunpowder, blankets and hoks of chickens stacked high—ready to be ferried across when all the wagons were safely on the far bank. The servants unharnessed the oxen, the wheels were removed and piled on one side of the raft, and then the men, sweating and grunting with effort, heaved the wagons aboard. Once each wagon was firmly fastened to the deck, we had to push the raft into deeper water so that it did not settle on the mud bottom on account of the extra weight. Jan took one long rope, I took another and together we waded into the water, pulling the raft behind us. Four men swam ahead to await our arrival on the opposite bank. Six men stayed behind, three to each of the stabilizing ropes attached to the bank. The ropes were played out inch by inch as we moved into the river but they would have to act quickly to pull the raft back to safety should the current begin to sweep it away. As Jan and I waded in, the riverbed fell away until we were chest high in swirling water.

"Swim for it!" I yelled to Jan and still holding the riempies but playing them out as we swam, we struck out for the shallows on the other side, now only about thirty yards away. The others were waiting for us, standing waist high in the waters of the far bank. They grabbed the ropes from us. "Pull," I shouted. We leaned back and started to haul the raft over the main channel. Each time it seemed that the current would sweep the raft away, the men on the far bank took up the tension, ensuring a smooth crossing for the precious cargo. The raft was awash with water but we managed to guide it safely into the shallows.

"Look! Look!" cried one of the men.

I looked across at the far bank. About forty servants were herding the cattle, sheep and goats to the water. The animals closest to the water's edge started to panic and tried to turn back. Whips cracked as herders shouted "Kom! Kom! Maak gou! Make haste!" There was a mêlée of cattle in front being forced by the pressure of the animals at the back. An ox fell into the water with a loud splash. A servant leaped into the river and swam next to the lead animal, pulling it by its nose ring. The others followed, preferring the water to the sticks and whips. There was a series of splashes as one after another the oxen were forced into the brown, rushing waters. They in turn were followed by the goats, sheep and horses. Within minutes the waters were wild with the threshing of thousands of animals. Men and boys dived into the river to help guide the animals safely across. By now the river was so full of animals that we had to wait before pulling the empty raft back across for the next load of wagons.

We sat on the bank and watched the amazing scene as terrified oxen swam desperately toward us, the whites of their eyes showing, their eyeballs rolling back in fear. The sound of cattle bellowing and sheep and goats bleating filled the air until, one by one, they felt firm land beneath their hooves and, staggering onto the bank, they shook the water from their coats, gave a last bellow or bleat of alarm before wandering off to graze.

For the rest of the day we toiled tirelessly and at last completed the enormous task of ferrying the wagons across. That night we set guards to watch over the empty wagons, which looked quite forlorn without their cargoes, while we slept, exhausted, on the bank. We began again early the next morning. The river had fallen further during the night, making our task easier and quicker. It took us ten trips to get everything, except the people, across. When the last trip was done, Jan and I took the raft back across to fetch the women and children. Arriving on the southern bank, I saw that the women and children were gathered together on a grassy knoll about fifty yards away.

"What are they doing?" asked Jan.

"Praying," I replied quietly.

The sound of sweet voices singing a moving psalm floated across to us in the still of the evening. It sounded beautiful. I remembered the singing of the Malay slaves in Cape Town and felt my eyes sting with sudden tears. We heard Potgieter's voice, leading the congregation in a prayer of gratitude: "Thank you, O Lord, for delivering your children to freedom."

"Amen," chorused the women. Then, clutching their Bibles, with heads held high, they marched down to the river and silently filed onto the raft. As it began to drift gently over the river, the women, led by Hester Botha, began to sing another hymn. Their voices soared as they offered their heartfelt thanks to their God. The sight of the sun slipping behind the western hills, daubing the clouds with streaks of peach and scarlet, the sound of the river lapping the raft and what sounded like the voices of angels, left a permanent imprint on my mind. As we reached the far bank, the border of a new country, the women leaped from the raft.

"Praise the Lord, we are free! We are free!" one called out.

The shout was taken up by hundreds of enthusiastic voices. "Now we are truly free!"

"Freedom!"

"Free from the English … free at last!"

That night the air was electric with excitement as we reassembled the wagons by lamplight and repacked the cargoes. Everyone was smiling, relaxed and happy. As Jan and I worked, helping Nikolaas and Dorothea Grobbelaar, Jan turned to me, beaming, "You know what, Rauch, even the air on this side of the river is cleaner and fresher than it is in the colony. What do you think?"

I laughed and carried on with my work. My thoughts were fixed on Marietjie as I wondered whether she and I would ever meet again. As I lay in my bed later that night, drifting off to sleep, the sounds that floated to my ears were the sounds of happiness, of music and laughter. Would my own happiness, and Marietjie's, ever be complete?

❧ ❧ ❧

Potgieter had asked me and Jan to ride on ahead, to scout out the land to ensure the safe passage of the wagon train. We set off next morning and travelled without stopping for about two hours. It was already hot as the sun beat down on us from a vast, cloudless sky, with not a breath of wind. We were about three miles ahead of the wagons when we cantered up a high, grassy koppie. We could see for miles in every direction.

I called to Jan, "Stop a minute. Let's have a look round."

In the distance we could see the wagons trundling through lush, rolling grasslands, so different from the land we had left behind. They were travelling four abreast, about ten yards apart, bobbing along in the tall grass, and at times disappearing in the folds of the veld. The white canopies were like the sails of ships at sea, rising and falling on the waves, an impression heightened by the rolling movement of the wagons as they wound their way around obstacles. Behind the wagons came the animals, creating a cloud of dust which hung in the still morning air. The tracks of the giant herd were marked by a broad swathe cut into the veld, about two hundred yards wide and stretching back as far as the eye could see. We could hear the crack of whips and the joyful shouts of the children who led the wagons.

"What a sight!" said Jan as he squinted into the sunlight.

But looking north I could see another cloud of dust, marking the path of three horsemen. They rode rapidly and, if I was not mistaken, they were moving in our direction. "Quick, load up," I said to Jan, as I primed my Sanna. "Could be trouble ahead."

Jan deftly poured powder from his horn into the pan as the trio drew closer. They were dressed like us and they were armed.

"Who are they?" whispered Jan. "Are they boers?"

"No, I don't think so. More likely Griquas, the people called the Bergenaars. The Bastards. Kok's people. Potgieter warned me that we might meet them. We are on their land. Be careful. This could be dangerous." I held my Sanna at the ready.

"Put down your guns," one of the men called to us in Dutch, when they were still some distance off.

"You put yours down first," I shouted back.

The horsemen drew to a halt. After a brief consultation the first man slipped his gun into its scabbard. The other two did the same. Jan and I followed their lead.

When they were a few yards off, one of the men spoke, "Greetings," he said in a strangled form of Dutch. I had to concentrate hard to understand what he was saying. "My name is Adam Kok. My brother Abraham is the Captain of the Griqua people, on whose land you now trespass." He waved his hand in the direction of an older man. "This is Hendrik Hendricks and this," indicating the third man, "is Pine Pienaar."

"Rauch Beukes," I said, my hand on my chest, "and Jan Greyling."

The men nodded in acknowledgement, unsmiling.

"We are from the church mission at Philippolis where the Reverend Archbell lives," said Kok.

The men's clothing was frayed and torn. The Griquas, people of mixed descent, had fled the colony some years before, tired of being treated as inferior by the whites. Many Griqua were the products of illicit relationships between white slave owners and their slaves, but some were fugitives from justice who lived by stealing and plundering. I was on my guard; I could sense trouble brewing. The three men sized us up, their eyes flicking from our horses to our guns and clothing.

"We mean no harm," I said. "We are just passing through on our way north. We were hoping to meet you so that we can take you to our leader. He is also Hendrik," I said with a smile. "Hendrik Potgieter." I jerked my head backward and noticed the men's eyes follow. They saw the wagon train, the vast cloud of dust and the animals crossing the veld far below us. They looked angrily at each other.

"This is our land," said Hendricks.

"That's fine. We're not here to take it. Nobody's disputing that this is your land. There is plenty of land north of here. In any event we are on our way to Blesberg ... is that your land as well?"

"Take us to your leader, then." said Hendricks, curtly.

Jan and I remounted and led the way back to the wagons, which lumbered to a halt with our approach. Hendrik Potgieter rode out to meet us. He held his hand up in greeting.

I overheard Pienaar say to Kok quietly under his breath, "Shall I shoot him now? It will save a lot of trouble later."

"Oh no, you will not," I snapped as I drew my Sanna from its scabbard.

Kok held up his hand, glaring at Pienaar. "There will be no shooting. I will discuss what they want with this man. We will see if we can come to some arrangement." Kok and Hendricks accompanied Potgieter to his wagon, while Pienaar stood guard outside, his weapon at the ready.

After two hours the three men emerged from the wagon. All were smiling, Kok and Hendricks each carrying an armful of Sannas cradled in their arms. Without laying down the guns, each man awkwardly shook Potgieter by the hand, climbed back onto their horse and galloped off.

Potgieter looked after them as they rode away. "Good riddance," he said.

By now a crowd had gathered round to hear the outcome of the discussion. "They have agreed that we can pass through this land to the land of Moroko. He is the chief of the Barolong people. In return for those guns, we have safe passage. Kok has also said that should any of you decide to settle in this area rather than travelling further, he is prepared to lease land to you for forty years in return for a few flagons of brandy. Is anybody interested?"

There was a murmur as the trekkers politely declined the offer and wandered back to their wagons. Some had already outspanned their oxen and were settling down for the night, setting up camp, gathering brushwood and lighting fires. Soon the air was rich with the smell of food being prepared.

⋖ ⋖ ⋖

Day after day, on and on, our ships of the veld slowly ploughed their way farther north through the rolling grassland, over koppies and through muddy streams … at times in dry, scorching heat and at times in torrential rain spilled from low black clouds lashed through with streaks of lightning. On and on and on … We made steady progress.

Several days after our encounter with the Griquas, as the sun was setting behind the hills, we crested a rise in the veld. Once again, Jan and I were scouting ahead. Suddenly, a strange thing happened and for a moment I thought that we had doubled back on our convoy. It took me a few moments to realize that in front of us was a smaller version of our own party. The canopies of fifteen wagons were clustered together on the bank of a stream some two miles ahead, shimmering in the heat of the day. Thin snakes of smoke coiling into the air signalled that cooking fires had already been lit. As we drew nearer a group of about ten horsemen galloped toward us.

We spurred on our horses to meet them. Jan shouted as he led the way, "These are boers. I think I recognize Sarel Cilliers." He waved his hat in delight, galloping toward them.

They were indeed Cilliers and his group from Colesberg. The two men riding behind Cilliers and slightly ahead of the others were immediately recognizable. My mouth went dry as I felt a wave of nausea sweep over me. It was Frans and Pa. I pulled on my reins as hard as I could. Grey came to an immediate stop.

Jan didn't realize why I had stopped. He reined in his horse to shout back at me. "Come on man! These are our people ... these are boers!" then galloped ahead again, waving his hat in greeting.

I wheeled Grey round in the space of a rix dollar, stirring up a cloud of dust and raced away from the approaching horsemen, hoping against hope that Pa and Frans had not recognized me. But it was too late. My mind whirled as I rode. What was I going to do now? Pa ... here? That meant Amelia was here too. They were going to join our trek. I would be travelling alongside them ... every day. I didn't know whether I could stand it.

It was getting dark as I approached the wagons with a heavy heart, knowing that a meeting with Pa—and worse, Amelia—was inevitable. The twinkling lights and the fires among the wagons seemed so bright and cheerful in stark contrast to my thoughts and feelings as I approached. I made my way to Potgieter to inform him that we had met up with Sarel Cilliers's trek party.

As I passed Piet de Wet's wagon, he placed the burning lamp he was carrying on the seat of the wagon before walking to the fire where his wife, Mieta, was cooking. Five-year-old Morné, the middle son of the five de Wet children, emerged from the wagon laughing, being chased by his brother. His left foot collided with the lantern. He tripped. With a yell he fell off the wagon. The lamp tipped on its side. I saw the tiny flame flicker, almost dying, before it flared and set fire to some dry cloth on the wagon seat. Within seconds the canopy was ablaze. Children screamed from the back of the wagon as I saw Piet de Wet running, shouting, "Help! Help! My children are in there!"

"Look out!" I shouted. "Look out ... the gunpowder. The gunpowder will explode!"

With a mighty 'Krrrump!' the bags of gunpowder secreted under the wagon's floor exploded. There was a blinding flash as the blast from the explosion slammed me to the ground. I saw the wagon lift a good six feet off the ground before it crashed down, blazing, on its side. Two figures etched in flames were thrown from the wagon. They hit the ground like broken, flaming dolls and lay still, flames marking a ghastly outline of each little body. People screamed and came running. De Wet tried to force his way into the blaze. He covered his eyes with his arm for protection against the dense black smoke pouring from the burning wreck. The intense heat pushed him back. He kept shouting, "My children! My children! Please, help me! Please help ... my children are in there!"

I crawled to my feet, stinging and bruised from the explosion. I grabbed a coat from one of the men and dashed to the two burning bodies. I rammed the coat down onto the flames in an attempt to smother them. There was a lot of smoke but the flames died. The stench of burning flesh brought back memories of how Ma and my poor sisters must have met their death. But I knew from the lack of movement beneath the blanket that it was too late.

Already the men had formed a line and were passing buckets of water, man to man, in a chain from the stream to the burning wagon. The light from the flames cast an eerie glow. It was all over as suddenly as it had started.

As the flames died down, Piet de Wet saw for the first time the mounds under the coat.

"No, no Oom Piet!" I shouted. "It's too late. They are gone."

There was no holding him back; he pulled the coat off the two bodies and when he saw what was left of his children the scream that pierced the night was as chilling and as terrible as anything I had ever heard.

"Oh my God! Mieta!" he wailed. Then louder, "Mieta! Mieta, where are you?"

Mieta, who had been cooking some distance away, appeared at his side. "I am here, I am here, Piet," she said, putting her arms around her distraught husband

"Gustav and Estelle have gone ... they are dead!" Piet sobbed.

Mieta stepped back. Her eyes widened in horror as she realized what the two burned bundles were. She clasped her hand over her mouth, "And the others? Where are the children? Are they safe?"

At that moment Nikolaas Grobbelaar approached with the three surviving de Wet children: Morné, his older brother Braam and older sister Nina, ashen faced and shocked. The two who had died in the inferno were the twins, Gustav and Estelle, just four years old. Piet de Wet stood staring at the tiny blackened corpses. I stepped forward and again covered them with a coat as Mieta watched in numbed disbelief.

"It is God's will," he said. "It is God's will."

I felt rage well up inside me as I looked at the tiny bundles, the broken father and mother beside them and the burned-out wreck of their wagon. Unable to control myself I said quietly, "No, that's not right, Piet. What God would will this to happen? It was a tragic accident. God had nothing to do with it."

I don't know whether Piet heard me for at that moment Jan Greyling made an appearance. "My God!" he cried. "What has happened?"

Behind him I could sense rather than see the others. Sarel Cilliers pushed his way to the front of the stunned crowd and put his arms around Piet and Mieta. "It is God's will," said Cilliers.

This time it was too much. "No it's not," I snapped. "No God does that to little children. Don't say that. It was an accident. No God planned this."

I turned and walked away. I could feel their eyes on me as I heard Jan say quietly, "Leave him be. He is in shock as well."

I looked back and saw that Sarel Cilliers was standing praying with his arms raised sideways, palms facing forward. Etched against the light from the wagons, with arms outstretched, he looked as if he himself was the cross.

That night I struggled to sleep as all my demons returned. I still had not seen Pa and Amelia but knew that a meeting was inevitable. I was in a state of shock from the tragedy and wondered how many more we would experience on this trek. I longed for word of Marietjie and wondered where this was all leading us. My last thought as I finally dozed off into a fitful slumber was, "I wonder how we are going to give the little twins a Christian burial? We have no ordained minister."

The next morning the trekkers mutely made their preparations. Jan and I made our way to Piet and Mieta to see if we could help in any way. As we approached the spare wagon that was now their home, we could hear the sound of women's voices singing softly, offering prayer and solace to the grieving couple and the children. Piet noticed us and detached himself from the group. His face was etched with grief, his eyes red-rimmed from a night spent weeping.

"We just came to say ..." I began.

"I know," said Piet. "Thank you for helping last night. I know that you did what you could. The only thing that needs to be done now is to bury the twins ... we need coffins and I have no planks ... do you think ...?" He left the question unfinished, imploring.

"We will get some planks. But who will bury them?" Jan asked.

"It will have to be Sarel Cilliers," answered Piet. We will do it tomorrow morning. We have no ordained minister of the church. For that we must thank the English. They made it so difficult for our ministers to come with us. It will have to be Sarel. I don't think it much matters that he is not ordained? Do you? As long as we commit the little ones with prayer into the hands and protection of the Lord, I don't think he will judge us because Sarel is not ordained, do you?" Not waiting for a reply he continued. "The women have been so good. Dorothea Grobbelaar is sewing burial shirts and making two caps and coverings for their faces. Even though we have no minister, they will still be dressed appropriately for their burial." His eyes brimmed with tears.

I had to look away and blinked furiously, suppressing my own tears.

"Nikolaas Grobbelaar is going to arrange everything." He turned and looked into the distance. My eyes followed his gaze and I could see three men, one of them Nikolaas Grobbelaar, digging the two graves in the veld about two hundred yards away. "If you two could see about the coffins ..."

We nodded, took our leave of the sad scene and went to the men digging. "Do you know of anyone who brought planks for coffins?" I asked.

The men paused. All three were sweating profusely under the hot sun. "Ja," one replied. "Old man Ferreira brought planks with him. He says he probably won't see the end of the trek himself. Go and ask him. I'm sure he won't mind giving up a few. Those are his wagons over there." He pointed at four wagons grouped together.

As we walked past the last group of wagons before Ferreira's, a man and a woman carrying a baby stepped out from behind a wagon into our path. They were no more than three paces away. The man was holding the woman's right hand while her left arm cradled a tiny infant wrapped in a shawl. Pa and Amelia! The moment I had been dreading had arrived. There was no avoiding them now.

Jan and I stopped in our tracks as did Pa and Amelia.

"Hello son," said Pa. He was still wearing the gold cross.

My throat tightened. I could barely speak. I looked him in the eye, swallowed and tried to control my voice, "Hello Pa .... hello Amelia," I said switching my gaze to her. Motherhood had matured her and enhanced her fragile beauty. Her figure was fuller than it was when I saw her last. She was not wearing her kappie, her blond hair braided on top of her head. Her blue eyes sparkled with pleasure at seeing me while her smile showed off her perfect white teeth. She was wearing a bright-coloured dress which, despite its unflattering lines, could not disguise her figure, her motherly breasts.

"Hello, Rauchie," she said with her distinctive English accent. "We heard that you were here with Potgieter. I'm so glad we're all together again."

Jan sensed my embarrassment, "You stay and talk to your family," he said. "I'll see if I can get those planks from old man Ferreira. I'm sure you have much to talk about."

There was a silence as we all looked at each other.

"Terrible thing that happened last night, wasn't it?"

"Ja, terrible, just terrible."

Again, silence.

"Come and say hello to your little brother, Rauchie," beamed Amelia, pulling down the shawl to show the tiny face of the three-month-old baby.

I moved closer and looked at the baby boy. My face was inches from Amelia's. I could smell her skin. My heart raced. Amelia, despite being married to Pa, still had that effect on me. "What's his name?"

"Jakob ... same as your Pa."

"What am I supposed to call you now?" I asked of her. "I'm *not* calling you Ma!"

"Don't be silly ... of course you aren't. You call me Amelia like you always have. But we're family now. Isn't that wonderful?"

Pa was watching us, a slight smile on his face.

"You must come and see us ... often," said Amelia squeezing my arm for emphasis. "Promise you will, Rauchie? We will be trekking together now so we can all be friends again ... just like we used to." She smiled at me, her hand lingering on my arm.

I didn't respond. I knew that things could never be the same. Too much had happened and in any event, Amelia was now Pa's wife. "Where is Frans?" I asked, changing the conversation.

"He's in his wagon with his new wife, Anna Laubscher ... you remember Annetjie?" Pa queried. "Anyway that's one of the reasons why we're here with Cilliers ... she is related to his family. Gieletjie is also here. It's God's will that we are all together again, isn't it?"

"I suppose so," I replied. "I must go now. Jan and I are to make the coffins for the twins so we don't have much time. They are to be buried tomorrow morning."

"Come and visit us soon," repeated Amelia.

"Yes," said Pa, "then we can catch up on your news ... we hear that you had your heart broken in Graaff-Reinet?"

I ignored his comment and turned away, "I will visit sometime," I said, although I had no intention of doing so. Amelia's presence still disturbed me.

As Jan and I were cutting and planing the planks Ferreira had given us, Jan imitated Ferreira's gruff voice in answer to his request, "... and then, what am I to do when it is my time? The old man was quite upset at having to part with his planks which he was quite sure he'd be needing sooner rather than later."

In the morning, Jan and I carried the coffins away from the wagon where the twins' bodies had been kept overnight so that the family would not hear us nailing down the lids. The sight and smell of the two little bodies, dressed for their own funerals but still blackened from the flames which had killed them, made me heave and more than once Jan and I had to turn away, our hands covering our mouths. Eventually I held a handkerchief over my nose to keep out the stench of burned flesh.

Then we carried the little coffins back to the wagons. The funeral was a sad affair. Mourners assembled at the de Wet wagons where burned grass marked the site of the explosion; the hulk of the burned-out wagon had been carried away. A sombre crowd of some two hundred, all dressed in black, formed behind the two coffins. Even the children were dressed in black. Piet and Mieta led the procession together with Potgieter and Cilliers, with the de Wet relatives carrying the coffins on their shoulders, followed by the men, then the wives and finally the children. The procession stopped at the graves. Slowly the two small coffins were lowered on riempies into the freshly dug holes. Sarel Cilliers read from Genesis 3:19. His strong voice rang out over the veld; even the nearby cattle seemed quieter than usual.

"In the sweat of thy face shalt thou eat bread, till thou return into the ground; for out of it wast though taken; for dust thou art, and into dust shalt thou return."

Then Piet threw a handful of earth on each of the coffins, the soil sounding like the rattle of a kettle drum on the wood. We all followed suit and then made our way back to the wagons for the funeral meal. I noticed Pa and Amelia on the other side of the tent. Once or twice I looked across at them and saw that Amelia was looking at me. In spite of the solemnity of the occasion I couldn't stop my heart from tripping slightly.

Chapter Thirteen

Four days after the funeral a meeting was held where we elected Hendrik Potgieter as our kommandant and leader and Sarel Cilliers as his deputy.

For the next few days Jan and I passed the time hunting game, which was there in great abundance, and talking to Potgieter about future plans. He had hinted that he might include the two of us in a small group which he would personally lead northeast to the sea. He also wanted to search for his cousins, the van Rensburgs, whose party had left with Trichardt the previous year. Jan and I took every opportunity to try and convince Potgieter that we should be included, although he was not the kind of man who was easily persuaded. We had to hope that he would himself decide it would be best to include us. In the end, God would advise him as to the right thing to do: Potgieter believed implicitly in divine guidance.

Early one morning, a week after the funeral, Jan and I set off to hunt lions that had killed three cattle the night before. We tracked the spoor of a pride for some miles until the trail ran cold at a small stream. We climbed off our horses and concealed ourselves behind some bushes. While we studied the terrain for signs of lion, a herd of some forty Cape buffalo emerged from the scrub about fifty yards downstream and across the river from us. Jan started to ready his Sanna for a shot but the buffalo became agitated and began to move farther downstream, tossing their heads and swishing their tails. I guessed they had picked up our scent as the wind was blowing in their direction.

Jan nudged me in the ribs. "Look," he said, pointing.

Five lions were stalking the buffalo through the long grass on the riverbank. They were thirty yards away when the buffalo started to move away, firstly at a walk, then at a brisk trot. The lions broke cover and the buffalo panicked, running wildly in different directions. A lioness singled out a buffalo calf. Totally focused, she ignored the larger animals as she bounded past. Within a few strides she leaped onto her prey, her claws gouging its sides. The whites of the calf's rolling eyes showed its terror. The rest of the pride joined the attack. The young buffalo crashed to the ground, surrounded, before slipping down the riverbank and splashing into the water. Standing in the shallows, the lions savaged the animal, with throaty roars and grunts until their coats were seeped with blood.

"He's had it," Jan whispered.

I nodded. We were totally engrossed in the scene until my gaze was drawn by a movement in the water, a few yards away. Two giant crocodiles were silently approaching the battle scene. The jaws of one crocodile emerged from the muddy waters. Mouth agape, it raced the last few yards, reared out of the water and grabbed the kicking, twitching back legs of the young buffalo. With a shake of its scaly head the crocodile started to pull the prey into the water. The calf had become the prize in a mortal tug-of-war.

As we watched in amazement the crocodile, realizing it was losing the struggle, summoned all its energy and power and heaved out of the water so that its jaws clamped the buffalo's rump. Shaking its tail, it began to pull the calf deeper into the water. The lions, angered by this intrusion into what should have been an uncontested kill, let out a barrage of roars and intensified their mauling of the calf's throat and then, almost as if by command, pulled together. The crocodile held on but was yanked up behind the buffalo until, with a shake of its head and a thrashing of the tail, it let go. The crocodile sank beneath the waters to sulk in the muddy depths below.

"The lions have won," exclaimed Jan.

"No they haven't. Look there," I whispered. "I can't believe this. It's not over yet. The buffalo have come back."

The buffalo had regrouped as a herd and returned. The lions looked up from their anticipated feast, aware of the approaching buffalo moving menacingly at a determined trot in their direction. There was no doubt what their intentions were. The lions clambered nervously to their feet, moving cautiously away from the approaching herd that had formed itself into a wall of muscle. As the speed of the buffalo increased, the nerve of a lioness broke as she slunk away from the others. A huge buffalo bull trotted after her, faster, then faster, and with a sweep of his horns, gored the lioness in the side and tossed her a full five feet into the air. When the lioness hit the ground her legs were like pistons which pounded the ground as she fled. The buffalo trotted back to the herd which had now surrounded the remaining lions.

At that moment there was a flurry of dark brown from among the lions and the buffalo calf—bitten, mauled and almost drowned—staggered away from the lions and disappeared into the protective ranks of the herd. Having dealt with one lioness, the buffalo drew closer to the remaining four, which slunk away along the riverbank. It was all over. The buffalo had won and the buffalo calf had survived … for the time being.

Jan breathed in one mighty rush. "Whew! That is something! I have never seen anything like that before."

I shook my head, "There's no point telling any of the others," I said. "They'll think we've had too many brandies."

�� �� ��

Jan and I rode back to camp, now consisting of sixty wagons and two hundred people, including sixty-five able fighting men. As we approached it was obvious from the activity that Potgieter had decided to move again. I was pleased as I found the breaks in our progress frustrating, although I knew they were necessary for grazing and lambing in season, as well as for restocking supplies of biltong, jam and bottled fruit.

That evening as I was bent over the hot coals, braaing the guinea fowl I had shot that morning, I felt rather than saw someone behind me. I turned.

It was my brother Frans. "Hello, Rauchie," he said with a smile, shaking my hand.

Standing next to him was an attractive woman of about eighteen, wearing a kappie, under which I could see dark brown curls nestling on a well-shaped neck. This was Anna, Frans's new wife. She regarded me with clear hazel eyes. She had a quick and ready smile. I warmed to her immediately.

"Hello Rauch. I'm pleased to meet you at last. Your brother is always talking about you." Her hand, when I shook it, was soft but firm.

I slapped Frans on the back, laughing. "Imagine all of you joining the trek with me. I can't get away from my family, can I?" I said, half in jest. "And now you're married as well!"

"Not only married, but ..." Frans patted Anna's stomach and I noticed for the first time that she was pregnant.

"Well done," I exclaimed. "It looks like it'll be quite soon."

"About three months, in July or August ... we are going to name him Dirk after your brother," she said simply.

I felt a stab in my gut at the mention of Dirk's name but I nodded. "That's good. Well done!" I wasn't sure what else to say, so decided to move onto more comfortable ground. "So we're off again tomorrow. I'll be glad to leave this place. After the twins were killed I never felt comfortable here."

"Oom Sarel says that we'll now make for a place called Black Mountain where we'll outspan for a few months. Maybe some will want to stay there permanently. What about you, Rauch, where are you going to settle?" Anna asked.

"Not sure really; I am trying to get myself included in the expedition Hendrik Potgieter is talking about, exploring up north and maybe even finding a route to the sea."

"Oh ... Oom Sarel is also going on that trip. He has spoken about it and I think your Pa might be going as well."

My heart sank at this news.

"Surely Pa won't want to go now, now that he has a little baby to worry about? Anyway whether he goes or not, I want to go. Apparently it will just be a small group. They aren't taking wagons so that they can move faster."

"Would you like me to speak to Oom Sarel for you?" asked Anna.

"If you can! Would you? Ask also for my friend Jan. We are both keen to go. If you can make Cilliers receive a message from the Lord, we would be forever grateful," I said with a grin. "I didn't realize that the Lord came in such an attractive body with such a pretty face," I added with a laugh.

Anna blushed gently. "I will see what I can do. They warned me that you were quite the charmer. Now I see why. At least Oom Sarel is open to persuasion, not like Hendrik Potgieter. I'll do my best for you."

She was as good as her word. The next morning, as Jan and I rode ahead of the wagons, Hendrik Potgieter rode up beside me with Sarel Cilliers.

"Good day Rauch," he said.

"Greetings kommandant," I replied touching my hat respectfully.

"I believe from your requests as well as from Sarel Cilliers that you are very keen to accompany us up north?"

"Yes kommandant!"

"Well, you are not married and you are a fine shot so I can think of no reason why you should not come. We will have to see how things develop but let us say that I will certainly consider you seriously … and your friend Jan, too."

"Thank you, kommandant." I was delighted at the news.

As he spurred his horse and made back for the wagons he called back, "We will have to see whether the Lord agrees. I will let you know my final decision when we are ready to leave. In the meantime, you and the others keep your eyes open and scout out the best route to Black Mountain."

Black Mountain was the translation of Thaba Nchu, the name given by local tribesmen to a large rocky outcrop. It was also known by the trekkers as Blesberg because many years' worth of droppings from vultures and other birds had covered the summit with a blanket of white. Thaba Nchu had been identified as the ideal rendezvous point for all who travelled north.

It took a few weeks of painstakingly slow progress for us to make our way to the plains that lay before the mountain. We arrived early in May. For a week the peak's white top had been visible, appearing misleadingly closer than it was. During the trek I tried to stay away from Pa and Amelia as much as I could. I felt ill at ease whenever I saw them and suspected that Pa felt the same. Amelia, though, seemed to go out of her way to be around me.

Our routine had settled into a pattern. Each day consisted of three or, if we were lucky, four skofs. Outspan for the evening, supper, prayers and bed. We woke early and after breakfast and prayers, always led by Cilliers with Kommandant Potgieter looking on sternly, we would repeat the pattern of the previous day. Except for Sundays, of course: on the Sabbath the women got out their best dresses and Sarel Cilliers made a church out of four wagons drawn into a square. We all attended his Sunday services which went on for most of the morning. There was no trekking on Sundays and people used the opportunity to cook and mend and get ready for the week ahead.

Our arrival at Thaba Nchu marked the end of the first phase of our trek; we felt a sense of accomplishment at having come so far. Our thanks to the Lord were conveyed to Him through prayers led by Cilliers. There ensued a festive atmosphere with the sounds of music floating through the chilly evening air from all parts of the encampment. I strolled round the wagons and was amazed as I passed Kommandant Potgieter's wagon, to see him sitting in the midst of a group of young children who were giggling and clearly enjoying listening to Potgieter's strong bass voice singing a love song. "Old Blaauwberg has a heart after all!" I thought to myself.

I came to a clearing where a group of young men and women were dancing the vigorous hanekraai to a two-three rhythm played on violins. I watched the dancing figures and spotted Frans and Anna, who moved well together. At the far end of the clearing, a couple was dancing out of the shadows and into the lamplight. It was Amelia in the arms of thirteen-year-old Douw Kruger. She had her head thrown back and was laughing gaily. She stopped dancing as soon as she saw me. Her young partner looked irritated; he was obviously enjoying the attention of this older woman. Amelia took his hand and started toward me. I moved away but she quickened her pace.

"Rauch! Rauchie, wait. Come and have some fun. Come and dance with me."

I hesitated which was all the encouragement she needed. She let go of Kruger's hand and reached out and took mine. Turning to her young partner, she said "Thank you, Douw. Now I will dance with my stepson."

The music had stopped for the fiddlers to catch their breath. We stood waiting for the music to begin again. Amelia was facing me; I could feel the heat from her body as she squeezed my hand.

"Where's Pa?" I asked.

"Back at the wagons; he told me to go and have some fun while he looked after little Jakob. Don't you think that was nice of him?" I noticed Frans and Anna watching as they too stood waiting for the music. Frans had a concerned look on his face as if realizing that no good would come of this encounter. I wished the music would start soon. Amelia was standing so close to me that I could feel her breasts touching my chest. She seemed aware of my unease and deliberately moved closer, increasing my discomfort. She pushed her breasts into my chest, all the while gazing directly into my eyes, with the corners of her mouth giving away just how much she was enjoying the game. She put her arms around me and for a moment I thought she was going to kiss me. To this day I think she was but just at that moment the strains of a polka filled the night air. I took her in my arms and began to dance, spinning her round and round. She was light on her feet and during the course of the next few moments we enjoyed the pace of the dance, twirling and laughing in time to the music. When the music called for her to move next to me she pushed her body closer than necessary. Our movements were in perfect harmony, moving as one when the dance demanded it. I was becoming aroused by her flirting and she knew it. Much as though I was enjoying being with her, I appreciated that her obvious flirting was not going unnoticed by my brother or his wife, or for that matter, by any of the other dancers. I was sure that everyone's eyes were on us as we whirled and turned with her skirts swirling to the rhythm of the polka.

When the music stopped she stayed leaning against me, her arms still holding me. I dropped my arms to my sides. I was breathing hard from the pace of the dance.

"Let's go for a walk," she said lightly.

"I really don't think that's a g …"

She broke away from me, walking slowly into the shadows, toward the towering mountain, its white top gleaming in the moonlight. She did not glance back. She knew I would follow. After twenty minutes of brisk walking, guided by the light of the moon, we had left the wagons behind and were moving up the lower reaches of the mountain. Grassland was replaced by rocks and boulders.

Amelia turned. "Let's go up the mountain. We will have a lovely view of the wagons from higher up."

"Shouldn't we go back, Amelia? Pa will wonder where you are."

"No he won't. He is busy looking after Jakob while he tells stories and talks and drinks brandy with the Krugers and the poor de Wets. Anyway," she smiled, "he told me to have a good time and that is exactly what I am doing."

I didn't answer, only followed her lead. We climbed about half way up the mountain and I looked down to see that Amelia had been right. We had a lovely view of the plains below us. She sat on a boulder and I perched next to her. For a few moments neither of us spoke. She took my hand and squeezed it tightly. I felt extremely uncomfortable. Lights from the wagons and the flares of camp fires dotted an area that must have extended a good few miles. The sounds of children laughing and shouting floated up to us as did the smell of meat cooking. In the distance we could hear the occasional sounds from the cattle as they settled down for the night. I could have sworn I heard the cough of a lion some distance away but didn't mention anything to Amelia.

We watched in silence for some time. Amelia still had my hand in hers, squeezing it quite hard. I squeezed back, looking up at the sky with its blanket of sparkling stars.

"No wonder they call this Big Sky Country," I murmured.

She looked at me. Her lips were slightly parted and she was smiling. I could see her perfect white teeth in the moonlight. She kissed me hard on my mouth. I felt her tongue slip into my mouth. Her taste was so familiar and so special. I felt myself responding. Her breath was quickening, her hands reached behind me and pulled me closer. Suddenly she slipped off the boulder and tumbled onto the ground, pulling me on top of her. Her eyes widened in surprise as she landed with the full weight of my body pressing her down. I could feel her warm body against mine. I remembered the last time I had been so close to her.

But as if the fall had brought her to her senses, she pulled her knee up into my groin and in one sideways motion wriggled out from under me. "No! No, Rauch. You can't do this to me. I am married to your Pa. He'll kill you ... and me too ... if he finds out you tried to fuck me!"

I couldn't believe my ears. "What do you mean? I didn't try anything. You're the one leading me on. My God, you *are* a tease. You never intended anything to happen, did you? You were just leading me on to see if I would try. I can't believe it! You did that to me on the riverbank long ago and tonight you did it again!" I glared at her, enraged, "Next time you play games with me you'd better know that I am not going to stop, whether you say you want me to or not. You'll have it coming."

Amelia stared at me silently.

"Come," I said, "we're going back. The magic is over and it is getting late."

We stumbled down the mountainside. A cloud passed over the moon and it was suddenly very dark. Amelia reached for my hand again and I jerked mine away as if it was a live coal. We were half way down the slope when the moon once again bathed the landscape in light.

"Stop!" I shouted.

Immediately in front of us the ground fell away, forming a deep hollow. It was filled with hundreds of skeletons, piled upon each other, some lying at strange angles. Strips of flesh dried by the sun hung in shreds where vultures had attempted to pick the bones clean.

"Rauch! What is it? Who has done this? My God! There must be more than a hundred skeletons. Whose are they? "

"They must be kaffirs. They can't be boers; there are too many of them. We would have heard about our people being slaughtered like this. There must have been one hell of a battle; there must have been hundreds killed … look at them!"

"No, I don't want to look." Amelia turned away and covered her face with her hands, "Oh my God, how horrible!"

We both became aware of the sickly smell of death. I grabbed her hand and pulled her along, skirting the mass grave. We stumbled away from the ghastly find, back to the safety of the wagons. We didn't talk on the way back. I had almost forgotten what had happened earlier as Amelia's teasing had been eclipsed by the grisly discovery. By the time we arrived back at camp the festivities had died down and all was quiet. I noticed that in spite of all that had happened; I was still holding her hand. I pulled my hand free lest someone should see.

Amelia stopped and turned to me. "I'm not going to say anything to your Pa about what you tried to do to me on the mountain, Rauch. Better that he doesn't know. He's a very jealous man."

I was about to protest but she reached up and put a finger across my lips, smiling. "And if you're smart you won't say a word either ... we don't want to upset anyone, do we?"

She disappeared into the wagon. There was a light on inside and I heard Pa ask in an angry tone where she'd been for the past two hours. I stopped in the lee of the wagon.

"I've been for a walk."

"Where and with whom?"

"Up the Blesberg Mountain with Frans and Anna and some of the others. You won't believe what we saw!" I heard her trying to change the subject. My stomach tightened as I heard her smoothly lie to Pa. I knew the truth would come out. I moved off as she started talking about the skeletons we had seen. I knew there would be a ripple effect from the evening but I didn't know then that it would become a tidal wave.

That night, after satisfying myself and asking forgiveness, I prayed that He would forgive Amelia's deceit as well, despite my thoughts being with Marietjie.

ᐊᙢ ᐊᙢ ᐊᙢ

A week later I received a summons from Kommandant Hendrik Potgieter. I made my way to the tent next to his wagon. Sarel Cilliers was with him.

"Good morning, kommandant."

"Morning, Rauch. Sit," he said patting the empty space on the bench beside him. "I need you to gather together a troop of six men to accompany me on a visit to Chief Moroka. He is the head of the Barolong people in this area. Our scouts tell us that he has suffered at the hands of another tribe called the Matabele. We need to make it very clear that we come in peace …"

Cilliers interrupted, "… and in peace as Christians, therefore in the protection of God Almighty under whom all men must live."

"I was up Blesberg the other night for a walk. Have you been up there?" I asked the two. They shook their heads. "Well, perhaps you should go and have a look. We came across what must be hundreds of skeletons up there … they must be Barolong. *They* certainly did not have the protection of God."

"Of course not; these people are heathens," Cilliers responded smugly.

"What is the fighting all about?" I asked.

"It's all on account of that savage, Mzilikazi," Potgieter explained. "He is wreaking havoc in this part of the world. He is power-mad. He is a fearless, brilliant military strategist and he commands an army of some sixty thousand bloodthirsty warriors. He belongs to the Zulu people but he apparently split from them about twenty years ago, after he, as one of Chaka's generals, refused to hand over cattle taken in battle. Since then, he and his people, the Matabele, are sworn enemies of the Zulu. They are on the warpath and have been for years. Being part of the Zulu tribe they use the same principles of attack. It is also said that they don't throw their assegais like other tribes but prefer short stabbing spears. They have swept all before them, causing many thousands of deaths. Most of the other chiefs are happy to live in peace but not this one."

He paused briefly, before continuing. "He must be stopped but there is no force strong enough to achieve that. I'm afraid that we will come up against him sooner or later." He stopped and looked at me as if suddenly reminded of something, "You served with Smith against the Xhosa, didn't you?"

I nodded.

"Well, don't you recall the Fingoes crossing into the colony?"

I nodded, "Yes, yes, I was there."

"Well, the Fingo were fleeing the same man—Mzilikazi—and his army of killer warriors. He is a tyrant. He has based himself farther north over a big river. I didn't realize that he had butchered these people here as well."

"Well, hopefully we won't meet up with him or his army," I said. "We wouldn't stand much chance with less than a hundred men against an army of sixty thousand."

"Ah, that's where you are so wrong, my son," interjected Cilliers, with a superior smile, as if I was rather slow. "You see, we have God on our side and He will be our shield."

I looked at Cilliers in amazement; surely he was joking. My heart almost stopped when I understood that he wasn't.

"Amen," added Potgieter, casting his eyes upward.

On the way back to my tent I caught sight of Amelia some way off. She looked as though she had been crying. We didn't speak.

Two hours later, eight of us rode into the kraal, the grouping of royal mud huts of Moroka II, Paramount Chief of the Seleka tribe of the Barolong people. We brought five fine oxen as a gift to ensure a friendly welcome. Moroka was accompanied by his counsellors and an interpreter, Jan Daniels, who had been educated by an English gentleman and baptized in Grahamstown. He smiled broadly when he was assured that Cilliers and Potgieter were men of God.

"Then you are friends of mine," said the chief, "and you are welcome to graze your cattle here on our lands as you pass through."

Cilliers interrupted the chief, holding his hands in the air, palms facing Chief Moroko. Cilliers closed his eyes. "If you listen to the teachings of our Lord and live according to those teachings, and you love God and your neighbours with all of your heart, then not only are you our friend but also the friend of God, our Father in Heaven."

Chief Moroka looked slightly taken aback at this outpouring, as did I, but he uttered, "We have suffered greatly at the hands of Mzilikazi. All we want is to live in peace with our neighbours but with the Matabele this is not possible. You are free to stay here as long as you wish and to graze your cattle and sheep with my blessing."

Chapter Fourteen

Two days were spent packing up the wagons and preparing for the next stage of our journey. The night before we left Thaba Nchu a stranger and two companions, carrying guns, rode into the camp. People stopped what they were doing and looked up as he greeted them in a friendly manner. He stopped beside Jan and me sitting next to our evening fire.

"Greetings. I am Reverend Archbell from the Wesleyan mission." He indicated in the direction of Chief Moroka's kraal, "I am looking for your leader."

"Over there," I said pointing out Potgieter's wagons. "You will find Kommandant Potgieter and Sarel Cilliers over there."

After he had gone Jan was silent for a few moments, while I gazed into the flickering flames.

"I need to talk to you, Rauch" he said suddenly, his handsome features solemn. I raised an inquiring eyebrow. "There is something I need to tell you. I don't know who else to speak to. I've got problems … of course, they are women problems." He picked up a stick and prodded the fire. There was a shower of sparks as he manoeuvred a log into position.

"Go on," I said. "I'm listening. I'll help if I can."

"This concerns … um … it concerns your family." I frowned in puzzlement as Jan continued, "Two evenings ago, I was down near the cattle enclosure, looking to hunt some partridge, when I met Amelia. She was out walking on her own; there was no one else about."

I got suspicious about what I was about to hear.

"Well," he said, embarrassed, "we talked for a while and she was very friendly. I mean *very* friendly." He studied me to gauge my reaction. "As you know she's a very attractive woman. She always has been but now, after the baby, she's even lovelier. Lovely enough to drive a man mad. Anyway … she talked about you and told me what you had tried to do to her on the mountain. But then … well you know … one thing led to another and we kissed."

My stomach contracted at the thought and I felt a pang of jealousy.

"Well, it didn't stop there. I started to … well … you know…" He was struggling to describe what happened in a way that wouldn't upset me. "I … I thought she wanted to make love!" he blurted out.

I felt as if I had been slapped in the face.

"But Rauch, I was wrong!"

A wave of relief swept over me.

"So, then, you didn't?"

"Well, no … no, we didn't. Whether we would have or not, I don't know. Things were getting quite hot and I was sure she wanted it."

"Well, what stopped you?"

"Your pa stopped me!"

"Pa! You mean he caught you? He caught you in the …?"

Jan didn't reply, just frowned and nodded.

"He threatened to tell Potgieter and have me kicked off the trek. You know what Kommandant Potgieter will do if he finds out I was with another man's wife? Particularly as the wife is your father's wife. I was caught with my pants down … literally," Jan added, ashamedly.

"You are joking! You had your pants down when he caught you?"

"Yes, that's right but Amelia had already said no. She started the whole thing and then she told me to stop!"

I had not spoken to Amelia since the night on the mountain but I remembered having seen her in the distance, just before we went to see Chief Moroka. I thought at the time that it might have been as a result of what had happened with me. I was wrong. "Well what happened next? What did Pa do?"

"He was furious, as you can guess. He started shouting at Amelia and calling her names. I thought he'd hit us both but he didn't. He was like a mad man; from what he was saying he has caught her out before this. Your name came up all the time, and so did your dead brother, Dirk. Anyway, Amelia answered back and he marched her away. I'm glad I didn't witness what took place in their wagon that night. Amelia was crying. I said I was sorry but I don't think anyone heard me. Do you think he will say anything to Potgieter?"

"I don't know. If he does then I think your trek is finished."

"Well, if he does then your father is finished as well," said Jan in a strange tone of voice.

"What do you mean?"

"Well, it's a bit like the pot calling the kettle black."

"Why?"

"Because the night you took Amelia up on the mountain I saw your pa trying to force himself on Anna, your brother's wife."

"You couldn't have!" I said angrily. "She is expecting a child and anyway Pa was looking after their baby in the wagon."

"That's where I saw them … they were in the wagon. I think Anna must have gone to the wagon to help him with the baby. They were kissing and your pa was … he was fondling her. Anna certainly wasn't trying to resist; it looked like she was playing along which really did surprise me. But then your pa started pulling her dress up and she was trying to stop him, holding it down. It didn't stop him though … he had his hand right up her dress."

I couldn't believe my ears. Pa again! First, he took Amelia from me and now, now Anna, my brother's wife! My thoughts were in turmoil. "What were you doing that you saw them?"

"The van Rensburgs had asked me for some saltpeter to make biltong and as your pa's wagon was nearby, I went to borrow some from him. I was at the wagon entrance and saw it all … of course, I couldn't ask for the saltpeter."

I thought for a while. "What a mess! What are you going to do about it?"

"Nothing … nothing. Unless he goes to Hendrik Potgieter and then I will tell Potgieter about your pa."

"Yes, that's fine but by then it will be too late. You won't achieve anything … Potgieter will still throw you out." I paused. "Unless of course Pa finds out what you'll do if he speaks about this. Pa has to know that he has been compromised. That will stop him. Otherwise you are finished. I can't believe what you've told me. The bastard … he knows no shame! But leave it with me," I continued. "I'll see he understands that if he opens his mouth about you, he will also lose out. This must be done quickly though, otherwise he will get to Potgieter." Even though I was horrified to hear the story about Pa, I think what disturbed me most was Amelia fooling around with Jan.

Early next morning the sixty wagons, thousands of head of cattle, sheep and goats and two hundred souls started off again to the sounds of whistles, shouts, cracking of whips and creaking of wagon wheels. Dust stirred up by the hooves of the cattle and sheep hovered over us like a protective red cloud. I rode on ahead as one of the scouts searching for the best route for the wagons and wondering how best to ensure that Pa would not tell Potgieter about Jan I didn't have long to wait before an opportunity arose. Half way through the first afternoon, I stopped Grey for a rest in the shade of a tree, allowing the wagons to pass, following Jan's lead.

Pa rode up to me, his face like thunder. "You had better tell your friend Jan to stay away from Amelia … and that goes for you, too," he said menacingly.

"I think he'll do that, Pa, as long as you keep your hands off my brother's wife." Unable to resist the jibe, I added, "Perhaps it is you who should keep your Amelia under control … maybe she has a taste for younger men."

Pa's face went white with rage. He glared at me, his sharp eyes narrowing. He was on the point of responding when we both became aware of horsemen approaching.

The riders were Potgieter and Cilliers. "Good morning Rauch. Good morning Jakob. The Lord has given us a fine day once again," said Potgieter, turning his eyes to the sky.

"Good day kommandant," Pa and I said in the same breath.

"What lies ahead, Rauch?" asked Potgieter.

"Just miles and miles of rolling grassland, kommandant; we met no one. Tomorrow we will reach a river which we will have to ford. Jan and I were there this morning. It is about fifteen miles from here. I have never seen as much game as we saw on the riverbanks today. Zebra in their thousands, elephant in giant herds and many varieties of buck … eland, impala, kudu … you name it. The banks are teeming with game … giraffe, as well."

"Well, I think we should call that river the Vet River, as it is fat with game," said Cilliers. He seemed to like naming the rivers we encountered. Earlier he had named a particularly muddy river that we'd had to ford the Modder, or Mud, River.

The scenery was very different from what we had experienced during the earlier part of the journey. This was good country for sheep and cattle. As far as the eye could see, gently rolling grasslands were broken by low koppies, small hills with flat tops and boulder-strewn slopes. The koppies were so flat they appeared to have been chopped off at the top by a butcher's knife. Away to the right, painted blue by the brush of distance, was a line of mountains running parallel to our route. Beyond them was another hazy range, much higher than the first, and covered in cloud.

"That is the home of Moshesh, the most powerful chief in the area," said Potgieter, gazing into the distance. "The Reverend Archbell tells me that Moshesh is a man of peace and that we shall have no trouble with him."

"Praise the Lord!" said Cilliers. He turned to Pa. "It's good to see you reunited with your son, Jakob. The Lord has led you to him and joined you all together again as a family. He is watching over us and protecting us."

Pa looked embarrassed, his face red. I enjoyed his discomfort and wondered idly whether it was the Lord who had led Amelia to Jan. I knew then that there would be no mention to Potgieter of Jan's brush with Amelia.

A few days later we crossed a sandy river and made camp on beautiful grazing lands.

Again, Cilliers showed off his creativity: "The Lord tells me that we should call this river the Sand River," he announced.

I heard Jan chuckle. "The Lord tells him everything he knows but the Lord obviously doesn't have much imagination," he laughed.

"I know. I find it all a bit too much," I replied.

As we moved onto the fertile land north of the Sand River, we came across small groups of trekkers who had independently made their way into the area and put down roots. Early in the afternoon, after passing many such groups of trekkers, we noticed, a hundred yards ahead, a group of blacks standing in our path.

Potgieter, Cilliers and three guards, including me, rode on to introduce ourselves. It was the local chief, Makwana, Chief of the Bataung, together with some of his counsellors. After brief introductions, Chief Makwana explained that his people were the only remaining tribe of thirty such clans that had once inhabited the region. All the rest had been wiped out by Mzilikazi. The Bataung still lived in constant fear of the warlike Matabele.

"If it is land you want," said Chief Makwana, "I can give you land."

Potgieter nodded in agreement.

"All I want from you," said the chief, "is your protection. You have guns and will be able to protect us from further attacks by Mzilikazi. In return for forty-nine head of cattle and your promise of protection, if you leave my people with enough land to live on, you may have all the land that lies between this river you have just crossed and the big river north of here … the one we call the Tky-Gariep."

"We will call it the Vaal River," announced Cilliers with a smile, as he translated the Bataung word for drab.

"Some of our people may wish to stay and settle here," said Potgieter.

"They are welcome as long as we can live side by side, in peace. You have my word on that," said Chief Makwana.

That evening around the fires, the conversation was about whether to stay and settle on this land. I heard many of our travelling companions discussing whether it would be better to move farther north.

"Why go any farther? The land here is ideal. Why don't we just stay here?" I heard Koos Robbertse telling his wife. He wasn't alone. A number of trekkers thought they had indeed found their promised land. A message went round the wagons that Kommandant Potgieter would address us all next morning.

The crowd that gathered on the banks of the Sand River to hear Potgieter's address included a number of independent migrants who appeared to be delighted with our arrival. By now there were more than two hundred and fifty of us. As always the majority of the party was children as it was customary for them too to hear the words of our leaders.

Sarel Cilliers opened the meeting with a prayer which concluded, "… and we thank you, Lord, for our safe deliverance into your Promised Land. You have sheltered us from harm. Protect your children from the evils of the heathen and continue, O Father, to guard and shield your chosen people from the enemy. Amen!"

"Amen," the crowd repeated.

I looked across at the faces turned eagerly, full of anticipation, toward Potgieter. Amelia's head had been bowed during the prayers but I saw her eyes were now open and she was staring straight at me. I shook my head in disbelief.

"People!" announced Potgieter in a strong, deep voice. "We have come to what truly must be the Promised Land. The Lord has led us safely here and delivered us into the lands of Chief Makwana, a good man who has himself found the Lord. He is a Christian like us …"

There was a buzz of surprise that a chieftain could also be a Christian.

"… Chief Makwana has made his mark on an agreement giving us the land between here, the Sand River and a river to the north that Sarel Cilliers has named the Vaal River. In return we have guaranteed him protection from his enemy, who is also our enemy: the one named Mzilikazi and his fierce Matabele warriors. They have already killed many thousands of other kaffirs. So, to those of you who wish to settle here and make this land your home, I say it is a fine place for a town. I can see, in the future, there will be churches, schools and an entire community living right here."

Again there was a hum of conversation as men and women turned to their neighbours to establish whether or not they intended to take up Potgieter's invitation. Someone in the crowd shouted out, "What about you kommandant? Will you stay here?"

More in the crowd took up the question.

"Yes. What about you, Meneer Potgieter?"

"Stay here, sir; this is indeed the Promised Land."

Potgieter puffed up his chest, pleased to have been asked to stay on.

"Not for the moment," he replied. "I am taking a small group of people farther north. I want to find a way through to the coast so that we can maintain total independence from the English. Until we have access to our own port we are still dependent on the English, even though we have left the colony. I also wish to locate the Trichardt and van Rensburg parties who travelled up north."

There was a murmur of unhappiness that the leader would be moving on.

"No, my people, don't worry. Sarel Cilliers and I will be back, either to stay here with you or to lead you to an even better land. That decision will be left to the will of God. Now please pay attention. The following men will accompany me …" He started with Sarel Cilliers and read out the names of ten other men. As the names were called, there much backslapping and shouts of congratulation. Eventually he finished off with "… and Jan Greyling and Rauch Beukes."

We were to be the twelfth and the thirteenth men.

Amelia's eyes were locked on mine. I grinned at her, delighted at having been named a member of Potgieter's party and pumped Jan's hand. Behind Amelia, I caught sight of Anna. She too was watching me, with the hint of smile on her lips. I nodded in her direction to express my appreciation for her putting in a word for me with her uncle, Sarel Cilliers. Anna didn't look at all embarrassed and I understood why: she had no idea that I knew anything about the incident between her and my Pa.

"One last thing," said Potgieter, holding his hand up for attention. "Do not cross the river to the north of us, the one that Sarel Cilliers has named the Vaal. If you do you will be moving onto the lands that the bloodthirsty tyrant, Mzilikazi, calls his own. Hear my words, I repeat: it would not be wise to cross the Vaal River. Stay here, where you are, on the land given to you by Chief Makwana and live in peace and friendship. There is plenty of good land here for all of us, so until I return, this is where you must stay. Cross the Vaal and you might well stir up a hornet's nest."

There was a buzz of excited conversation.

"To those whose names I have called, we leave to find the voorste mense, the people who went first, Trichardt and van Rensburg, on the day after tomorrow at sunrise. We will be travelling light with only two wagons so as not to slow us down. Bring your guns, ammunition and powder. Let us pray."

With that, he closed the meeting and we wandered off to discuss the latest developments. I saw Amelia walking ahead of us with Pa. Her head was bowed, she looked heartbroken. Just once she glanced back over her shoulder and looked at Jan and at me.

Then she walked on, head hanging.

Our party of fourteen left early on the morning of the May 24th, 1836. We followed the trail of the Trichardt and van Rensburg treks. It wasn't difficult. Their combined parties numbered around one hundred. There were only seventeen men, their wives and sixty children. The one thousand head of cattle, fifty horses and more than six thousand sheep and goats had cut a giant swathe through the veld which clearly marked their path, even though they had travelled this way many months before. All we had to do was follow the track which at times was two hundred yards wide.

Sometimes the path split into two where the groups had parted before meeting up again some ten to twenty miles farther on. As we rode I could see in my mind's eye what 'the first people' to travel over this vast empty space must have looked like to the local tribesmen just months earlier. Viewed from one of the mountaintops which flanked our path, the undulating grasslands would have been scarred by the brown and white wagons as they travelled in rows, four abreast, like a wave of flotsam in the surf, rising and falling, dipping into the folds of the earth. Out front, looking like minute specks, the scouts sought the best way forward. Behind the wagons, in a procession which would have taken some twenty minutes to pass a given point, would have been the cattle, sheep, goats and horses being herded along. It must have been a thrilling sight.

We were able to travel quickly as we had no animals with us. The days in the saddle allowed me time, at last, to take stock of my life. My thoughts frequently turned to Marietjie and I was surprised by my feelings of love for her. When I thought of Amelia or even Katrina, I thought only of their bodies, whereas I felt Marietjie was my soul's partner. I wondered how she was coping with Roddy and realized that by now I was probably a father. I wondered whether I would ever see her again. I wondered what had become of her plan to leave the colony. I longed for news of her.

I thought also of Katrina and her child. It would, of course, be a coloured baby. I couldn't help feeling sorry for her and I worried about what would happen to her. The last time I had seen her she had lost her allure; she had become sad, dull and listless.

Amelia, on the other hand, had blossomed and matured as a young mother. She was now as ripe as forbidden fruit and despite, or perhaps because of, her flirtatious nature, she still managed to excite me.

I wondered about Pa and whether we would ever return to the relationship we had enjoyed before Ma and my sisters had been so cruelly put to death. I also felt saddened that Pa's wandering eye had now homed in on Anna, his son's and my brother's wife. "Mind you," I mused. "She's a good looking woman; Pa certainly knows which ones to go for." I was surprised that Anna had responded as she had and wondered what the man of God, her uncle Sarel, would say if he heard that his niece appeared to be enjoying a bit of vrying with her father-in-law. Pa appeared to have few, if any, morals and I found it tragic, after what had happened between Dirk and me, that Pa showed so little respect for Frans or loyalty to Amelia. I felt anger and jealousy welling up as I pictured him with Amelia. Even though Amelia was a terrible tease and a flirt, Pa didn't deserve her. Now it seemed that the novelty of having taken her from me and being admired by a much younger woman had started to pall. I reflected on the fact that twice Amelia had led me on to the point of making love, only to spurn me. "The next time there will be nothing to stop me," I thought. "It would serve Pa right as well." I knew for certain there would be a next time.

We travelled north through a wide expanse of the grasslands, crossing the Vaal, the biggest river we had seen since the Orange. On the second day after the crossing, Kommandant Potgieter, who was riding in front with Cilliers, asked a question that briefly puzzled us.

"Do you notice anything strange?"

No one responded. Then the answer dawned on me: there were no people. Indeed, there was not a living creature to be seen, not man nor beast.

Potgieter had barely asked the question when there was a crunching sound, like that of dried mielies being ground on stone under wagon wheels. I looked down. My heart jumped and my mouth went dry. A human skull grinned up at me. In death, the bones of the hands looked like claws, as though the victim was still trying to fend off the attacker who had put paid to his life. Shocked, we moved slowly on, onto another skeleton and another and yet another until the crunching of wheels on human bone formed a continuous sombre refrain to our journey.

Potgieter and Cilliers pulled up their horses. "This is the work of the Matabele," said Potgieter.

We looked around anxiously, hoping they weren't still lurking in the area. "There must be thousands dead. It is no wonder that the other tribes are so afraid of him. We must pray earnestly to Our Lord for protection."

Cilliers held up his hand. "Let us pray."

We closed our eyes, sitting in our saddles, heads bowed. Cilliers prayed with what I thought even more fervour than usual as he read from Psalm thirty-seven:

Do not fret because of evildoers

Nor be envious of the workers of iniquity

For they shall soon be cut down like the grass

And wither as the green herb

Trust in the Lord, and do good

Dwell in the land and feed on his righteousness …

Amen.

"Amen!" we repeated.

I crossed my fingers as well, feeling that we might need more than prayer if we were to come across Mzilikazi and his troops. We rode on in silence, apart from the eerie crackle and crunch of human remains. Occasionally we passed burned-out kraals with only crumbling walls and a few charred roofing timbers remaining. In most cases the fields had been burned out around the kraals. There was a sinister, ghostly atmosphere of doom as we rode close to the wagons which still crunched and bumped over fields of bones that littered the barren landscape.

Only when we reached mountains several days later did we find any signs of life when we saw cultivated plants on the lower slopes.

"Sugar cane," said Kommandant Potgieter.

"The Lord names this place Suikerbosrand," proclaimed Cilliers.

Jan looked at me and grinned, "Our creative leader."

"That he may well be," I replied, "but he knows how to shoot, doesn't he?"

Jan nodded, "Ja, he can do that but then again, what would you expect? He has the Lord to guide his aim." Cilliers had proved time and again that when it came to shooting game he was without equal.

We had not encountered any resistance since leaving Thaba Nchu. Still travelling north after we passed the Suikerbosrand we discovered more and more villages. In some instances the natives, having never before seen a white person, fell to their knees as though we were gods. In others they dared not raise their eyes to look at us as we rode by.

Early on the morning of June 30th, after travelling for some four hundred and fifty miles and thirty-seven days, we were camped near the Zoutpansberg when I woke to the sound of distant gunfire.

"Quick! Arm yourselves!" I yelled as we leaped to our feet, grabbing our weapons.

"Who can this be?" asked Jan Bronkhorst. "The kaffirs have no guns."

"It must be Trichardt or van Rensburg. We've found them," said Kommandant Potgieter excitedly. "Fire a shot to let them know we are here."

Jan and I fired a volley and waited.

Answering shots from down the valley confirmed Potgieter's suspicion

"There they are!" called Jan. He pointed to three men on horseback, riding hard in our direction. We waved our hats and whistled.

The three had been out hunting, with two impala draped over their horses demonstrating their prowess. "Greetings," called the leader, a smiling young man who it turned out was Louis Trichardt's younger son, Petrus.

"It is wonderful that you are finally here! I cannot wait to see my pa's face when he meets you. We have been waiting for you for weeks now. Come, bring your things. We must go to camp straight away. We are staying just a few miles from here. Pa will be so pleased to see you all."

We gathered up our possessions and the enlarged party of sixteen men and two wagons made its way to the Trichardt settlement, only twenty minutes away. We passed several tribesmen who waved and smiled at us. What a relief: they appeared to be friendly.

"Look at that," I said to Jan. "Some of them are wearing what look like gold ornaments and arm bands."

"It *is* gold," said Carolus, Trichardt's elder son. "This is indeed the Promised Land, I tell you. It is rich in minerals and look, look over there ..." he pointed to some trees. "Fruit trees ... and over there are our vegetable gardens. Water is plentiful and the natives are friendly; this is indeed a fine place to which the good Lord has brought us."

The children saw us first as we rode into the camp. We fired our Sannas in the air in greeting. We were welcomed with squeals of delight. Children ran around laughing, shouting and clapping their hands with glee. All camp activity ceased as we climbed off our horses. We were greeted as heroes returning home from battle. My arm was pumped so much that I thought it must surely fall off. Backs were slapped, men hugged each other and women cried. Children were held aloft. There was a great deal of shouting and laughter.

Louis Trichardt and his wife Martha stood to the side. Trichardt's usually solemn face was wreathed in smiles as he watched the excitement. His camp consisted of nine wagons and a few wooden shacks which gave the place an air of permanency. Vegetable and flower gardens were flourishing.

Potgieter greeted the Trichardts affectionately, hugging them and kissing them both on their cheeks. "Where are the van Rensburgs?" he asked. "Do they have a separate camp?"

The smile disappeared from Trichardt's face as he reverted to his usual morose expression. He shook his head. "No. They are not here. We haven't seen them for about two months. I am ashamed to say that we had an argument. Hans was more interested in selling his ivory at the coast than he was in settling down. He and I had a strong difference of opinion. I felt he was wasting ammunition and he was offended when I told him he should pay more attention to the maintenance of his wagons." Trichardt shook his head. "Hopefully the Lord will forgive him for endangering us all. God knows what has happened to him. Have you not heard anything?"

Potgieter shook his head. "No, I am afraid not ..."

At that moment Sarel Cilliers interrupted, holding up his hand in his customary manner, indicating that it was time for prayer. "People, thank you for your joyous welcome but there will be plenty of time for celebration in the future. For now, we must first thank our Father in Heaven for our deliverance and for bringing us all together again."

We bowed our heads and held hands as Cilliers began to pray in the shadow of the mountain. "I pray from Exodus chapter three." Even the birds in the fruit trees seemed to fall silent as his voice, trembling with emotion, rang out:

And the Lord said

I have surely seen the oppression of my people who are in Egypt

and have heard their cry because of their taskmasters

for I know their sorrows

So I have come down to deliver them out of the hands of the Egyptians

and to bring them up from that land to a good and large land,

to a land flowing with milk and honey

We beseech you, O Father,

to deliver the van Rensburgs

back to the bosom of those friends who care for them.

Thank you, O Father for leading us to the voorste mense

and to this, your Promised Land.

Amen.

Chapter Fifteen

That night as we sat around the fire Kommandant Potgieter questioned Trichardt about his cousin, Hans van Rensburg.

"We parted on bad terms," said Trichardt. "And I am sorry to say we named the place where we had our quarrel, Strydpoort, the battle valley."

"Good name," said Cilliers, as Jan winked at me.

"I am sure you know Lang Hans can be difficult." Trichardt added.

Potgieter nodded and took another sip of his coffee. "Still," he said, "I think we should try and find them, difficult or not. They might need our help. So, you think that they will have made for the coast?"

"Yes. He wanted to sell ivory; they had a wagon full of it."

"Well, now that we are here, I really think it is one's duty to find him. I intend travelling farther north to see if we can pick up the trail to the coast … perhaps there is news of them up there. While I am gone we will leave a few men to guard the camp while you can scout on van Rensburg's trail to see what you can find out."

Potgieter then questioned Trichardt about living conditions in the area.

"Look, everything grows well here," said Trichardt. "The land is fertile. We have no problem with the kaffirs. We have even established contact with the Portuguese in Mozambique so we can trade. There is also gold here; it's just about perfect as a permanent home for us."

"And the best is that there are no English," Potgieter added with a chuckle. "It really does sound perfect. I think that after we have explored a bit more up north, we could come back, fetch those of our people who wish to come and set up our homes here."

"That would be wonderful," said Trichardt with a rare smile. Then a shadow passed over his face. "There is only one problem that I see but I'm sure if we move a little farther on, then that can be solved."

"What's that?" asked Potgieter.

"The mosquitoes around here are malarial. Also, some of the cattle seem to be sickening ... I think it's from the bite of a fly called the tsetse. The tribesmen call this sickness nagana, or sleeping sickness. I don't think it's a big problem though and if we change our site we will probably not be affected."

After further discussion Trichardt agreed to take a small party of men in an effort to pick up van Rensburg's trail while Potgieter and Cilliers headed farther north to find the route to the coast. That left a small group, which included Jan and me, to guard the camp. The time passed quickly as we explored the countryside with a view to settling in the area.

One morning Jan and I discussed the future as we repaired a wagon wheel. "I don't think I'll stay here," I said. "Much as I admire Potgieter, I find his religious fervour just too much for me. Also I prefer the idea of being near the coast. Of course, the downside is, as the kommandant says, that the English will probably be there too."

Jan looked up from the rim he was hammering, grimacing, "That's enough for me then. I've had more than enough of the English!"

"Listen, Jan," I said, cocking my head. All around were sounds of the veld: birds fluttered and chirped overhead, insects and crickets kept up a constant drone and I could feel, rather than hear, hoof beats approaching from the north.

"Perhaps it's Kommandant Potgieter and his group coming back," said Jan. But he was wrong.

Trichardt and five riders came into sight. They had been riding hard, the flanks of their horses glistening with sweat as they pulled to a halt, slumped in their saddles with an air of defeat. They swung themselves off their horses as Trichardt approached. We stopped working and waved but there was no return greeting, his expression that of a man bearing grave news. His eyes were red-rimmed with tears or dust or both, his face was haggard and his dark eyes full of pain.

"They're gone!" he said simply.

"What do you mean gone? Gone where?" Jan asked.

"He means dead," I said to the stricken Trichardt. "Is that right, Oom Louis?" I asked, hoping against hope that I was wrong.

"Ja," he replied in a flat, weary tone. "Of the forty-nine, every last one is dead." His voice faltered as he fought to keep his emotions in check. By this time a small crowd had gathered. Trichardt wiped the corners of his eyes and sniffed loudly, wiping his nose with the back of his hand.

"They are all dead," repeated Jan Robbertse, one of the riders. "Every single one has been killed by that kaffir, Sagana. A couple of the children might be alive though …"

He was interrupted by Lucas Bronkhorst, "We heard a cry, a white child's cry, from one of the huts when we were looking for van Rensburg. You know that white children sound different from black ones when they cry, don't you? Well, when we were at Chief Sagana's kraal we heard a white child crying. Later we were told by some tribesmen that Sagana's warriors had killed all the trekkers on the banks of the Crocodile River but that he was holding two of the children hostage. It was a close shave for us as well, I can tell you, because Sagana came after us He had his eye on our wagon, the evil heathen. It was only through Oom Louis' quick thinking that we lived to tell the tale."

"What about the children?" I interrupted. "Did you see them? Did you try to rescue them?"

Bronkhorst shook his head, "No, we couldn't. Sagana was trying to force us to stay so Oom Louis told him that we would come back and fetch the rest of our wagons and our people and then we would return. It is only because he thought he would have a bigger and better haul that he let us leave. No, those children are done for. We will never be able to save them."

Martha Trichardt and some of the other women had come within earshot. She held her hand up to her mouth in horror. "No Louis! Surely this cannot be! They can't all be dead … all forty-nine? Oh my God, preserve us all. What will happen to us?"

Louis Trichardt shook his head and put his arms around his wife, her body quivering with pain and grief. He patted her gently. The mood in the small community was one of dismay as the news sank in that more than half the original trekkers had perished.

The next day Potgieter, Cilliers and their group returned from the north with the news that they had found good land, had met with white trader families called Buys and that they had seen hard evidence of gold and processed iron among the natives. This was not enough, though, to lift the gloom caused by the loss of the van Rensburgs.

"It is God's will," said Sarel Cilliers.

"How can you always say that?" I snapped.

Cilliers looked shocked at my reaction, his face quite red. "Do not dare to challenge the ways of our Lord," he replied angrily.

But I'd had enough, "This is nonsense! Whenever something happens you say it's all part of God's plan. I say you talk nonsense, I can't believe that God has plans that include having people killed … forty-nine of them and some of them innocent children. If that is what your God does, I don't want him as *my* God," I shouted.

There was a stunned silence. The crowd seemed to be waiting for the ground to open up and swallow me, or for me to disappear in a flash of lightning and a cloud of smoke as the Lord punished me for my heretical comment.

Cilliers glared, "That is blasphemy. Don't you dare speak like that about our good Lord." Regaining his composure after a few moments, he held up his hands and closed his eyes.

I saw what was coming and turned and walked away, calling back over my shoulder. "I don't think that God is cruel enough to want to make us suffer … it's the kaffirs and what do they know of God's will?"

Behind me I could hear the voice of Cilliers leading the group in prayer.

Our party left Trichardt and his people to return to our main camp at the Sand River on August 17th, 1836. It was a sad farewell.

"Do not worry," said Potgieter. "I will soon be back with all our people who wish to settle here. You won't be alone for long. Have courage, have strength, my friend. We will return to join you in the Promised Land. This is to be our new home."

Cilliers shouted over the galloping hooves, "Have faith in the Lord, my brother, and he will protect you."

I said to Jan, riding alongside me, "Do you think that van Rensburg and his people had lost faith which is why they were all killed?"

Jan didn't reply but Cilliers had heard and glared at me.

Looking back I saw the forlorn figures of Louis and Martha Trichardt. He had his arm around her, waving us off. I waved back. We would never see the them again.

⊸⥃⊸⥃⊸⥃

Potgieter sent me, Jan and Lucas Bronkhorst on ahead to collect fresh horses from our camp between the Sand and the Vaal rivers. It was an easy ride and seven days later we approached the Vaal, curling its way lazily through the veld like a sluggish snake.

Lucas pulled on his reins. "Whoa!" he exclaimed. "What's that, there, in the water?"

We saw something large, close to the bank.

"It's a wagon … on its side," exclaimed Jan.

As we drew closer we could see he was right. Most of the wagon was submerged but two wheels and a torn canopy, flapping in shreds from the exposed metal hoops, were above the water. A hot, heavy silence filled the air as we tried to imagine what had caused this.

"I'm going up for a closer look," said Lucas. He rode to the bank and slipped from his saddle to examine something in the long grass, before calling, "Oh God, it's the Liebenbergs. The Liebenbergs … all dead!" He dropped to his knees next to a shape in the long, dry grass and taking off his hat, held it to his chest.

We rode up. I saw the bodies in the grass.

"It's old Barend Liebenberg and his son, Stephanus," Lucas announced shakily. The Liebenberg family had been in the group we had left behind at the Sand River.

"They must have crossed the Vaal in defiance of Kommandant Potgieter's orders," said Lucas, still on the ground beside the corpses. Both bodies were on their backs with the assegais that killed them protruding from their chests. Their eyes were wide open, staring deep into the blue skies above, searching in vain for their Lord's elusive protection.

"Where are the others, I wonder?" said Lucas, looking around.

It didn't take us long to discover six more bodies. All had suffered stab wounds. "We must get back and tell Kommandant Potgieter," he said, shaking his head in sorrow. "This is a disaster. Will the killing never end? Who did this? This must be the work of that Mzilikazi. Why, oh why, didn't they listen to the Kommandant? They were expressly warned *not* to cross the river."

Hastily we dug eight shallow graves in the soft earth at the water's edge and then rode, as if the Devil himself was after us, to break the tragic news to Potgieter. Potgieter immediately sent Nikolaas Potgieter and Piet Botha to inform the settlers farther along the river what had happened and to warn them of further attacks from the Matabele. We didn't know that it was already too late.

We rode south to our base on the Sand River. Shortly after crossing the Vaal we saw dust clouds rising from the veld ahead. The sight that met us made us pull up our horses to watch in amazement. It looked like the exodus of the Israelites from Egypt. Only this time it was Mzilikazi and the Matabele who had caused the mass departure. The veld was alive with wagons, people, cattle, sheep and goats. We gazed in stunned silence. Word had spread of the killings of the Liebenbergs and people were fleeing south, away from the danger. Long streaks of red dust hung in the air, marking the path of the panic-stricken settlers. The inspanned cattle heaved and strained as they pulled the brown-stained canopied wagons. A giant moving cloud of red dust, cloaking the cattle and sheep, followed the wagons.

We spurred our horses and rode up alongside a wagon. It belonged to the de Wet family. We galloped alongside the wagon; there was no option of stopping or even slowing down. De Wet glanced back over his shoulder and shouted, "We are getting away from here. The Matabele have killed the Erasmus family. They were hunting on the other side of the river with the Liebenbergs."

"Wait, wait … stop for a minute!" ordered Potgieter. "What do you mean? We know about the Liebenbergs ... we found their bodies. What is this about Erasmus?"

De Wet reluctantly drew his wagon to a halt. "They were on a hunting expedition and were attacked first," he said. "Then the Matabele killed the Liebenbergs and their party. All in all, they have killed more than fifty men, women and children in the past few days."

Potgieter gasped.

"And now," said de Wet hoarsely, "they are coming after the rest of us. I am taking my family south, away from the murdering heathen. We don't stand a chance against them. They say…. they say that Mzilikazi has over fifty thousand warriors." He cracked his whip over the heads of the oxen, breaking off the conversation and haring off in his desperate race for safety.

"God save us! The Erasmuses gone as well? We had better prepare ourselves for an attack by the bloodthirsty swine," Potgieter yelled to Cilliers with some urgency.

"Yes," answered Cilliers, "I think it's time to teach him a lesson. We have the Lord on our side."

I glanced at Jan, who looked as incredulous as I felt. He simply shook his head in astonishment. Potgieter told us to wait at a low koppie about two thousand yards long, a site that he had previously selected in anticipation of an attack by the Matabele. We climbed to the top. The view of the rolling veld stretched in every direction. Any approach by the enemy would be spotted well in advance.

"This is where I want the wagons parked," said Potgieter, pointing to an area below the hill where the ground sloped gently away, where there was little cover for the enemy.

Two days later we were joined by fifty ox wagons, thirty-five men and ten younger boys whose fathers felt they were old enough to shoot a weapon. Sixty women and children loyally accompanied them, despite the fact that an attack was in the offing.

Potgieter called us together. "People, you all know what has happened to the poor Liebenbergs and the Erasmuses. The Matabele are likely to attack again, so we must prepare ourselves for the worst. God is with us but you must know that we are against a mighty, mighty army. We must all be prepared to meet our Maker if indeed that is His will."

Cilliers, as usual, led us in prayer and after the defiant "Amens" had rung out, Potgieter said, "Let us now get to work, my friends, and ready ourselves for battle."

We began preparing our defences. First we herded the cattle and sheep to where we intended positioning the wagons, then we drove them over a wider, circular swathe around the site which flattened the grass as if cut and baled, leaving the ground flat and barren for a distance of half a mile in every direction. Forty-six wagons were then hauled into a square, each wagon lashed to its neighbour. At the two opposite corners we made schiet-hokken, or shooting slits, which enabled us to see and fire along all four sides of the square. We left two openings, each the width of a single wagon, with extra wagons ready to be rolled into position when we needed to secure the entrance. Inside the laager we drove thick wooden stakes into the ground to which we fastened the wagons with chains and ropes. It was slow, hot work as the fixed axles of the wagons meant that each wagon had to be lifted and carried into position. With the hot October sun beating down, we pulled four wagons into a smaller square in the centre and these we covered with skins and hides to provide a protective fortress for the women and children as well as a safe place where the wounded could be tended in the heat of battle.

Once the wagons were in position, we set off with axes and knives to cut down trees and thorn bushes, which were tied into bundles and packed underneath the wagons, filling the space completely. We secured the bundles to the wagons with chains so that they could not be removed. After a few hours our hands were cut and bleeding.

That evening Potgieter inspected our work. He tugged on branches from time to time to test their security. After walking around the perimeter twice, he declared himself well satisfied. "We are as ready as we will ever be, thank the Lord!" he said to Cilliers. "He has given us precious time in which to prepare. Now we must get the ammunition and powder into place. No matter how ready we may be, I still pray fervently that they will not come. We are just a handful of men and we would be very hard pressed to take on the might of the Matabele army." He sucked his lower lip thoughtfully as he gazed anxiously over the flattened grasslands.

Over the next few days Potgieter sent out groups of six to ten men early each morning to scout for the Matabele but there was no sign of them. The women busied themselves melting tin plates to make bullets and shot. They made small skin bags, each of which could hold about twelve lead slugs. These would be rammed down the barrels of the Sannas and burst in flight, providing a hail of hot lead from only one shot. Crosses were cut into the noses of the bullets. The four segments were then pinched together but these would separate when fired, each effectively becoming four bullets. Powder horns were filled and every spare Sanna was cleaned and readied for action.

Tables, chairs and kists were set up inside the laager and on these the women placed saucers of gunpowder, bullets and shot. Each man was allocated his own firing position next to his supply of ammunition and spare guns. Between the men were women who would keep the men supplied with loaded weapons. Each of us had two or three spare Sannas.

Abraham Swanepoel's wife was to stand between Jan and me. On the far side of Jan was the attractive Rachel Visser with her husband Floris next to her. There was an air of expectation in the laager as we waited for news of the Matabele.

For weeks, though, we heard nothing and so we settled into a pattern of mundane patrols and frustrating anticipation.

⊰ ⊰ ⊰

One evening as Jan and I were busy practising the loading and firing of our Sannas the other trekkers were attending a church service conducted by Sarel Cilliers. With hours of practice under my belt I had perfected my action to a point where I could load and fire six times in just sixty seconds. As we stood discussing our techniques, the wagons bathed in the light of a flaming red sun, I suddenly saw two black men running toward us. They were Bauteng tribesmen, their shouts carried to us on the gentle evening breeze.

As they drew near we saw their eyes, wide with fear. "Matabele! Matabele! The Matabele!" they shouted, pointing north.

Kommandant Potgieter, who was at prayer, was among the first to hear the warning. He stood and held up his hand, interrupting Cilliers. "The time has come," said Potgieter. "These men tell us that the Matabele are nigh. When we have finished our prayers we will send a small group to recconnoitre their position so that we may be ready for them. Sarel, lead us in the final prayer."

Cilliers sank to his knees, hands raised and eyes tightly closed, as he intoned, "Beloved Father. Grant us the courage to stand and fight in thy holy name. Please protect us Lord, from the heathen who approach. Grant us victory and protect our loved ones from all evil. Amen."

Twenty minutes later a group of five horsemen led by Potgieter and Cilliers galloped into the blackness of night in the direction of the Vaal in search of the Matabele. Jan and I sat up until midnight awaiting their return, but with no sign of them, rolled ourselves in our blankets to sleep.

The sun was already high next morning when the five tired riders returned. Their horses were damp with sweat; they had been ridden as hard as their hooves could pound the dry earth. "We have seen their fires. There are many thousands of them!" said Cilliers, as he swung off his horse and slapped the animal fondly on the rump, sending it off to drink.

"Thousands and thousands," added Potgieter. "We will watch their approach and we must make sure that we are ready. I think it will take a full two days for them to arrive. We must prepare. People, I will say it again: we must ready ourselves for the biggest test of our faith we have ever had to face."

The next day while we waited, Potgieter inspected his fighters and the positions over and over again. We checked and re-checked the thorn-bush fortifications. Disinfectant and bandages were placed at the ready in the four wagons of the inner fortress. Sannas were examined with painstaking care, gunpowder and shot were placed at each man's position and flagons of water filled to be ready at hand.

We readied ourselves to fight for our lives.

Chapter Sixteen

October 16th, 1836 dawned like any other day, with nothing to indicate the terrifying ordeal we were about to face. I woke while it was still dark and lay thinking about what was ahead as the deep blackness of night lightened slowly into a wispy light. A flare of red peeped over the eastern veld and I watched as it slowly ascended to wash the flattened, dew-covered grass in a soft morning glow. The veld sprang to life. Pigeons cooed, a loerie called, "Go-way! GO-WAY!" and small finches flitted, dived, chased and chirped as guineafowl called for companionship with cries that rattled like stones in a metal can. It was as if God wanted to show us goodness before demonstrating the evils of the world.

"Saddle up," I heard the command. All the horses were inside the laager, while the cattle and sheep had been left outside to fend for themselves under the watchful and sometimes not so watchful eyes of the Hottentots. I climbed onto Grey. There wasn't much talking and when men spoke it was in hushed tones. The air was thick with tension. Potgieter was taking twenty-five of us in a show of force to look for the Matabele and left but a handful to guard the laager with the women and children inside.

It was a beautiful, bright, blue-sky morning and I found it difficult to believe that anything could spoil such a day; not a cloud marred the immense space of the heavens above us. We topped a small rise and pulled up. I heard a sharp intake of breath from the men around me at the sight in front of us: a black sea, half a mile away, of thousands upon thousands of Matabele warriors, sitting on their shields in the veld. Their scouts had warned them of our approach and they were waiting for us. Sixteen thousand eyes watched as we stared back in horror. My heart raced. The massed warriors sat, row upon row, one hundred yards wide and one hundred men deep, a rippling, seething, black killing mass, with each regiment identified by different coloured shields with unique markings.

I felt fear like I had never felt fear.

Fear comes in many forms. It can be apprehensive butterflies in the stomach and the light moistening of the palms or heart-pounding dry-mouth fear. Then there is what I and probably all the others felt as we saw the Matabele that day: gut-wrenching, knee-shaking, vomit-making fear. We stank with fear. It smothered us with its claustrophobic cloak and seeped through our skin. I felt as if someone had slit open my chest, plucked my heart out and squeezed it, stopping the blood flow. I gasped as if an iron band had been placed around my chest. My gut heaved. I could feel sweat down my sides and I could hear my own breathing as if I had just run a mile as fast as my pounding lungs and straining legs could carry me.

I looked at Jan, his face ashen and his knuckles white as he clenched his reins.

"My God!" he said quietly.

Casper Kruger looked at Jan and replied in a hoarse whisper, "Call again Jan. We are going to need all the help He can provide. My God … I have never seen anything more terrifying."

Sarel Cilliers prayed, almost under his breath: "Our Father who art …"

And all looked as though they were staring into the very face of death.

The black army watched us. Nobody moved. Nobody spoke.

The heavy silence was broken only by the creak of leather and the shuffle of horses' hooves as they nervously shifted position. The rider next to me tried to swallow but his throat constricted and the silence was interrupted by a fit of coughing as he choked on his own spit.

The warriors were magnificent. Most of them wore headdresses of ostrich feathers, while the officers seated in front of their regiments were adorned with the feathers of the great blue crane. Around their shoulders they wore capes made of jackal skins or ostrich feathers and on their arms armlets of cow tails. Their kilts were made from the tails of monkeys and cats and their genitals protected by leather sheaths. Below the kilt a garter of cattle tails hung round their calves and on their feet buffalo-hide sandals with thongs securing them at the ankle. Each man had a five-foot-high ox-hide shield, a knobkerrie, a stabbing spear and two throwing assegais.

"God help us!" I heard a man whisper.

Cilliers looked at us and then back to the Matabele, "Never fear, God is with us." He didn't sound quite as sure as usual.

Potgieter held up his hand. "The rest of you stay here. Sarel and I will approach to parley for peace."

He called the Hottentot interpreter and the three of them walked their horses cautiously toward the Matabele, still sitting on their shields, silently watching. The three men stopped fifty yards from the simmering mass. Potgieter talked to the interpreter who nodded. There was dead silence. We watched, prayed and hoped against every faint hope that we would not have to fight.

The Hottentot translator addressed the Matabele in Zulu: "Why have you come to fight and kill us? We are here in peace. We do not wish war with you."

The Matabele stayed motionless. In front of the massed warriors a huge man, more yellow in colour than the rest, clambered to his feet. He wore a headdress of long blue-crane feathers. He waved his assegai in the air and roared. "Mzilikazi alone issues commands; we are his servants and we are here at his behest. We are not here to discuss or to argue. We are here to kill you … Mzilikazi!" he bellowed.

Eight thousand warriors leaped to their feet and as one roared out, "Mzilikazi!" The chant thundered across to us like an oncoming wave, immediately followed by a sound like water poured onto scorching-hot rocks: "Sssssssssssssssssssssssss …", the contemptuous hissing of thousands of warriors. Even the horses trembled at the sound. At the same moment, the mass of men started to move forward, breaking into two streams of angry blackness.

I heard Floris Visser say, in a voice hoarse as rough leather, "Oh, God! We don't stand a chance … Oh my God!"

The chilling bass cry of "Bulala ibhunu!" floated to us from the ranks of the approaching Matabele. Kill the boer, Kill the boer.

I noticed the front of Visser's breeches was wet.

"Pull back …" Potgieter shouted. "Quickly, quickly, pull back! Don't let them get behind us … if they do, we are finished. Look!" he said, pointing, "The horns of the beast. They are enclosing us between the two horns!" To ensure that we responded, he turned his horse, kicked its flanks and started to retreat in the direction of the wagons. We fell back, keeping ahead of the deadly embrace of the threatening horns.

Potgieter leaped from his horse, took aim and fired. I saw men fall. The seething mass paused and then as one screamed, rushing at us. We followed Potgieter's lead and dismounted. There was a volley of fire and as the acrid blue smoke drifted away I saw that at least another twenty warriors were down.

"On your horses!" shouted Cilliers.

We withdrew another fifty yards. "Reload," ordered Potgieter. We dismounted, reloaded and aimed again.

"Fire!" shouted Potgieter.

There was a roar from the guns. Smoke. Screams of anger and pain as another dozen fell. Again they paused and then again, "Sssssssssssss!" as we remounted and withdrew once more. Once out of range of the assegais we dismounted and again we fired. This time, when the smoke cleared another dozen warriors lay dead.

Retreat, dismount, load, fire, remount. Sixteen times we repeated this action before we neared the safety of the wagons. Hundreds of dead Matabele marked the route. My ears buzzed as though filled with cicada beetles from the repetitive hammering of the guns. I could smell myself: the smell of my own sour sweat—of fear.

The sun was directly overhead when the wagons hove into view. We galloped hard, our horses' hooves thundering over the dry ground, their ears flat. Bent low in the saddles, we whipped the horses for that extra ounce of speed that might bring us to safety as we raced toward the gap left for a single wagon. The Matabele had stopped on the far side of a small river, out of range of our guns.

As we neared the protection of the wagons and the horses started to slow, I heard a shout from Potgieter, "Hey! Where are you going? What on earth is going on?"

I glanced over my shoulder as I entered the narrow opening. Floris Visser, Marthinus van der Merwe junior and Louw du Plessis had galloped through the opening and were riding as fast as their horses could carry them in the direction of Thaba Nchu.

"Come back, you cowards," roared Potgieter.

Cilliers joined him, staring in disbelief after the departing men. "You swine!" he yelled, "Come back!" His shouts faded into the distance, making no impression on the departing trio.

We thundered into the ring of wagons and jumped from our horses amid a cloud of dust.

"Quick! Get ready ... the Matabele are here," commanded Potgieter.

Willing hands pulled the last wagon into place, sealing off the entrance. We crowded to the wagons and peered out. The Matabele were waiting on the other side of the river. A group of them could be seen rounding up about eighty of our cattle which had been left outside the laager. We watched as they slaughtered the beasts and shared out pieces of the raw meat, the fresh blood from the cattle running through their fingers and spilling from their mouths.

While we watched I heard Rachel Visser whisper to Jan, "What has happened? Why has my man run away?"

"He was scared ... we all were ... we are still scared, for that matter."

She snorted in derision as she gazed out at the Matabele sharpening their spears on rocks by the river while they gorged themselves on the warm, raw meat.

"The cowardly bastard!" she spat contemptuously, not bothering to whisper. "I should never have married him. He's not a man; he has never been a man. You and Rauch didn't run away, did you? And him with a family here! I always knew he was a coward but to run away and leave us all like this! I can't believe it. I'll get him for this. He has disgraced me!" She had a strange look on her face as she paused, looking first at Jan and then at me.

"You two are real men … it's a long time since I felt a real man. Maybe the two of you would like to show me what a man feels like?"

Jan glanced at me disbelievingly. I looked at Rachel. Despite being about twelve years older than us she was an attractive woman. Her brown eyes were wide and bright and her black hair, pulled back from her face and tied at the back, showed off high cheek bones and a full mouth which curled slightly at the corner. She was waiting for an answer.

My eyes glanced down to her large upright breasts which even her apron could not disguise. I glanced around the wagons. Men were staring out at the Matabele and getting themselves ready for the attack. Nobody else had noticed the exchange between Rachel and the two of us. After the morning's encounter with the Matabele and in view of what was still to come I was full of adrenaline.

"Why not?" I thought "She is certainly appealing enough even though she is a tannie. And anyway, this might be the last time I ever have sex."

Jan studied me as I looked at Rachel.

"Do you mean … you mean right now, Tannie?" I asked.

She nodded and her smile broadened, showing neat white teeth.

I swallowed hard. "Both of us?"

She nodded, "One at a time. Who gets to be first?"

Everybody had their eyes on the Matabele. Nobody had heard. I glanced at the warriors still sitting on the far bank of the river. We had at least an hour before the attack. My heart pounded with a different excitement. The tension in the air contributed to a hardness which I felt pushing against my breeches.

She nodded in the direction of one of the wagons and said, "I take it that's a yes? You will find me in there waiting for you. Be quick!" Without waiting for a reply she went, her long skirts swishing as her hips swung invitingly.

Jan looked at me. "Is she serious? Who gets to go first? I'm not too keen about second place."

I grinned. "I think she's deadly serious ... we'll soon find out, won't we? Let's draw for it." I picked two stalks of grass, shortened one and held one in each fist. "Short straw goes second." Jan tapped the hand with the longer piece of grass. I opened my hand and before he could compare the two, dropped the shorter one into the grass. "Bad luck ... you go second ... I go first."

Jan opened his mouth to argue but I turned on my heel and strode in the direction of the Visser wagon. I climbed into the wagon and pulled the canvas behind me. The interior was dark and for a second or two I stood waiting for my eyes to adjust to the gloom. A candle cast shadows which danced on the canvas ceiling above me. Rachel stood naked next to the bed. The flickering light played on her full breasts, highlighting dark brown nipples which stood out like corks.

"I'm glad it's you," she said with a smile. "Quick, take off your things. We don't have a lot of time." She lay down on the bed.

As I stripped I wondered when last Floris and she had used the bed as we were about to. I left my long underwear on and I could feel myself bulging in the front.

"No, take everything off," she whispered urgently. "I want to see you."

I pulled off my underwear and stood naked next to the bed. Her eyes widened in surprise as she took in my erection fuelled by adrenaline and lust.

"I really have been wasting my time. Come here, I have to have that." She was lying on her back, knees slightly raised. The desire in her face had flushed her cheeks. Her eyes sparkled as her lips parted. "Come here … I want you in my mouth. I want to taste you first." I could see that her hand was rubbing the dark patch between her legs.

She opened her mouth and I slipped the head into it. Her eyes widened as her lips tightened. She moved her head back and forth, sliding her mouth up and down the shaft. Her teeth nibbled the edge of the head and the sensation sent shivers up my spine. The sound of my breathing filled the wagon.

"Now … in me!" she commanded.

I knelt between her legs as she opened herself for me. One hand clutched my cock and guided it into the waiting wetness. As I pushed into her, she moaned in satisfaction, "Ahhhhhh!" Her legs came around me and for a few minutes we drove deep into each other, without emotion, just hard sex. She arched her hips and pushed against me as I pumped into her. Our breath came in short gasps. The sweat was running off me. I could feel it trickling down my back. She had beads of sweat above her lips and moaned with every thrust I made. Her hands kneaded my buttocks and her nails clawed them with delight as I slid in and out of her.

"Aggh!" "Aagh!" "Aagh!" she cried each time my thrust reached its hilt.

I heard Jan outside. "Hurry up. You're taking too long. I want my turn as well."

His pleas spurred us on. A new intensity crept into our animal lust. She arched her back higher and her moans became shouts. "Yes! Yes! More! Yes! Oh, yes! Oh, I never knew that it could be like this … Harder! Harder … pleeeease! Oh my Lord. Don't give me a baby, no, don't stop. Ahhhhh, go. Go! Go! I love it, please come in me … I am coming!" At this last shout she arched herself so high off the bed I was almost thrown off. I could feel the approaching orgasm. I came inside her. I started to shiver with ecstasy just as she cried out. "Now! Now! Go!" She pushed hard against me and shuddered. The waters burst from the canyon and filled her as she shouted "Gggg ... oo ... dddd! Agggghhhhhh!" Then it was done.

"Thank you! Oh my God" she said softly as she relaxed. Both of us were soaked with each other's sweat. "I hope you haven't given me a baby."

So did I.

The canvas across the doorway was pulled aside. Light flooded in. It was Jan. "Come on. I can't wait any longer. I want my turn!"

I was still lying between her legs and without looking up, I said, "Wait outside Jan. We haven't finished yet."

I lowered myself down her body. I heard Jan's clothes fall on the floor behind me. My mouth licked down her stomach and down to the wet, sticky patch between her legs. My tongue licked and probed. Rachel had one leg straight and the foot of the other resting below the knee. My tongue and lips sucked at her pinkness. I glanced up at her face. Her expression was one of absolute delight.

I felt a hand on my shoulder. Jan pulled me back. "Come on Rauch. My turn. Get off her!" He pulled me onto the floor and stood over me, naked, his cock standing erect above me. He lowered himself onto the bed and I saw Rachel open her legs for him. As he entered her with a shout of pleasure I grabbed my clothes and hastily turned away and dressed, disappointed that Rachel had responded to Jan as she had to me. As I dressed I couldn't resist a glance at the thrusting couple. Jan pumped two or three times and then with a groan collapsed on Rachel. The waiting had been too much; he was finished. My mind flashed back to the days when I used to watch Pa. I felt the same hollow feeling in the pit of my stomach and despite not wanting to watch, I was aroused when I saw Jan's hand and fingers move down to her black triangle as she widened her legs for him and lay waiting with a sensuous look on her face. He started to rub her. She was moaning. I put my hand on myself and started to rub. I looked at Rachel. Her sleepy eyes watched me.

She said to Jan, "Come on … again! I want you in me … not your fingers. I haven't finished yet."

I watched as Jan held his soft cock in his left hand and tried to guide it into her. Rachel wriggled and tried to assist but he could not enter her.

"Wait, Wait!" said Jan. He could see the impatience on Rachel's face. At this stage I had no sense of embarrassment and was enjoying my own pleasure.

"Come on Rauch, if he can't do it, I want you again," she said, dismissing Jan who looked crestfallen. I needed no further encouragement. As I pulled my breeches down again and my cock leaped out, I moved to her. Jan climbed off her and started to pull on his clothes. I knelt between her bent knees and had the tip against her waiting lips when the wagon was flooded with light.

The figure of Sarel Cilliers filled the entrance.

We made a strange sight. I looked around. Jan had his breeches around his knees, while I was kneeling in front of the naked Rachel.

"What in God's name is going on here?" he exclaimed as he looked at Jan and then at my naked back between Rachel's knees.

"Nothing, Oom Sarel," said Jan.

"Nothing? Nothing! Don't talk nonsense. Do you think I am blind? There is plenty going on. What on earth are you three doing?"

I blurted out the first thing that came into my head. "We are praying," I said as I grabbed my trousers. Rachel pulled the covers over her naked body and stared wide eyed at Sarel.

His face was red with anger. He looked as though he was going to explode. "Nothing? Nothing? Praying? Are you mad?" he shook his head with disbelief. "Praying? How can you say such a terrible thing? May God forgive you! And you," he said, looking at Rachel, "do you know no shame? First your husband runs away and now you are busy fornicating, not with one but with two young men! They are young enough to be your children. Shame on you! You have disgraced the name of your family. I came looking for you to tell you to get into position at the wagons. The Matabele will attack any time now. We need every person ... every person, even you!" With that he stormed out of the wagon.

Rachel covered her mouth with her hand but her eyes were laughing. Jan and I hurriedly pulled on our clothes and started to giggle. Soon all three of us were guffawing out loud. Jan lay on the floor, tears streaming down his cheeks while I was doubled over, clutching my aching stomach. When we could control our laughter we climbed from the wagon and took up our positions, too embarrassed to glance sideways at the other trekkers.

The excitement and lust of the last hour evaporated rapidly, quickly replaced by fear as we peered nervously out at the Matabele. They had crossed the stream and were moving in a great wave of many thousands toward the wagons.

Chapter Seventeen

The Matabele regiments were drawing nearer but Sarel Cilliers and Kommandant Potgieter found time to engage in an earnest whispered conversation before Potgieter came across to me. "God will punish you," he said. "And I will deal with you both when this is all over. With any luck I won't have to do anything; the Matabele might do God's work for me."

Rachel watched the exchange. She raised an eyebrow but I didn't respond.

Cilliers stood next to the wagons we had positioned in the centre. "Gather round everybody. Let us ask God for His protection."

Thirty-seven of us, including seven boys no older than twelve, formed a circle around Cilliers as he prayed. "No one is to make a sound, no matter what happens and no matter how frightened you are. Noise will only drive the savages to greater effort." He paused and then in a softer tone, said, "Let us pray … I pray from Psalm fifty, verse fifteen. He lowered his head and closed his eyes: "Call upon me in the day of trouble; I will deliver thee and thou shalt glorify me."

"Amen!" we responded softly.

As Cilliers walked past me he turned to me and said in a low voice. "I suggest that you read the next eight verses, so that you may know what God thinks of you."

"I will."

We went back to our positions. I glanced to my right. Rachel had again pulled her hair back and was wearing the severe kappie all the trekker women wore. I found it hard to believe that only half an hour earlier I had been lying between her thighs. I shook my head and smiled at the thought. Her husband's flight had been our good fortune.

We waited in the hot sun. Several hours passed. It seemed as if even the birds and insects had fled. All that could be heard was the hot silence broken by the tick … tick … tick of the contracting metal and wood as the wagons baked in the sun. We gazed out at the Matabele who had formed up smartly in their regiments, row upon row, surrounding the wagons. They sat on their shields out of range of our Sannas and stared. Still no attack came.

"Why don't they come?" Jan whispered across to me.

I shrugged and watched. The fear that I had felt earlier that day had replaced all lust and passion. I whispered, "I don't think we are going to get out of this alive!"

His face was white and the hands holding his Sanna trembled. I could see that he shared my view.

"If that's the case, I'm glad we did what we did," said Rachel, smiling at me.

"So am I," I said.

"Me too," added Jan.

The tension was becoming unbearable. "I wish they'd come," I said to nobody in particular.

Koos Potgieter, the kommandant's brother, leaped to his feet and shouted, "If die I must, die I will, but I cannot stand this waiting any longer!" He waved a piece of red cloth attached to a long pole at the Matabele. The massed warriors responded with a roar of rage. One of the lieutenants jumped up, waving a red shield at us. This was the signal for eight thousand warriors to spring to their feet. In front of them the giant, the lighter-skinned warrior danced, jumped and gesticulated as he encouraged the circle of warriors to attack. As one they shouted, "Bulala!" and surged toward us.

Cilliers sighted down his Sanna. "Wait for me to fire," he shouted to make himself heard above the noise.

Thirty yards from us, the yellowish warrior jumped into the air and screamed. He waved his shield in the air while the leopard tails swung and danced from his body as he incited his warriors. At that moment Cilliers fired the first shot. It smashed into the warrior's chest. He crumpled to the ground without ever finishing the dance.

A fusillade of fire from thirty-seven guns crackled out as the Matabele surged screaming over the body of their leader. The noise was deafening. We fired, reloaded and fired. Loaded weapons were constantly passed to us as the women loaded the waiting guns while we shot. There was a continuous staccato of firing.

I would fire, put out my hand and shout, "Gee! Give!" A newly loaded weapon would be put into my hand by one of the women. I would fire and again shout, "Gee!"

Matabele fell and lay twitching only yards in front of the wagons. Smoke and dust rose from the laager. Shouts and screams could be heard and despite Cilliers's warning I could hear the sounds of women and children sobbing in terror from the wagons in the centre. The smell of gunpowder seared my nostrils and I could taste the saltpeter on my lips. For the longest hour, the battle raged. Time and again the Matabele threw themselves at the wagons but the wall of fire from our guns drove them back. Thick, acrid smoke enveloped us, so thick it was hard to see. My eyes watered. I became disorientated, lost in a world of fear and determination, drowned in a wild sea of smoke, the rattle of gunfire, the screams and wails of terror.

The Matabele were close to breaching our defences. I saw a warrior hacking at the bushes we had tied together under the wagons. I shot him. As I did, I heard a shriek from Mrs Abraham Swanepoel nearby. I turned. Out of the corner of my eye I saw something black like a thick snake, with five moving heads, twitch, jerk and crawl in the grass in front of me. I swung my Sanna around and blasted the object which stopped all movement as the lead blew it to fleshy fragments. I looked at Mrs Swanepoel who was holding an axe with bright red blood dripping down the blade. She had her hand over her mouth, her eyes wide with horror as she gazed at the warrior lying in front of her. She had hacked his arm clean off. Blood gushed from the stump. I finished him off with a shot at point-blank range and went back to my rhythm of firing outward between the wagons.

A warrior clambered over a wagon canvas toward Rachel. "Look out Rachel!" I screamed.

She spun round. She saw the danger, grabbed a pot off the fire behind her and poured the boiling water over her assailant's head. His face erupted into a giant blister. His hands came up to cover his eyes and he screamed. His scream of pain died in his throat as the slug from my Sanna smashed into him.

"Gee!" Shoot. "Gee!" Shoot. The dead were piling up around the laager. And still the warriors kept coming. "Gee!" Shoot. "Gee!" Shoot.

The canvases of the wagons were punctured with holes where assegais had torn them. Two men and three women were lying on the ground receiving medical attention. When the Matabele realized that they couldn't penetrate our defences they began to throw their assegais over the wagons like javelins, raining down a shower of death, wounding horses and some of the women. We fired and fired and fired.

Over the din I heard the voice of Potgieter, as if from a great distance, "Cease firing! Don't waste your ammunition!"

We stopped. The silence was eerie. We stared out over the piles of bodies that surrounded the wagons like a black wall. Bodies lay piled several high in grotesque positions with frozen expressions on their faces, some only a yard from the wagons.

The Matabele were in retreat.

As they moved off they herded our animals with them. Great clouds of dust marked their progress as their leader, Kalipi, one of Mzilikazi's abler generals, led the remainder of his troops to safety with all our livestock. We looked around at each other's blackened faces as if seeing each other for the first time. Then someone let out a cheer, followed by another, and another. Soon we were all cheering at the tops of our voices, slapping each other on the back, waving our hats, hugging and kissing everybody with the sheer, blessed relief of being alive.

"Come people. Let us give thanks to our God," implored Cilliers. He whipped off his hat and fell on one knee in the middle of the laager, leading us in a prayer of thanksgiving. The background silence was broken by the sounds of more than one woman sobbing quietly in the hospital wagon.

Cilliers had scarcely started the prayers before Potgieter interrupted him, "It's not over yet," he shouted. "Get back to your positions!"

We hurried back to our places and peered out. The Matabele had withdrawn beyond the range of our guns. They were sitting on their shields while their leaders berated them.

Jacobus Potgieter stood up and shouted at the waiting warriors. "Come, you bunch of toothless old women … come, attack us again!"

Back came the response, translated by one of the Hottentot servants: "Come out from your houses on wheels. Come out and fight like real men."

We watched and waited. My shoulder ached, bruised by the repeated kicks from the butt of my Sanna. My hands and face were black with gunpowder as I gazed out over the wall of corpses which were already covered with buzzing green and black flies. The sun beat down.

"Dead men don't sweat," growled Potgieter as he discharged his musket into the body of a prostrate warrior.

We immediately began checking the bodies for signs of life. Jan, Flip Viljoen, Petrus Steyn and I went outside the laager with our Sannas charged and ready, inspecting each body for fresh sweat. When we found a live one, we put the barrel to his head and dispatched him into the next world, accompanied by hisses of contempt from the watching Matabele. Splattered with blood and flesh, we returned to our wagons.

There were two more attempts by the Matabele but our wall of fire drove them back each time. They had lost all heart for the battle; hundreds of warriors lay dead around the wagons. On our side, Potgieter's brother, Nikolaas, and Pieter Botha both lay where they had fallen.

Sounds of crying and wailing came from the wagons in the centre of the laager where fourteen trekkers lay seriously wounded. Their moans of pain were chilling to hear. I saw Cilliers limping out of the wagon with a bandaged thigh which had taken a Matabele assegai. He looked at me with contempt as he limped past, "You fought bravely, Beukes, but I can never forgive you for what you were doing beforehand. I only hope the Lord can."

I made no response.

Although we had driven off the Matabele the cost had been high. Apart from the few dead and the wounded we had lost all our animals. One of the small Liebenberg boys was missing. A child from a different branch of the Liebenberg family massacred on the banks of the Vaal, he had been herding cattle when the attack began and had not been seen since. We watched as the Matabele, with our six thousand cattle and fifty thousand sheep and goats, withdrew northward. A red dust cloud hung in the air, marking their path. We counted nearly twelve hundred assegais that had been thrown into the circle of wagons. Some of the canvas wagon coverings lay in shreds. Piet Niewenhuizen's wagon had three hundred and seventy-two holes from the attack, or so he told us later.

Sarel Cilliers stood on the back of a wagon and called us together. "Kom kêrels. Come, boys, come and give thanks!"

We assembled, men with white rings around their eyes sunk into blackened faces. Our clothes were stained with sweat and blood; women wore the white streaks of tear stains that trickled down their gunpowdered faces. Some moved like the living dead, their eyes vacant, as though the surreal events of the past hours had wiped from their minds any ability to think.

Cilliers held up his hands, closed his eyes and turned his face to the heavens. "I read from Psalm one hundred and eighteen ..."

O give thanks unto the Lord, for He is good

Because His mercy endureth forever ...

I called upon the Lord in distress

The Lord answered me and set me in a large place

The Lord is on my side

I will not fear

What can man do unto me?

They compassed me like bees

They are quenched as the fire of thorns

For in the name of the Lord I will destroy them

Thou has thrust sore at me that I might fall

But the Lord helped me

The Lord is my strength and song

And is my salvation …

I shall not die, but live

And declare the works of the Lord

The Lord hath chastened me sore

But He hath not given me over to death …

Amen.

A few hours later as the sun gently slid below the horizon, Cilliers conducted a burial service in the deepening dusk. Two graves were dug in a marshy area a few hundred yards from the wagons for the two men felled in battle. As he prayed for deliverance for their souls we stared at the two corpses wrapped in canvas, neatly positioned like logs waiting to be rolled into the fresh graves.

Jan spoke my thoughts as he whispered, "They could have been us."

"If Cilliers and Potgieter had had their way, it *would* have been us," I responded.

"Fortunately the Lord didn't heed their request," said Jan.

The moans of the wounded and the sobs of the women traumatized by battle and death could be heard from the wagons over the prayers.

That night Potgieter ordered us to stand to our posts in case the Matabele returned. I was peering out, seeking for any sign of Matabele late that night, when to my great shock a small figure appeared, his white face shining in the moonlight. Clambering over the wall of Matabele corpses, nine-year-old Barend Liebenberg was still carrying his cowhide sjambok.

"It's Barend! It's Barend!" I heard young Paul Kruger shout, "Barend. He's alive!"

Again a ragged cheer went up from the perimeter of the wagons as the young boy, sobbing with emotion, was returned to the grateful arms of his mother. He told an astonished but delighted audience that when he saw the Matabele massing he had decided to hide in a small cave he'd discovered next to the river.

"Praise the Lord. Praise the Lord!" cried Sarel Cilliers.

That same night another figure crept shamefacedly into the laager. This time there were no cheers of welcome; it was Floris Visser. I wondered how long it would be before he heard about us and his wife.

Two days after the battle Potgieter gathered us all together. "I have received news that the Matabele are still moving north. It is unlikely that they will attack us again. However, Mzilikazi must be crushed, so as soon as we are able, I will lead an attack against him and finish him off for good. In the meantime I am sending Jakobus Potgieter with two servants to Thaba Nchu to see if we can get assistance from Chief Moroko of the Baroleng. We have no cattle so we cannot trek further and I am told that the children are already in need of milk. Hopefully he can bring us some milking cows and some oxen. We will have to stay here until help arrives."

Cilliers again led us in prayer and as he concluded, he proudly announced that he would name the hill that overlooked the site of the battle. "I name this koppie, Vegkop!" It was apt: the hill of the fight.

Potgieter was right. We were stranded: without oxen we could not move our wagons. The first few days after the battle we busied ourselves cleaning up and repairing the damage caused by the Matabele. But morale was low. Many of the women were still in a state of shock. The sight of the corpses piled around the wagons, covered in flies and being eaten by jackals and hyenas, with vultures circling lazily above, added to the sombre mood. The stench of rotting bodies became overwhelming as the sun beat down relentlessly. By the fourth day we had to cover our noses with cloth.

That evening, as I walked over to the fire in the middle of the laager, I stumbled on something hidden in the grass. It was a black leg that had been dragged in by the dogs. I recoiled and landed on something soft: the remains of an arm with part of a man's shoulder still attached. My stomach heaved. I went to see Potgieter. "We have to do something about the stink and look over there …" I pointed in the direction of the torn-off limbs.

"We can't move the wagons without oxen; we have to wait till help comes."

"Well, I am going to do something … come on, Jan."

We mounted our horses and, followed by young Paulus Kruger and some of the younger boys and the Hottentot servants, rode over to the corpses with bandanas covering our faces. We hooked ropes around the bodies and dragged them two hundred yards downwind before dumping them in a donga. This ghastly task took us the next two days but at least the stench was reduced.

That night two new problems kept us from sleep: the desperate wails of babies needing milk and the sounds of lions, jackals and hyenas as they growled and fought over the feast of rotting human flesh. By next morning our situation had become so desperate that we manhandled the wagons, one at a time, closer to the stream and farther away from the open grave of the Matabele. Food was in short supply. We feared another attack from the Matabele—despite Potgieter's assurances that they had moved north—so we could not leave the wagons to hunt, and such water as we could get from the stream was contaminated by the rotting corpses dragged there by the predators. The situation deteriorated daily. We lay listlessly in the shade of the wagons. Barely anyone spoke and when they did it was in whispers. Our throats were parched, our lips were cracked and our tongues felt swollen.

Fifteen days after the battle of Vegkop, early in the morning, the cries of the hungry and thirsty women and children were broken by a hoarse shout from the sentry. "Get your guns! They are coming back."

But Potgieter shouted out: "They're not Matabele … they wouldn't come from the south … that's help from Thaba Nchu!"

"Praise the Lord!" said Cilliers as he gazed at the dust cloud over the approaching trek oxen and milking cows. "Praise the Lord! Let us give thanks to the Almighty!" Falling on his knees he clasped his hands together.

We whistled and waved our hats in the air. Some even fired shots of joy into the air which were quickly answered by the group accompanying the cattle. Salvation had come in the form of Reverend Archbell and our friend Moroko, Chief of the Baroleng. I ran to saddle my horse to ride out to greet the rescuers and I ran straight into Rachel. I hadn't spoken to her since the day of the battle. She and Floris had kept themselves very scarce and on the few occasions I had been close enough to talk, Floris was right there, next to her. Maybe it was only my guilty conscience but I was sure that he'd looked at me with hate in his eyes.

"Hello Rauch … how are you?" She forced a smile from her cracked lips.

"Hello Rachel … er … aahm… Tannie, are you alright, Tannie?"

"Yes, I'm fine now that help is here, thank you. As long as the two of you haven't made me pregnant that is." I was taken aback by her matter-of-fact tone. "Let me know if you would like to visit me again … I was most impressed," she said. "Just be careful of Floris … I think he will kill you if he finds out."

I made a mental note to stay well out of his way.

"It looks like it is all over doesn't it?"

"For now. For now, Tannie. I'll keep in mind what you've said. Hopefully everything isn't quite over yet."

She smiled as she got my meaning and strolled off to her wagon.

The women and children were the first to be transported to Thaba Nchu, the rest of us followed a few days later. As only two hundred trek oxen had been sent for our fifty wagons, the wagons had to be pulled in relays of fifteen at a time. Without a full span of oxen for each wagon, the going was much slower than usual. Potgieter ordered Jan and me to go with the first group. I think he just wanted us out of his sight. On our journey back to Thaba Nchu I pondered my future. I would soon be back with Pa and Amelia, a complication which filled my heart with dread. I also realized that I could not continue as a member of the Potgieter trek. He had made it very clear what he thought of Jan and me ... and, of course, of Tannie Rachel. In any event I had decided that I wanted to join the Natal trekkers. Besides, I reasoned to myself, Potgieter and Cilliers were too wrapped up in their God for my liking. My future was, at the very least, uncertain.

Little did I know that my whole world was about to be turned on its head.

ঙ্কচ্কঙ্ক

At Thaba Nchu there must have been close to two thousand wagons clustered, like a small town, on the slopes of the mountain. News of our victory against the Matabele at Vegkop had already spread like a veld fire. As we drew nearer, people stopped whatever they were doing and ran to give us a hero's welcome. We must have looked like a returning fleet of warships after a titanic battle, with tattered white canvases flapping in the breeze. People waved their hats as cheers floated above the creaking harnesses and the rumble of the wagon wheels. Gunshots were fired in jubilation. There were shouts of joy and excitement as people jumped up and down, craning their necks to get a better view of us. Fathers carried their children on their shoulders, while older children ran alongside as we rumbled to a vacant piece of land at the far edge of the settlement.

"Well done!"

"God has saved you!"

"You are heroes!"

"Welcome back!"

"Praise the Lord!"

"The Lord's will is done!"

"Thank you all!"

"You gave those heathen a proper hiding!"

The cries rang out as we passed. People touched our wagons with awe as if expecting some magical protection to rub off on them. Some of the smaller boys grabbed the lead reins to have the privilege of guiding our heroic convoy safely home. Near the open space where we had selected to outspan, the figure of a familiar man stood in front of a light blue wagon, waving his arms as if trying to catch the sky. And next to him, a bundle in her arms, stood a woman.

As we came closer, I recognized the woman. I couldn't believe my eyes: it was Marietjie! Gerrit Maritz stood beside her. As the wagons crawled across the veld surrounded by well-wishers I did not take my eyes off her. She saw me and shifted the bundle she was carrying onto one arm so she could wave with the other. A warm smile lit up her face, which was a great deal thinner than when last I had seen her. My heart hammered a greeting against my chest and my stomach tensed with excitement. I jumped off the wagon and ran to Maritz and Marietjie. Roddy was nowhere in sight. Marietjie stood smiling, waiting for me to reach her. I stopped in front of her.

"Hello Rauch," she said.

I was on the point of grabbing her and kissing her when I stopped myself. Instead I smiled. I gazed at her and then at Maritz: "Hello Marietjie. Hello Meneer Maritz. I wasn't expecting to see either of you here!"

Maritz answered. "Good to see you, Rauch. Sounds like you all had a lucky escape at Vegkop?"

"Not according to Sarel Cilliers. Naturally luck had nothing to do with it. We were protected by the Lord."

Maritz, who as usual looked very dapper, raised an eyebrow with a cynical smile. "I was hoping that he and Potgieter had softened their religious fanaticism but I suppose that's too much to expect, isn't it?" When Maritz saw my eyes were still on Marietjie and that I was not paying attention to anything he said, he added, "The Bronkhorst family and Roddy and Marietjie came up with me. We arrived here a few days ago and we will join up with Potgieter and Cilliers. There is much unhappiness in the colony; as we speak more people are on the way. I've heard tell that Retief is also likely to arrive."

I could feel Marietjie's eyes on me as I tried to appear unflustered, focused on what Maritz was saying. I wished he'd disappear so that I could talk to Marietjie alone. I guessed what was in the bundle and could hardly contain my excitement.

Maritz went on. "Where is Kommandant Potgieter? I need to talk to him. There are strong rumours that the English, the missionaries in particular, turned Mzilikazi against the trekkers and that is why they attacked you. I need to talk to the kommandant."

"He's in the second wagon, there," I said, pointing to a wagon thirty yards away.

"Ah, so he is. We will talk again later, Rauch. We have much to catch up on."

I nodded without taking my eyes off Marietjie as he took his leave. "I wish I could hold you and kiss you. I thought I would never see you again," I said softly.

"Me too, but it would not be wise. We are being watched. Later perhaps. Look!" she said as she opened the blanket covering the bundle in her arms. I leaned forward to see the baby. Two little faces peered out at me, blinking in the bright sunlight. One baby was much larger than the other.

"Twins? But why are they so different in size?"

"No, not twins, Rauch." She looked down at the babies. "There is seven months between them. André was born in December … on the twenty-fourth, to be exact, very soon after you left. And Anton was born on the tenth of July … he is only four months while André is nearly a year."

"I don't understand. How could you …?" I left the sentence unfinished as I began to guess the answer.

"They are both your sons. The older one is Katrina's and the younger is mine. Rauch, you are their father."

I didn't know whether to laugh or cry. "My God! Two sons! I don't believe it!" I laughed out loud. "How come you have both of them? Where is Katrina? Is she also here?"

The smile that had lit Marietjie's face disappeared. "You don't know?"

"Know what?" I said, still chuckling.

"Katrina is dead."

My knees turned to jelly and I felt sick. "Dead?"

Marietjie nodded. "Did no one tell you? Oh, I'm so sorry Rauch. I assumed you knew. It was a few months back."

"How? What happened?"

She looked away as she tucked the blanket around the little bodies. "She was working for us at the time. Do you remember her family had worked for us a long time ago? After you left she started drinking heavily and of course she was trying to earn a living … in the way, in the way you know. Anyway, we decided we would help her and we took her in as a servant."

"Yes, yes but how did she die?"

Marietjie looked at me with sympathy in her eyes. "She killed herself, Rauch."

I went cold. "Oh my God! Are you sure? Why, why?"

"Look, we can't talk now. Meet me at eight tonight … next to Maritz's wagon. I will try to get out … by then Roddy will be drunk and hopefully asleep. If I am not there tonight go there every night at the same time until I come. I must warn you, Roddy knows that you are the father ... but he is the only one. He beats me because of it and hates your sons, particularly little André. He calls them 'Rauch's little bastards'. I think he will try and kill you if you are not careful ... look here ..." She pulled up her sleeve; her arm was black and blue, bruised from the shoulder to the elbow.

"The bastard!" I breathed.

As she turned to leave, I implored, "Before you go, Marietjie, tell me, how did she die?"

"She hanged herself ... I will tell you more when we can talk properly. She adored you ... you know that, don't you?"

A wave of overpowering guilt and sadness swept over me as Marietjie turned on her heel and disappeared into the maze of wagons that covered the plains beneath the mountain.

I had to wait three nights before she came to the rendezvous. I was about to give up when she emerged from the shadows. I took her in my arms and pulled her close to me. Our mouths met in a long and tender kiss. I could feel her body against me, her arms tight around my neck, pulling me to her.

"Oh Rauch, I love you so. It is so wonderful to see you again. I thought you had gone forever and now here you are. I can't believe it!"

We kissed and held each other close for a long time. I pushed her gently away, held her hand and looked into her eyes. "Tell me first about Roddy. Does he really beat you?"

She nodded, bit her bottom lip. "Ever since he was injured he has had terrible mood swings. One day he seems fine then the next he behaves like a madman. When that happens he hits me and hurts me ... always on the body so that it can't be seen. Usually after he has been drinking ... which is every day ... sometimes worse than others. Even when he is not violent he shouts at me and ridicules me. He hates the boys because they are your sons. One day I thought I caught him trying to drown André. I fear for our sons' lives and I hate him. He's a pig and a coward. I should never have married him but I felt so guilty at the time and so sorry for him. Now there's no escape. He is evil and I can't get away from him. It's not really his fault, I suppose. He is sick. His injuries have made him mad. He keeps saying that if your paths cross he will kill you for fathering the child he couldn't give me … now you are here. I am scared for you … and for us too."

I felt helpless and changed the subject. "Tell me what happened to Katrina."

"She used to get fits of depression. You know what she was like. I mean, she was as rough as hippo hide but underneath her tough exterior she had a heart of gold. She loved you and I always felt guilty because she knew that I loved you as well. Because you wouldn't accept her child as yours, she got more and more depressed. She drank heavily and of course was the delight of many, many men." She glanced at me to gauge my reaction. "There were lots of men and lots of stories … including, so I am told, your pa, before he and Amelia went north."

"My Pa … my God! He can't keep his hands off a pretty woman."

"Anyway, after one drinking spell she was found hanging from the rafters in her room." She paused and then added, "Found by Roddy."

"By Roddy? … surely not? He can't, I mean … isn't Roddy impotent? What would he have been doing with her?"

She shrugged and looked at me. "He is … as far as our relationship is concerned … but who knows? We have never made love; he was injured before we were married."

"What a terrible story. I seem to leave a trail of destruction behind me, don't I? First I killed Dirk and now I'm responsible for Katrina's death."

Marietjie did not reply.

"And now? Why are you here? Where will you go from here?"

"We came with my parents … you remember my pa was friendly with Maritz … he even helped get you a job there, didn't he?"

It all seemed so very long ago.

"Well, my pa was asked to join Meneer Maritz ... there was nothing there for me after you left, so Roddy and I came with Maritz as well. He has been good to us."

"And now, will you go north or over the mountains to the coast ... to Natal, as they call it?"

"I don't think that's decided yet. There seems to be a great deal of discussion. For me it makes no difference ... except now that I have found you I want to be near you ... even if I am married to Roddy. Also, I have the two boys to care for. I am not going to let Roddy force me to give them up. What will you do?"

I shrugged. "All I know is that the religious fervour of Potgieter and Cilliers is too much for me. I think Jan and I might link up with Maritz. I like Maritz; he is more my type of person ... and anyway, Potgieter and Cilliers aren't too fond of Jan and me." I didn't explain further and certainly didn't mention Rachel.

We talked in whispers for an age as we held each other close. I was troubled by all that Marietjie had told me. I was ashamed by the news of Katrina and saddened by Marietjie's desperate life with Roddy. Before she left we made passionate love under the blue wagon. We arranged to try and meet at the blue wagon every second night. I kissed her for a long time before she slipped away into the darkness.

Chapter Eighteen

For a brief few months there was calm and normal daily life prevailed for the pioneers on the Great Trek. More than two thousand wagons were spread out over a vast area, each group's wagons huddled around its leader's. Potgieter and his supporters gathered near the Modder River while Maritz and others were congregated in the lee of Thaba Nchu. Life settled into a routine. Days were spent hunting and fields were planted with crops. There was an air of permanence. Some people talked of staying in the area. There was enough water, the natives were friendly and land was plentiful.

Our tranquillity was to be short lived.

Petty jealousies arose with an ensuing power struggle between the two major leaders, Potgieter and Maritz, over the appointment of a minister to administer to the trekkers' religious needs. The argument about whether to go north and join up with Trichardt or over the mountains into the land of the Zulu, split the migrants into factions. Debates raged and frequently erupted into fist fights. The most contentious issue was the appointment of the minister. Maritz had arrived with Erasmus Smit who was married to his sister. Smit was not ordained but was well qualified in every other respect, although he had a severe drinking problem. Smit wanted the position and had the support of his brother-in-law. Potgieter preferred the Englishman, Archbell, because he was an ordained minister and had been very supportive of us, particularly as our saviour after Vegkop.

Early in December 1836 a meeting of the trekkers was held and much to our delight, Gerrit Maritz was elected as our President and Hendrik Potgieter as kommandant of the field force.

Potgieter immediately started to plan his revenge against Mzilikazi and called for volunteers to attack his stronghold at Mosega.

During this time Marietjie and I met secretly at Maritz's blue wagon every second night, although she sometimes missed a meeting if she was unable to slip away from Roddy. We fell deeper and deeper in love. Sometimes if Roddy was in a drunken stupor, Marietjie managed to bring the two babies with her and I was able to develop something of a bond with my sons. André, my son by Katrina, was already a strong, happy child. While I could see that he had my features his black hair and large brown eyes were Katrina's. The younger Anton had my fair hair and blue eyes and looked a great deal like Amelia's son, my half brother, Jakob. He showed a stong will and determination but was quieter and appeared more serious than André. The shadows under the blue wagon became our sanctuary

I saw little of Pa and Amelia. When I did see Amelia her eyes shone with promise when she looked at me. She had a habit of licking her top lip as she smiled, almost like a cat, never trying to disguise her flirting. Despite being in love with Marietjie I lusted after Amelia's ripe body. So too, I knew, did Jan. Motherhood suited Amelia. Pa was close to Potgieter and kept his distance from me. I think he saw me as a threat. Whenever I did see him the gold cross hanging from the chain around his neck twinkled mockingly at me. Frans and Anna, with their baby girl, Frieda, had moved with a group of other trekkers to an area farther north. I suspect that Frans also kept his distance from Pa.

In the early part of January 1837 two hundred and thirteen of us set off in two commandos to attack the Matabele to end their reign of terror once and for all. One hundred and seven whites were supplemented by Griqua, Koranna and Barolong tribesmen. Potgieter and his supporters rode off first, followed the next day by our squadron under Maritz. We wore red bands around our hats to show that we were with Maritz, such was the animosity between the two groups.

After a two-week ride we surprised the Matabele at Mosega and attacked fifteen settlements spread over a wide area. We set fire to the kraals causing the heavens to blacken above us with thick billows of smoke. I was reminded of the time, two years before, when the boot had been very much on the other foot during the sixth Frontier War. It felt like a lifetime ago. The Matabele, without the opportunity to prepare for battle as they had at Vegkop, fled. We killed as many of the retreating Matabele as we could, about four hundred warriors, and we recovered seven thousand head of cattle and thirty thousand sheep and goats without losing one of our men. Our triumph was tinged with sadness because we'd hoped to find the two children who had gone missing when the Matabele massacred Hans van Rensburg's party the previous year. We found no trace.

On the way back to Thaba Nchu the lingering disagreements between Potgieter and Maritz erupted into open hostility. When we arrived back to a hero's welcome, Potgieter gave some of the recovered cattle and sheep to the Griquas, Korannas and Barolong who had helped us. He then announced that people who had lost their livestock at Vegkop would receive compensation from the cattle that were left and that the rest would be divided equally between the Potgieter and Maritz groups.

Maritz bristled when he heard the news. "That is absolute nonsense! What is done is done. The battle of Vegkop and the cattle lost that day has nothing to do with our taking cattle from the Matabele. Without us those cattle would never have been recovered. We should share the cattle equally. Potgieter's people get half and we get half. If they want to give their half to those who lost cattle before, that's their decision. We want our half of the cattle."

The argument raged for days before a compromise was reached. Only a quarter of all the cattle would be given as compensation to the victims of Vegkop, the largest recipient being Potgieter himself. Another quarter would go to Potgieter's commando and Maritz, who refused to budge, would receive the half he demanded. The argument was settled but the rift deepened.

It wasn't only cattle that caused dissent. By far the most sensitive issue was our final destination. Potgieter was adamant he was going north.

One evening a crowd gathered around Potgieter and Cilliers. The people listening were Maritz supporters. I joined the back of the heckling crowd and listened.

Potgieter was holding forth: "The Lord intended us to go north. That is the land He has chosen for us. That is the Promised Land. Where our Lord commands, that is where we must go."

"Amen," intoned Sarel Cilliers.

"And besides, the English have passed a law that states we will still be governed by their laws up to twenty-five degrees south. That means anyone in Natal will still fall under them. Only by going north can we escape their evil laws."

"What about the Matabele?" someone from the front shouted out.

"We will finish them off soon enough. God will see to that. But you had better know that in Natal you have the Zulu under Dingaan. I hear that he makes Mzilikazi look like a Christian by comparison."

The ongoing rivalry between the two groups was like a burr under a saddle. Along with the division in religious devotion, the Potgieter supporters even dressed differently, more severely. The dissent eventually led to Potgieter moving farther north with his wagons and supporters to an area between the Vet and the Vaal rivers where they started a small settlement. In honour of the victories at Vegkop and Mosega, Potgieter—no doubt assisted and guided by his creative master, Sarel Cilliers—named the settlement Winburg, or the town of victory.

Even with some distance between us, the bitterness increased as the days passed. In late March a small group of trekkers arrived and informed us that the great man, Piet Retief, with twenty-four families, servants and oxen had crossed the Orange River and was heading our way. The news spread and caused us to focus on his arrival instead of our petty disputes.

Retief was already a legend, highly respected both as a military man and a businessman. With his arrival we would have a real leader and he would hopefully put an end to the political stand-off between Maritz and Potgieter. Maritz went to meet Retief and his party and accompanied them to Winburg where a big crowd turned out to welcome them. People jostled and elbowed their way through the large crowd of over a thousand people to get a better view. I caught a glimpse of Amelia in the crowd and then she was gone.

"Here they come," someone shouted excitedly, as the convoy of wagons rolled into sight. Cheers broke out and the children ran to escort the wagons over the last few yards of their trek. Whistles and cheers filled the air as Retief, accompanied by a smiling and hat-waving Gerrit Maritz, drew near. Potgieter and Cilliers stood side by side, waiting to welcome Retief. Potgieter's face was like thunder. The leaders shook hands and disappeared into one of the wagons, engaged in earnest conversation. Maritz was talking. It looked as though he was trying to convince Potgieter and Cilliers of something, gesticulating with his hands. Potgieter listened intently, occasionally shaking his head.

On June 6th, Piet Retief, much to everyone's joy—with the exception of Potgieter and some of his followers—was elected Governor and Head Kommandant of our united laagers. He in turn confirmed Erasmus Smit as Trek Clergyman in the hope that this would put an end to the conflict over the ministry. Retief was sworn in by Smit, a constitution was adopted and the name 'The Free Province of New Holland in South East Africa' was selected for the Promised Land.

Retief began planning the trek to Natal while Potgieter prepared another military assault against Mzilikazi. "This time will be the last. After this there will be no Matabele left to trouble us again," he explained.

The arrival in August of the fiery, red-haired and bearded Pieter Uys along with another hundred souls caused rivalries and jealousies to flare up again. Uys refused to recognize Retief and his new government. He found a ready ally in Potgieter.

One evening in early September, on my way to meet Marietjie, I walked around a wagon and encountered our kommandant, Retief. He was deep in conversation with Maritz but I saw that he recognized me.

"Isn't that young Beukes?" I heard him ask. Maritz nodded. "Rauch … Rauch … it *is* you! Greetings, my young friend. I am glad to see you here. It's been a long time,"

"Good evening Your Excellency," I replied. "Yes, sir, it is I, Rauch. Much has happened since we fought together on the frontier. It's good to see you again, sir." I hesitated in case I sounded too familiar, adding, "We are all happy to have you as our Head Kommandant."

Retief smiled. "I hope you are going to come with us into Natal. Will you?" He turned to Maritz, explaining, "Rauch and I fought against the Xhosa together. He's a good man. We could do a lot worse than to have him with us."

He turned to me. "I am putting together a small group to travel to Port Natal and from there to meet with Dingaan, King of the Zulu, to try to persuade him to give us some land. Interested?"

I thought quickly. I would far rather throw in my lot with Retief and, if he was going, with Maritz rather than Potgieter. I nodded.

"Good," said Retief. "I'm leaving in a couple of days. Come to my wagon tomorrow and we can discuss the final details."

"You had better start saying your many goodbyes," Maritz smiled.

I wondered what he'd heard. I felt my face go red, thankful it was dark and they couldn't see me blush. My heart sank though at the thought of leaving Marietjie behind again.

She was waiting for me behind the blue wagon. We kissed tenderly. That night our conversation focused on the future.

"If you are going to Natal then that is where I want to be. Pa is one of Maritz's people so we will go where Maritz goes … I don't think I could bear not being near you again," said Marietjie.

I squeezed her close and felt her involuntary jerk as she breathed in sharply in obvious pain as my arms tightened around her.

"What is it? What's hurting you?"

"My ribs hurt."

I felt a surge of helpless rage. "My God ... I have to find a way to get you away from him. What does your pa say?"

"My pa doesn't know. In any event, whenever I try and say anything about Roddy's treatment of me and the boys he dismisses it, saying it's my own fault for being loose. He doesn't know the boys are your boys ... at least, I don't think he does. He still refers to the day we went up the mountain. He says it's my duty as a wife to care for Roddy, that it's God's will."

Later, as we made love, Marietjie was particularly passionate and responsive. At the height of our passion Marietjie called out my name in a loud whisper, "Rauch ... oh Rauch!"

"Sssshhhh!" I whispered.

I stopped moving and lay very still. I heard footsteps in the darkness next to the wagon. They walked slowly by and then stopped. I could see shoes only a yard or so from my head. For what seemed like hours the feet did not move. My heart hammered so hard I thought that whoever it was must hear. Marietjie's eyes were wide with fear. Then the feet shuffled on. I exhaled deeply.

That was the end of our lovemaking on our last evening together. We promised to stay in touch. I kissed her tenderly and wiped the trickle of tears from her cheeks with my handkerchief.

Sleep was slow to come that night as I lay under the stars in the corner of the camp where Jan and I had made our home. I had just entered the in-between phase of half-sleep when something startled me; I jerked up involuntarily. I opened my eyes. A figure was crouched above me. In the moonlight I caught the flash of light on the blade of a hunting knife, raised above the assailant's shoulder. The knife came down in a flash, aimed at my chest. I rolled aside, shouting, "What the hell ... what do you think you are doing? Christ! You're trying to kill me!"

The knife plunged into the bedclothes where I'd been lying a split second before. I lunged at the figure and felt a slippery body in my fingers but I was unable to hold on. Everything went black for a couple of seconds as a fist crashed into my face. Groggily I heard rapid footsteps fading away.

"Stop, stop! You bastard, I'll get you!" I chased after the footsteps but the attacker slipped between the wagons, gone.

Jan arrived a few minutes later. I suspected that he'd been seeing Rachel. "You look as if you have just seen a ghost!"

"Forget about seeing one ... I was nearly a ghost myself." I related what had happened.

"Good grief. Who do you think it was?"

"I didn't see him. But I'm sure it was a kaffir."

"Well, that's okay," said Jan reassuringly. "I thought it might have been Roddy ... or Floris ... or maybe even your pa ... they all have good reasons, don't they?" he said with a wry smile.

"Who says it wasn't? None of them would be so foolish to try themselves. Whoever it was probably paid the kaffir to do it." I gingerly touched the swelling under my eye.

"Anyway, I don't think it was Floris ... he would more likely be after you than me. And Pa, well ... he might not like me but I don't think he'd try and kill me or have me killed. No, I think if it was anyone other than an intruder, it was Roddy. He hates me."

"With good reason," Jan said.

Two days later I left with Retief and his fifty-eight wagons to trek to Natal. Jan decided to stay behind and join Potgieter's commando for the attack on Mzilikazi. I think he wanted to stay near Rachel.

It was an arduous journey and by the end of September, when we reached the foothills of the uKhahlamba mountains, the barrier of spears, with peaks more than eleven thousand feet high towering above us, our convoy was down to thirty wagons. Each time we encountered new difficulties or dangers one or two of the wagons would scurry back over the harsh veld to the safety of the main laagers between the Vet and the Sand rivers.

Another great frontier leader, Andries Pretorius, came to see his friend Piet Retief while we were camped next to the great mountains. Pretorius was a man I admired even more than I did Maritz and Retief. He had been active in the frontier area where he had proved his value as a military strategist and a fighter. Retief told us that Pretorius was travelling north to join Maritz, Potgieter and Uys in what they hoped would be their final assault on the Matabele. After that, though, he thought a future in Natal was far more attractive than settling in the north. I was pleased that such a great man's opinion agreed with my own.

A few days later, we left the main body of wagons behind with Retief's stepson, Abraham Greyling, in command. Retief gave him instructions to follow our tracks over the mountains at the pace of the remaining wagons. Our advance party of sixteen riders and two wagons ascended a pass through the uKhahlamba, which scouts had identified for Retief a few weeks before. After toiling up the pass we found ourselves at the top of the mountains. We gazed in wonder at the land below us. It had been raining and everything was green, lush and fertile. We stood on the peak, drinking in the astounding view. For as far as the eye could see, the land below was a patchwork of colours, terraced in giant steps to the hazy pale blue ocean in the far distance. Spring flowers painted the landscape in bright hues and streams meandered like lazy brown ribbons. The fields were rich green, dark and so different from the arid brown veld we had left behind. Large herds of game grazed peacefully, undisturbed by man. We could see gemsbuck, buffalo, eland, kudu, giraffe and elephant.

"Look at that!" said Retief, passing me his binoculars. "That soil must be deep and rich … made in heaven to grow grass as lush as that. Can you imagine farming here? Look at those beautiful trees; they seem to have been shaped by the angels themselves. Fertile soil, water, rich grass and game in plentiful supply … what more could we ask? And it looks as peaceful as can be. This is truly land fresh from God's hands; it is His own country."

I looked at him questioningly.

He laughed. "Don't worry, Rauch. But I think you'll agree that if ever a man has witnessed God's handiwork, this must be it."

I smiled, nodding. For a second or two my mind went back to Marietjie and our visit to the Valley of Desolation all that time ago. As the sun slowly sank behind the barrier of spears, the shadow of the mountain crept across the scene below, casting a soft darkness over the colours that a few moments before had appeared so bright.

I heard Louw Lourens say quietly under his breath, "I wouldn't be so sure. A land so marked by the shadow of the Lord may well be cursed."

We didn't realize at the time how accurate his prediction was.

The next day we made our way down the steep slope of the mountains, a difficult and hazardous descent which we completed without mishap. We continued our journey to Port Natal, two hundred and twenty miles away, to meet with the small group of English settlers there. Retief then planned to visit the mighty king of the Zulu, the invincible ruler of the most powerful, warlike people in southern and eastern Africa, to ask for land. Ominously, our journey to Port Natal was marked by a succession of burned-out and deserted kraals. There was no sign of life other than the herds of wild animals that roamed the empty landscape.

"Strange," remarked Retief.

"Not really, sir," I replied. "We saw the same thing when we went looking for the Trichardts up north. There, hundreds of kraals had been burned to the ground. That was Mzilikazi. This must be Dingaan. It doesn't say much for our chances of getting land from him, does it Your Excellency?"

Retief was pensive as we rode. Then he grimaced, "They say he rules by fear ... and it looks as if the stories are true. However, the word is that he's well disposed to white settlers. We will have to see for ourselves. It's a pity; I'd hoped the stories were exaggerated."

After riding hard for twelve days there was a shout from one of the scouts who was riding ahead, "We're here! There's Port Natal directly ahead."

I looked east toward the haze that hung over the sea and saw a small cluster of some two dozen shacks. As we approached, people waved their hats in greeting. Welcoming shots were fired.

"Respond with fire!" ordered Retief, as we drew nearer.

We fired a volley into the air. A ragged cheer from a small crowd of about thirty reached us. "Well, that's a good start," said Retief with a smile, "at least the English are pleased to see us."

Two of the settlers stepped forward to greet us. "Welcome ... welcome. We're so glad that you're here," said a man who introduced himself as Alexander Biggar.

The other was John Cane. "This is truly wondrous. We had word that you were on the way. Where is the rest of your party?"

"They are well behind us," said Retief. "We're going ahead to see the king to request permission to settle on his land. If we are successful, the others will follow."

"How many have you left behind?"

"Depends, really; all in all we are more than a thousand wagons. Not all of them will come. Some might head north. I think the majority will come this way, though. Perhaps as many as two thousand people. We will have to wait and see."

Biggar pursed his lips and whistled, "That's wonderful news! This is just what we've been waiting for. If you're able to get agreement from that treacherous Dingaan, we'll have the making of a wonderful settlement. Of course under your own control," he added hastily. One or two among the crowd exchanged glances. It was clear that not all the settlers were happy with the idea of living under boer control.

It did not take long for us to establish our camp.

"They are no different to us, Rauch," Retief said with a smile. "Just because they're English doesn't mean that they don't have conflicts. Anyway, I think that we can expect full co-operation from them. It just shows you how wrong Potgieter was. There's nothing wrong with an Englishman, only their governors. We have nothing to fear from them. If anything, they need us."

That night we sat around the fire eating and drinking with our newfound English friends. It was a noisy, happy celebration. An Englishman produced a fiddle and I recognized the merry strains of English tunes from when Brian Thompson used to entertain us. The entire settlement of traders and hunters had turned out. It was obvious that our arrival had lifted their spirits.

One of the Englishmen, John Kemble, flask of brandy in his right hand, slung his left arm around Retief's shoulders. "Sho', " he slurred, "Going to call on me mate Dingaan, are youse? All I can say is good luck ... Good luck, me matey!" He stumbled slightly before recovering his balance. "When you shake 'ands wiff 'im you'd be wise to count your fingers after. 'E's not to be trusted, that devil isn't."

"Come on, John," said Biggar, laughing. "He's not that bad. He hasn't attacked us, has he?"

"Not yet, 'e 'asn't! Who says 'e aint going to, though? 'E's always threatening us, in't he?"

Biggar appeared slightly embarrassed. "Well, Mister Retief might find that things are different, now. There are two white people with him. Dingaan has allowed the missionary, the Reverend Francis Owen, to live there to convert his people. Owen's there now with his family."

"No chance of that," said Kemble. He burped behind his hand as he lurched off into the darkness, seemingly bored with the conversation.

"There's also a young boy up there. Quite a story actually," said Biggar. He took a sip from his beaker, shaking his head. "He's only twelve years old but he speaks Zulu like a native … it's quite remarkable. Dingaan wanted to see a white child, so young William Wood went up to Umgungundlovu, the place of elephants, and lives there now. They say that he even translates for the Reverend Owen."

"Well, that gives me an idea. I'm going to write to Dingaan and request a meeting with him. I will send the letter to Owen and he can get young Wood to translate it for me," said Retief.

"Good idea. A few of Dingaan's warriors are camping down near the beach. I'm sure they'll take the letter for you when they return tomorrow. We can ask them."

Retief stretched his arms above his head and yawned. "Right, I must take my leave. I'm tired but before I sleep I will write to the king requesting an audience as soon as possible. I must also send a note back to my people who are camped at the mountains to tell them that we have arrived safely. Of course, I will tell them of the wonderfully warm welcome we have received. Thank you and good night."

A chorus of friendly "Good nights" rang out from the English and Retief, content, disappeared into the night.

Chapter Nineteen

Umgungundlovu was the great kraal of the king of the Zulus. Oval in shape and fully two miles in circumference, surrounded by a thick fence of thorns, it contained two thousand straw huts which housed more than thirty thousand of Dingaan's warriors. At the upper end of the oval, looking down on his subjects, were the king's royal huts which housed several of his ninety wives. The palace overlooked a three-acre parade ground. Half a mile to the east, beyond the Umkhumbane stream was a ridge known as Hlomo Amabuto, or Soldiers' Hill, where Dingaan assembled his troops before deployment.

The northern spur of this hill was known as Kwa Matiwane where the king's enemies, and a few former friends, were routinely tortured and executed. Victims were dragged to the hill where they'd have their skulls crushed by stones and sticks. Some unfortunates suffered a slow, agonizing death with a pointed stake two inches in diameter rammed up the anus to be skewered like kebabs. When the wind blew from the direction of the hill one was only too aware of the smell of the rotting corpses. Growing on the sides of the hill were aloes and giant euphorbias whose branches reached for the sky like hands uplifted in seeming horror at what they had witnessed.

The entrance to Umgungundlovu was marked by the decayed trunk of a giant tree under which Dingaan's father had died and which nobody was allowed to touch. With a view of both the king's city and Kwa Matiwane were the recently erected huts where Dingaan had allowed the Reverend Owen to set up house while he attempted to convert lost souls to Christianity.

Dingaan had ascended the throne nine years earlier at the age of thirty-one after he'd had his half-brother, Shaka, murdered. He was tall and powerfully built but carried too much fat having lived a life of over-indulgence. Despite his bulk, he was a light-footed, agile dancer who loved and composed music. He anointed his body with the oils the women used; his features were effeminate. He habitually played cruel jokes on his subjects, displaying a childish sense of humour with a cynical streak. His robes were brightly coloured and he often wore a red band around his head with a red tasseled veil that hid his face. He laid down strict rules of conduct for visitors who were not allowed to cough or spit in his presence. They were forbidden to make a sound or even to clear their throats. No one was permitted to stand taller than the king and all were enjoined to move silently on pain of death. He never led his troops in battle, leaving this task to his trusted generals, Uhlele and Tambuza. He was always accompanied by at least two mbongos, or praise-singers, with rasping voices, ensuring that they could be heard singing his praises from many miles away.

I was part of the group that rode to Umgungundlovu. Led by Retief, the group was made up of Barend Liebenberg, Coenraad and Lucas Meyer, Daniel Bezuidenhout, Roelof Dreyer and Thomas Halstead, an Englishman who spoke fluent Zulu and who would act as our interpreter. Leaving the rest of our party at the Tugela River, we made our way on horseback toward the Royal Kraal. In the afternoon of Sunday, November 5th, after a nine-day journey, we approached the Great Palace. Retief, who was in the lead, held up his hand as the seven of us pulled up.

"There it is," said Retief, arm outstretched. "Look at it!"

We halted in stunned silence, gazing in wonder at the impressive sight. Smoke curled lazily into the sky from giant cooking pots. The spacious kraal was a hive of activity and from a distance it looked as though thousands of black ants were swarming among the straw huts.

"Let's hope they're happy to see us," I said.

"Well, if they aren't we won't stand a chance," said Retief with the hint of a smile. "Don't worry men; I'm sure all will be well."

We cast nervous glances at each other as our horses shifted uneasily.

"We'll soon find out. Here come some warriors," announced Roelof Dreyer.

"Whatever happens, do not appear threatening," said Retief as a group of Zulu warriors with assegais and shields approached.

They were accompanied by an older, unarmed Zulu, who held up a hand in greeting. "Bayete!" he said: 'I salute you'. "You will make camp here. The king will see you tomorrow. Tonight you may slaughter one of our oxen to feast on." Halstead translated the message.

Through Halstead, Retief responded, "Greetings. Bayete! We salute you and the great king, Dingaan. Tell the king we thank him for the generous gift of an ox. Tell him also that we come in peace and that we will do as he commands."

Next day we waited outside the entrance to Umgungundhlovu, sitting under the shade of one of the milkwood trees near the sacred tree stump. All day we waited. Late in the evening a white man and a boy, presumably William Wood, approached. We stood up and dusted off our breeches to greet them.

"Hello!" the man called when he was still some distance away. "It's good to see a few white faces again. My name is Francis Owen. I am a missionary and King Dingaan has given me permission to convert his subjects … if I am able to, of course," he added ruefully. "And this," he said, laying a hand on the boy's shoulder, "is William Wood who is staying with the king."

The blond boy smiled pleasantly and I asked myself what kind of boy would be brave enough, at only eleven years old, to live in the kraal of the Zulu king. That night Retief and I joined Owen, his wife and sister for a meal in their hut overlooking Kwa Matiwane.

Owen poured his heart out to us while his wife and sister sat quietly listening, nodding agreement from time to time. "Dingaan is like nobody you ever met," said Owen. "He is totally heartless. I must warn you to be very careful. He ridicules me and our Lord at every opportunity. I daren't argue with him when I see how he disposes of anyone who crosses him." He gave an involuntary shiver, peering through the dark to Kwa Matiwane.

"I have tried to give him religious instruction but it's all a bit pointless, I fear." He shook his head. "I keep praying with him and preaching to him but he's only interested in getting his hands on guns and gunpowder. Unfortunately, the lad William Wood, with the best of intentions, I am sure, has shown Dingaan the power of the musket. Now he is fixated with guns. I'm not getting very far with his religious instruction … he comes up with the most extraordinary arguments. To be frank, his logic exhausts me. The other day, I tried to explain the Crucifixion to him …"

I had a sudden vision of the gold crucifix I had given Amelia which now rested on Pa's wishbone.

"And when I'd finished explaining, he asked me whether it was God who had died. I replied, 'No, the Son of God.' Then he asked me, 'Did not God himself die?' I repeated, 'No, God cannot die.' Do you know what he said then?"

We shook our heads.

"If God does not die why has he said that people must die?" Owen looked on the point of bursting into tears.

I held my hand over my mouth to smother a chuckle. It didn't sound to me as if Dingaan was stupid.

Owen continued, "I explained to him that all people are sinners and that death was the punishment for sin but that our Lord would raise us all from the grave. Well, he received that news with great alarm. Of course, the idea of his enemies, of which there are many, being raised from the dead must have been quite an alarming thought!"

At this, I took my lead from Retief and joined in the general laughter.

"Well, there was worse to come!" said Owen. "He then asked me how long Jesus Christ had been dead before he rose again. When I told him he merely said, 'Well, it's clear to me that in all probability he wasn't really dead … he was just pretending.' He finished off our lesson by saying that God couldn't have liked his only son if he allowed him to be nailed to a cross."

He shook his head sadly. "I'm afraid I am not making much progress with him, other than teaching him to paint. He likes the bright colours of the paints. I took it upon myself to explain to him about a diving-bell … but I gave that up as a hopeless task."

I kept very quiet at this point. I didn't know what a diving bell was either.

Owen concluded the evening by telling Retief, "I know you have come to petition for land. Quite frankly I don't think you have the slightest chance of getting anything from Dingaan. Be careful though, be very careful. I don't believe he is to be trusted."

Next day, a Tuesday, we received the summons to see the great king. Dingaan's induna announced, "I am instructed by our king to tell you that you are to leave your weapons here … outside Umgungundlovu. It is not permitted to take weapons inside."

Retief looked surprised and with a little smile, pointing to his own graying hair, retorted, "Do I look like a child to you? We take our guns inside." The induna looked completely taken aback. Retief turned to us. "Take your guns with you, men, and make sure they are primed. I am not being caught by surprise here."

We did as ordered. The induna marched us into the main entrance and across the parade ground. Dingaan was seated in a carved armchair, his enormous bulk shiny and slick with oil. His eyes narrowed against the sun as he watched us approach. The king's generals, Tambuza and Uhlele, stood on either side of him. Behind them was a bevy of attendants. The king smiled as we drew near, exposing three rotten teeth in the middle of his upper gum.

Retief greeted Dingaan through the interpreter. There was a long silence as the king glanced from one to the other of us, his shrewd eyes swivelling as he sized us up. Then he smiled broadly again and the rotten teeth seemed even more noticeable than before. "Sanibona!" he said, nodding. "I see you. Which of you is the leader?"

Retief replied "It is I."

Dingaan looked surprised, his eyes widening in mock horror. "You! You? You are too small to be a captain of men. You do not look like a chief at all."

Retief looked unsure of himself. "I can assure you, your Majesty, it is I. I am elected by my people."

Dingaan looked amused, "How do they call you?"

"Retief."

"Litivu ... Litivu," said Dingaan, finding it difficult to pronounce the name correctly. "You do not know me, or I you. So, before we talk of what brings you here, we must become better acquainted. You have travelled a long distance to see me, so first you must have rest, food and amusement."

Retief stood slightly in front of us while we watched the exchange. Dingaan clapped his hands, summoning an attendant to his side. He whispered secretively into the man's ear. The attendant nodded and disappeared, only to return a few minutes later carrying a telescope and an eye glass, which Dingaan had been given as gifts. Dingaan called another of his attendants forward and held the eyeglass over some dry grass until the grass burst into flames. He looked up at us, smiling proudly. He ordered the attendant to extend his arm. He seized the man's hand and held the eye glass over his arm until a hole was burned into the wrist. A thin spiral of smoke rose from the man's arm with a sickening smell of burning flesh. The wretched victim squirmed and tried to pull away. Tears ran down his cheeks but he uttered not a sound lest he annoy the king. Dingaan smirked and nodded, satisfied that he had impressed us.

He clapped his hands again and the arena was suddenly filled with two thousand warriors with muscular, oiled bodies gleaming in the sunlight. They wore kilts of cat and leopard tails, beads and feather headdresses, tails and skins hung from their ankles and wrists. Each man carried a shield as tall as himself and a bundle of fighting sticks. It was a formidable sight. The warriors formed up in their regiments in front of us. There was perfect silence until, suddenly, a sharp whistle blew. The warriors leaped into action, their bare feet blurring with movement, stirring up the dust. The ground trembled and shook beneath the stamping feet. With shrieks, yells and whistles, they leaped into the air, drumming the fighting sticks against their shields, making a noise like thunder, entertaining us to a swirling, dancing, dusty, noisy display of mock battle. The noise was deafening, the sight awesome.

Lucas turned to me, having to shout above the noise, "Thank God they are playing around. I would hate to face the real thing."

I nodded. Their actions were so realistic that on more than one occasion I imagined a fighting stick cracking open the skull of an opponent.

Dingaan turned to Retief, smiling in apparent modesty, "These are my smallest regiments."

Retief nodded, deeply impressed. Soon the arena filled again with a group of fresh warriors, dressed much the same. This time we were entertained to a singing and dancing display. Again the dust swirled, covering us in a red cloud as two thousand legs lifted high above their heads and stamped down into the ground time after time in perfect unison. With their fighting sticks held out in front of their chests, at arms' length and parallel to the ground, they seemed to form a continuous, sinuous line when viewed from the side. After the dancers left the arena came the thunder of approaching hooves. Into the arena through the swirling dust that hung like a veil in front of our eyes, came four hundred red oxen, followed by four hundred warriors with red shields. After them came four hundred black oxen followed by four hundred warriors with black shields and finally, after them came the elite regiments consisting of four hundred men with white shields and four hundred white oxen. Astonished, we stood applauding and whistling, captivated by the spectacular display.

Dingaan looked mightily pleased by our reaction. "Now let me show you my smallest herd of oxen," he said, clapping his hands.

The marching warriors were followed by thousands upon thousands of oxen in two groups. Half were red, the others black. Each ox had a white strip down its back and was identical to the next one in its group. Again we applauded until our hands hurt.

"Two thousand, two hundred and twenty-four oxen by my reckoning," said Lucas quietly, "Just imagine the organization that put this together."

"Now come, Litivu. Let me see what you can show us," taunted Dingaan, with a self-satisfied smirk and a flash of his blackened stumps.

Retief indicated we should mount our horses. Some five thousand warriors now surrounded the arena. There was a buzz as they realized that we were about to demonstrate some of our own skills.

Retief turned to us. "Let's show him what we can do, kêrels. Kom nou!"

We withdrew from the arena, turned and then galloped at full pace onto the parade ground. In unison there was a loud exclamation of "Haaauw!" from ten thousand lungs. We whirled around in a dust cloud, split into two groups and mock charged each other, riding at full speed and missing our opposite numbers by the narrowest of margins. We wheeled, raising another cloud of dust and charged again. And at each charge we turned so sharply that our horses almost sat on their haunches.

"Haauw, haauw, haauw!" from ten thousand throats filled the dusty air, spurring us on to greater feats of daring. We continued in this vein, enjoying the adulation of the crowd, until there was so much dust we were lost to our spectators. We then lined up our mounts and amidst roars of astonished laughter from the spectators, we danced the horses. The warriors were noisily shouting, laughing, clapping and nudging each other. Their amusement was punctuated by the stamping of bare feet on the hard ground. We enjoyed the display every bit as much as the appreciative crowd.

Retief dismounted with a flourish and through Halstead requested eight calabashes. There was a murmur of curiosity from the audience. With the help of a few warriors, Retief directed us to place the gourds on eight poles, two yards apart. He motioned to the warriors standing behind the poles to move to one side. There was a buzz as the spectators tried to ascertain what we were going to do next. Dingaan smiled broadly, his hand covering the blackened teeth, thoroughly enjoying the display. We positioned ourselves fifty yards from the calabashes, cocked our Sannas and took aim.

"Fire!" shouted Retief.

The assembled warriors leaped in fright as the guns roared, spitting angry flames. Every shot was true: pieces of calabash sprayed into the crowd as they simultaneously shattered into tiny pieces.

There was a second or two of stunned silence and then the shouting began! This time the "Haauws!" were continuous: "Hauw-Haauw-Haauw-HAAUW!" Whistles and shouts rent the air and then slowly died away to an ominous silence. I looked at Dingaan. He was scowling, staring at us with hate or anger or both. The black teeth seemed even more prominent. His face wore the sullen look of one who has lost a bet. He waved a dismissive hand and the crowd of warriors turned and quietly left the arena. Our demonstration had ended on a sour note.

The next morning we returned to talk business with Dingaan. I felt when we were shown into his presence that he regarded us with a new respect: "What is it you want from me?"

Retief replied, "We come to purchase land from you. We come from afar. Our country is small and we are many and can no longer live there. We see you have a large country which lies empty from the big mountains to the sea. We wish to buy that land from you."

"How can you ask me this?" responded Dingaan angrily. "You have recently shot some of my people and you have taken their cattle!"

"No. Not us. We have not done anything like that. Who told you that?"

"Some of my people say they were attacked by the Maboena, the boers, and that they were riding the oxen without horns. They attacked our people and stole three hundred oxen."

"That was *not* us," retorted Retief. "There is only one chief with horses and that is Sikonyela, the son of Manthatisi, Chief of the Tlokwa people. You know them as the Wild Cat people … it must have been done by them."

Dingaan rubbed his chin thoughtfully and for a full minute there was silence while he weighed up this piece of information. "Litivu, I will sell you the land if you can prove that you didn't take our cattle. Go back to your people near the mountain and take with you four of my indunas who will check your herds to see if our cattle are among them. If they are not, then you are to recover my cattle from the Wild Cat people and bring them safely back to me. Then, and only then, will I give you such land as you desire."

Retief smiled and looked around at us. He turned back to Dingaan and nodded, "Yes. Thank you. I accept your terms. We will leave immediately and we will return with your cattle. Thank you for your generous hospitality."

Dingaan waved his hand and turned away. I saw Reverend Owen whisper to William Wood, shaking his head, looking worried.

⊰ ⊰ ⊰

We departed early next morning for Port Natal and then on to the pass where over a thousand wagons had crossed the great mountains at the rate of more than a hundred a day, following the earlier positive reports from Retief. The trekkers had settled in various laagers covering a vast area between the Blaauwkrantz and the Tugela rivers. On the way we'd called at a mission station run by George Champion. Retief told him what had transpired with Dingaan.

"No good will come of this, let me tell you," Champion said. "I have lived and worked among these heathens and they are not to be trusted, least of all that ogre Dingaan. Are you aware that the land he has promised you has also been promised to others?"

Retief laughed. "I am sure you're wrong about that, Mister Champion. You see, we boers understand the kaffirs better than you Englishmen."

"That may well be," said Champion testily, "but I am an American, not an Englishman."

"There is little difference between the two, it scarcely makes a difference," retorted Retief with a wry grin.

Dusk was rapidly falling on November 27th as we finally arrived at the vast encampment. As we rode in I heard my name called. It was Jan.

"Rauch! Hey! It's good to see you again."

"Likewise," I responded. "When did you get here?"

"A few days ago. Everyone's come over the mountains. More than a thousand wagons have made the crossing and you know what? We lost only one. Your Pa and Amelia are here and your brother and, of course, last but not least … guess who?"

I grinned, "Marietjie?"

He nodded. "Yes, but unfortunately she's not alone. She's with Roddy. The rumour is that he beats her?"

I grimaced, "Yes, I know. Where is she? I must see her as soon as possible."

"Their wagon's over there." He pointed to a group of about thirty wagons on the banks of a stream. I turned Grey's head in that direction, longing to see Marietjie just as soon as I could.

"Wait!" called Jan. "Don't you want to hear how we finally defeated Mzilikazi? What a battle!" said Jan. "We have finished him off for good!"

We had heard the cheering news already but Jan was so keen to share the details that I really couldn't disappoint him. For the next hour Jan told me all about the epic battle that had been waged over nine days. "Potgieter, Uys and Cilliers were fantastic leaders. They bravely led from the front and we gave those kaffirs the hiding of their lives. We'll have no more trouble from Mzilikazi. The tribe has been driven north and their kraals destroyed."

"What about Maritz and Pretorius? We heard they were also there?"

"Ja," said Jan. "Maritz was sick so he didn't take part … he's here now but I don't think he's a well man. Apparently Pretorius said he wasn't going to interfere with Potgieter's plans and that he'd just observe. Not that that made any difference. We gave them a hell of a fright."

It was dark by the time he finished telling me everything. I arranged to meet up with him later and made my way excitedly to the wagon Jan had pointed out as Marietjie's.

As I rode off Jan called cheerfully, "Rachel's here as well!"

I wasn't too sure which was Marietjie's wagon. I tethered Grey and picked my way between the wagons, my heart in my mouth. It was supper time so most of the occupants were sitting around their fires. The smell of home-cooked stew filled the air and the atmosphere was relaxed. Each group I passed called out in greeting. It took a while before I caught sight of Marietjie on the far side of a wide circle of fires. She was stirring the contents of a large iron pot. I quietly made my way to her, hoping to surprise her. I smiled to myself.

Suddenly a rough hand fell on my shoulder, grasping it so hard that it hurt. "Looking for someone, Rauch Beukes?" hissed Roddy softly.

I shook his hand free and turned to face him. We glared at each other. In the light of the fire he looked gaunt but seemed in better health than when last I'd seen him. There was silence as we sized each other up.

"Hello Roddy. Yes, it's me. I was coming to say hello to Marietjie."

"Stay away from her," he spat. "If I hear that you have been anywhere near her, I will kill her. Not you, I will kill *her*. Do you hear me? Do you understand? I will kill her and those two bastard boys of yours. If you want them to live, stay well away from all of us!" He jabbed his crutch like a wooden arm against my chest, forcing me to take a step backward.

I could see that he was deadly serious. "Well, know this Roddy. I will stay away from Marietjie. But if I hear word that you've laid a finger on any of them, it is you who will suffer. I will track you down and you *will* pay."

"Piss off, Beukes! And don't you dare come near us again." He turned and limped swiftly away.

Marietjie looked up and I saw her face in the light of the fire. She looked so beautiful. She could not see me as I was in the shadows. I wanted to go to her but knew that if I did she would be severely punished by Roddy. I went back to the camp Jan had set up for us and told him what had happened.

"What are you going to do?" he asked.

"I don't know. I must get a message to her to explain the danger she's in and the reason why I haven't made contact with her. She'll know soon enough that we are back and she'll wonder why I haven't called on her."

The next day Retief called a meeting to discuss the plan to recover the cattle from Sikonyela. It was decided that a commando of fifty men would accompany him. Pa and Amelia were at the meeting. I volunteered to accompany Retief only to learn that Pa had done so as well. After the meeting was done, while Pa was talking to Retief, I saw Amelia watching me, leaning casually against a wagon.

"Hello Amelia."

She smiled widely, turned her face up and kissed me, not on the cheek as a normal greeting but on the lips. "Hello Rauch, it's good to see you again."

I looked over at Pa. He was still talking to Retief but at the same time he was watching us intently. "Ja, Amelia. So, how are things with you and Pa?"

"We are well, if that's what you mean. Your brother is well. Everyone is fine. We're just so relieved to finally be here." She glanced around and saw that Pa was still engaged with Retief. "Although I must say I'm getting quite bored with your father." She looked at me with a coquettish smile. "Though I don't suppose you're prepared to do anything about that, are you? Still waiting around for Marietjie? I think you'll have a long wait. That Roddy isn't going to let her out of his clutches. Have you seen her yet?"

I shook my head. Pa was watching us and an idea struck me. "No I haven't … I've seen Roddy and that's the problem. Roddy has threatened to kill her if I go anywhere near her. So I'm afraid to talk to her in case he finds out and hurts her and the boys … or worse. In the meantime I need to let her know why I'm staying well away."

Amelia was standing so close to me I could smell her muskiness mixed with a delicate sheen of perspiration, it being midday on a very hot day.

"Do you love Marietjie?"

I nodded. "Yes I do, very much."

"Love her more than me, Rauchie? Surely not; that's just not possible," she teased. "You seem to have a short memory span. Don't we still have … don't we still have … um … unfinished business?"

I looked at her and didn't know what to say, so I shrugged without replying. I had a vision of her lying on the grass that night, just a few years earlier, her luscious thighs exposed to my gaze. My mouth felt like a dry well.

"It's a pity, really, that you're so devoted to Marietjie. We could have had fun, you and me. I believe that you like a mature woman."

This was an obvious reference to Rachel. I wondered who had told her about that and I thought, of course, it must have been Jan. He was clearly still seeing Amelia! "Are you seeing Jan?" I asked.

"So, what if I am … jealous, Rauch?"

She was right. My stomach had done somersaults at the very thought that Jan was still seeing Amelia, seeing her and much more. "Amelia, do you ever speak to her … speak to Marietjie, I mean?" I asked.

"Yes, often … I've made it my business to befriend her. That sort of keeps me close to you, my Rauchie." Again she smiled, tauntingly.

"Well, maybe you would do me a great favour. Speak to her for me, will you?"

She looked surprised. Out of the corner of my eye I saw Pa approaching, his conversation with Retief at an end.

"Please tell her, tell Marietjie that I am back … tell her that I still love her more than ever and tell her that she is in danger. If she's able to get away without being caught I will meet her down there, next to the river, at eight o' clock tonight. If she cannot make it I will be there every night at eight until she comes. Tell her that I can't be seen even speaking to her as Roddy has threatened to kill her and the boys if I make any contact. She must be very, very careful."

Amelia looked thoughtful and then nodded: "Alright, Rauch, I'll do it for you. And maybe, in return, I could have a favour from you some time?"

"What, what's that?" said Pa as he approached. He looked at me coolly. "What sort of favour?"

"No, nothing, Jakob, well nothing that concerns you."

Pa turned to me and without any form of greeting, addressed me angrily, "You, tell your friend Jan to watch himself. I am warning the two of you that I am not Floris … and Amelia here is not Rachel."

"What do you mean?"

"You know what I mean. Stay clear of us. Come on Amelia. Let's go." He grabbed her firmly by the arm and in a voice that carried, "My son or not; if he pesters you again he'll know all about it. I'll flay his hide."

That night I waited at the designated spot for Marietjie. She did not come. I waited every night for six nights. On the seventh night I was about to leave when a woman's figure approached through the shadows. As she drew closer, I could see that she wore a shawl over her head.

"Marietjie?" I called softly.

"Shhhh! Rauch. It is me, Amelia."

My heart sank. "Where's Marietjie, where is she? She hasn't come at all. Did you give her my message?"

"Yes, of course I gave her the message." She kissed me on the cheek this time, appearing quite brisk and businesslike. "Yes, Rauch, I said I would and I did."

'Oh … well, she hasn't come."

"No, Rauch, and that's why I have come down here to tell you to stop wasting your time, Marietjie is not going to come."

"What do you mean?"

"You'd better get her out of your mind. I gave her your message."

"Well, what did she say? Come on Amelia … stop torturing me."

"She doesn't want to see you again. I'm sorry but it's the truth. I thought it might be the case but I didn't want to say anything in case it wasn't true. But Marietjie confirmed it herself."

I felt an icy hand squeeze my heart. "You can't be serious. She loves me … and I her … you, you're surely joking, Amelia, aren't you?"

"No, I'm afraid not, Rauch. She told me to tell you that things are better between her and Roddy. From what I hear from some of the other women, that much is true. Roddy seems to have quite a lot of energy nowadays."

"What do you mean?"

"Well, according to Margarieta Strauss, the story about his being impotent is not true, or if it was, it no longer applies. Also, and this is important, Marietjie seems to be really quite fond of him which means that he's probably stopped beating her." She watched me closely, gauging my reaction.

The blood drained from my face, my knees turned to jelly and I felt sick to my stomach. "Amelia, I can't believe what I'm hearing."

She placed a gentle hand on my arm, "Sorry, Rauch. I know how you must feel. But never mind." She patted my arm.

I shook my head as if to shake the words from my ears. I gazed at her in shock. She looked back at me, questioningly. "Well, maybe you and I …" She left the sentence unfinished.

"No, Amelia. For God's sake, no! You know I love Marietjie … No, just leave it, will you."

"I'm not talking about love, Rauch. You owe me something and I want it. If not right now, well, some other time. Rauchie, you did promise …"

What seemed to be a giant bull animal suddenly burst from the reeds with a crash. "I thought as much!" trumpeted the animal. It was Pa. Pa, with one hand held behind his back. The gold crucifix twinkled in the moonlight. "You! I told you to keep your hands off her."

"I wasn't touching her. We were just talking."

"I heard you talking and I heard what you were talking about ... stay away from Amelia. Keep away from my wife!"

Too late I saw his hand shoot out from behind his back as his arm lifted skyward and flashed in a blur. The sjambok caught me across the cheek, cutting through my flesh like a knife. I could feel warm blood trickling down my chin. I held my hand up to the cut as blood oozed through my fingers.

"You sod!" I shouted.

"Come on you, you little bitch in heat," he said evenly as he grabbed Amelia's arm, pulling her away in the direction of their wagon. I could hear them arguing fiercely as they strode away into the darkness. I held a handkerchief to my cheek and stumbled back to my camp.

Chapter Twenty

After a long month of not having seen or heard from Marietjie, Jan and I left with Retief and forty-eight others, including Pa, Frans and Floris, to recover the stolen cattle from Sikonyela. We crossed back over the Drakensberg. Two of Dingaan's indunas showed us the way until we picked up the spoor of the stolen cattle and Sikonyela's warriors.

For the first few days there was a great deal of tension, bordering on outright hostility, between Pa and me. Things came to a head after six days when we were half way to Sikonyela's kraal. We were sitting round the fire after supper, drinking coffee and talking. Jan and I had stayed out of Pa's way so were surprised to see him walking over to us.

"Evening Oom," said Jan politely as he glanced up at Pa.

I said nothing, staring into the fire, sipping my coffee.

Pa ignored Jan's greeting. He looked at me. I looked back at him without a word.

"That's going to leave a scar on your face. It'll be a reminder to you: don't mesh around with another man's wife, especially my wife."

I could smell alcohol on his breath. His speech was slurred and his eyes were bloodshot. I ignored him and returned to the glowing embers of the fire.

"I am shpeeking to you," he said. "Don't ignore me!"

Jan was watching us closely. I continued staring into the fire.

"Answer me!" Pa shouted. I looked up and saw that a few others were watching, including Floris, who was smiling broadly.

"Have you learned your lesson, you little cur?" Pa taunted.

My blood boiled. I had intended keeping quiet. "Maybe it's you who should learn a lesson and keep that wife of yours who you can't satisfy under better control."

Pa let out a roar of anger and leaped at me, hands outstretched to grab my neck. But he was off balance. I stepped aside and as he lurched past me I punched him in the side of the head. He fell like a log. I was about to kick his head in when I was grabbed from behind and my arms restrained.

It was Retief. "Stop this you two. Right now! What's all this about? I suppose I can guess. That's enough now, Rauch. I won't have you and your father fighting like cat and dog. This sort of thing will disrupt the whole expedition."

"It's not his fault.," said Jan. "We were sitting here, just talking, when his father came up and started to taunt him … you can see, Your Excellency, that Oom Jakob has been drinking."

"Be that as it may; Jakob and I go back a long way. Look," he said to me, "I think you and Jan had better return to Doornkop and the other wagons and wait until we get back. You and your father are like fire and water and it is not going to work having you on the same commando."

I began to protest.

"I'm sorry, Rauch. I like you and you're a good youngster. But I cannot place the lives of my men in danger by having you and your father fighting. That's how it is. I have made up my mind. You'll leave in the morning."

Two men helped Pa to his feet. Something glittered on the ground. It was the gold crucifix. One of the men saw it and bent down, picked it up and handed it back to Pa. He glared daggers at me as he hooked the chain around his neck.

The next morning before the sun came up Jan and I were in our saddles heading back to Doornkop, where we had to wait until the commando returned. More and more wagons arrived from the north. Both Jan and I were delighted to welcome our friend Gerrit Maritz and his familiar blue wagon. It seemed as if everyone had decided to come to Natal and that word of Retief's successful negotiations with Dingaan had spread. Even Hendrik Potgieter had joined the growing group, of course accompanied by Sarel Cilliers. The great man, Andries Pretorius, also arrived, followed a few days later by Piet Uys who now seemed to have accepted Retief as our leader.

Maritz pumped my arm when he saw me. "Hello Rauchie. My God, it's good to see you again. I thought you'd be away with Retief recovering those cattle. Hey, what happened to your face?" I explained and Maritz listened intently, then said with a smile, "Well, well Rauch, you'd better be careful. It sounds like half the men here are after the two of you for chasing their women. Floris, Roddy and now even your Pa. I don't know where you get the energy!"

A fit of coughing accompanied his last comment. I looked at Maritz more closely. He was pale; he didn't look at all well but was putting on a brave front.

During the days spent waiting I frequently saw Marietjie from afar. I was sure she saw me but she always looked away before I could make eye contact. It appeared that Amelia had been telling the truth. She too seemed to be keeping her distance. The only woman who seemed to be on friendly terms with me was Rachel. She made it clear that the fruits of our first encounter were there to be picked whenever I was hungry.

The sound of gunshots signalled the return of Retief and the others. They rode into camp with joyful shouts of victory. The group was herding about eight hundred cattle and over sixty horses recovered from Sikonyela. Four hundred head of cattle belonged to Dingaan. It transpired later that Retief had tricked Sikonyela into wearing a pair of handcuffs which he had described as "lovely silver bracelets". He kept the chief in the 'bracelets' until he handed over Dingaan's four hundred cattle. Not content with that, Retief had taken an additional four hundred cattle and sixty horses as a fine to punish Sikonyela. He had also confiscated a dozen guns. There was much jubilation at the return of the party. Retief rewarded his commando with eight head of cattle and a horse each from the stock he'd brought back. He kept the eight confiscated rifles. Jan and I received nothing.

The day after Retief's return a meeting was held to distribute the cattle and raise a commando to return the cattle to Dingaan. After much debate it was felt that Retief personally should return the cattle.

"I will take two hundred men with me," declared Retief.

A warning voice rang out over the noise of the crowd. "Beware!"

We turned to see who had called out. There was silence as an old man, Herklaas Malan, ashen-faced, shouted again to Retief. "Yes. I say beware! I have dreamed of a massacre. You will all die. That Dingaan is not to be trusted. Believe me, you will all be killed." People nearby tried to hush Malan up but Retief made it clear that he did not take the warning seriously.

Ignoring Herklaas he called out, "Men, who is with me?"

There was a roar from several hundred voices as everyone wished to be part of an expedition that looked as if it would be a joy ride. Jan and I joined in too; we'd had enough of hanging around camp.

"No, no!" shouted Maritz. "Under no circumstances should so many men go. Dingaan is not to be trusted. If something does not go according to plan we will lose too many. I think you should take far fewer men. In fact, Your Excellency, we cannot afford to lose you should things go badly wrong. Please let me go in your place. My illness is getting worse and I fear that I have not much time left."

Retief looked furious. He glared at Maritz. The meeting fell silent, the tension palpable. "No. I go, I am your appointed commander and I will go. Nobody will take that privilege away from me, not even you, Meneer Maritz. I will, however, take a smaller group than the planned two hundred. Here, volunteers may put their names on this sheet of paper. From the list I will choose a body of men to accompany me." He turned again, giving his old friend Maritz a cold stare: "I find your attitude unacceptable. Dingaan has agreed to make land available once we have fulfilled our side of the bargain. I am surprised that you should try and take the glory of the occasion away from me."

Only sixty-eight of us signed up as volunteers; many had indeed heeded Herklaas's and Maritz's warnings.

Retief sent for Jan and me. "Sorry, I am afraid your pa is coming, Rauch. That means you stay behind. I cannot have any in-fighting."

As we left his wagon, Jan looked at me saying, "Are you thinking what I am thinking?" I shrugged, not sure what he meant. "Think about it, Rauchie, Floris is away—he and Rachel are not talking—and your pa is going with Retief. So is Frans, your brother. Who will be left behind? Why, all the women of course!" He chuckled and dug me in the ribs.

I ruefully rubbed a hand across the scar on my face but had to laugh.

A few days later, when Reverend Smit had said prayers calling on the Lord to protect them, sixty men with thirty coloured servants, including Gieletjie, were set to leave. The four hundred cattle which belonged to Dingaan had been sent off the day before with herders. Te party planned to catch up with them before they reached Umgungundlovu.

Retief rode up to Maritz's blue wagon and called out, laughing, "Goodbye, you old coward!"

Maritz came out, "Please, Piet … I'm warning you. Dingaan is not to be trusted. You'll be riding to your death. I will wager your wagons against mine that we will never see you again."

Retief, looking dashing in a crimson waistcoat, threw back his head and laughed uproariously, "I accept the wager. We will be back, safe and sound and I'll take great pleasure in accepting that blue wagon from you."

Maritz waved his hand in farewell, shouting, "I say to you … not even one of you will return!"

Even Hendrik Potgieter was concerned for the safety of the group. He turned to his close friend Jan Robbertse who was accompanying Retief. "Jan, I think Maritz is correct. I must bid you a sad farewell. I do not expect to see you again."

Robbertse laughed, clapping Potgieter on the back. "Don't be silly

Hendrik, what could Dingaan do to us? Farewell my friend, I'll see you in a few weeks time."

A volley of shots rang out as we fired a salute to the commando of ninety laughing, relaxed men and boys who, accompanied by eight dogs, rode off. They stopped briefly, firing a return volley, before waving their hats and disappearing over the hill. I saw that Pa and Gieletjie were laughing too.

ക്ക ക്ക ക്ക

Jan and I were disappointed that Retief had not included us in his group but there was nothing that could be done about it. For the next few days we busied ourselves with hunting for the pot and exploring the area around the wagon settlement. The wagons were spread over a wide area between the Tugela and Bushmans rivers and, just as at Thaba Nchu, there was an air of comfortable permanency. People had started planting crops and some had even erected small picket fences around their wagons.

A few days after the commando had left, Jan and I returned from two days of hunting with a kudu and three impala slung over the back of a spare horse. We topped the rise approaching our camp and gazed down at the peaceful scene on the plain below. The rolling grass that stretched as far as the eye could see, stirred slightly in the evening breeze; blue smoke from evening fires snaked lazily into the sky. The wagons were outspanned haphazardly in groups of four and five, far enough away from each other for privacy but close enough for communal safety. The happy sounds of children laughing and dogs barking floated up to us. Near the wagons were over ten thousand head of cattle and ten times that number of sheep. The animals too looked content feeding on the abundant grazing.

The two encampments were spread over an area of more than five hundred square miles. We were part of the Maritz group near the Bushmans River. The other major group—Retief's followers, including Erasmus Smit and Sarel Cilliers—was some distance away between the Blaauwkrantz and the Tugela rivers. In between the two major laagers were smaller, scattered settlements of trekkers, grouped for the most part as families. Piet Uys and Potgieter had gone back north to collect their followers.

"Looks so peaceful, doesn't it?" called Jan.

"All we need now is for Retief to get the final agreement from Dingaan and then we can make this our home. It looks as if we've reached the end of our journey," I smiled.

As we rode past the first of the wagons, I heard a call. "Hello Rauch. Hello Jan." It was Amelia, sitting by her wagon, her baby crawling on a blanket on the ground. "We're getting some exercise before he gets put down for the night," she said with a laugh. We stopped. "At least I can talk to you now without your pa getting jealous … how's your cheek?"

I touched the scab. "Ag, it's nothing really. He had no right to hit me, though."

She picked Jakob up who squealed with delight, his little legs kicking the air with excitement. "No, but you know what he's like. I'm going to put little Jakob down to sleep now. What are you two doing this evening? Come and have some supper with me." She addressed the question to me. Jan looked at me, questioningly.

"Thanks Amelia," I said. "But I've some things I must see to. Another time, perhaps." As soon as the words were out of my mouth I regretted it. A part of me still found Amelia very attractive … and Pa was away.

Amelia appeared annoyed, quickly switching her attention, "Well, what about you, Jan? Do come and have a drink. It's lonely for me on my own … or are you looking to visit Rachel?"

Jan smiled and climbed off his horse, glancing apologetically at me. "No thank you, Amelia. But I will sit here with you for a while and keep you company, if you wish."

I felt a twinge of jealousy. The feeling was worsened by the fact that I could see there was a bond of intimacy between them as I took my leave.

I hadn't spoken to Marietjie for weeks so I decided to look for their wagon and see if, somehow, I could get to talk to her. I missed her but at the same time didn't wish to give Roddy any further cause to hurt her. I hadn't gone far when I recognized the wagon. I stopped, unsure what to do. I dared not risk calling her in case Roddy was at hand. The evening had swiftly deepened into darkness. I heard voices, argumentative voices. The voices rose louder as tempers flared and I heard Roddy's drunken shout, "Come here, you whore. Come here and get your clothes off!"

"Leave me alone!" snapped Marietjie. There was the sound of tearing fabric as the babies started wailing. "Get away from me," shrieked Marietjie.

There was a sound like a gunshot—a flat hand on a cheek—followed by another and another. "This will teach you, you bitch. You listen to me! Lie down on the bed!"

I heard Marietjie's sobs and the metallic clatter of a belt buckle as it fell to the wooden floor of the wagon. I could not control my rage a second longer. I yanked open the flap of the wagon cover and rushed in. Marietjie was lying on her back, her full breasts spilling out of her dress which was torn half way to the hem. Her eye was already swelling from the blows. Her hands were in front of her face, desperately trying to fend him off as he, trousers round his ankles, made ready to rape her.

"What the hell ..." he gasped, turning to glare at me.

"Leave her alone!" I shouted. The boys were bawling. I grabbed at Roddy but he evaded my grasp.

"Get out of our wagon," he ordered as he swung a fist at my head.

I ducked and clenched my fist to deliver a punch to his head when I heard Marietjie whisper, "Get out! Get out! What do you think you are doing? This has nothing to do with you. Get out of our wagon. Go back to your whores. I don't want to see you again ... ever ... leave us alone!"

I couldn't believe what I was hearing, stunned that it was me she was hissing at. I stared at Marietjie in blank disbelief. "But ... but ... but!"

"Get out! Leave us … now!"

I stumbled blindly into the darkness, Roddy's sneer imprinted on my mind as he pulled his trousers on and followed me outside. "And if you dare come back again I will kill her first and then you! Do you understand?" he snarled.

He went back into the wagon and I heard the buckle hit the floor again. This time there were quiet sobs of resignation … which were smothered … and then stopped. The only sound I could hear from the wagon was the crying of the two boys. I made my way back to my own camp, my heart heavy and my thoughts in turmoil.

As dawn was breaking, I was jerked from my half-sleep by Jan climbing into the bedclothes next to mine.

"You awake?" he asked quietly.

"Ja."

"Whew! I'll sleep for a week. I'm exhausted. Your stepmother is really something else!" he said with a lecherous grin. "Your pa isn't doing his job so we had to make up for lost time. Just look at my back." He rolled over, exposing his bare back: red fingernail scratches showed just how much Amelia had enjoyed her evening.

"Shut your bloody mouth!" I snapped as my jealousy, rage and frustration spilled over. Seething, I pulled the covers over my head and turned my back on him.

ᷛᷛᷛ

Next morning Gerrit Maritz called a meeting. He looked pale and ill at ease. "I am concerned about our governor. There are reports that Zulus have been heard shouting across the hills and that they—the governor and everyone in his party—are dead. Of course, this cannot be. But there is some cause for concern as they were due back, at the very latest, two days ago, on the fifteenth of February. There is not the slightest sign of them. I am sending instructions to all the camps, warning everyone to draw their wagons into protective laagers … just in case. I need a party of ten men to scout for signs of any Zulu attack."

Jan and I were joined by eight others as we rode off in search of the Zulu. After some hours we crossed the Tugela River into Zululand and came across a lone, elderly Zulu man.

He held his hand up in greeting, "Bayete!"

"Bayete!" we replied.

"Where are you going?" asked the old man.

"We are hunting buffalo," answered Landman, our leader.

'Well, you need to go in the other direction," he said pointing away from a small hill two hundred yards to the north.

"No, we think that the buffalo are behind *that* hill." said Landman, pointing in the other direction.

"They are *not* there. I have just come from there. The buffalo are over that way." He pointed again, insistently. As we hesitated, he added, "Or is it not buffalo that you are seeking?"

Not wishing to alarm the old man, Landman turned us away. Only later did we find out that the massed ranks of ten thousand Zulus were waiting to attack us, hidden behind that very hill. We turned back to camp. That night reports started coming in that many of the trekkers had ignored Maritz's warnings and had not put in place any protective measures. I felt uneasy and couldn't settle down.

After supper next to the fire, I left Jan on his own. We had hardly spoken since his boasting about his night with Amelia. I made my way through the wagons and wandered down to the Bushmans River. It was a warm, balmy evening. I sat on the bank, listening to the rhythmic croaking of the bullfrogs in the reeds. The sliver of moon in decline started to peek over the horizon as the darkness was replaced by a gentle, silvery light.

Suddenly I was aware of a rustling in the grass behind me. The figure of a familiar-looking woman approached. My heart beat faster at the thought that it might be Marietjie.

"Hello Rauch. Catching moonbeams, are you?" It was Amelia.

"What are you doing here? Who's looking after your baby?"

"Oh ... I saw you walk down here so decided to join you. It's been a long time since we were on our own. It's a lovely evening, so I asked Sandra Hattingh to watch out for Jakob. Anyway, he's asleep now. So, here I am, and there's no one to disturb us."

I looked at her. Her golden hair tumbled down over her shoulders. She was wearing a brightly coloured, square-necked dress. She was barefoot. Her full figure looked ripe and tempting with her breasts straining against the fabric of the dress.

I swallowed hard, "I suppose that you have no news of Pa? There are whispers that something dreadful has happened to them. They should have been back by now."

"No, there has been no news. But you know what these people are like; they are always worrying about something. Anyway, I am sure they're fine. And now we have a chance to finish our business, don't we? They'll no doubt be back tomorrow or the next day, and then who knows when we'll get another chance."

"Don't start something that you don't intend finishing," I warned.

"Don't be such a silly boy. Of course not!" She came to me and turned her face upward.

I put my arms around her. I could feel her warm body against mine, her breasts pushing against my chest. I held her close. She nuzzled against me.

"Well, you have led me on before and then stopped me," I said. "What about Pa?"

"He's not here, is he? ... and I'm certainly not going to say anything."

She felt so warm and so soft. I could feel myself become aroused. I ran my hand down her back and stroked the cheeks of her buttocks through her dress. She wasn't wearing anything underneath. Her upturned lips found mine and she hungrily kissed me, her tongue moving in and out of my mouth.

"I have waited a long time for this, Rauch," she whispered urgently.

I felt her hands feeling the front of my breeches. She moaned as she felt the hardness under her hand. I lifted her dress up around her waist. She used one hand to help me while the other rubbed me harder.

"Well you should have let me before," I whispered into her ear. "Maybe then you wouldn't have married Pa if you knew what you were missing, would you?"

"This way I can have you both, can't I?"

I placed my hand around her bare buttocks. Her skin was smooth and cool. I pulled her against me. She gasped as she felt my erection hard against her through my breeches. She was breathing heavily, as was I. She turned and I undid three buttons at the back. She wriggled and pulled the dress over her head and threw it on the grass, standing naked in the moonlight. My breath caught in my throat at the sight of her. I felt dizzy as I took in her sculpted outline, her breasts taut and erect and the dark triangle between her legs, which I had dreamed of for so long, clear in the moonlight. I pushed her down onto her dress at the water's edge. She leaned back, resting on her hands and raising her knees, opening her legs for me. I stood and unbuckled my belt, dropped my trousers and pulled off my underwear. Her gaze never left me and her eyes widened when she saw all of me. She ran her tongue under her upper lip in anticipation. I knelt down in front of her. She lay back and with one movement placed her legs over my shoulders. I knelt and slid into her hotness, feeling sheer delight as I filled her with my hardness. She gasped. For the next few minutes everything was a blur through barriers of ecstasy and sensual delight. We exploded together in a frenzy of movement and sound. Our groans filled the night air but neither of us cared. I had never experienced such delicious sensations. She was like a wild animal and made love with total abandon. As we climaxed she squeezed her legs hard around my neck, shuddering and screaming. I collapsed next to her on the grass.

"That was wonderful, my darling. That was truly wonderful. I want more … come on Rauchie … let's see how quickly you can give me an encore."

Three times more, in the time that it took the moon to make its journey across the heavens that night, Amelia took me to places I had never experienced before. I fell asleep, with my shirt on, holding the naked Amelia, exhausted, tender, sated.

I woke with a start. Early morning dew dampened my shirt and drops of moisture had formed on my forehead. Amelia still lay naked in my arms on the ground, dead to the world. Her hair was plastered to her skin from the damp.

"Amelia," I whispered. "Wake up."

She started, opened her eyes sleepily and yawned.

"You'd better get up. It's nearly morning. Sandra Hattingh will be furious. They are probably looking for you." The sky was starting to change colour. Sreaks of light marked the arrival of a new day.

She looked at me through half-closed lids like a gecko about to catch a fly. She rolled onto her back, held her arms up and smiled with lips slightly swollen from the night's activities. There was no mistaking what she intended. I felt myself stirring and responded. We rolled on the wet grass and satisfied each other. Birds called from the trees, the frogs slept and the early morning insects started their high-pitched noise to signal the start of a hot summer's day as we made our way back to the camp.

"Come to my wagon tonight … after the baby is asleep … we can do it again." She kissed me lightly on the cheek. Then she was gone.

Jan was still asleep when I climbed into my bedclothes and within seconds I was asleep, exhausted.

The sun was high in the sky when I finally rose. I spent the day reflecting on the night with Amelia and anticipating the night ahead. I hoped that Retief, and Pa, would not return that day. I felt confused. I wanted Marietjie but Amelia had introduced me to another world and one that I was anxious to stay in.

After dusk, I made my way to Amelia's wagon. Little Jakob was already asleep and she was dozing on her bed. She smiled as she saw me, and pulled the covers down, signalling me to join her. I slipped out of my clothes and fell into her arms. She was naked and warm. I blew out the lamp. We made passionate love, this time only once before we fell asleep, our lips pressed against each other's. I woke with the feeling of Amelia's hand stroking me. I felt sleepy and warm in her arms, smiling as she skilfully manipulated my erection.

"That's nice," I whispered and rolled onto my back to give her hand freedom of movement. She slid down my body and I felt her lips on me. Her head moved up and down as she sucked and licked. The sensation was exquisite. I allowed myself to float into heaven.

Above the sound of our heavy breathing I heard noises in the distance. Gunshots! I sat up.

Amelia looked startled, her eyes wide with surprise as she knelt between my legs. She wiped her lips with the back of her hand and looked up at me. "What are you doing ... don't you like that?"

"Shhh," I said, putting a finger over my lips. "Listen!"

We craned our heads in the dark like two watchdogs alert to danger. More shots. This time there was no doubt about it ... and they were much closer.

"My God, it's them, they're back. Quick, I must get out of here. They're back! Damn it! Pa will be here any minute. Sorry my darling. You'd better pretend to be asleep. What a shame ... I was really enjoying that." I grabbed my clothes and dressed hurriedly.

Amelia giggled "You'd better hurry otherwise you'll get another cut."

I pulled a face.

"Oh well, I'll just have to finish off with your pa, I'm sure he'll enjoy it after being away for a few weeks," she said with a smile.

"You know how to tease me, don't you?" I retorted.

She sat on the bed, knees drawn up under her chin as I kissed her upturned mouth and left.

Chapter Twenty-one

The darkness was broken by the distant flare of a fire as I stepped out of the wagon. There were gunshots. Closer to the camp, I saw lamps being lit in a few wagons and then figures emerging clad in nightgowns and shirts.

"It's them. Retief is back," said Cilliers as another fusillade of shots rang out.

"No... I don't think so," I replied. "Look there." I pointed in the direction of a fire which lit up the distant sky.

There was another rattle of gunfire and then the faint, terrified screams of women and children and the angry barking and alarmed howling of dogs. "My God, it's the Zulu! We are being attacked. Look out! Get your guns. Those screams are coming from the Bezuidenhout camp!" I shouted.

The mood changed from curiosity and excitement over the expected return of Retief to one of terror, as if a cold wind of evil had swept through the camp. There was no doubt that I was right. I ran back to our camp and grabbed my Sanna, shaking Jan awake.

"Get up! Quick! Hurry! We are being attacked by the Zulu!"

Jan jumped up, startled. I ran off and grabbed Grey. Our wagons were already in a circle in laager formation, Maritz having had the foresight to take precautions a few days earlier. Most of the other wagons had paid no heed to his warnings and were scattered here and there, vulnerable. I galloped as hard as I could in the direction of the flames which lit up the sky with an orange glow. The sound of screams and gunshots grew louder and seemed to be spread over a wide area. As I drew near to the flames of the Bezuidenhout wagons, a figure darted for cover, pursued by three dark shapes. It was Daniel Bezuidenhout carrying something wrapped in a blanket.

"Daniel, Daniel ... here!" I fired at the figures chasing after him. They stopped dead while he scrambled in my direction, covered in blood. He was gasping for air as he placed the bundle down on the ground in front of him. He held one hand against his side to stem the blood gushing from a gaping assegai wound.

"Our baby," he cried in anguish. "Here … but she's dead too." The shaft of an assegai protruded through the blanket. "My God! We are finished. They have killed all our family except for my brother and me. There are thousands, thousands of them. I have to warn the others along the Blaauwkrantz before it's too late." He left the blood-stained bundle on the ground and ran wildly into the darkness.

All around me the blackness of the sky was lit up by the flames of burning wagons. People came running out of the dark, dressed in their night things. Bodies lay spread-eagled on the ground. Zulus were everywhere. The shouts of "Bulala ibhunu!", "Kill the boers!" that I had last heard at the battle of Vegkop, rang out across the scene of carnage. Zulu warriors moved from one group of wagons to the next, killing and burning as they went. Confusion and panic reigned, with terrified screams preceding the shouts of the Zulu: "Gahla!", "I have eaten!" Each time I saw a black shape I fired and turned to fire again even before I saw the effects of my previous shot. Zulus chased the fleeing trekkers, cutting them down with their stabbing spears.

In one group of burning wagons I saw a group of Zulu warriors holding three women on the ground while they hacked off their breasts before disembowelling the bodies to free their spirits. Again the bloodthirsty shout of "Gahla!" A little girl, no more than four years old, was picked up feet first by a towering warrior who swung her against a wagon wheel with all his might. Her brains splattered over the wheel. He tossed the lifeless body to the ground and moved on to his next victim. Bodies lay all about. The smell of burning wood from the wagons filled the air amidst the chilling screams for mercy. I saw the bodies of the Greyling and Engelbrecht families lying in grotesque positions, slaughtered as they'd attempted to flee. I learned afterward that all thirty-six members of these families had been killed. The grass under my feet was sticky with blood. The Bothmas had held the Zulu wave back for a while until the warriors, using the cattle as cover, sneaked in and mercilessly slaughtered them all.

Gradually, after the initial onslaught, we began to fight back more effectively. I rode on to see where I could best help. A figure cantered toward me in the dark and I recognized Marthinus Oosthuizen who had been camping alongside the van Rensburg family.

"Quick, quickly, help! The van Rensburgs are surrounded. We are holding them off but we are fast running out of gunpowder and bullets. Quick! I have to get supplies to them at once." I looked around. The Terblanche wagon was close by and not on fire. I whispered a quick prayer under my breath and leaped onto the wagon. In the flickering light I could see gunpowder and a large pile of shot. I swept it all into a bag and passed it to Marthinus.

"Thanks Rauch." He spurred his horse on, crashing through a barrier of warriors who had moved up to attack us. They leaped aside, Marthinus bent low in the saddle as he rode to the relief of the van Rensburgs.

"Make for Maritz's laager!" I shouted above the screams of terror and the war cries of the Zulus. As I passed a wagon I saw a white man dressed in Zulu skins rifling through a moneybag. I fired without warning. He dropped dead to the ground, the empty bag still clutched in his fingers. I never found out who he was but there was some talk that he had originally been part of another group of trekkers.

I rode back to the Maritz laager, the early morning sky streaked with ribbons of light. As I approached, the sound of gunfire was almost deafening. I passed the corpses of men, women and children who had not followed Maritz's advice of forming a defensive laager. The people in the laager saw me coming and manoeuvred a wagon aside to allow me in. I galloped at full speed, hunched over to present a smaller target. The Zulus scattered as I ploughed through their ranks. I held my Sanna by the barrel, turning it into a whirling club that crunched with a sickening thump against the skulls of the Zulus as I battered my way through. I rode into the circle of wagons in a cloud of dust. The women were positioned alongside the men, passing bullets and gunpowder. I found a space and immediately started to shoot at wave upon wave of Zulu fighters. Their cries of "Bulala ibuhnu" resonated above the din.

It was mid-morning by the time I noticed Roddy to my right, with Marietjie passing powder and shot to him. Out of the corner of my eye I saw a dozen Zulu warriors wriggle their way under the wagons, through the thorn bush defences and into the laager. Hand-to-hand fighting broke out. Roddy was in the thick of the mêlée. I ran across to him but was grabbed from behind by two Zulus. I tried to turn but was held fast. A shot rang out, then another and the two fell dead to the ground. I looked across and saw Rachel, gun in hand, smile thinly as she acknowledged my unspoken gratitude. Roddy was fighting off three Zulus. He was backing away toward a wagon in the centre of the laager, stabbing and slashing with a knife. Two fell. Roddy jumped up into the wagon to escape the third. I chased after them. As I entered the wagon, the Zulu lifted up his arm to stab Roddy with his assegai. Roddy drew his pistol and the stabbing spear clattered to the floor as the Zulu fell lifeless, blood pumping from a great hole in his head.

Roddy and I looked at each other. We were both panting from the exertion of the battle. I glanced down at the assegai and Roddy's eyes widened as he realized my intention. I swooped down and lifted the spear in my right hand and in one movement, pulled my arm back and plunged it into the 'V' below his Adam's apple. He staggered backward, his hands clutching at the assegai. Blood was running from his mouth and the hole in his throat. His eyes stared, unseeing, as he tried to yank the shaft out, but to no avail. He fell; his legs jerked once and there was a rattling in his throat as his spirit left him. I jumped down from the wagon. My hands were shaking with the realization of what I had done. I ran back to the perimeter. Marietjie herself was now shooting at the Zulus, the Sanna to her shoulder. I stood in the space where Roddy had been and fired out at the advancing black hordes.

"Where's Roddy?" asked Marietjie.

I fired a shot and another Zulu fell. I carried on shooting, hesitating before I said quietly, without looking at her, "I'm sorry Marietjie … Roddy is dead, stabbed by one of the kaffirs."

There was a sharp intake of breath as she looked at me, her eyes wide. "Dead? Dead? Surely not … no, that cannot be!" Her hand shot up to cover her mouth. She dropped the gun and ran to the wagon where Roddy's body lay.

I continued firing, not daring to look back in case she deduced what had really happened.

The wave of attacks finally came to an end. I heard a shout from behind as Sarel Cilliers entered the laager. "Come men, get your horses. Let's go after the savages."

He led a charge of twenty of us on horseback, chasing after the Zulu, shooting and killing as we went. Their ranks broke. Some dived into the river looking for cover and I saw many swept away by the raging waters of the Bushmans River. The rest of the horde retreated, taking thousands of our cattle, sheep and horses. Some of us wanted to pursue them farther.

"Leave them," commanded Cilliers "We have our own to tend to first."

It was late afternoon when we returned to the scene of devastation that had been left behind. The grass surrounding the laager was caked with blood. Burned-out husks of wagons still smoked. Canvas coverings hung in shreds from the metal ribs of the wagons, fluttering like flags of surrender in the evening breeze. Personal possessions and household items lay scattered over the veld. Ripped mattresses and torn cushions, many stained red with Zulu and trekker blood, were scattered about. As we passed I stared in horror at one of the wagons, the site of a bloody massacre. Blood still dripped through the floorboards and onto the grass beneath the wagon. We searched for survivors in the wagons and among the piles of corpses.

A slight movement caught my eye, "Come quick," I called. "There's someone alive in here!" Willing hands assisted and we pulled aside the dead to reach an arm that seemed to have moved. We dragged bodies aside and found two teenage girls, Johanna van der Merwe and Margareta Prinsloo, both alive but each with more than twenty assegai wounds.

The sounds of wailing were too awful to bear.

I saw Marietjie watching me. She had been crying. "You killed him, didn't you?"

I stared at her without answering and felt my stomach tense. "The kaffir was already dead. Roddy shot him. You must have killed Roddy," she said in a quiet voice. "You have his blood on your hands, Rauch."

She turned and walked away, head drooped in silence as I watched her go.

After all the final reports had come in, we began to count the cost of the battle. It was horrific. Over five hundred of our people had been killed, including one hundred and eighty-five children, fifty-six women, forty-four men and more than two hundred coloured servants. Never before had we experienced such a disaster. The sun itself appeared stained with blood as it silently dropped behind the western hills. We made preparations to bury the dead in a mass grave near the laager. We wrapped the bodies in karosses, canvas and blankets, the children so pathetically small. Men and women sobbed unashamedly as they sat on the hard earth next to the bodies of their children. Some sat in vacant silence, too traumatized to show any emotion. Some would remain in a state of shock for the rest of their lives and more than one would never speak, or even utter a single sound, ever again. Some of the men climbed down into the grave as others gently passed them the bodies. Occasionally a body had to be prised from the arms of a loved one desperately attempting to delay the final parting. The sounds of weeping and despair accompanied proceedings. Sarel Cilliers and Reverend Smit said the prayers as we shovelled soil into the grave.

Then Maritz spoke. "Today, the seventeenth day of February, 1838, is a day that will be marked in the history of our people as a day of infamy. This is indeed our darkest hour. But the sun shall shine again. Do not despair. We will avenge this horrific day and the vile atrocities visited on our people. Their blood that was spilled shall be remembered and honoured for all time. We will mark this place and we name it henceforth a place of weeping ... Weenen."

I saw Amelia standing nearby and I moved to stand next to her.

Maritz was still talking. "We are going to take care of the wounded and of course those left behind. We have a number of orphans now, so I will be looking for homes for them." He paused, glancing around at the sombre faces, "I think you must all now know, or suspect, that it is not only those buried here whom we have lost. There can be no doubt from what happened today and from reports coming through, that our beloved governor, Piet Retief, and all the brave men who accompanied him to visit the treacherous Dingaan have perished."

I heard a sharp intake of breath from Amelia. Her face went ashen. My mind whirled. There was an anguished wail as one of the widows collapsed to the ground, sobbing. Anna's eyes widened in horror. She covered her mouth with both hands, realizing that my brother was dead. Jan put his arm around her shoulders as tears trickled down her cheeks.

Maritz continued, "I will be sending news of what has happened to our brothers, Hendrik Potgieter and Piet Uys, asking for assistance, as well as alerting the authorities in the colony of these events. Until we get aid, be strong and keep your faith in the Lord for he will protect us against evil. We must all work together to help those who have lost their loved ones."

For the next few hours, working in the dark under the tireless leadership of Maritz and Cilliers, we dragged the piles of Zulu corpses away from the wagons. It was late when we finished. I made my way to Amelia's wagon. Marietjie was there with her. The two women looked forlorn, with the three little boys playing at their feet, little knowing how the events of the day had changed the course of their lives. Both women looked up as I entered. They had both been crying. I wondered whether Marietjie had told Amelia that I had killed Roddy.

"What will become of us now?" asked Amelia.

I shrugged. "I don't know ... I suppose we must go on as before ... a lot of the men are talking about getting out of here ... it's too dangerous now that Dingaan has shown his true colours."

"Well, I am not giving up," said Amelia. "Where would I go? I have nothing anywhere else. Anyway, at least I still have you, Rauch ... come here." She held up her hand to take mine. I did not respond.

Marietjie was watching me. "Nor I, the men mustn't be cowards. We women are staying put, so they had better stay as well. They should concern themselves with killing that swine Dingaan instead of moping around talking about giving up."

A few days later Maritz led us all on a trek to join up with what was left of the Retief laager at Doornkop. We positioned our laager next to the Retief family's, now under the command of Piet Greyling.

᰾ ᰾ ᰾

Early in March the gloom was lifted by the arrival of Piet Uys and his party and two weeks later we were further strengthened by the arrival of Hendrik Potgieter. Both men and their supporters had responded promptly to Maritz's call for aid. We named our new laager Vechtlaager, or fighting laager. It consisted of Greyling's, Uys's and Maritz's laager, the latter by far the largest. Potgieter's had merged with ours so that we were ensured of an excellent defence. We felt comfortable that we'd be ready should we be attacked again.

For the next few weeks, while I worried that the truth about Roddy's death would emerge, I busied myself helping Maritz care for the orphans, the wounded and the bereft. It soon became apparent that his health was rapidly deteriorating but he did not allow his failing strength to slow him down, working tirelessly to assist the trekkers. He arranged a series of auctions where we sold the possessions of those killed with the money raised being given to the survivors' families. We arranged for the adoption of the orphans by relatives and willing friends. Gradually, over the period of a few weeks some semblance of normality returned.

Amelia made it clear that she now expected me to be her man. She seemed blissfully unconcerned that I knew about Jan and her.

For a full month I avoided Marietjie, not knowing what to say, but aching to be with her. Finally, just before a commando led by Uys and Potgieter went off to attack Dingaan, I could stand it no longer and decided to speak to her. I made my way to her tent. She heard my footsteps outside and pulled the entrance open. She said not a word.

"Hello, Marietjie," I said softly.

She nodded, tucking the boys into their cradles. She kissed one then the other. Then she looked at me sadly and said, "What do you want with us? Amelia told me about the two of you ages ago. Of course, I could see it whenever you were together. What you did to me was cruel … I loved you so. How could you end it with a message … you didn't even have the courage to tell me yourself. Now you have killed Roddy. For what? You have left me with no one. Why did you kill him when you don't even want me?"

"What do you mean … don't want you? Who told you that? It is I who should be upset. You wanted to go back to Roddy and you didn't want to see me at all. You sent me a message saying just that …" I cut the sentence short as the realization struck me: "Amelia! The bitch, Amelia!" I shouted, suddenly furious. "I asked her to get a message to you, a message saying that we should meet and she, Amelia, told me that you didn't want to see me. I'll wager anything that she told you I didn't want to see you."

Marietjie nodded, "Amelia told me that the two of you had been having an affair for months, that you were both very much in love. She also said she was going to run away from your pa, with you."

"That's a lie. I had not touched Amelia. There was no affair. She just didn't want me to be happy with you. Amelia always wants everything for herself. My God! What a mess. Now Pa is dead and I have killed Roddy." As I said the words I drew breath sharply as if to suck them back.

Marietjie's expression did not change. "I know you did. Don't worry, Rauch, I'm not going to tell Maritz or any of the others. Only you know and I know what truly happened. I hated Roddy and I can't pretend I didn't. Many were the times he hit me and the boys. I wanted him dead. I don't mourn him at all, in fact, I feel relieved. But this is all too much for me to take in now. Go now. I need time and space to think all this through. For so long I believed that you didn't care for me."

I shook my head, "Marietjie, how can you think that?" I bent over the two cribs and looked at the peaceful faces of my sons. One white and the other coloured and both of them such beautiful children. My heart swelled with love and pride for all three of them. I left the wagon.

⚜ ⚜ ⚜

It did not take long after our defences had been strengthened by the arrival of Uys and Potgieter for the old jealousies to break out again. Uys and Potgieter challenged Maritz's leadership, considering themselves better equipped to lead the attack on Dingaan.

In the early morning of April 6th, 1838 Piet Uys, his twelve-year-old son,

Dirkie, Sarel Cilliers and Potgieter, after prayers led by Erasmus Smit, rode out of Veghtlaager with three hundred and fifty men, to avenge the killings at Weenen by attacking Dingaan. Jan went with the commando. I stayed behind with Maritz.

"They should have taken wagons with them … we have proved that wagons in laager formation offer the best possible protection," Maritz told me, shaking his head. "Still, they know best." His expression made it clear that he didn't think so.

Ten tense days later, shouts and gunshots heralded the return of the commando. "They are back … they are back!"

I looked to the northwest and saw horses approaching. There were two groups. Out in front was Potgieter and his men, followed by Uys's supporters. Several horses had bodies slung over them. I could see by the way the men were riding, slumped in their saddles, heads down and bodies sagging, that they were tired and beaten.

I called out to Maritz, "They are back … they are back, Maritz. But I'm afraid it doesn't look good."

Maritz ran to greet the returning commandos. "What's happened? Where's Piet Uys?" he demanded of Potgieter.

"Piet is dead … and young Dirkie too. Both killed by Zulus."

"But surely that cannot be? What on earth happened?"

"Piet led his men into a trap. The Zulu used the horns of the beast to entice them into a valley at a place called Italeni, five days' ride from here. Piet was badly wounded but he went back to help another man and then fell to the ground from loss of blood. Dirkie rushed back to try and save his father but they were overrun. They fought so bravely …"

"And you?" asked Maritz. "How is it that you were not caught in the same trap?"

"I saw what was happening and I led my men away to safety."

Maritz looked aghast. "You didn't go to his aid?"

"There was no point. I couldn't endanger the lives of my men."

I looked around and it dawned on me that the commandos remained separated into two distinct groups.

One from the Uys group yelled out in fury, "You could have helped. You ran away. You and your vlug commando, your flight commando … you, you are the cowards!"

Potgieter's face went red with rage but he said nothing further.

"Now, now, it wasn't like that, it was merely God's will," said Sarel Cilliers.

"So, you think it was God's will to have Hendrik run away?" the man called angrily. "That's rubbish. How could God will the death of a twelve-year-old child who is brave enough to try and save his father? Is this how your God rewards bravery? Hendrik and all his people are damned cowards. The vlug commando has brought shame on our people. I want nothing to do with Hendrik Potgieter and his vlug commando … nothing at all."

"You won't have to," retorted Potgieter. "I plan to take my people away from this accursed land. I always said it was wrong to come to Natal. I am going back over the mountains with whoever wishes to follow me, to join Trichardt. Take my advice, we should all go now."

True to his word Potgieter left ten days later with a small group of supporters. Maritz was once again our leader, this time unchallenged, but he was in poor health. He decided to lead a delegation to Port Natal. The English, who had themselves been attacked and defeated by the Zulus, gave us help in the form of provisions and a small cannon which we towed back to camp. We were visited by many people bringing aid after they'd heard of our plight. Two of the visitors, Jacobus Boshoff and Gideon Joubert, saw that Maritz was struggling to fulfil his duties and that his illness was getting steadily worse. So they took over as our leaders.

However, it was Maritz who instructed us to move to a new position near the Little Tugela River for better security in the event of another Zulu attack. He encouraged us to lash the wagons together. We shoved robust thorn bushes under and between the wagons and then built a six-foot-high wall of grass sods around the laager, providing a double line of defence.

Sarel Cilliers, who had stayed with us, called out when we had completed our wall of sod, "We will have to call this laager Sooilaer!"

Maritz looked at me and smiled at the name Sods' Laager, shaking his head.

On August 3rd the Zulu warriors came again. This time we were ready for them. Despite the fact that they now had a few guns, taken from Retief, they were poor shots. After two days of repeated attacks, they gave up, although not before again driving all our cattle away. Maritz and I had become firm friends and I could see that he regarded me almost as his own son. I spent time talking to him as he lay in his tent, too ill to go about his onerous round of daily tasks. He confided his plans to attack Dingaan once again.

"This time," he said, eagerly, "we will take fifty wagons with us. The Zulu cannot penetrate our wall of wagons … that's where Uys and Potgieter made their mistake and that's why Uys is now dead. They thought they could defeat Dingaan using the same tactics they employed against the Matabele. They were wrong."

I nodded. I was determined to be part of the final battle plan against Dingaan.

"I am too weak to go, Rauchie. But I trust Karel Landman as a field commander, so he will be in command when the time comes."

I had not spoken to Marietjie since the day we had uncovered Amelia's wicked lies. Nor had I challenged Amelia as to why she had not faithfully delivered my message. Whenever I was near her she made it clear that she wanted me to call on her again, leaving left me in no doubt as to what might happen if I did.

On the evening of September 23rd I was sitting beside my fire, carving a new walking stick, when I was called by Rachel Visser. "Rauch, Rauch, you had better go to the commander … I know that you are fond of him and he of you. They say he's sinking fast."

I went quickly to Maritz's tent. It was dimly lit, candles and lanterns casting grotesque shadows onto the battered canvas. Death was present. Wheezy old Erasmus Smit was just finishing a prayer as I entered. I looked around at the grave faces of the knot of people who stood motionless next to the bed. Some had tears in their eyes. Maritz waved a pale hand in greeting and gave me a weak smile. I nodded and tried unsuccessfully to return his smile. But my throat was tight.

He spoke in a thin, reedy voice, "Like Moses," he said softly, "I have seen the Promised Land but I am not destined to live in it."

He paused, struggling for the strength to continue, "It would have given me great joy to see the rise of my people … but this is not to be. I advise you all to be faithful to the Lord and to your government. No matter what difficulties are still to be surmounted, you will surely still see our people prosper in this land so full of promise." His voice tailed off. Then he began to sing, although so quietly that the words were difficult to hear:

The Lord is my shepherd

I shall not want

He maketh me to lie down in green pastures

He leadeth me beside the still waters

He restoreth my soul …

He stopped singing and silence fell. Then he coughed, paused and started his song again, his voice even feebler. "He leadeth me … " The whispering faded away. The silence was thick. Maritz was dead. He was forty-one years old. One of the women let out a quiet sob. We stood in silence, heads bowed in sorrow while cheeks hardened and roughened by the sun and the wind glistened with tears. The only sound was the drip, drip, drip of rain plopping on the canvas roof of the tent. My eyes burned with tears.

Retief was dead. Uys was dead. Potgieter had left us and taken the vlug kommando north. And now Maritz was dead. We were like a captainless ship in a storm. We had no leader and we had suffered much at the hands of the Zulu. Our spirits sagged.

❦ ❦ ❦

It took two weeks after we had buried Maritz before the general mood lifted slightly. Once again we heard the sound of shots being fired from an approaching party. We scanned the veld to see who it might be. There had been rumours that the great man, Andries Pretorius, and his party were on the way from Graaff-Reinet but it was too soon to expect them. A group of some sixty horsemen came riding into sight. Two of their horses towed a carriage with a cannon mounted on it. There was a wild cheer from the people.

"It's Pretorius!" someone shouted excitedly.

"So it is," came the response "They have come on ahead of their wagons."

"Praise the Lord," declared Sarel Cilliers as he strode out of the laager to greet the new arrivals.

Pretorius rode in, beaming at the warmth of his reception. Willing hands took care of his horse as an excited crowd clamoured around him. Pretorius was tall and good-looking, with dark piercing eyes. His mouth turned down slightly at the corners when he wasn't smiling which made him appear more severe than he actually was. Wherever he stood, because of his height of well over six feet, he seemed to dominate those around him.

He knew me from the days on the frontier and the Xhosa wars. Despite the crowd shaking his hand and clapping him on the back, his piercing glance caught my eye. There was a quick smile of recognition.

"So, we meet again. Hello ... Rauch, it is Rauch Beukes, isn't it?"

I nodded and warmly shook the outstretched hand.

"Yes it is, Meneer Pretorius. How have you been? We are pleased to see you here."

"And I am pleased to be here," his deep voice boomed.

Some of the trekkers turned admiring glances to me with traces of envy.

Three days later, at a meeting of all the trekkers, we elected thirty-nine-year-old Andries Pretorius as our Commandant-General. After being sworn in by Erasmus Smit, Pretorius held up his hand for silence. "Citizens!" he called. "You have all suffered grievously. It is time for change. We will now avenge the killings of our leaders and punish the barbarians who have ripped our children from our bosoms and made others fatherless. I need volunteers. This time we march to war against the Zulu and we will not return until we have the head of that scoundrel and murderer, Dingaan!"

There was a roar of approval and men rushed forward, eager to be part of the new commando. Jan and I found ourselves near the front and to our delight, were promptly accepted. Johannes de Lange became my officer and I was honoured when Pretorius came over, laid a hand on my shoulder, and said to de Lange, "Johannes, I want this youngster to be one of your veldt kornets."

I beamed with joy. Jan looked quite put out.

"We leave in two days," proclaimed Pretorius to the cheers of the assembly.

His arrival and prompt action had lifted our crushed spirits. For the next two days the camp was a bustle of activity. Pretorius instructed us to load up the fifty-seven wagons we were to take on commando. The women helped make extra ammunition by melting tin plates and lead items and loaded the prepared bullets into bags. Waste iron was bound into vet lappies, or oiled cloths, to make small bombs which could be fired from the Sannas. The women worked for many days and late into the evenings making veghekke, or fighting gates; these wooden hurdles, covered with skins and hides, were to be used to seal the openings between the wagons if there were no thorn bushes available at the battle site. Food, water, gunpowder, extra weapons and medical supplies were carefully checked and loaded.

The night before our departure I went to see Amelia in her tent, her body in the soft lamplight looking more appealing than ever before.

"Hello Rauch," she said sweetly. "Have you come to stay?" She smiled, holding her head coquettishly to one side.

I kissed her softly on the mouth and felt her respond passionately. With difficulty I pulled myself away. "No Amelia. Not tonight. We are off early in the morning." She looked taken aback. "We're going to attack Dingaan."

"Oh no, no, don't go Rauch." She reached up and clutched my shirtfront. "Please, not you, don't you go now, I couldn't bear to lose you too. Please don't do this to me."

"I must go, Amelia. This will all soon be over and then perhaps we can talk about the future."

She looked at me with wide blue eyes. "Come then ... stay with me tonight. Just one last time, before you go, please do this for me."

A feeling of panic flooded over me. I wanted to find Marietjie and tell her that I was going. I looked at Amelia as she pulled her dress open at the front. Her milky, white breasts spilled out with rose-red nipples protruding. "Here, Rauch. This is for you .... Please, please make love to me." Her hands tugged at my belt.

I couldn't resist. We made love. As always I was amazed at the force of her passion, her total abandon. Amelia, my first love, my greatest betrayal, the source of my passion, the focal point of my hate—yet always, for me, irresistible.

Early in the morning I kissed her on the forehead while she slept and made my way to Marietjie's tent. I pushed aside the entrance flap; it was pitch dark inside. I could hear her breathing, softly rising and falling.

"Marietjie ... it's me ... Rauch." I whispered.

My eyes strained to accustom themselves to the dark as one of the two figures in the bed stirred. I lit my tonteldoos and held it up. Marietjie opened her eyes and smiled when she saw me in the flickering light. Greta Carstens, whose husband had been killed on commando with Uys, lay beside her. The two were naked and only a light sheet covered them to their waists. Greta held her hands over her bare breasts which had a slight sheen of perspiration. Her mouth shot open in shocked surprise.

"Greta was lonely; she was upset and needed warmth and company, so I suggested that she sleep here with me," said Marietjie with a dismissive smile. "Anyway, Rauch, what brings you here at this hour?'

"I've come to say goodbye."

"Wait, step outside. I'll put on some clothes and talk to you there. We are disturbing Greta."

I did as asked and a minute later she emerged from the tent. "So, you are going? When will you be back?" she asked softly.

"I don't know. Pretorius is adamant that we're going to defeat Dingaan once and for all ... they've made me a veldt kornet," I blurted out proudly. "We leave in a few hours."

"God speed, Rauch!"

"What's Greta doing here ... in your bed?"

"Sshh, Rauch. It's none of your business. We're merely keeping each other company. Anyway, come back safely. I will pray for you."

She put her arms around my neck and kissed me softly on the lips. I could feel her firm breasts against my chest and her warm body under the flimsy gown she had thrown on. I started to respond, kissing her harder. I pulled her close.

She responded for a few seconds and then pushed me away firmly, both hands on my chest. "What about us, when you get back?" she asked.

"I'm not sure ... I can't be sure."

"Don't you love me? Is it Amelia?" She studied me closely. "So .... Amelia was right. You never did answer me all that time ago when I asked if you were over her."

"No, no. I really, I really am not sure of anything anymore."

She looked at me with deep sadness in her eyes. "Is it … what you're thinking about Greta?"

She was right. I had come this time to declare my love for her and had found her in bed with another woman. I remembered the first night I had met her, way back in Grahamstown. Then she had been in bed with Katrina.

"Sometimes I find that a woman can be more comforting than a man. Roddy is dead. You're with Amelia. I needed someone … and so did Greta … I sometimes ache with the need …"

"I must go now. Goodbye, Marietjie. Look after André and Anton." I kissed her gently, turned away and left her there, standing in the dark.

"Come back safely, Rauch," she whispered.

Chapter Twenty-two

As the sun struggled to break though the early morning rain clouds on November 27th, 1838, three hundred and forty-one men stood before Erasmus Smit. Stricken by rheumatism, he hobbled to stand in front of us to offer up one last prayer.

"Kneel, kêrels!" Pretorius ordered. As one we sank to our knees on the grass beside the wagons.

Erasmus Smit closed his eyes, holding his arms up to the sky: "Oh my God, incline Your ear and hear; open Your eyes to see our desolations and that of the city which is called by Your name; for we do not present our supplications before You because of our righteous deeds, but because of Your great mercies …"

I looked round at the kneeling men, hats clasped on chests, eyes squeezed tight as if the Lord would not hear should an eye display the tiniest chink. I wondered how many of us would not return. When Smit had finished, we clambered awkwardly to our feet.

Pretorius stepped up: "Men, we go forth in the name of our Lord. We are God's soldiers and we go to avenge the killing of our women, our children and our brothers under Governor Retief. Know this …" He paused, scanning the expectant faces, "… I am in charge here. I will be obeyed. Our lieutenants are under me and the veldt kornets under them. I expect every man to obey his orders. I expect all of us to stand together. We have to win, win or die. Remember, men …" He raised his voice and shouted, "Unity is strength!"

"Unity is Strength," we roared back with one voice.

We mounted our horses and rode off to do battle with the mighty army of the Zulu. Karel Landman and his men joined us at Klip River a few days later. The party was further swelled by the arrival of Alexander Biggar, the Englishman from Port Natal, with over a hundred friendly Zulus. We were a fighting force of four hundred and sixty-four men, more than a hundred servants and sixty-four wagons. As we trundled over the veld the wagons were lined up in four rows so that the convoy was not overly extended and vulnerable to attack. Discipline was strict. Every night as we travelled east toward Umgungundhlovu, Pretorius made us form the wagons into a laager, placing veghekke in the gaps between them. He posted sentries and dispatched scouts to look for the Zulus. He also made sure that the five commandos of men prepared their weapons for the battle which lay ahead and were regularly inspected by the officers. I felt proud to have been appointed a junior officer, a veldt kornet. Pretorius gave orders that only the officers would wear pistols, so as to identify them. I wore mine as a badge of honour. Among the men there was a new air of confidence: they sat erect on their horses, followed orders promptly and walked with a spring in their step. Pretorius had infused us with a renewed sense of purpose.

The health of Erasmus Smit did not permit him to accompany us but we had Sarel Cilliers to provide spiritual guidance. As we crossed a range of steep hills, Cilliers suddenly exclaimed, "Look out!"

I looked in the direction he indicated and to my horror I saw a wagon plunge into a ravine after its wheel skidded off the path. "It's Biggar's wagon," I shouted as I galloped off to inspect the damage.

Ten minutes later I reported back to Pretorius and Cilliers. "All is well, no one is injured and the only damage is to the wagon but they are busy fixing it as I speak."

Cilliers looked at me with the hint of a smile. "I hope you are not praying as hard as you were with Rachel Visser."

I had a vision of how I must have looked between Rachel's legs before the battle at Vegkop. I could feel my face burning with embarrassment; I couldn't think of a riposte.

Cilliers's smile broadened as he noticed my discomfort before thankfully changing the subject: "I think we should name those hills the Biggarsberg in memory of old Biggar's wagon that just went over. " He chuckled, "Trust an Englishman to lose his wagon."

Jan grinned at me. "Old Cilliers is naming the world again … it's just like old times."

On the Sunday we laagered next to the Wasbank River, named by Cilliers because the men washed their clothes there and went swimming.

In the morning we assembled for divine service. Pretorius stood in front of our small army and waited for silence. "Men! Our scouts have sent word that a mighty Zulu army has left Umgungundhlovu and is making its way to meet us. What lies ahead is a task of monumental proportions. We estimate that there are fifteen to twenty thousand warriors. Our scouts tell us that they are being led by Dingaan's leading general, Uhlele. Prepare yourselves, men. Prepare your weapons, your bodies, your minds and your souls. To help us in these preparations, Sarel Cilliers will now lead us in prayer."

Cilliers climbed onto a gun carriage: "My brethren and fellow countrymen. At this moment we stand before the Holy God of Heaven and Earth to make a promise. If our God will be with us to protect us, and to deliver into our hands the enemy so that we may triumph over him, we shall observe this day and date as an anniversary. This will forever be observed as a day of thanksgiving, like the Sabbath, in His honour; and we shall enjoin our children and our children's children to participate in this. Now, if there is anyone among us who sees a difficulty in this observation, let him retire from this place. For the honour of His name shall be joyfully exalted. To Him must the fame and the honour of the victory ever be given. Amen!"

Jan and I exchanged glances as five men we didn't recognize walked away, not sure that they could honour a promise made on behalf of their children. I watched sadly as they collected their clothes and bedding and rode off, back to Sooilaar.

Every evening thereafter, when we had laagered our wagons for the night and gathered for prayers, Sarel Cilliers repeated word for word the vow he had made. Whenever he uttered the words I could see that the others present felt as I did: with God on our side, how could we lose?

With each day we saw more evidence of Zulu activity. In one encounter, in light rain, Hans Dons, one of our commanders, captured five Zulus after shooting a further three. Among the prisoners was a young maiden. Pretorius approached her. She stood before him with her head bowed, looking at the ground. She wore a skirt of beads. The upper part of her body was naked. I saw that the men's eyes were glued to the same spot as mine, to the pert, ebony breasts with large black nipples standing stiffly erect with raindrops trickling between her breasts.

Pretorius wrote his name on a piece of white cloth, handed it to her and said through an interpreter: "Take this to your king. Tell him that I am coming to punish him for the murders he has committed against my people. Tell him that I am still willing to make peace if he will. If he chooses peace then he must return to us the guns, sheep and cattle he has taken, and he must apologize for the atrocities he has committed against our people. But if his choice is war, he must understand that the white man will never give up … even if it takes ten years. Now go! Tell him that I, Pretorius, come!"

The Zulu maiden took the cloth, stared hard at Andries Pretorius, then turned and trotted away slowly in the direction of Umgungundhlovu.

It was drizzling again. Jan was, as usual, riding alongside me, drops of rain trickling off the brims of our hats. In every direction there was a fine mist over the hills. Everything was grey and wet.

I had a sudden thought: "This is not good, Jan. Heaven help us if we meet the Zulus in the rain. It won't be long before our powder's wet … we will be defenceless."

Jan looked at me, concerned, "Well, we'd better make sure that we stay well away from them until we get some dry weather."

By Saturday, thankfully, the rain had stopped. The skies were still heavy and grey above us as we approached a hill the Zulus called Gelato. Ahead of us Hans de Lange led six scouts to track down the Zulu army. After passing the hill we drew near the river the Zulus called the Ncome, or Cow River, when two scouts came galloping into view.

From a distance, cupping his hands to his mouth, Jan Robbertse, called out, "They are here, just half an hour's ride from us. The whole Zulu army is waiting behind those hills!" He pointed in the direction of the Nqutu mountains. "God save us!" gasped Robbertse, as he drew closer, ashen-faced, "I have never seen anything like it."

The moment of reckoning had come.

He jumped from his horse, his hands shaking and looked up at Pretorius, still mounted. "Even with God's help we simply cannot take them on."

"Be quiet!" said Pretorius sternly, "We are not running from these heathens. Where's Piet Moolman?" He looked around for his lieutenant and addressed him: "You stay here with two commandos and prepare the wagons. I will take three hundred men to look for the Zulu army. Place the wagons in a semi-circle here." He indicated an area where the base would run parallel to the river with part of the 'D' running next to the deep donga, the ditch created by a stream that had practically dried up and carried but a trickle of water into the Ncome. The donga was deep with high walls which would be difficult to climb. The river ran from north to south and where the donga entered the river there was a deep hippo hole, making it impossible to be attacked from that direction. The wagons could therefore only be attacked from the northeast. I looked at the site Pretorius had chosen and could not help but admire his tactical acumen.

"Chain the wagons together," he ordered, "and put the veghekke in place. Move all the oxen into the laager for protection. Place the three cannons there …" pointing northeast, "there …" where the donga merged with the river, "… and here," he added, indicating west.

"But they can't attack from there?" questioned Moolman studying the donga.

"Possibly, but we must make sure that the noise is distributed evenly around the laager otherwise the cattle and horses will bolt from the noise and charge into the wagons."

Moolman nodded.

"Right! Come on, the rest of you, we'll show these savages that we're not scared of them ... unity is strength!" he yelled, spurring his horse forward as we all roared in unison, "Unity is strength!"

It was late afternoon when we trotted round a small hill and saw, for the first time, the massed ranks of the Zulu army. Twenty thousand warriors were sitting on their shields some five hundred yards away. Row upon row, regiment by regiment, each distinguished by the colour of their shields. Their commanders stood regally out in front.

As we rounded the hill, with Pretorius in the lead, he called back to us: "Keep in your commandos of fifty men ... leave a space of fifty yards between each commando ... and keep circling that hill. That way they will never be able to calculate our full strength."

We did as commanded. The Zulu army sat on their shields. Once they had realized we were not going to engage, the sound of their derisive hisses was carried to us on the evening breeze. They were massed in their numbers, shoulder to shoulder, looking from afar like a rippling black sea.

Cilliers shouted to Pretorius, "Come. We are in God's hands. Let us attack them now!"

"No," replied Pretorius. "That is just what they want ... to lead us into a trap. Let them come to us. Better to return to the wagons. Let them attack us there."

It was dark when we arrived back at the laager. A heavy mist blanketed the wagons and the surrounding hills. Moolman had placed lanterns around the sixty-four wagons, one to each wagon, diffusing an eerie orange light in the mist. Piet Moolman and his men had done their work thoroughly. The wagons were bound together by leather riempies and chains, with the three ammunition wagons positioned inside the laager. The veghekke were in place, with all the cattle and the spare horses inside a hastily constructed kraal in the centre of the laager.

There was an air of solemnity in the camp that night as we ate our evening meal. Men spoke in low voices. A line of men had silently formed near one of the wagons. At the front of the queue, bent over and scribbling furiously, was the Scot, William Cowie. Men who could not write were dictating hasty letters to loved ones in case they did not return from the battle.

Cilliers called out, "Gather round, men. Our Chief Kommandant wishes to address us."

Pretorius stood in front of us, calm and confident: "My brothers! This is the moment. Tomorrow is the Sabbath so I am hoping that the enemy will not come on the Lord's Day. But if they do, we shall be ready for them. You must all get a good night's rest; however no man shall sleep until he has checked his weapons and made ready for the attack. I want eight men between every wagon. The three cannoniers will be Piet Rudolph, my brother Bart Pretorius and Gerhardus Pretorius." The three men exchanged proud smiles. "I want every man ready and in position two hours before sun-up ... whether you have slept or not." He looked anxiously up at the sky. "When Sarel Cilliers leads us in prayer, I suggest we ask the Lord for sunshine tomorrow. Sarel?"

Cilliers stepped forward and again repeated the vow. We sang hymns, prayed for sunshine and sang Psalm thirty-eight as loudly as we could, as if the very volume of our singing could intimidate the Zulu ...

Forsake me not, O Lord

O my God, Be not far from me

Make haste to help me

O Lord, my salvation

Amen.

From a distance and through the mist the ensuing silence was pierced by faint shouts which floated to us from across the river. One of the servants translated: "They say, 'Cry, cry! You sound like children crying for their mothers. Tomorrow you will have something to cry about!'"

The laager fell silent. Then the night was filled with the bloodcurdling sound of twenty thousand Zulu warriors chanting from across the river:

We journey to war

Over the hills yonder

Over the hills where the sun sets

To a country we do not know

We journey for you, King and Father

Lion! Elephant! Liberator!

King of Kings! King of the Zulu! Dinga aa- aane!

We salute you!

Zeee … zeeeeee … zeeee

"Oh Lord, be with us," whispered Hans Bruwer next to me. In the dim light of the lantern I could see that his face was as pale as death. Terror was written on all our faces as we made our way to our positions between the wagons.

Jan was in my commando of thirty-two men. We settled ourselves between four wagons, facing northeast. We prepared our weapons for the coming onslaught. Each of us had three Sannas. Beside each man lay stitched bags containing lead bullets, plates of shot, piles of gunpowder, fresh water and biltong. On my belt I carried my voorlaaier pistol and a knife with a twelve-inch blade. Once satisfied that there was nothing more to be done, I called out, "Right, men. Make sure your guns are cleaned, loaded and ready for action. Then get some sleep. Each man is to stand guard tonight for two hours and all must be at his post two hours before sunrise. Goodnight."

At midnight I was still wide awake, tossing and turning restlessly in my blankets. I thought of Amelia, of Marietjie and my small boys, wondering whether I would ever see them again. As I lay, desperate for sleep, the mist seemed to grow ever thicker. A few men moved around inside the laager, their shapes made ghostly by the swirling fog.

In the early hours of morning I thought I heard a faint noise like small rocks tumbling against one another in deep water. It seemed to come from the northeast. I wriggled out of my bedclothes and peered between the wagons.

"What's that noise?" I whispered to a sentry. "I heard a noise."

A continuous low swishing sound was coming from the direction of the river. The sentry shrugged nervously, staring out into the mist which was now so thick that the river was hidden from view. All the sentries strained their eyes, trying to pierce the murky darkness of the night.

"It sounds like the wind in the trees ... but there are no trees here," said one of the men, rubbing his eyes.

"Maybe it's just rain on the way," whispered Jan in a tone of false optimism.

"It's them!" whispered a sentry in a hoarse voice. "The Zulu ... they are crossing the river ... sshhh! Listen!" The rumble continued. It was the sound of thousands of bare feet walking across the smooth rocks of the riverbed. "My God! There must be ... there are thousands coming! Do you think they will attack now?"

No one responded. I heard the man next to me swallow hard. A man began to pray, "Our Father, who art in heaven ..." His voice shook audibly.

By now everyone was awake and there was a soft bustle of activity as men moved cautiously into their positions. The tension was palpable.

"I hope they don't attack in the dark," whispered Jan.

The soft swish of the warriors making the river crossing had stopped.

"Holy Father," said one of the men breathlessly, "They are out there … I can feel they are out there. Maybe they are getting ready to attack right now. O dear God … save my soul."

The mist had started to lift. I glanced at the sky. A thousand thousand stars twinkled overhead.

"Look!" I whispered loudly, pointing, "It's going to be a sunny day."

"Praise the Lord," a voice uttered fervently.

We could see no sign of the enemy in the dark but knew they were out there, like a terrifying, tangible presence. I could hear quiet gasps of fear in the darkness around me. I heard the sound of retching as a man vomited. Horses snorted and shook their manes. Cattle shifted nervously in their kraal. Some men prayed, others sat staring out into the night. Some cleaned their weapons for the umpteenth time. It was a long, long night.

As the dawn began to break I peered out of the laager. I could just make out the shapes of the flat-topped thorn trees in the distance. A bush pigeon started to coo. A guinea fowl replied raucously. Everything looked so peaceful.

And then I caught sight of them. A solid black mass, only forty paces or so from the wagons, stretched back for a hundred yards. As a cold hand squeezed my gut and another gripped my throat.

"There they are!" Cilliers cried. "Get ready, men! Have faith in the Lord. He has ordained a day made in heaven for us."

Indeed He had.

As the sun began to rise it washed the scene before us with a bloody pink glow, climbing higher and higher until it broke the silhouetted line of the horizon and ascended into the sky.

"Do not fear their numbers," called out Pretorius. "And do not shoot until I give the word."

The veld was now bathed in sparkling light. Forty yards from us sat the Zulu general, Tambuza, wearing a headdress made from the long distinctive tail feathers of the blue crane. His commanders sat in front of their regiments: the Impohlo, the Izinyozi, Ufazimba, Udlambedlu, Umkutyana, Ukhokothi, Ihlabe, Bulawayo, Dukuza, Belebelini, Mnyame, Khangela, Imkulutyani, Dlangezwa, the Imvokwe and on and on …

The frightful sight made my blood run cold. All around me I could see the white, drawn faces of my men. Pieter Hamman was biting his lip so hard a trickle of blood ran down his chin. Sybrand van Niekerk had covered his eyes with his hands and his lips moved quickly in fervent prayer.

Dirk du Plooy thrust into my hand an envelope addressed to his sister. "Here, Rauch. Give this to my sister if you make it and I don't." I nodded. Four more letters were shoved into my hands, each with a similar request. I realized with sudden sadness that I hadn't even thought to write my farewell to anyone.

The Zulu warriors sat patiently on their man-sized shields, wearing a variety of feather headdresses. Their upper bodies were naked but glistened with perspiration, early morning dew and animal fat. Hands gripped spears and fighting sticks as they stared at us. The now familiar but still terrifying "Hisssssssssss" of contempt emerged sibilantly from more than ten thousand throats. General Tambuza turned his back on the wagons. He faced his men and shouted a command. As one they rose to their feet, their shields next to them. My mouth was dry and my hands were clammy, slipping on the butt of my Sanna.

"Ready, men!" yelled Pretorius, his weapon in his shoulder, finger lightly squeezing the trigger as he took aim.

Tambuza began by driving the warriors into a killing frenzy. "Bulala ibhunu!" he screamed.

He was answered by the roar of ten thousand voices, "Bulala ibhunu! Bulala ibhunu! Bulala ibhunu!" Their rhythmic chant washed over us as the rippling black Zulu wave began to creep toward us. There was a sound like pouring rain as they drummed the hasps of their spears against their shields. They were trotting. Faster. Then faster still.

And as they ran they shouted the chilling cry that went right through us: "Usuthu! Usuthu!" The war cry of the Zulu warrior.

"Zee! … zee! … zeee! …. zee!

"Fire!" came the command from Pretorius. Five hundred triggers were pulled. The noise of the simultaneous explosions was deafening. My ears sang and warriors fell dead as our lead cut a swath through their ranks. Choking smoke filled the air. The surge halted momentarily but more surged forward to replace the fallen. Again they charged.

"Fire the cannon," yelled Pretorius, who could scarcely be heard above the noise of the approaching impis.

"Boom! … Boom!" The two cannons fired, spurting deadly flames. One cannon recoiled, somersaulting backward and causing the men nearby to dive for safety. The earth trembled. Acrid smoke thickened around us. The cannon balls crashed through the front rows of the Zulu regiments. Dozens of broken bodies flew into the air and tumbled to the ground. Again the dead were replaced by fresh warriors as the wave came crashing on. There was a continuous sound of gunfire. A chunk of wood from one of the wagons flew past my head.

"Look out!" I yelled. "Some of them have guns."

The sharp smell of gunpowder filled the air and my eyes stung from the cloying, thick blue smoke.

Pretorius's voice rang out. "Cease fire!"

A few desultory shots rang out. A slight morning breeze shepherded the smoke away.

Cilliers shouted, "God be with us all! This is just half their army. The white shields under Uhlela are still on the far riverbank … look! Some of them are starting to cross!"

The Zulu had retreated some five hundred paces. Between us and them lay the bodies of many hundreds of their fallen, some still moving. Shots rang out as some of the men fired at the wounded who tried to crawl away.

"I said cease fire!" commanded Pretorius.

We stopped firing and all was quiet. We could see fresh divisions of white shields joining the ranks of the black shields. Some of the Zulu had climbed down into the donga in an attempt to launch an attack from there.

"Get ready, men," said Pretorius. "They will come at us again."

I checked my weapons and waited, my heart pounding against my chest.

The Zulu commanders were berating their men, urging them on, fuelling their anger. Tambuza, strutting at the front, shouted again, "Bulala ibunhu! Bulala ibunhu! Bulaaala ibuuunhu!"

As one they stood. We braced ourselves as they charged again, cat tail skirts swirling, shields held high and stabbing spears ready to thrust.

"Fire!" shouted Pretorius.

One of the servants from Biggar's group helped me by reloading and passing my Sanna to me. I fired and fired. My shoulder ached from the kicks of the voorlaaier. I was totally lost in my own world, responding automatically with but single thought: shoot, hold out hand, grab, shoot as I shouted, "Gee!" … aim, shoot, "Gee!" … aim, shoot, "Gee!"

The barrels of the guns became so overheated that I was afraid they'd explode when a new charge of gunpowder was rammed down the barrels. The noise was deafening. The pall of blue gunpowder smoke became thicker, burning the hairs in our nostrils. Flashes and spurts of fire from the five hundred guns punctured the dense cloud of smoke. The flash and roar of the cannons, the crack of the Sannas firing repeatedly, screams of anger, pain, terror and shouted commands from both sides made for a hellish inferno. The fresh Zulu horde was almost upon us. Every time triggers were pulled, men fell. It was impossible to miss. And still they came. The flash of assegais distracted me. Faces contorted with hatred loomed up at me through the smoke. Grab—aim—fire! The enemy charged like lions only to drop like stones. I found myself screaming at one stage, unaware that I was doing so. The stench of battle was overpowering: smoke and sweat and fear and gore. Wave after wave washed toward us. Not one, thank God, breached the wagons' defences.

"Look out," warned Cilliers. "They're climbing out of that donga ... they're standing on each other's shoulders!"

A group of more than fifty men ran to repel the new threat. The Zulus were trapped in the donga. They were packed so tightly it was impossible to throw a spear. Some of the warriors managed it but they were so few it hardly mattered. Suddenly Philip Fourie screamed in agony as a flying assegai sank into his thigh. He grabbed the hasp and pulled the blade out, blood spurted and ran down his leg but still he continued shooting. A hail of slugs found their targets in the packed bodies wedged in the donga. The warriors tried helplessly to defend themselves by holding their shields above their heads but to no avail. Hot metal scythed through them. Again and again the volleys rang out. The bodies piled higher and higher in the donga until not one Zulu was left standing.

Pretorius shouted out a command. "Turn the cannon on the white shields across the river!"

Willing hands helped Piet Rudolph roll the heavy cannon to face the river.

"Fire!" yelled Pretorius. The shot crashed into the middle of a group of senior Zulu officers, missing Nhlele but killing what appeared to be two Zulu princes.

"Cease fire!"

The smoke again started to clear. The silence weighed heavily in the still air. The highly trained Zulu had retreated five hundred paces and were again seated impassively on their shields. The veld around the wagons was covered to waist height with perhaps over two thousand Zulu bodies. The ranks of the living had been swelled by the regiments of the white shields.

There were still more than fifteen thousand able warriors ready to do battle.

Someone let out a cheer which was picked up by others.

Pretorius fired a pistol shot in the air to get our attention. "It's not over yet, men. Be ready! They will come again. Use this time to prepare your weapons."

We watched as messengers ran from one regiment to another, their commanders conferring, planning their next attack. We waited.

Pretorius called his brother Bart to his side. They talked briefly and then Bart, with an interpreter, left the safety of the laager and walked to a distance of one hundred paces from the massed ranks of the Zulu.

"What are you doing, you men of Dingaan? Are you afraid? We have come to fight men, not women and children. Why will you not attack? Is it because you are scared?" he taunted. There was no response other than the "Hissssss", that bloodcurdling sound we would never get used to. Bart fired two shots into the massed ranks but still they sat.

Pretorius ordered the two cannons to be fired again. A shower of grass, dust, bones and blood erupted, before being engulfed in thick black smoke.

Brightly painted sangomas, medicine men, some wearing hideous wooden masks and skirts made of jackal and hyena tails, administered muti, or magic medicine, to the warriors. Roots, animal blood, leaves and holy water were splashed on their bodies in a valiant attempt to protect them from our bullets and bombs. The sound like that of trumpets, bellowed from the commanders' cow horns, floated across to us like the plaintive cries of a wounded beast. The warriors leaped to their feet and charged again. The war cry "Usuthu!" and the answering "Zeeee … zeee … zeeee!" sent a chill down my spine. Then the familiar "Bulala ibhunu!" signalling that we would be shown no mercy.

The charge brought the front ranks to within feet of the laager. We stood firm. A wall of fire and lead met the assegai attack. Hundreds more warriors lay dead. The Zulu losses were horrific but still they came. I saw some of the black-shield warriors turn away from our devastating fire, holding their shields in front of their heads for protection. Warriors with white shields tried to reach us but were blocked by the black-shield warriors who were starting to retreat. Out of frustration at not being able to attack us, some of those with white shields attacked those carrying black shields, beating their own brothers in arms with fighting sticks; I saw more than a few stabbed to death by the assegais of the white-shield troops.

Pretorius stopped shooting. He was talking to Bart Pretorius, his brother, "We cannot hold them off much longer. Our ammunition won't last. We'll have to go on the offensive now."

Bart nodded and beckoned to me. He explained what he wanted us to do. I called my commando together and we ran for our horses. When we were all mounted Bart Pretorius shouted, "Now!"

A wagon was rolled aside by twenty men as my commando, with three hundred men led by Bart Pretorius, galloped out of the laager straight at the Zulu, firing from the saddle as we rode.

He yelled, "Come on, men! Unity is strength!"

We responded, shouting in the thick of the charge: "Unity is strength!"

The warriors scattered before us, creating a path for our horses. Bodies fell and by dint of firing continuously we were able to drive a wedge between the ranks of Zulu. At our third charge we were able to break through the last of the enemy ranks and we began to attack them from their rear.

The cannon shells were decimating the warriors nearest the wagons while we shot from horseback at the rear. Caught in a trap between two walls of fire, the Zulu started to break ranks.

"Keep firing," shouted Bart Pretorius above the noise.

The crackle of gunfire from the front changed pitch, growing in volume as it came closer. It was our leader, Andries Pretorius, leading a large group of men on horseback in another frontal attack.

The Zulu were now in full flight. They ran wildly, scattering in all directions. Many fled toward the river, leaping into the swirling brown waters. Andries Pretorius pursued a fleeing warrior, who turned to face him, stabbing spear in hand. Pretorius fired at the warrior but his horse reared in fright and the shot missed. The Zulu stabbed at Pretorius who fended off the blade with his rifle butt. Again the Zulu stabbed, again Pretorius deflected the assegai. A third thrust pierced Pretorius's left hand. Blood spurted. Pretorius threw the Zulu to the ground and tried to draw his knife. The Zulu put his hands around Pretorius's throat and squeezed. Pretorius went red in the face, eyes bulging. Beads of sweat stood on his brow as he struggled for breath. Piet Rudolph saw what was happening and ran to the two men rolling on the ground. Piet Meyer also ran to them. Rudolph pulled the assegai out of Pretorius's hand and thrust it into the Zulu's throat; the warrior let go of Pretorius and sat up tugging at the shaft, blood gushing. I took my chance and shot him between the eyes. He fell back dead, vacant eyes staring at the smoke-filled heavens.

"Thank you, men, thank you. You saved my life," said Pretorius, his right hand cradling his wounded left. Blood trickled through his fingers.

"You had better get that cared for, kommandant," said Meyer.

I looked at the dead Zulu. My eye was caught by the sun glinting on a piece of metal around his neck. I looked closer. Alongside the wooden necklace—umNyzene, the necklace awarded for bravery by the Zulu king—a small gold crucifix dangled from a thin riempie. My heart pounded as I knelt beside the body to examine it. Zulu blood smeared the crucifix but the engraving was clear: 'Amelia'.

I decided to take it back to Amelia. I pulled it off, wrapped it in my handkerchief and pocketed it. The battle still raged around us with the Zulu now in full retreat, pursued by our men on horseback. Bodies littered the veld, with blood, guts and gore everywhere. Most of our men had gathered by the river where many of the Zulus had sought refuge. I kicked Grey's flanks and galloped to join them. Hundreds of warriors were in the water, seeking its fragile protection. Some dived under to escape the bullets. As the bullets found their mark, little clouds of blood swirled, marking the spot. We stood on the banks and picked them off, one by one, with bodies half submerged in the reeds.

By the time we called it a day there was not one Zulu left alive in the river … and the waters of the Ncomo River ran red with blood.

Slowly Grey and I made our way back to the laager. A wave of exhaustion swept over me. Despite the fact that we had won the battle, I felt flat. The killing had been too much, too intense. The scene of thousands of bodies, many still warm, lying where they fell would be imprinted on my mind forever. The midday sun was high in the sky and beat down mercilessly. In every direction all one saw were corpses. Where they had managed to get close to the wagons the corpses formed a bank, just as they had done at Vegkop. The smell of death permeated my every pore. Dozens of black specks circling in the sky signalled the arrival, en masse, of the vultures.

As I entered the laager, I encountered a scene of joyous celebration. Men were shouting to each other, laughing shrilly, some hysterically, as if they couldn't believe they were still alive. Some wore dazed expressions on their gunpowder-blackened faces with teeth shining a startling white when they grimaced or smiled.

Someone clapped me on my back and I turned to see Sarel Cilliers. He had a broad grin on his face as he grabbed my right hand and pumped it vigorously. "Praise the Lord, Rauchie! Well done … well fought! You helped save the kommandant's life, so he tells me. Praise the Lord, praise the Lord." I felt as though my arm was going to be yanked from its socket. Cilliers finally let go and stared out at the broken bodies surrounding the wagons. It was as if he saw them for the first time. He said suddenly, "It looks like pumpkins on a rich soil that has born a plentiful crop."

Pretorius approached, his left hand bandaged and the arm in a sling. "I've given that heathen Dingaan one more chance to make peace," he said to

Cilliers. "I have sent two Zulu prisoners to Dingaan with a white cloth that I have signed. I told him again that if he will apologize and return our cattle we can live in peace. If not, we will come after him at Umgungundlovu."

Cilliers nodded, sagely.

"You must lead us in prayers of reverent thanksgiving, Sarel. This victory was truly the Lord's. Do you know that we have not lost a single man? There are three wounded but not one man is dead."

"Our God is a merciful God," answered Cilliers solemnly. "Praise the Lord!"

The men were trickling back into the laager. Shouts of "Praise the Lord!" echoing Cillier's sentiments were heard over and over, as friends recognized each other, rejoicing at being alive.

Some of the men had not yet returned from chasing Zulu stragglers when Cilliers called out, "Come, my brothers. Come near, so that we can thank the Lord for granting us victory."

The tired but elated men gathered round as Cilliers knelt in front of us, holding his Bible up to the sky. "I read from Chronicles two, chapter twenty, verse five …" We bowed our heads.

And Jehoshaphat stood in the congregation of Judah and Jerusalem, in the house of the Lord, before the new court and said: O Lord God of our fathers, art thou not God in heaven, and rulest not Thou over all the kingdoms of the heathen, and in Thine hand is there not power and might, so that no one is able to withstand Thee? Art Thou not our God, who didst drive out the inhabitants of this land before Thy people Israel, and gavest it to the seed of Abraham, Thy friend forever … Thank you, dear God. You are indeed merciful. You have protected the righteous and granted us victory over our enemies. We made a vow to You that we will treat this day as a day like the Sabbath, for all time. And so be it that this day, December the sixteenth, 1838, shall be carved into our history as the day when we renewed that vow to You and in remembrance of the river which ran red with the blood of our enemies. From this day, it will be known as Blood River and those that fought here will be remembered as the Wen Kommando, the Victory Commando. We will build a church in honour of the victory you have given us.

Amen.

He then led us in hymns and we repeated the vow. On this day it had a very special meaning. Even I felt that we had been protected by the Lord and this time I prayed as fervently as the next man.

After prayers men sat drinking brandy to celebrate, although sentries kept a watchful eye in case Uhlela's warriors returned. Someone started to play a fiddle. Laughter and jubilation went on late into the night, accompanied by the snarling of hyenas and wild dogs squabbling over the corpses.

When eventually I wrapped myself in my blankets I lay awake listening to the noise of scavengers while my mind whirled with confused thoughts of Amelia and Marietjie and the boys. Sleep came to me only in short bursts. I fingered the crucifix before I finally slid into a restless sleep.

The next morning we counted the bodies, marking each with tar so as not to count them twice. In the immediate area of the wagons we counted three thousand, five hundred. Many had been devoured during the night and many more must have been killed by the commando which had pursued the ragtag remnants of the Zulu army late into the night.

The total Zulu dead numbered more than five thousand. We felt we had honourably avenged the massacre at Weenen.

Chapter Twenty-three

After the battle we broke camp. We cleared a path between the corpses and rode out to attack Dingaan at Umgungundlovu. We made rapid progress over the eighty miles to the royal enclosure and two days later our scouts reported that we were close.

We were startled by the sudden sound of a gunshot. I looked round in time to see a crow plunge to the ground with Jacobus Uys waving the smoking gun.

We were all still laughing when Barend Boshof called out, "Look, look over there!" He pointed in the direction of Umgungundlovu where a thick, black cloud of smoke rose from behind the hills.

"It's Dingaan!" yelled Pretorius, "He must have heard the shot and it seems he has set his kraal alight. Come quickly. I am sure he is fleeing."

Pretorius was right. When we arrived several hours later tendrils of smoke still rose from the ruins of the royal settlement. A few of the flimsy structures were still burning. We sat on our agitated horses and stared at what had been Dingaan's palace. The wily old devil had beaten us to it.

"Maybe we will find some trace of Retief and his men," said Pretorius solemnly.

We picked our way carefully through the smouldering ruins. There were no signs of life but we managed to recover ivory tusks, copperware, farm implements, jewellery, pottery and other valuables and also, sadly, the familiar guns taken from Retief's slaughtered men.

"We will take these. We can sell them," said Pretorius. "The money will go to the families made destitute by the Zulu attacks."

"What is that, over there?" asked Pretorius, indicating Kwa Matiwane hill about a mile away. "That is … that must be … the hill of death," he said quietly, answering his own question. He kicked his horse and cantered toward the hill.

We found the remains of Retief and his party among the many bodies on the foul-smelling hill. As we approached the open mass grave in silence, men gagged at the ghastly smell that rose from many thousands of skeletons, some with lumps of putrefying flesh still clinging to them. The skeletal frames and other pieces of evidence showed us how valiantly Retief and his men must have fought before they had been so cruelly cut down. With tears in our eyes, we shovelled our way through the piles of bones, some with bits of skin and hair still attached, dried bronze by ten months of baking under the merciless sun. Men were silently weeping as they found a shred of cloth, a belt, any evidence of a family member or a friend killed. Many skeletons still had stakes protruding from their pelvises, thick stakes that had been driven up their anuses. Skeletal legs were still bound with leather thongs.

One skeleton lay some distance from the others, still with the remnants of a pale blue waistcoat that I recognized as Pa's. I felt nauseous as I stared down on the skeleton of Jakob Beukes. It was my turn to cry. Shaking with emotion, I dismounted and sat next to the skeleton of my father.

"If you can hear me now, Pa," I said, with tears coursing down my cheeks, "know that I am sorry. I am so very sorry for all the wrongs that I have committed against you. I will look after Amelia and little Jakob for you. That I promise, Pa." Cold with shock and grief, I cast about for any sign of my brother, Frans, who had died so young. Not a sign could I identify. I said a silent prayer for my brother.

Suddenly, Pretorius cried out. "Here's Retief!"

After one last sorrowful glance at Pa's hideously grinning skull I went over to Pretorius. The skeleton at his feet was draped with the tatters of a satin waistcoat. Nearby was a water bottle bearing the Masonic emblem and a leather bag. Pretorius knelt and opened the bag and pulled out a sheaf of papers.

He waved a page triumphantly over his head. "Here it is! It is signed by

Dingaan's own hand. Here he grants us all the land between the Tugela River, the mountains and the Umfolozi River." He folded the paper and stuffed it into his breast pocket. The bag and the water bottle he placed in his saddle bag. "Come, kêrels, to work. We cannot leave our brothers out in the open like this. Get going … together we will honour them with a Christian burial."

We dug a large hole in earth that seemed as hard as rock and dragged the pathetic remains of my father and the nameless others into it. When we had completed the gruesome task, Sarel Cilliers led us in a prayer for the dead.

Pretorius had two of the men engrave a large rock which we used to mark the grave:

21ste Desember, 1838 A.W.J. Pretorius.

Die hoofstad van Dingane, Koning van de Zulus

Heb ik, Andries Wilhelmus Jacobus, Kommandant-Generaal met mij

Onder Kommandante, Veldkornette en Manschappe

op 21ste Desember ingeneem

Here I, A.W.J. Pretorius, Kommandant-General, with my officers and men, took occupation of the capital town of Dingaan, King of the Zulus, on 21st December, 1838

That night we started to make camp near Kwa Matiwane but the sight of the bone-covered charnel hill unnerved us all. So Pretorius ordered us to move some distance away, closer to the White Umfolozi, where we stayed until Christmas Day. While resting our scouts captured three Zulu men who told us that Dingaan was without power, that his people and his army had scattered. They also said that many of our cattle were in the valley near the White Umfolozi.

We decided to recover the cattle. Guided by the Zulu scouts, we eventually reached the top of the deep gorge carved by the White Umfolozi River.

Jan clutched at my arm, "There, look Rauch, there are our cattle," he pointed.

Squinting against the sun, I followed Jan's finger, way, way down into the valley where I could see the huge herds of cattle.

"Come men, those animals belong to us," said Pretorius. "I am afraid that you, Karel Landman, must take command. My hand is giving me a great deal of pain and I must return to the camp. But, be careful. There are quite a few Zulu warriors hidden in the hills. They might just be spoiling for another fight."

Led by Landman we had descended deep into the valley before realizing that we too had been lured into a trap. On the slope above, our retreat had been cut off by thousands of warriors who had materialized out of the bush still in their battle dress. Even the so-called cattle near the river were now standing on two legs, actually Zulu warriors who had been crouching under their shields.

Hans de Lange shouted, "Manne, it's a trap! Look at them all. How many do you think we can kill? How long will our ammunition last? It means certain death to go to that hill. Forward, men, forward! He who loves me will follow me!"

We galloped behind de Lange and crossed the drift, shooting as we rode, with the Zulus attempting to cut off our escape. Three of our men fell. We soldiered on, forming a wide circle before finally crossing back over the river to the northwest. It was a terrifying ride. We were hotly pursued by bloodthirsty warriors, many of whom were now on horseback and carried guns. As we made the crossing we heard a shout, "Here they come!" Hundreds and hundreds of Zulus were closing in on us. On the perimeter, some of the men were already engaged in hand-to-hand combat. In the heat of battle I saw six more of our men fall in the shrieking, screaming mêlée.

"Help me!" screamed the Englishman, Biggar. But it was too late. Two warriors dragged him from his horse as a mass of Zulus stabbed at him, his bloodied corpse soon still in the shallow water.

Zulu cries of "Gahla!" rent the air as more than fifty of Biggar's coloured servants were struck down. We fired and fired our Sannas in an attempt to cut a swath through the Zulu horde before we managed to make it through. Then we, the survivors, galloped as hard as we could for the safety of the camp.

The sun had already set as we staggered, exhausted and much subdued into camp that evening. We had suffered heavy losses: more than nine of our own trekkers and over seventy of our loyal attendants.

The battle of Blood River was now finally over.

⨳ ⨳ ⨳

A few days later we arrived back at the main camp, Sooilaer, on the banks of the Tugela.

As we approached we fired shots of greeting into the air, which were returned as people came running. The evening fires had already been lit and the camp exuded an air of peace and tranquillity.

"I never thought I would hear that wonderful sound again," said Jan as we heard the happy laughter of children. I nodded. We had been to the brink of hell.

Then I saw her. Amelia! I leaped from my horse, leaving the reins dangling, and ran to her. She held out her arms to me and I enfolded her in mine.

"Oh Rauch, Rauchie, I'm so happy you are alive. Thank you, thank you God for bringing him back."

I held her close and kissed her cheeks, streaming with tears. She felt warm and full in my arms. "I too am glad to be back," I said. I kissed her lips, then pushed her gently away. "I have something for you, Amelia, something very special." I reached into my pocket and took out the crucifix. "Here, this belongs to you. I want you to keep it. Pa would have wished that. I made a promise to him, when we ... when we found him, that I would care for you and baby Jakob. And so it shall be. I could not promise that I would love you, though."

Amelia looked stunned. She stood with her hand open, the crucifix in her palm. "But you do, Rauch .... don't you? You do really love me, I mean?"

"I do Amelia, I do love you but not in the way that you would want me to. You betrayed me and try as I have, I just cannot forgive and forget. There was a time when you could have had me for your own. You didn't want me and now it's too late. I love Marietjie and I will go to her ... if she will have me."

Tears welled in her eyes as I turned away.

Marietjie stood nearby, holding the hands of our children, silently watching Amelia and me. Her anxious face lit up suddenly and her fearful expression was replaced by her most beautiful smile. My heart pounded with happiness as I walked slowly to the woman I loved. My woman and my two boys, one white and one coloured. I smiled as I thought of their future in the sun as equals in this new country, this land of endless opportunity.

I folded Marietjie into my arms and kissed her gently.

"Welcome home, Rauch. Welcome home, my love."

I was home.

Acknowledgments

Thank yous are always boring except to the people mentioned. However trite they might sound, each of these people contributed in some way: Chris and Kerrin Cocks of 30° South who had the faith in my writing and the story to publish it, and inspired me to write another book on the history of South Africa; Margie who never once refused to read "the next few pages" and who constantly encouraged me with her comments; John Gordon Davis who agreed to having his name on the cover and wrote a shout for the book; Colin and Romy Bryden who mentored me and taught me how the world of books works; Alexandra Fuller who inspired the book still to be written; Eve Yohalem who took time out of her own writing to read, comment and suggest improvements; Mike Hook whose enthusiasm was catching (as always); Astrid Schwenke and Professor Jackie Grobler who read and commented on the accuracy of the history; Jimmy and Glenda Rangouses whose assistance in making the book a success is immeasurable; Bearnard O' Riain who wept into his coffee with me at every publisher's rejection and shared in my joy at meeting Chris and Kerrin; 'Skip' Jooste who introduced me to Kerrin and Chris and who read and commented on the story; Michael and Samantha for their support and encouragement and Jacques who still doesn't believe the Voortrekkers smoked marijuana; Doug Sutherland who most Friday evenings listened unflinchingly over a beer as I recounted blow by blow the trials and tribulations of an aspirant writer; Peter Harris who encouraged me and raised the bar with the standard set in his books; the late David Rattray who taught me what a difference storytelling can make to history for which I am forever grateful; Roger Webster who introduced me to the rich tapestry of history that is South Africa and enriched my life; to all my friends who took the time to read the manuscript and who gave me wonderful support and encouragement; to all my guests on my tours—I hope you will buy this book; to the Voortrekker Monument with its wonderful story—to the great men and women who trekked in those wagons in their search for freedom and who not only inspired this story but also my forthcoming book, *The Great Trek*; and finally to this wonderful country where each day is an incredible journey and privilege.